On the Threshold

M. Laszlo

AIA PUBLISHING

On the Threshold
M. Laszlo
Copyright © 2023
Published by AIA Publishing, Australia
ABN: 32736122056
http://www.aiapublishing.com

All characters in this publication are fictitious and any resemblance to real persons, living or dead, is purely coincidental.

All rights reserved. No part of this publication may be reproduced, stored in a retrieval system or transmitted in any form or by any means electronic, mechanical, audio, visual or otherwise, without prior permission of the copyright owner. Nor can it be circulated in any form of binding or cover other than that in which it is published and without similar conditions including this condition being imposed on the subsequent purchaser.

ISBN: 978-1-922329-58-5

To E.A.

I

Chapter One

Autumn, 1907.

Late one morning some kind of torrid, invisible beast wrapped itself around Fingal T. Smyth's body. He exited the castle with toes twitching fiercely and scanned the distant Scottish Highlands. *Go back where you came from.* The entity wrapped itself tighter about his person, and Fingal blinked back his tears. *I'm melting, I am. Aye, it's the heat of fusion,* he thought.

Gradually, the beast's heartbeat became audible—each pulsation. At the same time, the illusory heat of transformation emitted an odour like that of oven-roasted peppercorns dissolving in a cup of burnt coffee.

Over by the gatehouse, Fräulein Wunderwaffe appeared—the little German girl wore a plain-sewn robe and square-crown bowler. In that moment, she no longer seemed to be a sickly child of seven years; her inscrutable expression resembled that of a wise, indifferent cat.

Perhaps even some kind of lioness. Fingal cringed, and he recalled a fragment of conversation from three weeks earlier.

'She suffers from a most unnatural pathology, an anguished, maniacal obsession with cats,' Doktor Hubertus Pflug had explained. 'Ever since the poor girl was a baby, she has always regarded it her fate to one day metamorphose into a glorious panther, for she believes herself to be *ein Gestaltwandler*. Do you know this word? It means *shapeshifter*, and refers to someone who possesses the power to take the form of anything in nature.'

The heat radiated up and down Fingal's spine, and his thoughts turned back to the present. *Aye, it's a change of phase. I'm melting into a chemical compound.* Despite all, he greeted the girl and willed himself to flash a grin.

Fräulein Wunderwaffe did not return the smile. Hand on heart, the little girl drew a bit closer. Then, as the hot animalistic presence undulated across Fingal's body, the little girl's eyes grew wide until her expression turned to that of a vacant stare.

He waved. 'Please, hen. *Listen*. You're too clever for your own good. A prodigy, you'd be, *ein Wunderkind*. How much better everything would be for you if you was like all the other children, eh?'A moment later, her feet pointed inwards, and she removed her hat and undid her long, flaxen hair.

Again, he cringed. 'If you've noticed something, ignore all. This hasn't got anything to do with you.'

A most ethereal, lyrical, and incomprehensible hiss commenced. At the other end of the winding, decorative-brick driveway, each clay block shining the colour of blue Welsh stone, a sleek Siamese cat with a coat of chocolate-spotted ivory appeared. The creature raced toward his shadow.

Fingal looked into the animal's large blue eyes, while the chocolate Siamese studied the off-centre tip of his nose. Then the animal turned away, as if to compare the peculiarity with that of some disembodied visage hovering in the distance.

Out on the loch, meanwhile, a miraculous rogue wave suddenly arose and crashed against the pebbly strand.

Less than a moment later, a cool flame crawled across Fingal's throat. The strange fire rattled, not unlike the sound of fallen juniper leaves caught up in the current and dancing against the surface of a stone walkway.

Crivens. By now, the alien, pulsating presence held him so tight that he could barely breathe. He fell to the earth, and as the dreamlike flame continued to move across his throat, he rolled about until the illusory sensation of cool warmth wriggled and twisted and dropped into his neck dimple.

He crawled over to the little girl and grabbed her ankle. 'Get on up to your physician's room, eh? *Please*. Go on and wake Doktor Pflug and tell him what's happened.'

Fräulein Wunderwaffe only turned to study the castle grounds. When she turned back, she fixed her gaze upon the postern-tower.

A sense of compulsion made him do the same. The flourishes of coral pink in the masonry served to remind him of his bygone school necktie—each stripe a soft, velvet-rose hue. *How long has it been? Twenty-three years since me school days ended.*

He reached up and tapped her wrist. 'Go back inside the castle, lass. Aye, find that fine physician and tell him to come quick.'

A deep crease appeared upon the little girl's brow. Fingal gasped for breath and tapped her foot. 'I know you might be a wee bit green about the gills, hen. Still, this wouldn't be a good time for you to stand there fiddling about.'

He should not have raised his voice in that moment, for now the chocolate Siamese drew close and glowered at him, as if he must be the worst kind of profligate. The creature's soot-black pupils grew as large as could be. Then, as the breeze kicked up such that several pink, threadlike chrysanthemum petals entangled themselves in the cat's whiskers, the chocolate Siamese stood on its hind legs, as if preparing to do battle with him.

'Aye, look at this mouser here. She's a bit of a snicket, eh? Came from out of nowhere, she did.'

The chocolate Siamese licked the very tip of its tail, as if someone had stepped on it, and then it darted off toward the rowan tree and up into its lush crown.

Fräulein Wunderwaffe knelt to the earth. '*Brennst du?*' she asked Fingal.

'The heat, it's bloody unbearable. I got to leave this place.' He picked himself up and raced back into the castle courtyard, where he cupped his hands and then reached into the blue-limestone fountain that stood in the heart of Mother's chrysanthemum garden. Some five times over, he splashed his face, and then he slumped to the earth, facing the castle's south wall. A thin ray of sunlight reflected off a quartz vein in the black-fossil limestone such that a shimmery spark blinded him—just for a moment.

Thankfully, Doktor Pflug happened along. 'Are you feeling sick, delirious?' His frame all so imposing and stocky, the physician pointed toward the centuries-old castle. '*Na gut.* Do you know where you are? Tell me. Do you recognise this place as your home?'

Fingal nodded. 'Aye, acquired by bequest.' A memory awoke: at once, he recalled that harrowing moment when Mother had breathed her last, not long ago on his thirtieth birthday.

'Promise you'll stay and run the hotel,' she had told him.

'Don't let Bonnie Castle go to rack and ruin.' At that point Mother had closed her eyes, and, without a goodbye, the elderly woman had slipped away.

Fingal sat up now and leaned against the fountain's basin. 'What's wrong with me?'

For a time, the physician stroked his beard. 'I'd say it's nothing more than high anxiety, *angst. Sturm und Drang.*'

From the other side of the chrysanthemum garden, Fräulein Wunderwaffe walked forward and dropped her bowler at Fingal's feet.

He collected her hat and slipped the brim back into her trembling hand. 'You've noticed the visitor, have you? Aye, you're a shrewd lass, so you are. Still, you've got nothing to fear. The good doctor has told me true. Like enough, the fiendish bogie wisnae onythin more than the stuff o' me own hysteria. And because I believed him to be real, so *you* did as well.'

'No, it's not a daydream. *Es ist dein doppelgänger.*' The little girl burst out laughing. Then she collapsed and writhed about—almost as if she believed that a profusion of flames had only just ignited all over *her* person.

Doktor Pflug grabbed her hand. '*Lass es bitte.*'

Whilst the physician tended to the girl, the hot, oppressive presence wrapped itself all about Fingal's body once more. This time, though, as the spectral beast's heartbeat recommenced, he even smelled the creature's breath: it reeked of smouldering holly leaves. Despite all, he forced himself to focus on the girl, and careful not to crush her bowler, knelt beside the child. 'Come to your senses, hen. Don't let the caller nettle you none. No, no, no. He's only the stuff of dreams, nothing more than fantasy.'

Fräulein Wunderwaffe's delicate body continued to thrash

and flail and contort, and when the excitable girl managed to kick Fingal in the belly, he rolled to the side. 'If you'll not behave good and mannerly, I'll have no recourse but to tell your father.' Like a badly-abused animal, Fräulein Wunderwaffe chortled loudly—and the ironic, bestial laughter made him shiver.

'You're not well, lass.'

Her convulsions grew worse. How long before the poor girl managed to bite through the tip of her tongue?

Doktor Pflug gestured toward Fingal. 'Go find her father. She'll respond to him. *Ja*.'

Fingal stood and hurried across the castle courtyard and into the grand hall, where he cried for help.

Herr Wunderwaffe failed to respond, so Fingal recited a torrent of Scottish Gaelic curses and then raced upstairs. Several times over, he knocked upon the gentleman's door. 'Do forgive the trespass, but you've got to tend to your daughter. She'd be acting most contrary.'

Slowly, the sound of footfall approached the other side of the stile. 'We're busy,' a woman's voice told Fingal. 'Why don't you come back later? We'd be plenty obliged.'

He recognised the speaker as Jean Selwyn, the selfish American woman who had travelled all the way from London, Kentucky to work with the German scholar and to study his pioneering film theories.

The burning sensation crawling up and down his arms and legs, Fingal took hold of the pressed-glass knob—only to find that Jean had locked the door. 'Please, sir! Come along now posthaste. You must tend to your daughter.'

'No, you ain't got no cause to worry,' Jean continued. 'That girl, she's always doing things hindside first. I featured it the moment I got here. She's always losing her religion.'

On the other side of the stile, Jean's footsteps trailed away—as if the American woman must be walking over to Herr Wunderwaffe's writing table.

Fingal sighed. 'Hurry, won't ye please? We haven't got much time.'

Eventually, Jean's footsteps returned. 'Herr Wunderwaffe says he'll come for to tend to things a little bit later.'

Fingal grabbed the knob again, and like a wintry breeze, the pressed glass numbed his fingertips. He gasped and withdrew his hand. '*Please!* Time would be of the essence.'

'No, we got to think on our work. Herr Wunderwaffe ain't got the luxury to lay the back of his hand on that daughter of his just now.'

Fingal smote the jamb so forcefully that his knuckles smarted. Jean must have intuited as much, for at last, she opened the door. A gleam in her thyme-green eyes, the young lady twitched her long, inelegant nose. 'I can tell you one thing. If you don't bring us to ruination, it sure won't be for lack of trying.'

Finegal placed his hands on his hips and sought to look over the loathsome woman's shoulder to catch a glimpse of the celebrated German scholar.

'Never in all my born days,' the insufferable American woman said. 'You better don't disturb Herr Wunderwaffe any further.'

Fingal stomped his heel. 'You're a scold, so you are. That's right, I said it.'

Jean poked his lapel. 'You think I travelled to Scotland to tend to some petticoat whenever she raises Cain and runs wild the way she do?'

'Please!' Fingal cried out, still peering over the American woman's shoulder. 'Come quick, *Mein Herr*. Let's bustle off and collect your daughter.'

'Hush up already,' Jean shouted. 'You suppose Herr Wunderwaffe done came to live in this castle here to run through his childrearing routine? No, he went and came here to get himself some liberty because he's onto something big. Have you clean forgot he ain't nothing less than the father of film theory?'

'But even so—'

'Do you know how come cinema has the power to bewitch peoples here and there and all but everywhere? Herr Wunderwaffe could learn you the answer. He reckons humankind favours picture shows and celluloid photoplays only because ever since the Lumière brothers went and came along, the public can't help its unconscious hankering to evolve into beings fit to live within realms of fantasy. Just like players in the frame.'

Fingal shook his head, and then he turned to consider the natural glow streaming in through the window at the end of the corridor. 'Enough with movies. Let's face *reality*.'

As he spoke, the glow came to resemble the art of undiffused side lighting—as if a filmmaker had resolved to create striking shadows up and down the length of the hallway.

Fingal turned back and looked into the American woman's eyes. 'Me happy home would be a splendid establishment. We get sundry lodgers. From far afield, they come. Most wend their way here from Glasgow, everyone looking to have themselves a fortnight's holiday. Be that as it may, lately we got nothing but strife. Yet *you* only compound the trouble and make it worse.'

Jean's breathing grew louder. 'You're more stubborn than a Tennessee walking horse racked with seedy toe. Go *away* already.' Without another word, the American woman shut the door and locked it anew.

Bloody hell. Fingal cursed all the distinctive shadows up and down the hallway, and then he raced back downstairs.

Outside, he found Doktor Pflug sitting beneath the rowan tree, holding the chocolate Siamese in his arms. A gust of wind blew across the castle grounds, and the cat broke free from his embrace. Doktor Pflug turned to Fingal and studied him awhile. 'The poor little girl, she's gone off. *Ach du meine Güte.*'

Not thirty minutes later, Fräulein Wunderwaffe reappeared upon the bridle path—the little girl riding bareback upon a wild, silver-grey pony foal, the creature running along at a training gallop.

The torrid presence returned all across Fingal's person, but even so, he raced forward and sought to stop the animal—to no avail, however.

Moments later, when he returned past the rowan tree, he could not locate the creature anywhere. 'The steed from before ought to be buzzing about, eh?'

'It went *inside*,' Doktor Pflug told him.

'Not bloody likely.'

'*Nein*,' the physician insisted. 'I think Fräulein Wunderwaffe opened the door for the visitor. Why? Because she hungers for its flesh.'

'Stuff and nonsense.'

'*Nein*. I've told you a thousand times. She cannot overcome her obsessions. Truly, she believes she's growing into a hungry cat.'

'So why don't you heal her of such whimsy?'

'For three long years, I have struggled to do just that. Nevertheless, I have failed.'

'Well then, what if she goes blinders? Could it be you'll not have any means to restore the lass?'

'Some alienists might approve of such a result. You must realise that the little girl embodies what we call the fetish of primitivism. The desire to do as the ancients or go even further and do as the beasts of the field. That's a strong urge for some. Why? Because some people long to leave behind the sombre life of Man, the plainness of modernity. And who's to say the primitivists *shouldn't* do so?'

Arms crossed, Fingal walked back to the castle and continued into the grand hall. And no sooner had he done so than a shattering of glass resounded from the gallery, as if the foal had only just knocked over one of the lamp tables.

He chased the wayward animal into the kitchen. Then, as it raced off toward the pantry, he stumbled into the rubbish bin and spilled its contents—an oilskin barn coat that once belonged to his mother. At once, he became lost in memories—for she'd worn that coat whenever she tended to her garden, all throughout her final years. *Maw.*

Doktor Pflug followed along into the castle and physician drew near. 'You look pensive. Like your mind must be brimming with . . . the incalculable.'

'I'm feeling unsettled, that's all.' Fingal bit his lip and touched his mother's coat. 'I do wish Herr Wunderwaffe would take his daughter home to Prussia before she wrecks this bloody keep. Think of what she's already done. Aye, she invites wild animals to come live here in me beloved lodging house. What's she hoping to do? Drive me around Cape Horn?'

'Don't despair,' Doktor Pflug told him. With that remark, the physician held his hands with palms up and called out for the little girl.

Moments later, they discovered Fräulein Wunderwaffe in the stair hall, the little girl checking the pony foal's teeth.

'I think we ought to take the beastie outside,' Fingal

whispered. 'We'll put your mount in the stables, eh?'

Three times over, Fräulein Wunderwaffe blinked. Then she dropped to her knees and caressed the animal's hind leg.

'I'll not let no innocent lass like you change into no woeful panther running wild about the moor,' he continued.

The little girl ran her hands up and down her arms and legs. 'I feel something all across my body. *Ja*. Some kind of energy … some kind of heat … some kind of ghostly being.'

'Yes, I feel it as well.' Without another word, Fingal grabbed hold of the pony foal's silky mane and walked the beast through the hallway.

Outside, not far from the fountain, a staccato purr rang out—the chocolate Siamese. The soft, autumn light and absence of shadows made Fingal hold out his hand and let the pony's mane slip through his fingers and thumb.

Fräulein Wunderwaffe came along and blew a kiss to the cat—at which point the chocolate Siamese guided the pony foal out across the castle grounds and back into the wild.

Fingal fingered his kilt pin. 'You got me worried sick,' he told the girl. 'Let me take you into town, eh? We'll consult a proper Scottish castor-oil artist, and he'll find a remedy for whatever ails you.'

Open-mouthed, Fräulein Wunderwaffe contemplated the loch, then walked over to the rowan tree. With a series of eyelid twitches, she looked into the crown.

Fingal drew close and admired the girl's pointy Germanic chin before taking hold of a fallen rowan berry. 'Back home in Heidelberg, did you ever affright your neighbours? Might that explain why ye travelled all this way? Aye, you and your old man would be *exiles*.'

She did not respond. Instead, she looked to the earth, then lay amid the rowan tree's elongated roots and curled into a ball.

An array of thistledown sailed by on a current of air, and then the purple tufts were gone—the same way Fingal's dreams had always vanished upon awakening. *Aye, that's right.*

Hours later, once darkness had fallen and the burning sensation had recommenced all across his body, he returned to the rowan tree.

The autumn night grew impossibly quiet, the only sound the ticking of his extravagant timepiece—a Frédérique Constant with poker hands of gold. He reached into his waistcoat fob pocket to check the time. *Nine o'clock.* As he returned the timepiece into his pocket, a cold, seemingly-magnetic charge pricked the tip of his nose.

No sooner had the bolt of electricity continued up into the treetop than the physician happened along and greeted Fingal in German.

Fingal raised his hand. 'Did you feel a spark of energy a moment ago?'

Doktor Pflug made a face. 'What's this? A spark of *die Kraft*? No, sir.'

Again, Fingal checked his timepiece, and he realised that the hands no longer functioned. 'Me kettle and hob has gone dead.' Three times over, he struck the dial. 'That goddamn bloody electrical current, I do believe it went and killed one of the wheels within the case.'

Doktor Pflug scowled. 'It's only a pocket watch. You have no reason to be heartbroken.'

A memory seized hold of Fingal, and he recalled the first young lady who he had ever fancied—a guest at the castle, Felicity Mingus. The tall, comely, buxom maiden had come from the Isle of Islay to malt the barley at one of the local distilleries. Powerless to think up any better way to introduce himself, late one evening, he had resolved to concoct a story and had feigned having misplaced the Frédérique Constant so he could ask her if she had noticed it anywhere.

Three nights later, the corridor softly lit, he had showed up at her door to tell her about his seeming discovery of the precious timepiece—as if their inconsequential first encounter had provided a sound pretence for another.

The scullery maid had wandered by then. 'The island girl travelled off to Port William an hour ago,' the scullery maid had explained. 'The lass felt homesick, aye, so she booked passage aboard a steamship bound for the Outer Hebrides or wherever it was.'

By now, something like nineteen years had gone by, but the ache of those unrequited affections still burned deep inside his gut. *What have they done to me?* The answer was plain enough: they had driven him to a life of introversion and estrangement from nature. And now he studied the rowan tree standing before him and imagined it something artificial—a great, terrible machine, the stuff of technology and heartlessness.

Chapter Two

In the morning, Fingal returned to the rowan tree and cocked his ear; like rusty machine parts, the boughs above creaked and bent. *Aye, something like two whole decades has gone by since love came into me life.* All over his body, the burning sensation recommenced, until he doubled over and reached in vain for someone's hand. The cold, fiery presence commingled with the ache of his unrequited affections, and a ponderous weight seemed to take its place upon his shoulders.

He placed his hands over his face. *What's come over me?* Beneath his increasingly shallow breath, he cursed all his introversion and estrangement from nature.

A second time, the boughs of the rowan tree creaked and bent. He pointed at the crown. 'What's the trouble, eh? You feeling frustrated? You feeling impatient to perform some grand chore? Maybe you'd be yearning to metamorphose into some bloody mechanical device fit to serve the world. Might that be so?'

The burning sensation seemed to melt below the surface of his skin and onward into the furthest reaches of his very being, his psyche.

In time, the sun blinded him—just like the ancient Mediterranean sun sinking behind the audience during an afternoon performance, only to blind some Athenian actor. The fiery presence inside Fingal conjured an array of fantastical sensations upon the tip of his tongue. He tasted something like thyme honey drizzled over white cheese, and at the back of his tongue, something like olive oil drizzled over sea-salt brine.

Almost drooling, he staggered off across the castle grounds, and when he reached the pewter works, he dropped to his knees. Someone had left the front door ajar. All the more peculiar, sinister even, the structure shone Aegean blue, the gold veins in the ironstone walls almost blinding bright. The glimmery flashes numbed the tip of his nose. Nevertheless, he crawled forward and gasped at the sight of Fräulein Wunderwaffe's bowler lying against the weatherboard. 'Anyone here just now? Hey, little girl. Are you hiding? Come out, please.'

With the uncanny heat racing through his bloodstream, he crawled forward and placed the brim of the little girl's hat into his mouth. He breathed in the aroma lingering upon the weatherboard—the scent of wildflowers, Greek peonies.

Inside the pewter works, a storm of feathers lay strewn about. And each one shone the bright marble white of a pied oystercatcher's plumage.

He placed the little girl's hat into his hands and sat up. 'Listen up, hen. If you're hiding somewhere, you must take heed. Don't let them shorebirds inside here. They'll be fluttering all the way from their Arctic breeding grounds, and them shorebirds, they'll be looking for all kinds of repast. That's why you can't entice them to come inside. No, no.'

If the little girl were hiding somewhere, she did not speak up.

He returned to his feet, and no matter of the heat flowing through his body, staggered forward—until he stood before his revolutionary invention, the apparatus by which he had always hoped to prove true Plato's theory of innate knowledge.

The oblong power source did not look promising. If anything, it resembled a tall, cumbersome steam boiler.

For a moment or two, the heat inside him intensified so much that he staggered back into the wall. With a grunt, he staggered forward a second time. Then he turned and looked up to the long, thin, metallic spring extending across the room.

The bestial presence inside him burned even hotter. *Does it hope to reduce me heart to ashes?* He followed the spring to the far side of the room, where the ribbon cable plugged into the arched, tin-bronze gateway. 'Hey, little girl. Do come out from wherever you'd be hiding and come collect your bonny hat, eh?' He hung the bowler from one of the tin-bronze rivets protruding from the gateway. '*Behold.*'

If she were hiding somewhere, Fräulein Wunderwaffe did not reveal herself.

He scanned the large room—the heaps of machine parts, the heaps of papers, the darkened alcoves and weathered doorways. 'Please come out. I got some right crucial news to share with you. Just last night, the answer came to me. *Honest.* I think I know what went all so wrong yesterday. That whole disturbance, it wisnae onythin but the side effects from me recent failed experimentations. Aye, the side effects from all the sparks flying about. Don't that make sense then? That's what had me feeling discomfited the other day. And because I were feeling bad, so *you* took a wee bit ill. Aye, a very bad influence I was.'

If the little girl were hiding somewhere, she did not respond.

Meanwhile, the heat of the bestial presence inside him

seemed to seep out through his ears. And now the warmth spread out across his left breast and all down his left arm.

He lay upon the floorboards and, before long, turned to some of the charcoal sketches strewn about to his right. 'Please come out. You mustn't fear me any. What's happened to me, it's not some grave condition. I'd say it's nothing but a case of exhaustion sickness. Don't that sound right?'

No response came, not even a nervous yelp. The crackle of illusory fire resounded, though, and soon enough the invisible flames emitted the scents of medicinal herbs and mountain tea.

He took one of the charcoal sketches into his hand—a detailed study of an 1888 electric data-processing mechanism, perhaps the first computer he had ever operated. His muscles tightening, he touched the image and left a smudge. *Confound it.*

A strong gust came through the pewter works, and the charcoal sketch sailed from his hand and glided off some four feet away.

He turned upon his side. A second time, he studied his revolutionary invention—both the power source and the arched gateway. *Oh, to prove the truth of inborn knowledge.* He rested his temple against the floor. 'Hey, little girl. Do you wish to know why I builded all this?'

A second gust blew, and as a few more charcoal sketches glided off upon the wild current, Fräulein Wunderwaffe climbed down from the beamed ceiling and exposed rafters, at which point she walked off without so much as a word.

Early that evening, once he had already returned to the castle, the chocolate Siamese tapped him twice upon his knee—at which point he suddenly tasted the illusory sensation of herbal tea upon the very tip of his tongue. 'You got me mystified,' he told the animal. Then he followed the creature into the billiard hall, where Doktor Pflug stood as if he himself had just come inside—the physician still dressed in his long, grey, double-breasted frock coat.

'I've been looking all over for you there,' Doktor Pflug told Fingal. 'Where have you been? Have you been hiding from me?'

'Aye, that's it.' Fingal approached the billiard table, worked the chalk around the tip of the cue stick, and then struck the cue ball into the corner pocket.

Before he could do anything more, the chocolate Siamese hopped onto the billiard table and curled up into a ball beneath the glare falling from the Victorian ceiling pendant light.

A frigid draft swirling about his kilt, an illusory blaze awoke up and down his arms and legs, the flames as fragrant as wintersweet.

He turned to the physician and looked to the floor. 'I've brought great calamity into the world. It's infected me. Aye, and it's gone and sickened the little girl as well. Much worse than anything that might've afflicted her way back when.'

Doktor Pflug pressed his lips together into a frown, scratched at his scalp, and then dug his hands into the pockets of his frock coat.

The ghostly fire spread over Fingal's back and chest, and the touch of the flames crawled across his skin as softly as an ancient tunic—an overfold made from the finest flax linen.

Meanwhile, the chocolate Siamese studied Fingal. The cat looked into his eyes and then leapt from the billiard table. Twice, the creature circled him. Had the animal sensed the fiery presence upon his person?

After a while, a scent like that of Greek octopus crept through the air, and the cat must have sensed it. Just like that, the creature exited the billiard hall and guided Fingal down the corridor and onward into the castle's throne room.

He came upon Fräulein Wunderwaffe, who sat on the chesterfield dressed in her bedgown. She looked up at him with blood-shot eyes and recited sensual, German-language poetry—what sounded like a piece from *Des Knaben Wunderhorn*.

He shook his finger at her. 'Don't think I don't know what you'd be doing. In point of fact, you'd be singing some kind of invocation. Maybe you wish some devilish cat god ought to come and help you change into some glorious, wild animal. But no, don't you do nothing of the kind, lass. No, no. We've to battle the watch *against* such things. You and me and everyone in this world, we've to champion the cause of intellectualism.'

The sconce flashed, and, for a fleeting moment, the glow assumed an impossible shade of *chartreuse* yellow.

'Maybe you believe the chocolate Siamese here might help you in your endeavours. Might that be so? No, no. He only means to make mischief. Aye, but I'll not let him harm you any. No, no. I'm quite fond of you. Honestly.' The bestial, fiery presence wrapped itself around Fingal's thigh—and now his eyesight blurred some.

Fräulein Wunderwaffe's breath grew laboured, and she dropped to the floor and crawled off behind the high-back settee. Just like an affrighted cat might do.

Fingal departed the throne room, at which point Doktor Pflug confronted him at the foot of the stair. 'Tell me about your experimentations.'

Fingal rubbed his eyes. 'You don't want to know.' All the time shaking his head, he climbed the stair and continued into his darkened bedchamber.

When Doktor Pflug followed him inside not long afterward,

the physician very nearly walked into the white-oak *armoire*.

Fingal apologised, then walked over to the bedside table, struck a match, and lit a thin, blue taper. Little by little, the bedchamber assumed the romantic glow of a Greek taverna. The air filled with the scent of candle grease, and a ghost moth fluttered out of the wardrobe and hovered above the solitary blaze.

Fingal gestured toward the alluring insect. 'Don't it come across all so godlike the way it floats there?'

'*Godlike*?' The physician drew close to the bedside table, the floorboards silent beneath his feet.

The ghost moth descended too close to the flame—and the fire consumed all.

Doktor Pflug stepped back. '*Unmöglich*.' The insect's sudden absence plainly mystified the physician. Did he assume that the warm wax trickling down the length of the candle and into the socket pan ought to contain at least a measure of the organism's remains?

The chocolate Siamese appeared in the bedchamber doorway. Twice, the cat cried out—a distress call perhaps. Had it espied the illusory fire wrapping itself tighter and tighter around Fingal's thigh?

Fingal followed the creature down the corridor, up the spiral staircase and out into the deserted rooftop café.

Fingal snapped his fingers. 'Come you here, mouser.'

Oblivious, the cat sniffed at a few of the butter-cookie crumbs strewn about the console tables and accent chairs.

Pflug came along then, and the physician gestured toward Fingal. 'Tell me all about your experimentations. It's imperative that I know.'

Fingal walked over to the railing. 'Just look at the narrows. They're behaving peaceful tonight. As mild as maiden's water.'

With a loud sigh, Doktor Pflug approached the railing. 'You do not fathom the gravity of our predicament. Why? For all I know, you feel guilty. And because of that, perhaps you prefer to misjudge the dreadful circumstances that face us. *Please*. Tell me what you've been doing.'

Fingal gripped the railing. 'I wisnae hoping to harm no one. I only hoped to prove the idea of natural knowledge, *innata scientia*. That's why I builded what I builded. To prove Plato's theory that the whole of the learning process would be little more than the recollection of inborn facts and figures and such.' His thigh burning more and more, Fingal gripped the railing a little bit tighter. 'I only ever wanted to prove precognition. Foreknowledge. That kind of thing.'

The physician looked to the stars. Did he presume that his silence would fill Fingal with shame?

Fingal walked off along the railing with a shudder. He had to stop when the warmth unwrapped itself from his thigh. For a moment or two, the uncanny heat swirled all around his body—something like a cloud of deadly microbes, or lethal toxins, some kind of pestilence, an assemblage of spores. *No, no*. Suddenly, he imagined the unnerving heat all around him to be something artificial—an agent powerful enough to spread much faster than anything natural. *Aye, a manmade weapon. Poison gases*. He arranged his hands over his temples and slowly returned to the physician's side.

By now the physician seemed lost in thought. On and on, he muttered in a chaotic combination of German and Scots.

Trying to get free from the warm aura, Fingal ducked to the rooftop, then raced to the other side of the café. Though he repeated this several times, all his efforts proved futile.

The mysterious presence enveloped him like a fog of dead skin cells, cat dander. For a moment or two, the entity even made a series of catlike trills and snarls.

The chocolate Siamese drew close and hissed. Then the hisses turned into a low, whispery growl.

'You've espied the presence, so you have.' Fingal knelt by the cat and stroked its coat. 'Don't be alarmed, mouser. And please don't mistrust me none. If I could put an end to all this hooliganism, I'd do it. Expeditiously. Like the wind. That way no harm would ever come to you, nor the little girl.'

A few times over, the chocolate Siamese circled Fingal's person, then it hissed again.

'What you blethering about?' Fingal asked it in a whisper. 'At the moment, I can't do onythin about the trouble at hand.' He turned to the physician. 'Don't let your heart catch in your throat, but I haven't got the technology to make things right just now.'

The physician cursed in German and kicked the base rail. 'So you didn't even think of these things *before*hand? *Ach*. You commenced with your experimentations without pondering the perils of trying the psyche.'

The cool flames lifted from Fingal's body and drifted off through the railing. The faint, fiery presence descended to the loch such that the spectral glow suddenly illumined the shoreline.

Haste ye back. Slowly, Fingal returned to the physician's side. 'Forgive me folly.' His arms and legs atremble, Fingal looked to his feet—until a round of childish laughter resounded. *Could it be some kind of aural hallucination?* He closed his eyes and recalled his school days—all the short, impish lads out in the schoolyard, the ecstasy with which they had always laughed in his face. And now he opened his eyes, only to find the cat from before shamelessly expelling a load of excrement at his feet.

For the first time in years, he recalled the evening tea reception in which dozens of boys and girls had gathered around to offer him a custard cup filled with animal droppings. *Why did the other children deride me so?* Even then, the children must have intuited his heresy—for he had always regarded the Church of Scotland as lacking and imperfect in its ability to explain the way of the world. *All them boys and girls, aye, they despised me devotion to blessed Plato.* His skin still smouldering, Fingal returned to the railing. In that moment, he pictured himself as a snake longing to crawl out of its own skin—the same sensation that he had registered all those years ago, standing there speechless and benumbed by the children's cruelty.

The mysterious aura, the light, had vanished, so he studied the loch. *How poetic it'd be if the light were to shine from somewhere* below *the waters.*

A monkey barge emerged from around the bend, the vessel's engine churning and groaning as if with all her might.

How poetic it'd be if the light were to suddenly reappear at the tiller. The monkey barge continued along on her course, and Fingal turned to consider the structure looking out over the waters: Boleskine House, the manor where the notorious Aleister Crowley lately conducted his questionable 'magick' rites. *Might* he *be to blame for everything?* Fingal shook his head.

A series of catlike trills and snarls resounded at his back, and the chocolate Siamese hissed as if it had detected the presence of evil.

Little by little, a pulsating presence tapped a languid, erratic tempo against the nape of Fingal's neck. He tilted his head back, ever so slightly. *It's nothing.* Then he raised his chin a little bit more and studied Boleskine House. *Aye, Crowley.* Perhaps the ill-famed sorcerer had decided to trifle with him at this very moment. Perhaps he had mastered the art of necromancy, and now he had summoned some airy spirit to rise from a fissure adjacent to his property.

The presence wrapped itself tightly around Fingal's forearm, and he almost wept. *Aye, it's back. I'm guilty of arrogance against the gods, I am. Crowley hasn't done onythin.* Fingal yelped, twice. *Me experimentations have gone wrong, that's all.*

The chocolate Siamese looked into his eyes, scowled, and then darted off.

Damn. Fingal could not risk the possibility that the creature might wish to hector the little girl, so he chased after the cat. Once downstairs, he opened the door and let the creature walk off into the night—and then his intuition told him to follow along.

The chocolate Siamese guided him ever closer to the shattered remains of a witch elm.

How long had it been since the night a bolt of lightning split the tree in two? The storm had raged almost a decade ago, the very night he had walked into the pewter works to investigate Plato's writings—the ones pertaining to *innata scientia*, inborn knowledge.

The witch elm glowed now, the decaying wood agleam with foxfire. Then, as if some heavenly force had commanded the spark to dissolve into the ether, the disturbance suddenly discontinued.

From somewhere in the cool darkness of night, the chocolate Siamese yowled a few times over.

The physician pounded upon the railing of the rooftop café. 'Forget the accursed cat and come back up here. We've yet to determine a stratagem for preserving the poor little *fräulein*.'

'Yes, I know.' Fingal walked back through a stretch of

dying chickweed and stopped before a puddle of rainwater. The puddle happened to be just big enough to accommodate his face, so he studied his reflection.

A pair of footsteps resounded. And like some kind of ghostly nymph, the stuff of mythology, Fräulein Wunderwaffe emerged from the fog. 'What a glorious night,' she told him.

'What've you been doing out and about?'

'I've commenced to metamorphose into a laughing, luxuriant leopardess.'

'That can't be true, hen. No, no. You mustn't say such things. Affectation don't become a good German lass like you.'

For a moment or two, the little girl did not say a word. She only gave him a tight-lipped grin. 'No, I'm quite sincere,' she announced then. 'I feel it in my ribs. Yes, it feels like some great animal spirit has seized hold of me.'

'That can't be true.'

'Oh yes, it's true. Mother Earth has planted the seed inside me, and there's no going back. I'm *possessed*.'

Chapter Three

The next day, Fingal exited the castle and returned to the very same puddle of rainwater from the night before. The reflection of his face shone all so *brightly*—something like the powerful glow of a key light. He wrapped his hand around his kilt purse and sought to recall the dream that had only just visited him in the darkness before dawn. *What was it?*

The bestial presence, the sensation of fire, reignited within the reflection's left eye and then arose from the dark waters and enveloped Fingal's right shoulder.

The late-morning breeze made a chuffing sound, not unlike a snow leopard's breathy way of greeting one of its cubs. And the chocolate Siamese came forward, a rowan berry in the animal's mouth. The creature stopped some three feet from the puddle and dropped the offering into a patch of almond willow.

'What do you suppose I might've dreamt last night?' Fingal asked the cat. 'I want to say that maybe I imagined myself a phoenix enkindling a jumble of laurel leaves and destroying myself in the blaze. Aye. A dream of rebirth, it was.'

He closed his eyes and imagined that he held the power to discern the odour of the dream fire. *A moist, metallic, sulfurous stench, it was.*

A burning sensation awoke in his throat, and the cat studied the soft light flickering from his person. With its teeth bared, the cat retreated several steps and then arched its back.

Deep inside Fingal's waistcoat fob pocket, meanwhile, the timepiece recommenced to count the seconds. *Me ticker, it's working again.*

And then the dream revisited him; he recalled Fräulein Wunderwaffe assuming the form of a leopardess and explaining to him the one last adjustment that he must perform so as to make his curious invention back in the pewter works function properly. *Aye, the whole delay would be owing to a poor connection with the circuit panel, nothing more.* Without the least bit of hesitation, he walked back to the pewter works. His breath coming in spurts, he approached the power source and replaced one of the circuit breakers—just as his unconscious mind had suggested. Then he stepped back and clasped his hands together. *Might that be all then?*

The chocolate Siamese appeared in the doorway, crouched, and flattened its ears back against its head. Did the cat regard him as lacking forethought? He had heard such criticism before. *So what? Fortune favours the foolhardy. I'm quite sure Plato would agree.* Fingal held his body stiff and activated the machine.

An effusion of energised matter flowed up into the spring that connected the power source to the arched gateway standing on the other side of the room, and the portal filled with a powdery, blue-grey light streaked with jade green.

He smoothed out his kilt and thought back to his school days. Back then, everyone else had dreamt of succeeding in *conventional* endeavours. One lad had yearned to exhibit a row of mercury lights at Trades Hall, and another pioneering chap had always hoped to illumine the whole of Merchant City with electric lampposts. *But I dreamt of all* this.

The powdery, blue-grey light assumed the colour of snowflake obsidian.

No reason to dawdle. He moved into the glow, which enveloped him like a cool ghost rain. *Aye, a Scotch mist.* And now the glow filled him with a curious sensation—perhaps the gut reaction that a baby must have that very first time the infant exercises its sense of touch and feels not just something of the phenomenological world but also registers a concurrent, inner *emotion.*

Fingal braced himself, for the uncanny feeling could only mean that a projection of his primeval core had in fact manifested itself. With that in mind, he continued through the light to the other side. Then he looked all about. At first glance, though, he seemed to be alone. 'Are you here? If so, a thousand welcomes.'

A royal-yellow sunbeam streamed through the cracked casement window, but no visitor appeared—nor did any disembodied voice speak up.

A billowing pall sailed through Fingal's short brown hair, and he detected something like charcoal ash on the tip of his tongue. Gradually, the otherworldly dust diffused—but his throat burned even more. Three times over, he sought to swallow. The sulfurous taste in his mouth did not abate, though. Indeed, the taste grew into a moist, acidic, sour presence all throughout his nasal passages.

Flaring his nostrils, he deactivated the machine, and, as the luminescence that had filled the gateway melted into nothingness, he walked outside. 'Where'd you go?' he asked, hooking his thumbs into his waistcoat pockets. 'Why don't you show yourself? Don't be bashful. You'd be a projection of me innermost self, that's all. Me inborn knowledge.'

Other than the rush of the morning breeze, a stubborn, undying silence prevailed.

Fingal polished his kilt pin with his coat sleeve. 'Could it be you're feeling perplexed because you don't know how you got here? But it's all quite simple. I liberated you with me artifice, I did. And that's no fib. I went and conjured you with me humble invention, aye, international patent pending.'

The burning presence that had earlier enveloped Fingal's right shoulder went free in a burst of yellow-opal light, and now the glow guided him across the castle grounds and past the loch and all the way back to the rowan tree—where the light vanished into the crown.

Fingal looked at his feet. 'I know what you'd be hoping to ask me. Why'd you summon me this day? And that's a good question. Well, I wisnae aiming to vex you. And I wisnae just having me a good laugh. No, I builded that bonny contrivance back there in the pewter works and brought you forth so that you might help me fathom whether all them theories associated with Plato might be factual.'

A quiet, ghostlike presence tapped three times at his heel.

Fingal shuffled his feet. 'You got me burning with curiosity, eh? Just what do you look like? I always thought you'd appear the way a person's image might manifest itself in either a collodion or silver plate.' Almost hopping, Fingal placed his left hand upon his right shoulder and then turned around.

No fantastical entity stood there: it was only the chocolate Siamese, the animal standing alert with its fur lying flat.

For three hours Fingal traipsed all about the castle grounds, checking the pewter works five times.

Jean Selwyn discovered him down by the boathouse. 'Ain't you got the foggiest notion what's cooking around here? It's Herr Wunderwaffe. He ain't acting like himself no more. I'll be working the charcoal iron, and then I'll bring him a sporting dress shirt, but the damn fool won't wear it. And I'll get him some cheese pudding from the buttery, but he won't touch nothing. And to look at him, hell, you'd swear he's become just about as lost as last year's Easter egg.'

Quietly, Fingal fussed with the wreath of Michaelmas daisies hanging on the boathouse door. No matter how awkward the silence, how to speak to such a disagreeable woman?

Jean studied his shoulder—the place where the light had shone not long before. Then she circled him several times over. 'You got hard feelings for me, don't you?'

'Aye. You'd be a woman of three-and-twenty years or thereabouts, yet you pout like a self-absorbed maiden. That's because you don't know right from wrong.'

'You think I don't know right from wrong? How you figure that? I only ever came to these parts for to learn me what Herr Wunderwaffe has to say.'

'He knows his business, does he?'

'Yes, but near as I can tell, *you* ain't never once so much as said a good word for him, and he's hurting bad these days.' Without another word, Jean marched back to the castle and slammed the wicket gate behind her.

Once more, Fingal detected a presence at his heels. *It's got to be the entity.* When he shot a glance over his shoulder, he found himself alone. *Goddamn, me bum's oot the windae.*

At dusk he returned to the castle. And no sooner had he stepped inside than he snorted and retched—a stench as of burning human flesh lingered in the air.

With his ears ringing as if someone had only just called

out his name, he continued upstairs, where the ghastly odour stopped him in his tracks.

Ashen and all atremble, Jean emerged from Herr Wunderwaffe's room and slumped to the floor. 'He's off to eternity,' the American woman announced, grinding her teeth.

Fingal sought to control his breath. Then he went inside. A tin of kerosene lay beside the writing table, and a body lay aflame out on the balcony. The German scholar had immolated himself.

Once the shock had diffused some, Fingal raced off to collect the soda-acid extinguisher that he had purchased at a hoteliers' convention one year before. Quickly, he doused the fire.

Doktor Pflug happened along then, and peering over his glasses, turned to Fingal. 'I'll tell you what happened. A strange manifestation appeared before the poor scholar.'

'How do you mean?'

'It was a burning man, a fiend swathed in hot, ignited gases. And because of this most remarkable outward aspect, the puzzling *phantasma* must have inspired Herr Wunderwaffe to mimic its appearance. I'll tell you something else. A burning man like that, he commands the power to entrance entire multitudes. Especially the meek, anyone given to . . . emotional contagion.'

Fingal knelt on the floor. *The burning man; might* he *be the projection that I released this very day?* Fingal flinched. 'How did the entity persuade Herr Wunderwaffe?'

'The power of suggestion. That's how.' Doktor Pflug turned his back to the scholar's charred remains. 'Many contradistinct disorders afflict peoples all over the world. *Ja*. What of dementia, all those madmen holding forth the way they do? And think of how omnipresent the scourge of anxiety. No, many people *cannot* ignore the hypnotic power of suggestion. *Kämpft*, struggles, everyone has them. *Ja*. And there's no anguish quite so common as debasement, the torment of memory, traumas impossible to forgive. Deep down, almost everyone must be some kind of unstable derelict.'

'Aye, and Herr Wunderwaffe detected something of himself in that fiery, mesmerising similitude when it appeared before him. Would that be so?' Fingal asked.

'Yes, it was only a matter of time before the hapless soul felt the urge to kindle a fire and destroy himself by immolation, *ja*, a horrible rite to mirror the way the visitor appeared.'

Fingal looked into the physician's eyes. 'The projection of all me inborn knowledge, that's what must've brought this about. Which means *I'd* be to blame.' Before Doktor Pflug could respond, Fingal returned into the corridor.

Jean walked forward, her face bathed in a glow something like fill light. 'Did I hear you right in there? You went and released some kind of damn fool projection? A living image?'

'Aye, as I'm sure you know, all me life I'd been engaged in esoteric investigations into proving or else disproving Plato. That's why I had to release a reduplication of that godly part of me being, for there'd be no other avenue of inquiry by which to—'

'So you finally done it?'

'That's right, so I did.'

'In dead earnest?'

'Aye, me inborn knowledge has gone free. And the bloody bounder promptly went and bruised the fine scholar's psyche. At first sight, he did. Who knew Herr Wunderwaffe should be so damn fragile? Subject to the worst kind of influence, he'd be. His daughter as well.'

Three doors down, Fräulein Wunderwaffe appeared.

'What's that odour?' the little girl asked, shaking the fringe out of her eyes.

Fingal forced a smile. 'It's nothing,' he lied. 'We're cooking up some wild boar for supper. Aye, we've still got such beasties in these parts. "No farrow of spotted swine has chased about the Highlands for a thousand years or more," they say. But that's a fib.'

The little girl breathed in and winced. 'Has *Papa* gone home to Heidelberg? Where's my father?'

'Never mind, lass. You can't speak to him just now.'

'*No*? For what reason? Please tell me why.'

'Something right direful has happened.' Fingal wrapped his hand around his throat, until the sulfurous taste in his mouth grew warm and dry.

The little girl wrung her hands. 'If my father cooked the pony foal, I don't mind. No, not at all. When I change into a leopardess, I'll be hungry for so much more. Yes, I'll probably crave a snowflake-dappled mare.'

'You mustn't haver like that, lass.'

'No, bring me a strong, savoury racehorse. One descended from Darley Arabian, the best sire ever there was. Bring me a purebred, with the same kind of blaze on its muzzle and the same kind of coronet. And . . .'

'Your father's dead, little hen. Gone to his reward. But I'll not forsake you. If you got no family back home, I'll raise you as me own daughter and never let no harm come to you.'

Fräulein Wunderwaffe blinked several times. Had she gone into shock? The little girl descended the stair, every movement precise, and stopped before the newel post.

Fingal followed along. 'Please accept me humblest apologies. Aye, me heart bleeds for you. Do forgive me. Honest, I never thought anything like this should happen.'

Did she even hear a word? The little girl walked to the door, grabbed her hat, and continued outside into the garden.

In the evening the inviting crackle of fire resounded from the armoury hall, so Fingal continued into the darkened chamber, where he paused before the plate armour mounted atop the wooden horse. *Something's afoot.* For the longest time, he studied the slit in the helmet resting atop the breastplate. Then he grabbed a broomstick and placed the dusty bristles up against the headpiece. 'You in there yet?' he asked. The helmet fell to the floor, the sudden shrill clamour sounding like a wind-driven whirligig. With his throat burning even more, Fingal turned toward the opposite end of the hall.

A naked figure wholly enshrouded in flames of blush scarlet stood there all ablaze.

The very idea. Fingal shivered, for he had never imagined that his likeness might assume such an oddly-unnerving appearance. 'You got me feeling goddamn perplexed. Why must you appear like you've just immolated yourself?'

The spectre raised its hand. 'You betrayed our maw, eh? Instead of contenting yourself to master the principles of hotel management and to live the Scottish life, you reverted back to your childhood passions. The art of electricity. Aye, and you dreamt up the absurd machine by which you brought me here … against my wishes.'

Fingal pointed at the entity. 'Do you know what you've done? Damn, you've gotten the measure of Herr Wunderwaffe. And don't say I'd be to blame. I brought you forth for the best of reasons intellectual, I did.'

The spectral figure levitated a foot or so. 'You do not prize wisdom. Rather you seek glory, renown.' With that remark, the burning man returned to the floor and continued outside.

Fingal followed the spectre into the castle courtyard. Then, as the fiery, ghostlike being raised its arms to the nighttime sky and purred, Fingal slumped beside the well and drew his legs up. *Why'd I bring the bloody projection forth?* With the back of his hand, he brushed his brow, and for a moment, he shook and wept and groaned—and it was all that he could do to keep from rending his coat lapels.

Doktor Pflug walked into the castle courtyard with the chocolate Siamese cradled in the crook of his arm. 'Whatever you do, you must not alert the authorities,' he told Fingal. 'Why? If you reveal what has happened here, countless newspapermen should come along. And then their sensationalist communiqués should serve to give people ideas.'

'Ideas?'

'Terrible ideas. Before you know it, a suicide cluster could commence. *Ja*. A contagion event. The whole travesty would resemble *der Werther-Effekt*.' With a sigh, the physician peered into the well. 'Everyone prizes lucidity, presence of mind. But this thing we call perspective, it tends to be fragile.'

'Fragile?'

'Very fragile.' The physician released the cat. 'Remember, almost everyone tends to be susceptible to any kind of agitator. *Ja*. And then, once unnerved, we feel shock, confusion, rage, emotional disturbance. We make mistakes. We contradict ourselves.'

Fingal kicked off his shoes and rubbed his toes. He turned to the burning man, who walked off across the castle grounds.

Doktor Pflug snapped his fingers. '*Na gut*. We must not fritter away the time. No, we must find the girl before the visitor imperils her.'

Fingal returned to his feet at once. 'I'll collect the lass and bring her back.' All the time shaking his head, he darted off in the same direction as the spectre.

Down by the rowan tree, the fiery figure paused, shining as darkly as a person standing in shadow. At the same time, a phenomenon not unlike backlight illumined the tree trunk and its crown, lighting up each one of the boughs.

Fingal stopped not three feet away. 'What're you doing, you bloody miscreant? Would you be looking for the girl?'

'I am your foe,' the spectre answered, without even turning back. 'Why should I tell you what I aim to do?'

Fingal looked to the earth. 'You listen here. I unleashed a projection of me knowledge primeval, I did. And maybe that was a daft thing to do, but even so, I'll just go on and send you right back inside me. Aye, and you'll become one with me psyche again, and that'll be that, do you hear? Aye, I got me the right keen wish to put you back where you belong. Firstly, though, tell me why you take such menacing form. Why so harrowing?'

A purple lily beetle crawled past Fingal's heel, swivelled toward a fallen rowan berry, and proceeded to scurry about in circles, as if the dumbfounded creature could not decide just what to make of the bitter feast.

Meanwhile, the night turned dark—and by the time Fingal looked up, the burning man had vanished.

The crown of the rowan tree stirred ever so slightly, even though the night had grown impossibly still.

At last, Fräulein Wunderwaffe climbed down from the boughs and bowed the way little girls sometimes do. '*Guten Abend*.'

'Me wretched miscreation has wrought a most unhealthful impact upon you, eh? Don't you pother though. Soon enough, I'll have me the ken to force me ill-natured mate to stay away from you for good. Do you hear? Don't you fret none. No, don't take things to heart. One way or another, I'll find some way to restrain me accursed playfellow. No, I'll not let the visitor affright you no more. Me solemn vow, I pledge.'

The little girl removed her hat. 'I think it'd be good to let a wondrous fire enfold my body. Yes, I'm happy that I've learned the magical rite of sacrifice.'

Fingal clenched his fists. 'No, I'll not have you talking like that no more,' he almost shouted.

'*Nein. Noch nie.* Once I gather the nerve, I'll do as my father did. I'll bathe myself in a cloud of fire and leave this terrible world and then come back as the most beautiful leopardess ever there was.'

An orange-coloured berry dropped from the rowan tree's crown and bounced off Fingal's sloping shoulder.

The little girl pointed at the berry and let out a dissonant shriek. Then, her hand all atremble and her big, blue eyes growing wide, Fräulein Wunderwaffe snarled like a hungry, merciless cat.

Chapter Four

At eight o'clock in the morning, Fingal returned to the rowan tree and knelt before the berry that had impacted against his shoulder the night before. With both the little girl's shriek and snarl still ringing in his ears, he placed the berry in his hand. *Why must inborn knowledge be so violent? Why so destructive? How could I let this happen? The worst of sinners, I'd be.*

The morning breeze came sailing across the castle grounds, and he almost melted into tears. *Bloody hell, I'm feeling wistful for a time and place unknown to me.* For ten minutes or more, he became lost in daydreams. More than anything, he envisioned his destiny—the sense of jubilation sure to come upon him in that moment he triumphally returned the projection inside him. *What then? I'll tell everyone me invention works just right. Aye, but then I'll admonish everyone just how gingerly we must make such images. Perilous, they'd be.*

Little by little, an aroma something like the sweet scent of genuine Scottish-heather perfume drifted down from the rowan tree.

A hopeful sign, that. A second time, he envisioned his future—his renown. Then he laughed the way he had when he was a little boy of Fräulein Wunderwaffe's age. *I've had me a fleeting glimpse of victory, and now it's time to act.* In a sprint, he raced all the way back to the pewter works.

A dim glow as that of oil lamps welcomed him, and when it drew him inside, the soft gleam assumed the mysterious energy and radiance of Shakespearean stage lighting.

He approached his worktable and removed a few leaves of sketch paper from the little pull-out drawer. *I know. I'll dedicate all me faculties and fashion a novel handheld device by which to control the unruly projection. Aye, that's what I'll do. Now then, where to begin?*

The autumn breeze kicked up, and his mouth filled with the taste of butterscotch blended with something like Scottish thistle blossom.

A second hopeful sign. He made a crude sketch, and then he scanned a few of the spare machine parts strewn about the floor. *Where to find all the vital materials I'd require?* Before long, he made his way into the store room.

While he surveyed the various surplus parts, a pair of footsteps raced across the gable rooftop. *It's me double up there.* He collected a broomstick and tapped the ceiling. 'Enjoy your freedom whilst you may.'

Over in the corner, an experimental system unit stirred to life. An odourless wisp of blue smoke emerged from the strange contraption's electro-mechanical ventilation fan.

Just where and when did I get me that primitive apparatus? If memory served him right, he had procured the contrivance at the Glasgow Electrical Exhibition, just a few days after his fourteenth birthday. *Why not cannibalise the computer?*

Another nebulous blue fume drifted into the air, but the

second vapour reeked of tap root and curdling milk.

Lovely. Fingal removed the pipe wrench from his toolbox and forced open the computer's mainframe. *Aye, this'll do. Or should I say* thistle *do?* Methodically, he collected a heap of machine parts from inside and then returned to the worktable.

For twenty minutes or more, he toiled away—until Doktor Pflug invited himself into the pewter works and pointed at him. 'Please, friend,' the doktor said, 'tell me that you're on the verge of returning that mesmerising projection into your being.' The physician fussed with his collar. 'Your mirror-image, there's no limit to its malevolence.'

Fingal held up the diagram. 'Have no fear. I'd be ready to fashion a trusty weapon. Aye, and I'll even give it a German name. For want of a better word, I'll call it the Instruktor. And if the damn thing works right, I'll soon have me the power to command me ghostly double.'

'*Wunderbar*. I wish you success, for our troubles extend far deeper than you realise. Not unlike some depraved, alien substance yearning to spread its life force, your double possesses the potential to impact and destroy the whole world. Perhaps every living thing in the universe.'

'Don't say that.' A fragrance as of Scottish thistle tea sailed through the pewter works, and Fingal closed his eyes. *Soon, very soon, I'll be right acclimated.* The sweet, earthy fragrance died out, and he opened his eyes. *Onward to victory*.

Doktor Pflug looked to the ceiling. 'I'll tell you something more. The projection of your unconscious mind up there on the gables, he wields even greater influence over the little girl than you appreciate. In confidence, I tell you. Any day now, your twin stranger *must* inspire our poor little Fräulein Wunderwaffe to destroy herself. Why? *Na gut*, I'll tell you why. The poor thing has no other way to remedy her ongoing failure to transform into a cat. What a pity.'

Fingal placed his hands over his face. 'I had good reason to do what I did. It's only right to study the psyche, for it's the most mosaic of machines. Barring no technology nowhere.'

The light streaming through the windows grew much too bright, but the effect did not last long, and the illusion of archaic stage lighting returned along with the fragrance of Scottish thistle tea. Fingal arranged a few of the more intricate, sensitive pieces. *Let's do this. Onward to destiny.*

Over the course of the next two days and nights, he continued to toil away. Even on the day of Herr Wunderwaffe's funeral, when Doktor Pflug stopped by to insist that he attend the services, Fingal continued with his work.

One afternoon, the physician called upon him, and, in a kindly manner, pulled him away from his worktable. 'I think you should rest. *Sleep*. Take a little pill, *ein Hypnotikum*. Otherwise, you'll strain yourself.'

'No, no. You'll not stay me hand.'

'Come back to the castle,' Doktor Pflug insisted. 'I'll give you a psychosocial study that explains the issues confronting us, the bond between thought and physiology, the bond between wisdom and pathology.'

Fingal fussed with his kilt purse. *Why* not *lose myself in a good book?* Soon enough, he slipped into his coat and followed the physician outside.

A discordant wail rang out—either the chocolate Siamese or Fräulein Wunderwaffe, or both in unison. And then the burning man materialised before Fingal and wailed even louder, before turning and striding off across the castle grounds.

Fingal followed the burning man down the winding, rutted road to the cemetery—where the fiery spectre promptly vanished.

At twilight Fingal had still not departed. He stood with his arms crossed seeking to picture the funeral services for Herr Wunderwaffe. *Were the ceremony honourable enough?* For the little girl's sake, Fingal hoped so. If nothing else, Fräulein Wunderwaffe must have appreciated the fine music. After all, the beadle had secured the services of an accomplished piper—and he had performed two solemn, stirring songs from the Church of Scotland hymnal. For a time, Fingal pretended to perform a piece and fluttered his fingers up and down an imaginary melody pipe.

At eight o'clock, the gravedigger came along to bury someone. For a moment or two, he peered into Fingal's eyes. 'You look so *sad*. Aye, just the way a proper Scotsman looks when he espies his wraith.' With that, the old man plunged his trench shovel into the fill and dropped a bit of the earth into the fresh plot.

The bit of earth failed to make much of a sound when it hit the casket. Still, from somewhere not so far away, the fierce, vengeful cries of a dozen Highland tigers rang out.

'You'd better stay away from your wraith,' the gravedigger continued. 'Any Scotsman knows his semblance only ever stops by to forewarn of his impending death and damnation.'

'You're talking bollocks.' Fingal walked over to the family tomb, where he paused to whistle the tune to a sacred piece that his mother had always loved. *How I miss you so, Maw.*

A few brown, brittle and tattered witch-elm leaves tumbled by, and back along the winding country road, the breeze grew strong enough to rattle the wooden lychgate's weathered posts—so much so that two of the shingles fell to the earth.

In his bones Fingal felt the languid change of seasons—the heartrending beauty of life slowly dying, the approach of another harsh winter. The witch-elm leaves blew back, and as they collided against the vault, he intuited the return of his double. As quickly as possible, he stood up straight. 'Face me then, why don't you? Tell me just what in the world could ever justify what you did to that fine German chap.'

Like a mischievous spirit hoping to incense its prey, the entity failed to respond. Instead, the ghostlike being walked off very slowly, beckoning Fingal to follow.

The creature guided him a mile and a half down the winding, rutted road, past the charity school and Scottish Aluminium Limited with its malodorous smelting furnace. When they reached the village, the fiery figure disappeared from view a second time.

A moment or two later, a distant applause resounded. And then the sound of music suddenly blared—the pub band performing a time-honoured jig and reel.

'Show yourself,' Fingal cried out. When nothing happened, he peered into the narrow, begrimed alleyway to his left.

A cold flame seeped through his coat and shirt, licked at the small of his back, and then seemed to merge with the subatomic particles surrounding his flesh.

He patted his belly. 'Would you be hiding inside me? Well then, you might as well stay there. For there's no way for you to alter your miserable fate.' As he spoke those words, the cold flame departed through his left ear—or so it seemed. Determined to look unconcerned, he stood tall and continued into the pub.

The establishment seemed unusually dark that evening, the only light a faint glow from the candle standing atop the Victorian pier cabinet. Despite the darkness, Fingal paused to admire a few of the medieval spirit decanters that the publican had recently put on display. He breathed in all the pleasing scents lingering in the air—haggis and roasted turnips, cream stout and old ale. Then he turned toward the pub band and gestured toward the fiddler.

Just like that, the fiddle scraped and screeched to a halt—at which point all the other instruments let up in a cacophony of peeps and grunts and honks and whistles.

He approached the barmaid and offered her a crooked smile. 'Give me a pennyworth of something smooth and mellow, eh?' When she poured him a pint of malt whisky, he paid the tab with the last few coins in his kilt purse and then walked over to the far corner.

Thankfully, the chap on penny whistle broke into a time-honoured tune. And soon enough, the rest of the band joined in—the fiddler producing all the wrong chords, as if the poor fool had lost the power to play.

A local drunkard and sometime clock winder by the name of Iain Galbraith stumbled over to Fingal's table. 'Why you here?'

'Come to lay the dust, I have.'

'Aye, sometimes there's nothing to do but drown your thoroughgoing sorrows and get yourself pickled. These days, I'm blighted as well but nothing like *you*. And I know, for I've heard the rumours. Aye, you'd be the talk of the town. Not two hours ago, Hamish Macfadyen told me the whole tale. "Fingal's got doubtful company dwelling in that castle of his, a fiery ghost aiming to drive away all of his lodgers." Aye, that's what the fine chap said.'

Fingal turned to the window. 'Don't you pother. I know what's what, and I got me a stratagem for victory.'

Down by the watchmaker's shop, some two blocks away, a bright purple glare the colour of cotton thistle suddenly shone.

Me kindred, no doubt. Fingal returned outside into the

street. 'You're not long for this world,' he spoke up, the door closing behind him quietly. 'I've almost cobbled together me right fine Instruktor, and when I complete me toils, so you'll be me captive. And I'll not permit you to spread your abominable influence. No, no. Believe me. There won't be no kind of no emotional contagions abounding here and there and hither and thither.'

A few blocks away, a light shone from the picture window two stories above the tallow chandler's shop. On the other side of the curtain lace then, a figure appeared in silhouette—the candlemaker himself. Slowly, deliberately, he took hold of what appeared to be a length of thread and then dipped it into what must have been a mould filled with hot wax.

The heat of a cold spark trickled past Fingal's shoulder. With the back of his hand, he felt at the base of his spine and pulled at his shirt, only to find that the uncanny fire burned even more. *Jesus wept.* Sweat dripped down his spine. Fingal knelt to the walkway and breathed in. He grew still then and made his body rigid. With the palms of both hands, he smote the cobblestone.

'Come face me if you'd be so inclined,' his double whispered. 'I'll not hide from view. No, I'll stand right here because I'd prefer you get a sense of my adeptness for mayhem and malfeasance. I'm sure once you do, you'll be pleading for dear life.'

Fingal belched. *I got to be dead calm.* He turned westward and fixed his gaze upon the quiet lane where the morphine pushers and the addicts congregated from time to time.

His twin reappeared on the edge of the village, the nightmarish figure standing between a dying cherry tree and a slanted fingerpost.

Fingal chased the spectre back along the winding country

road—until the elusive entity vanished not far from an ancient Celtic passage grave.

A pair of meadow mice with pink noses happened along then. For a moment or two, the voles studied Fingal. When the two pests finally wandered off into a patch of knotweed, he continued along for another quarter of a mile, until a nagging twinge awoke deep in his gut.

The anguish served to remind him of a night ten years earlier when a deceitful tenant had sought to leave the castle before settling the bill. Fingal had pursued the scoundrel to this precise spot. 'You aim to bury the landlady, eh?'

Immediately, the shameless thug had socked him in the gut. Then the reprobate had raced off into the ruins of the Roman marching camp—and now the fiery figure reappeared just there, in the heart of the archaeological site.

Me quarry. Fingal marched off into the field, fragments of cotton thistle scratching at his ankles—but when the figure vanished a second time and left nothing behind but the faint scent of burnt heather, Fingal paused beside a little juniper tree. 'Where did you go? Come back and face me proper, I say.'

On and on, the watching and waiting continued, until the two combatants stood face to face.

Fingal shivered. 'We've never stood so close as this, have we then?' Irrespective of the glare, he studied his nemesis. How perfect their resemblance: each one even had the same flesh-coloured mole on the thumb side of the left wrist. 'To beguile the time, I suppose you must *look* like the time,' Fingal whispered. 'Wouldn't that be so?'

The other leaned forward and sniffed Fingal's neck. 'I got me a favour to ask of you this autumn night.'

'No, I'll not favour you. No, not never. I got me a

conscience, haven't I? No, I'd never do nothing for the likes of you.'

'Stop calling yourself by my forename,' the fiery figure said loudly.

'How's that? Have you forgotten how you got to this world? Properly, *I* should be the one asking *you* to stop calling yourself by *my* Christian name, for I'd be the sole true Fingal, and just so you know, I do much regret liberating you from me deepest reaches, and I solemnly swear that one splendid day, someday quite soon I hope, I'll puzzle out the way to bring you back into the pewter works. And then I'll send you back inside me where you belong.'

'Do what you must. Persecute me. But I'd be guilty of no crime. No, I'd be a perfectly natural breed.'

The moonlight grew warm and inviting, and as the yellowy fog shifted, a vast array of constellations shone like the little white sprinkles that a traditional Scottish confectioner might drop all over a fresh batch of melty mints.

'Look at them lights up there,' Fingal whispered. 'Carbon stars, the dazzling Vega, dozens and dozens of luminous bodies. Wondrous planets.'

The flame-enshrouded projection dropped its hands to its sides. 'You feel the stardust alighting upon the good earth, do you? Aye, all them chemical elements and ionised gases what fall through the Milky Way, every last measure must run its course here, and then all that wee stardust fashions itself into discrete living things, flesh and blood, plants and animals.'

Fingal wrapped both hands around his rival's neck. 'Tell me whether Plato's theory of innate knowledge would be true. Then get back inside me. Let me realise the essence I seek. Let me distinguish myself as someone worthy of Scots engineering.'

The spectre grabbed Fingal's neck, and both fell to the

earth, where a struggle ensued amid a cloud of red dust.

At one point during the melee, Fingal felt the primal being's heartbeat. What power the steady pulsations—as if the entity must surely possess the heart of a lion. *How to battle a ghoul like this?* Fingal eased his grip, and when his opposer did the same, Fingal crawled off a few feet and held his palm over his left breast. *I'm bloodless, I am.* Despite the sensation, he forced himself to stand. 'You're in robust health, so you are.'

'Right, right. And it's no mystery why. Inside the furthest recesses of anyone's psyche dwells something like an angry god, a fallen angel, a renegade, a *savage*.'

All so nimbly, a Highland tiger emerged from the shadows, and when the wildcat paused to study the two figures, the creature's eyes shone a faded green.

Fingal thought of Fräulein Wunderwaffe and turned back to his double. 'Don't harm the German lass, eh? That girl, she's already got herself so many troubles.'

Fingal's double offered a blank stare that made it seem as if the entity lacked the power to register any feeling.

Fingal raised his hand. 'Regarding that German lass, ever since she were a baby, a fair few delusions have plagued her. Don't ask me why, but she thinks she's bound to change into some kind of panther. And there's nothing me nor anyone else should do about it.'

Like a nefarious character in a children's puppet show, the apparition laughed. 'Either the girl destroys herself by fire, or else she goes mad.'

'*Please*. If only you could permit yourself to sympathise, then Doktor Pflug could rescue the wee lass from the frowns of fortune.'

The wildcat from before growled at a purple star shimmering in the northern sky, and then the alluring animal retreated back into the shadows—and for *its* part, the fiery spectre floated off to the side of the road.

No matter all his bruised and strained muscles, Fingal pursued the diabolical figure for two miles or more, until the fiend climbed into the boughs of a majestic field maple.

Fingal shook his fist. 'Why you acting like a Guinea baboon? Come you down from there this bloody instant.'

The whole of the brightly-coloured crown shook such that a storm of pineapple-yellow leaves rained all over, which must have spooked the herd of Scotch Highlands cattle dwelling in the petting zoo standing off to the side. Soon enough, a few of the heifers bolted and tore through the fence, and then a dozen more followed, until the whole herd joined the stampede.

Chapter Five

At the break of dawn, a series of confounded grunts, snorts and bellows awoke Fingal and brought him to his balcony doors. Down below, a Highland cow raced about in circles.

Indeed, the whole herd of cattle from the night before wandered about the castle grounds. Time and again, each beast turned this way and that—as if it could not precisely discern the parameters of the phenomenological world itself. Had the creatures lost the power to feel the temperature? Perhaps they could no longer discern weather patterns.

Dressed in nothing more than his wrinkled, grey nightshirt, Fingal walked downstairs and continued outside.

One of the Highland cows drew close and studied him awhile before turning its muzzle back toward its crops. Three times over, the animal snorted—as if it wished to communicate with its unborn calf.

Something stirred in the crown of the rowan tree, then, dressed in a long, pink camisole, Fräulein Wunderwaffe climbed down from the boughs. 'I'm dying. *Ach*. Your sharer has bathed me in a stream of invisible fire.'

For the first time in days, a burning sensation crawled across Fingal's forearms—and now the uncanny heat continued up and down his legs. More than that, the warmth emitted a scent as of persimmon. Despite all, he walked forward some. 'Go inside, lass. *Forthwith*. The evildoer would be buzzing about the treetops, wherefore you shouldn't be out and about.'

Some of the cattle brushed past the little girl's side, but she did not respond. Instead, she breathed in. 'I feel the approach of a storm. It's come all the way from the tropics, maybe the jungles of India. Can't you taste the jackfruit in the air? *No*, I think it's Caribbean lime.'

No matter the dawn light, the fog refused to dissolve, and now the length and breadth of the castle grounds assumed the colour of black-and-white cinematography. As the lines and shapes of the cattle materialised and then dematerialised here and there throughout the mist, Fingal shook his head. *Aye, the art of shadows*.

For her part, Fräulein Wunderwaffe returned to the rowan tree and climbed back into the boughs. When she peered down, the sensual girl made a series of melodic purrs. Then she held herself still, as if she detected some intrusive creature breathing sweet scents into her left ear.

Fingal paced awhile, and then he looked upon her. 'Please, lass. You got to come to your senses. You and me and all, we got to make good choices now and not let the burning man get the better of us. That's right, we'll harden up. Together, you and me and all, we'll find some way to get the burning man to resolve the riddle of inborn knowledge. He'll tell us whether it's true, and then we'll send the projection back inside me noodle. Aye, and then we'll tend to all your infirmities.'

The little girl vanished into the crown for a moment and then climbed back onto the same bough as before. Now she held in her lap a pendulum clock, its once-immaculate brass weight as black as *café noir.*

Fingal scowled. *Aye, look there, the metallic surface has oxidised. Someone must've touched it. Must've been the goddamn burning man.*

The little girl placed the clock to her side, letting the antique teeter upon the bough. He studied the clock more closely and realised that even the count wheel was gone. *The striking mechanism as well.* His knees smarted. 'Grandmaw Mackenzie gave us that lovely ticker,' he told the little girl. 'And now look what the burning man has gone and done. Spoiled our family heirloom, he has.'

A soft, wild breeze stirred the boughsand. The rowan berries should have emitted a scent as sweet as treacle tart, but Fingal breathed in the scent of something tropical instead, and then he waved to the girl. 'Serve as me friendly witness, would you? Hear me as I pledge to face me nightmares and learn what's got to be what for me to make the Instruktor work right and orderly.'

She did not respond, but from out of the mist a delicate figure appeared and nudged his foot. The visitor proved to be the chocolate Siamese. It licked its whiskers, then gazed off toward some of the cattle wandering past a rolling cloud of fog.

Fingal turned back to the little girl—how tattered her robe, and how greasy and how matted her long, golden hair. He pointed at a laceration cut deep into her forearm. 'You ought to cease wandering about the night, eh? Looks like you've been fiddling about like a Chinese mountain cat. I suppose you wish to prepare for your metamorphosis. Would that be so?'

For a time, Fräulein Wunderwaffe studied some of the

cattle wandering about the fog-laden earth. Then she turned away, as if to consider the faint light of dawn. 'Today's the very last Sabbath before Advent begins.'

'Aye, we call it Eternity Sunday.'

'Back home, we say *Totensonntag.*'

'Please, lass. Hear me now. You haven't got no cause to worry about onythin. Like I told you a thousand times before, I'll save you. Once I wield me fine Instruktor and I've detained me wretched adversary, you'll no longer scheme to throw yourself onto some funeral pyre and burn your wee body into oblivion. No, because me familiar, he won't have no influence over you no more. Aye, and the honourable Doktor Pflug, he'll talk to you, and he'll get you feeling like yourself again, so that you no longer daydream about changing into some kind of beast.'

At Fingal's side, the chocolate Siamese trilled softly, and the little girl rasped in perfect concert with the creature.

Fingal stepped back. 'What're you doing? Come down from that mountain ash. You're no mouser, and you're not bound to transform into one neither. That kind of thing, it's not even bloody possible.'

The pendulum clock fell from the bough and landed with a soft thud that made the chocolate Siamese yelp before darting off. Fräulein Wunderwaffe vanished back into the crown, so Fingal returned into the castle. Upstairs, he heard footsteps coming from Herr Wunderwaffe's bedchamber. "Who's in there?" he asked, standing alongside the jamb. .

The sound of someone's languid footfall approached the other side of the door. Then the footsteps fell silent. 'What the hell do you want?' the American woman, Jean Selwyn, asked in her distinctive Kentucky accent. 'Do you always wake up the womenfolk at sunrise? Can't you let me rest my weary bones? Judas priest.'

Fingal fumbled with the locked, pressed-glass knob. 'What're *you* doing in Herr Wunderwaffe's bedchamber?'

'What am I doing in here? I was flying up the roost till *you* came along.'

'Help me with the girl, won't you? Not a short time ago, the delicate lass went and got herself up a tree. And that's why you got to help me, eh?'

'I don't got to do goose eggs. And another thing. Just remember, there ain't nothing so foremost as Herr Wunderwaffe's work. He knew the proper way to bliss, like no bible-thumping, honey-tongued preacher man ever could've imagined. Because Herr Wunderwaffe, he knew that someday each and every last one of us ought to evolve into flattened images fit to live in realms of fantasy, a world of endless adventure. Don't you get it? Herr Wunderwaffe wrote about the promise of tomorrow and the founding of cinematic worlds what offer everlasting life and the fulfilment of all desire. Yeah, he wrote about honest-to-goodness *utopianism*.'

Fingal turned the knob as forcefully as he could and sought to open the locked door. 'Was it you what let the girl purloin me pendulum clock? Confess, I say,' he said to the American through the door.

He heard Jean blow her nose and then say, 'Listen here. Tell me why a great scholar like Herr Wunderwaffe would go and set himself on fire. What did that damn devilish apparition say to him? How does the scourge of emotional contagion play out? Tell me true.'

Fingal tried to break through the door. He kicked the bottom rail several times over but only managed to stub his toe.

'Go away,' the American woman told him. 'I got to get

some sleep, so's I can think on futurism and carry on with Herr Wunderwaffe's research.'

For the rest of the day, a host of farmhands worked to corral the cattle, and as they did, Fingal toiled away in the pewter works. For an hour or more, he examined the experimental weapon. As much as anything, the device had come to resemble one of those pioneering handheld instruments by which a lineman measures the electric flux in the air. Fingal activated the mechanism, but it failed to summon the entity. *Just what would I be lacking?*

At three o'clock, he exited the pewter works, favouring his stubbed toe. He limped and hobbled and ambled his way back to the rowan tree.

Fräulein Wunderwaffe, still dressed in her tattered robe, approached his side and greeted him. Oddly enough, the little girl held in her hands the zoetrope that Mother had presented to him on his fifth birthday.

'Where'd you find them tricks?'

'Beneath my bed.' The little girl balanced the toy upon one of the rowan tree's long, thick roots. Then she worked the wooden crank to make the zoetrope spin around.

He knelt to the earth and looked through the slats. Just as he remembered, the animation reel depicted a Nepalese leopard cat running along with a powerful stride.

'Where did you get this?' the little girl asked. 'Do you remember?'

'Aye, me maw got this plaything for me on the highway to Inverness. She got it from a clever, pioneering toymaker what knew all about precinema technologies.'

Fräulein Wunderwaffe lay down on her belly, peered through the slats, and batted her eyelashes. *'Es ist so schön.'*

'You shouldn't be so fond of panthers and such,' Fingal told her. 'If your old man was here, he'd be quite cross with you.'

'Forget him already. Let me watch the kitty. Oh, it's as wondrous as a cherub.'

'Maybe so, but in consideration of the foregoing, I do feel it'd be me duty to—'

'Have you ever noticed the leopard cat's miraculous spots? What a magical shade of admiral blue. Wouldn't that be just about the most perfect, graceful, supreme, angelic colour ever there was? What do you think?'

'I can't be asking myself such precious things just now, lass. *No*. Haven't got the time, have I? Just now I got to acculture myself and work me fingers to the bone and find the way to make me whimsical Instruktor work good and artful. That'd be the only way to save you.'

A cold, autumn breeze sailed by, swaying the rowan tree, and as a shower of brittle, crimson leaves and rotten berries pelted the toy, Fingal turned away and staggered straight back to the pewter works.

In the evening, hungry, barefoot and yawning, he finally returned to the castle. Not an hour later, a nightmare invaded his sleep.

Suddenly, a thick fog rolls across the moor. Fräulein Wunderwaffe emerges from the glen and pauses before a patch of meadow grass.

A murder of carrion crows takes flight from atop the tithe barn's roof. Out beyond the millpond's far shore, a down of hares retreat into their warren. And then, from the direction of the Highlands, a soft breeze dances and twists through the fields and stirs one of the ash trees.

Fräulein Wunderwaffe prostrates herself and crawls into a patch of dying heather. By the time she reappears, she has transformed into a leopardess with blue spots—each one shaped like a sensuous woman's hooded eye.

The scent of miracle berries wafted into the bedchamber, the aroma so strong that Fingal almost fell out of bed. Before long, though, he returned to deep sleep.

The leopardess races out into the countryside and continues along the border of a neighbouring townland, where the jungle cat consumes the last of the Highland cattle and then saunters back toward the castle.

Not far from the rowan tree, a deerhound confronts the beast. 'Tell us the secret what'd make Fingal's Instruktor work good and hearty and proper. Aye, we beg you.'

Plainly indifferent, the jungle cat refuses to answer. Instead, the creature climbs into the rowan tree and becomes lost in the lush crown. Then, a vengeful red fire crackling in its eyes, the leopardess commands a solitary moonbeam to illumine the castle walls.

Fräulein Wunderwaffe appears alongside the easternmost parapet and grins at the leopardess. The beast roars, at which point the girl recites some kind of Old-Saxon healing incantation.

A soft autumn rain commences, obscuring the dreamscape, and when the cloudburst ceases, the leopardess spews up the zoetrope.

With a yelp, Fingal awoke. And soon enough, no matter the darkness, he intuited the approach of something inhuman—a beast drawing ever closer through the bedchamber. *Aye, it's only the mouser.* When the chocolate Siamese climbed over his belly, he let the animal's tail slip through his fingers, the soothing sensation lingering in his palm. He sat up and rested his back against the headboard.

The cat returned to the heart of the moonlit room, leapt onto the drum table and struck a pose something like a circus animal posing for a black-and-white glamour portrait.

After donning his dressing gown, Fingal staggered off to find Doktor Pflug. *Got to get me a wee bit of succour.* He found a handwritten note thumbtacked to the lock rail the physician's door:

MEET ME BENEATH THE ROWAN TREE

Fingal arrived at the tree as dawn broke.

Doktor Pflug bowed. 'I had a feeling some deep trauma must visit you last night.'

Fingal crushed a rowan berry beneath the ball of his foot and then related the vision in minute detail.

The physician yawned and stretched his arms. 'I think your nightmare must be a good portent. Why? Because the trauma means to *inspire* you.'

'How so? Put it in plain English, eh?'

'Very well. Your unconscious mind afflicts you with such fantasies for no other reason than to help you fashion the Instruktor. That's why you must embrace these dreams. If you do, they should teach you how to complete the device and control the fiendish projection.'

Fingal breathed in and exhaled. Then he knelt to the earth and wrapped his hand around one of the rowan tree's gnarled roots, where it reached through a patch of dead hogweed. 'Tell me more.'

The physician dug his hands into the pockets of his long, grey frock coat. 'The answer must be the beloved zoetrope.'

'How do you mean?'

'When you sleep, you observe the way your unconscious mind celebrates the zoetrope's capacity to beguile. Why? I'd say your very deepest impulses seek to compel you into implanting a like effect within the Instruktor, for only in this manner should the device serve to ensnare your prey.'

Fingal shook his head. *Could that be the answer?*

The entity in question rematerialised some thirty feet away, the figure enshrouded in flames of pale turquoise.

Fräulein Wunderwaffe hurried forward from the direction of the gatehouse, the little girl draped in her lamb's-wool blanket.

'Get yourself back in the gaff,' Fingal shouted. 'Go indoors, lass.'

'*Schnell*,' the physician added. 'Don't look at the deceiver whatever you do. Go back to your room.'

At last, she turned back, but the uncanny transgressor blocked her path. Fingal raced over and he and Doktor Pflug brought the girl away from it, right down to the loch.

The flaming projection reappeared in the shadow of the rowan tree. 'Behold,' it called out, pointing toward the waters. 'Look at all those beautiful, silvery faces floating upon the waves.'

'Don't listen,' Fingal told the little girl. 'Ignore the burning man.'

'Each one of those faces must be the countenance of some immolated soul,' the spectre continued. 'Listen, fräulein. Can't you hear the silvery faces calling out your name?'

Fingal patted the little girl's wrist. 'There's nothing out there on the placid firth. Me unwonted projection only means to wind you up, he does.'

The girl dropped her blanket and turned to the narrow lake. 'Don't faces *always* appear in the most peculiar places?' she asked in a whisper.

The physician tapped the girl's shoulder. 'The malevolent spirit only hopes to implant a suggestion inside you. Why? Because the vile being feels the urge to compel others to delude themselves.'

Fräulein Wunderwaffe studied the waters and cried out, '*Ein Vexierbild!*' A picture puzzle. Then her bladder gave way such that the little girl wet her linen sleeper.

'There's nothing out there,' Doktor Pflug insisted. '*Nichts.*'

'How do *you* know?' she asked in a whisper. 'Maybe the silvery faces wish to come ashore and dance a folk waltz.' Her knees wobbling, Fräulein Wunderwaffe motioned toward a place out along the strand where the blustering wind had a multitude of fallen chrysanthemum petals swirling around in a terrific circle. 'Maybe some of the dead souls wish to come ashore and dance just like that.'

Fingal shook the girl. 'Listen, hen. *Please*. The entity would be ribbing you. Aye, the infernal defrauder would be hounding you in the hope that he might someday soon goad you into destroying yourself. Like your old man done.'

Doktor Pflug knelt to the earth and studied the girl. 'Listen, please,' the physician told her, speaking in the becalming tone of a mesmerist. 'Even if you were to witness scores of faces rising from the waters, what would any of it prove? Those hidden faces, they'd be nothing more than shadows, optical illusions.'

Fräulein Wunderwaffe's eyes grew wide. '*Sind Sie im Ernst?*' Are you serious.

Doktor Pflug returned to his feet. '*Ja. Hab keine Angst.*' Yes; have no fear.

With neck and shoulders stiff and tight, Fingal glanced back at the burning man and cringed. The fiery apparition's lips shone parchment white—the ongoing efforts to undermine the projection had plainly inspirited *it* with great fury. Fingal turned back to the little girl and tapped her arm. 'Let's go inside, eh? You'll have yourself a sip of spring water, and then it's off to bed.' When she failed to respond, he turned back.

The burning man waved at him, and then the whole of the entity's body turned the colour of a king's robes—a hue as of purple guava.

Fräulein Wunderwaffe pointed at the spectre and laughed like a woman. She turned back to Fingal. 'Don't worry about me any,' she said. 'No trick of the light could ever deceive me. No, I'm a clever girl. And in the coming days, I'm to become the most cunning creature of all. *Ja*. Soon enough, I shall change into a magnificent leopardess.'

The castle grounds grew quiet, and Fingal considered the burning man; given the regal hue, the entity had never appeared so impressive. 'Why you looking like some wise king?' Fingal asked. 'Are you hiding something? If so, share with us your secret. Aye, share with us all your wisdom.'

The burning man coughed uncontrollably, as if he had breathed in a silky strand of a horse's forelock and it prodded the back of his mouth.

Fingal's muscles grew tense. He walked forward and pointed at the spectre. 'Share with us your wisdom, I say.' When he stood not three feet away, the burning man vomited, and the discharge resembled the same kind of warm, damp hairball that a cat might spew onto a Persian rug, the precious silk ruined forever.

Fingal's abdomen tightened. *Today I complete the Instruktor. Today, aye, today . . .*

Chapter Six

Night found Fingal overcome with burdens. He had to pay a heap of overdue bills that he had sworn to pay. More than that, he had to tidy up the accomodations. Only after he had completed all the busy work did he make his way into the pewter works. *Tonight, I complete the Instruktor.* He felt at his scalp, and a big clump of hair came loose in his hand. *What's this? Am I going bloody mental?*

The chocolate Siamese followed him inside, sneezing all the while, and then fussed with a few of the mechanical sketches strewn about the floor.

'Mind you don't bollocks up all me goddamn papers,' Fingal protested.

At dusk, he switched on every lamp and lit a whole chandelier of candles. *Tonight, I imprison me twin.*

Fingal returned to his work, and, eventually, the Instruktor produced a flashing orange light that assumed the shape of a starfish. The fantastical light reeled all about the pewter works, not unlike an animated image spinning around within a zoetrope.

It's the answer to all me prayers. Fingal turned slowly to the cat. 'I got the bloody Instruktor working. Do you hear, mouser? Aye, this instrument should give me the power to overcome me double once and for all.' He walked over to the windowsill, where he had placed a pewter urn. 'As bloody quick as possible, we've got to get me goddamn projection into this jar.' He lit a lantern and carried it outside with the Instruktor in his other hand, and the urn resting in a loop of string tied to his belt.

Despite the moonless night, the fog shone oyster white—the colour of frost smoke. Even more unlikely, a dozen or so fairy stones scattered about the strand glowed softly.

Far off to the south, from somewhere out across the loch, a church chorus performed a tune from Georg Philip Telemann's *Weihnachtskantate*. And then the tenors grew quiet, and a soprano's voice broke into a double cackle.

Once the last of the voices had died out, an almost-imperceptible, twofold crackle of fire resounded in the December breeze.

There. Fingal studied the dark, rolling hills. He tapped the urn's foot and fillet against his thigh a few times over. *Am I ready for this?* His stomach protested, and he dry heaved a couple of times.

At last, he marched off toward a light shimmering not two miles up ahead, but when he arrived at his destination, a farmhouse, he noticed no sign of life other than the aforementioned gleam shining from the garret. 'Are you here? Would you be hiding out in this gentleman's cow farm? Come out, eh? Please, I got a surprise for you.'

The sky filled with flashes of silent lightning, or had Fingal only hallucinated the whole effect? He listened for the peal of thunder; it should have resounded a dozen times over, and it should have echoed like an orchestra's vessel drums. *The kind what Telemann employed in his remembrance of the dead following the earthquake what razed Lisbon.*

The Instruktor trembled with the energy of oscillation in Fingal's hand. For a moment or two, the fluctuations almost sounded like little beads sliding back and forth along the grooves of a medieval abacus.

A gust reeking of sour wine and vinegar cooed and whistled like a songbird, and as both the wind and its odour grew stronger, Fingal lay the lantern and Instruktor down for a moment and buttoned his coat.

'What're you doing on this farmstead here?' a man's voice asked from behind him.

Fingal spun around. Some twenty feet away, an old huntsman stood by a hobbled horse, a lantern sat on the ground beside him and a lever-action sporting rifle rested on his gut, aimed at Fingal.

'Don't shoot,' Fingal pleaded, shaking his finger. 'I'm looking for me goddamn double.'

'Oh? That's what I'd be doing as well.'

Fingal shook his head. 'Please, you'd be wise to let *me* tend to things from this night forth. I don't mean to get on your wick, but this here's no paper chase.'

The huntsman lowered the rifle, and then the old man turned to a furrow wheel lying over to the side. 'You've unleashed great tumult into this world. Rumour has it your double could very well bring about the fall of British civilisation, one quiet market town at a time.'

'Nothing of the kind should happen,' Fingal said. 'I'll bully up the beastie tonight, before he menaces anyone else. There shall be no more immolations. No, no.'

The huntsman laid his rifle down and wrapped his hand

around the furrow wheel. His breath came in what sounded like tortured gulps. 'What've you *done*?'

'I've done wrong. I now know that it was a foolhardy thing for me to make a projection of me deepest unconscious self. For that, I'm sorry. Aye, but how was I to know the realm of inborn knowledge should prove to be so goddamn fiery and ruinous?'

Twice, the huntsman rattled the furrow wheel. 'Why must inborn knowledge appear and act the way it would? For what reason? Have you any answer? *Why*? *Why*?'

'If I knew the answer, I'd be as wise as King Solomon. Alas, I haven't got the answer, mate.' Fingal picked up the Instruktor and gripped it tightly. *I don't even know if me weapon here should work proper.*

A swathe of thick fog descended and, after a brief farewell, he picked up his lantern and marched off along a pathway that led towards a gleam of light. He wound his way through a stretch of hawkweed and stopped in the potter's field beside a rotting wooden Celtic cross that seemed suffused with light somehow. A pack of big, mink-grey rats hurried by. 'You here?' he asked. 'Show yourself and say something. We've so much to talk about, haven't we?'

His fiery likeness materialised some thirty feet away. Six ribbons of flame wrapped themselves around its head, not unlike a golden wreath.

Fingal lowered the lantern to the ground and, with the tip of his thumb, felt for the Instruktor's fluorescent-blue activation switch. 'So how would you be feeling this evening?'

'Fairly good,' the spectre answered, the ribbons of flame transforming into something resembling a series of waveforms. It moved nearer, head tilted, a curious gaze on the object Fingal held. 'What've you got in your hand?'

'What have I got? Come a wee bit closer, and I'll show you.'

The spectre stopped. 'No, if it's all the same to you, I'll be on my easy way.'

'No, no. Don't go.' Fingal held the Instruktor between his teeth, dried his palms against his kilt, and then transferred the weapon back into his hand.

The projection threw its shoulders back, and the boldness of its movements made Fingal tremble and gasp for breath.

As if to mock his condition, the spectre huffed and puffed awhile. Then the creature stopped and grinned. 'You sound fair puckled, so you do. Powerless to control your nerves, eh?'

Fingal did his best to collect himself. *Buck up then.* He activated the Instruktor and the device vibrated in his hand.

The burning man laughed—albeit in a feigned manner. 'What's the meaning of this?' the fiery figure asked. 'What're you doing?'

Fingal checked the Instruktor's flash shield and then pointed the weapon at his double's heart. 'I've come to answer the bugle, haven't I?'

Like a wary cat, the fiery figure walked forward and bowed his head. 'Why'd you even bring me into this world? The ancients never did. Not even Plato … nor any of his disciples.'

Fingal averted his gaze. 'Listen, regarding my work, I had to do what I did. Any right, proper gentleman of science and philosophy would've done the same. Aye, it all comes down to *enterprise*. That's how the most curious of visionaries learn what they would.'

The burning man let out a childlike hiccup and then excused himself.

Fingal sighed. 'I had no choice but to endeavour to consult you. Aye, for you'd be me second self. You possess the answers. You know all the workings of the psyche, and you know whether the mind would be comprised of inborn knowledge. Sure, you comprehend all that fine, esoteric business. Nevertheless, you behave bloody malevolent. Why, though? Maybe you're so damn wicked, you won't even say.'

The burning man let out a second childlike hiccup. Then he knelt to the earth and, like a newborn baby, crawled this way and that. Time after time, he paused and cocked his ear, as if he heard something. How innocent he seemed—like a baby boy who calls upon his senses to learn something about the surrounding environment but finds all phenomena overwhelming, confounding.

At last, the burning man sat up some and felt at his body here and there. Did he hope to convey some kind of intuitive power? Perhaps he wanted Fingal to believe that a person might teach himself how to feel the subatomic particles surrounding his flesh—the exquisite cloud of electrons that shield a person from head to toe.

Fingal felt at his own chest. *How to fathom the illusion of touch?* For a moment or two, he longed to ask his double just how it could be that the mind makes a person register the sense of touch even though nothing ever penetrates any field boasting an electric charge. When he attempted to speak, though, his tongue swelled, and he could not produce a sound.

The burning man looked into Fingal's eyes. 'Do you hear music? Might it be a double flute? Oh yes, it sounds just like the incidental music from a Greek tragedy, maybe even that great one by Euripides, the one about Medea. Don't you love the moment her wedding dress bursts into flames? Ah, but who doesn't fancy tales of combustion?'

Fingal intuited his twin's inclination toward deceit, and suddenly able once again to speak, he retorted, 'I don't hear any goddamn music.'

The burning man looked to the sky. 'Oh, what a soothing voice. Yes, just listen. That double flute there, it sounds like a narrow, wind-tossed bridge swaying in the night.'

'That's enough of that, eh?' Without any further ado, Fingal depressed the control button such that the orange light flitted about—again, just like some fanciful personage reeling around within a zoetrope.

Almost immediately, the fiery miscreant dissolved into a pulsating, shapeless presence no bigger than a puff from a tobacco pipe. Little by little, the pall coiled itself together with the light, and then the whole concoction drifted close enough to nudge the tip of Fingal's nose. He knelt to the earth, set the Instruktor beside the lantern and opened the urn's threaded lid. 'Get inside,' he whispered to the entity playing about his ear. 'Go on. Gently now.'

It seemed as if hours passed by before the puff of smoke finally descended into the vase.

There we are, just like a genie in a bottle. Fingal screwed the lid back on. *Cheerio.*

In the darkness before dawn, he trudged back onto the castle grounds, lantern and Instruktor in hand and urn swinging at his belt. No sooner had he arrived than Fräulein Wunderwaffe called him over to the rowan tree.

He marched forward and placed the Instruktor and lantern at his feet. 'I bring good news. I've trapped the accursed one. Out for blood, I was. Aye, I've put the fitful bastard in his place. Who knows just how long it'll take him to puzzle his way out? So you've got nothing to fear no more.'

The little girl circled the rowan tree a few times over, then she paused to smooth out her tattered robe. Finally, Fräulein Wunderwaffe pointed at the pewter urn and, oh so softly, she whispered something in German—something wholly unintelligible.

Fingal imagined the poor little girl having already changed into a leopardess. If it were to happen, she would come back to this very spot. Here, she would mark her territory. *Just like any leopardess might do. Aye, night after night, she'd fear the notion that some other jungle cat, a cheetah perhaps, might come along to encroach upon her territory.*

'If you was to change into a jungle cat, would you still remember me?' Fingal asked.

Once again, Fräulein Wunderwaffe muttered something beneath her breath—a dozen or more German-language profanities.

'If you was to change into a leopardess, and if you was to espy me drawing nigh, you'd up and bolt, so you would. Aye, that's what you'd do.'

The little girl rested her brow against the trunk of the rowan tree and held her chest tight—almost as if she had lost control of the muscles that governed her lungs.

What could it be? Fingal presumed that she must be lost in reverie. If nothing else, she likely imagined herself transforming into the leopardess. One with a fine, rarefied, frilly, colour-point coat. *Aye, and reflective eyes what shine blue sapphire whenever the glistering glamour of the moon hits them right.*

The little girl lifted her brow from the tree trunk. Then, her expression wholly inscrutable, she closed her eyes and licked her lips.

'Would you be thinking of all the horrors you wish to bring about? Aye, you must be thinking all about the mauling you wish to visit upon the land, the bloodied carcass of a shire horse here, the remains of a seed ox there.'

She opened her eyes and moved her right foot back, as if

preparing to kick him in the ribs. She did not do so, however. A second time, she pointed at the pewter jar.

As she did, he lost his balance, tripped over a few of the rowan tree's roots and then fell into a patch of dead clover. In the process the urn escaped from its loop of rope on his belt and nearly fell over. *Curses.*

The little girl grabbed the urn, opened the lid and slammed the jar down against Fingal's scalp, so quickly that as he suspended consciousness he never even witnessed that moment when his double went free.

Some two hours later when he awoke, he found himself back in his bedchamber. *Doktor Pflug must have brought me here.* Fingal studied the footboard. *How many years has it been since the garret-master travelled from Drumchapel to build the bed frame?*

At last, Fingal recollected all that had happened that day, and his thoughts turned back to the crisis at hand.

Before he could even manage to climb out of bed, Jean Selwyn marched into the room and cast an almond-butter cookie at his feet. 'Ain't you got no wholesome fare down there in the pantry? Hell, you ain't even got any gingerbread crumbs. And hey, just what kind of hotel don't serve eggnog-cream tarts this time of year? And just when do you mean to slaughter a Christmas goose?'

'*Enough.* We've got ourselves a wee lass in distress, and though there's no virtue like the call to preserve innocent life; you do nothing to help.'

'Even if what you say was true, it ain't my fault no how.'

'How can you be so bloody hardhearted? Don't you never think about onythin but yourself?'

The American woman shook her head. 'How do you like them apples? Here I am, working to complete them precious papers what Herr Wunderwaffe left behind, and you do me like that. If we was in the Old South, I'd shoot your rawboned arms off. Goddamn, ain't you got any notion about how hard I work on behalf of all peoples everywhere? Already, I've calculated the very year that all of Mankind should be ready to evolve into flattened little beings fit to live in a fantasy world of picture shows. Won't be the seventh day of November, 7700 C.E., nor the ninth day of November, 9900 C.E. No, sir. The whole damn thing, I say it's bound to happen on the eighth day of November, 8800 C.E. Yup, that'll be the day.' Jean kicked Fingal in his right shin, and then the American woman marched off.

Fingal checked the night table, and then he looked beneath the bed. *Bloody hell, I can't find the Instruktor.*

Doktor Pflug appeared in the doorway holding the pewter urn. 'I put the Instruktor inside your kilt purse.' He strode inside and placed the urn upon the windowsill.

Fingal stared at the jar and prayed that it might rock and wobble—as if the zealous captive were still inside, throwing a tantrum. *But no.*

The chocolate Siamese sauntered past Doktor Pflug. Though the cat's soft, soothing coat of spotted ivory brushed past the physician's ankle, he showed no emotion. The animal stopped before the pewter urn and arched its back as if affrighted.

Fingal pushed and pulled and gasped and grunted until he had climbed out of bed. Then he pointed at the jar. 'Go on and rattle, I say.' He prayed that a great, terrible cacophony might suddenly resound from within the jar—a noise not unlike the violent commotion of an ice-slab avalanche, a thousand or more vast, half-frozen boulders falling from some quake-damaged summit.

When nothing happened, he placed his hand over his left breast and lurched across the room and tapped upon the pewter urn's neck ring a few times. 'You think I'd ever let you out of there? No, I'll never do so.' He jerked the urn right and left, until he remembered that his twin had gone free some time before. 'Why don't I go get some blended malt Scotch from the rooftop café?' he asked, turning to the physician. 'A strong spirit like that ought to cure me collywobbles.'

A few minutes later, up in the rooftop café, Fingal advanced through the maze of console tables, but suddenly forgot what had brought him there. In the end, he dumped two shovelfuls of sand into the chimney and doused the flames burning within the hearth. *Why'd I do that?* Puzzled, he returned downstairs to his bedchamber. Both the physician and the chocolate Siamese had departed the room.

Again Fingal tapped upon the pewter urn's neck ring. *Aye, how to deny the compulsion?* With the tips of his fingers, he tapped out a sequence of numbers—just as he had done as a child whenever he had felt unduly confounded or overexcited. In those moments, he had always displayed such urges. Time after time, he might sit here or there for two hours or more as he counted out some intricate, arithmetical pattern. *But that were then and this be now.*

Little by little, the arithmetic sequence grew erratic, until his tapping sounded like little more than a drunken musician's frenzied, experimental percussion.

Chapter Seven

Late the next morning, Fingal realised that Fräulein Wunderwaffe had gone missing. He brought the pewter urn down to the hotel desk and resumed tapping upon the neck ring. *What if the poor lass never returns?*

At eleven o'clock, he finally forced himself to forgo tapping the urn in arithmetical patterns. Several times over, he wiggled his toes, then he stood, slipped his feet into his smoking slippers, and wrapped his hand around the Instruktor. *I've got to find the spectre.*

The telephone rang, but just as he turned toward the receiver, Doktor Pflug walked into the room in a state of undress.

Doktor Pflug's slurred speech surprised Fingal, so he caressed the physician's big, bony shoulder—as tenderly as possible. 'You're acting a touch erratic, mate. Would it be the little girl what's got you feeling such bemusement?'

Doktor Pflug passed his hands over his naked body in the same way that Fingal had once done when he'd felt that uncanny, bestial, burning sensation up and down his arms and legs. '*Ach du meine Güte*'—good gracious—the physician announced, his voice raspy as if his mouth must be very dry.

Fingal placed the Instruktor onto the reception desk. 'Maybe I'll look through the little girl's room and find me a clue as to where she went. How's that?' He walked upstairs into Fräulein Wunderwaffe's bedchamber and looked around, but found nothing, so he continued out onto her balcony to survey the castle grounds. The sound of someone passing by below drew his attention. *Pflug*.

Naked yet, the physician ducked into the woodshed and then reappeared with a tin in his hand and a coil of rope over the opposite shoulder.

'What're you doing?'

'I must kindle a fire.'

'No, get yourself into shirtsleeves, eh? We got to find the lass before the spectre finds her.'

'No, I can't go anywhere just now,' Doktor Pflug almost shouted. Chest out, the physician marched back into the castle.

Fingal returned inside and lay upon the little girl's bed. 'Come home,' he whispered several times over.

The chocolate Siamese jumped onto the bed and meowed insistently, then leapt off and wandered to the door where it meowed again. Fingal sat up and stared at the beast. It left the room, but meowed again, as if calling. Fingal pulled himself off the bed and followed the creature downstairs to the private hallway and then onward into its hidden room.

Oddly enough, someone had rolled back a section of the tartan rug so as to open the trapdoor to the bottle dungeon. *Aye, the good doktor went and climbed down into the goddamn oubliette.* Fingal peered deep into the impenetrable blackness. 'Just what're you doing down there, sir? Come along now, please. We'll saddle up me best horses, and we'll ride off into the village. Aye, we'll get a right stalwart search party together, and then we'll make door-to-door enquiries until we locate the poor girl.'

The physician, carrying a tin of kerosene, reluctantly climbed the ladder and returned into the light. Then he raised the oil tin and poured the kerosene all over his person. 'I have succumbed to your noble creation's influence, and there's no going back.' He dropped the tin at his feet. '*Ich bin schon tot.*' I am already dead.

For the first time in his life, Fingal experienced a grave hand tremor, and his belly churned, almost as if he had consumed a ton of sea-salt caramel fudge. 'This can't be. No, my friend, you'd be practiced in the art of the medical sciences.'

The physician tapped his feet. 'Today, I make a burnt offering of myself. Why? Because no other sacrifice should ever suffice. How should a bag of spelt flour placate the gods? Do they hunger for a mere crust of Scottish shortbread?'

'Please, mate. There's no reason why modern man should be seeking to come by no primitive god's good opinions.'

'*Bald bin ich in Frieden.*' I'll be at peace soon.

'Listen, sir. At present, you'd be a wee bit overcome. The spectre, he's got you drowning in a torrent of foul memories. Ignore the bastard, why don't you? Come have yourself a cup of cock-a-leekie soup, and on the morn's morn, you'll be in good fettle. As ever.'

The physician swayed a little and then decended back into the darkness. Fingal shrieked for the American woman, and she came running. 'Please get help,' he told her. 'It's the leech. He means to immolate himself this very day, he does.'

'What a dirty shame.' Jean's eyes narrowed, and she laughed like a mischievous old woman, and then she marched off as if she disbelieved all.

Fingal turned back to the dungeon. 'Pray come into the light.' When the physician failed to respond, Fingal shook the rope ladder. '*Please.*'

The chocolate Siamese walked over to the other side of the hatch, looked into Fingal's eyes, and squealed. Did it mean to chide him for not climbing down? The belligerent cat even raised its tail and slapped it hard against the floor, repeating the gesture until Fingal took hold of the rope ladder and descended some fifteen feet to the stone floor.

Somewhere amid the darkness, Doktor Pflug howled like an animal that has detected the presence of some intruder in its burrow. And what a shrill, dissonant echo it had.

Fingal removed his coat. 'Where would you be? Come here, into the goodly light. Let's talk, shall we? Remember, we've got so much to do. Aye, we've got to save the innocents from me projection's deathly influence. Remember all that talk about emotional contagion? Think of the many delicate peoples in this world. Each one would be sorely afflicted, aye, with spiritual scars.'

No response followed, and the silence made Fingal shiver. Even worse, the stale, mouldy air had him gagging. As soon as he recovered, he dropped his coat to the side and advanced into the blackness, hands reaching before him. 'I hope you're not feeling too cross with me for calling upon you, eh? If so, why not beset me? Aye, we'll wrestle all day long. Maybe I'll teach you the Scottish back-hold.' A soft thud echoed through the murk. Fingal scanned the darkness. 'What happened? Did you fall down, friend? Give a wee shout, and I'll come collect you then.'

In a wavering voice, Doktor Pflug recited a Gaelic-language chant—what sounded like a necromancer's invocation.

Fingal shuffled his feet across the floor and stopped when

his toes discovered an elongated crack. *Bloody hell, what next?*

Suddenly, a numbing glare shone from above and behind him. Final spun around. The burning man had suddenly appeared alongside the trapdoor. 'Forget the Hun, do you hear?'

Fingal's belly felt cold, and his hand tremor grew worse. 'I don't care three damns what a roaster like you says.'

'Come out of here this instant,' the apparition shouted. 'Don't you dare defy my entreaty.'

'No, you can't menace me none,' Fingal shouted right back. Then he forged ahead, further into the darkness.

The spectre laughed, the outburst sounding reminiscent of a dog panting. Then, as if hoping to mock Fingal's resolve, it made the sound of Fingal's beloved timepiece ticking.

Despite the ongoing hand tremor, Fingal reached into his waistcoat fob pocket, removed the Frédérique Constant and held it tight. Without even considering the danger that his actions might present to Doktor Pflug, Fingal hurled the timepiece towards where he could hear the docktor muttering to himself. But the beloved Frédérique Constant did not hit the physician and knock him from his stupor. The timepiece shattered against the masonry with a metallic explosion, and several parts rolled back as noisily as a broken toy.

Shite!

A soft, subdued buzzing commenced. *Might that be a warble fly?* Fingal opened his mouth in surprise and inadvertently swallowed the gnat, which filled his mouth with the taste of thick fat. *The kind what floats about in a bottle of milk.* He smacked his lips to clear the sensation, but it did no good.

The glare from above shone a little more brightly. 'You'll not triumph in your efforts,' the burning man said.

'No, I'll save me friend's life. And someday I'll take the

crown and learn the answer to me question regarding inborn knowledge and all that.' The taste in his mouth having grown much worse, Fingal spewed forth a bit of vomit and saliva.

'You ought to realise how pointless is the whole matter of inborn knowledge,' the burning man continued. 'Whatever the answer might be, it disnae change onythin. *No*. But I could share with you the greatest of revelations, for the limitless energy of inborn knowledge happens to be something all so *godly*.' The entity screamed, its primal voice reverberating all throughout the dungeon.

Fingal inched further into the darkness. 'Do you hear me, doktor? Let me know where you'd be, and then I'll come collect you. Please, sir, where'd you go?'

'The Hun can't hear you none,' the spectre continued, its voice reverberating all throughout the dungeon. 'Already, the physician has lost himself in a meditation rite. That's what anyone must do if he hopes to gather the nerve to strike the match. For pity's sake, let the fool ready himself for his great sacrifice.'

Fingal continued forward until the floor felt smooth and the odour of coal oil grew stronger—as if the physician must be kneeling no more than three feet away. 'Do you hear me?' Fingal asked.

'Yes, I hear,' the physician answered.

'Come, let's get on back to the ladder. Aye, and if you can't lift your weight up, I'll go on ahead, and whilst you hold fast, I'll hoist you up like you was a bag of Scottish seed potatoes.'

'No, I shall not go anywhere with you. *Nein*.'

'But I'm asking polite. So follow me voice.'

'Why don't *you* succumb? Let the gentle phantasm fill your thoughts with the glory of immolation.'

'No, that's what me baneful bastard miscreation wants me

to do. Aye, but I'll not grant him the satisfaction.'

'But don't you wish to be at one with the gods?'

'What's this?' Fingal asked, his voice cracking.

'*Eins mit den Göttern*'—one with the gods—Doktor Pflug whispered. He struck a match. An orange glow illumined his naked body sitting on the floor, his skin glistening with the coal oil. '*Hier geht,*' he whispered, and dropped the match into his lap. The physician's body burst into flames, and the dungeon filled with an obscene sulfurous odour.

Fingal's astonishment precluded any response. He neither cried out nor whispered some quaint prayer; he only coughed and wheezed and spat. With the torrid smoke billowing in all directions and the stench of burning human flesh growing warm and wet throughout his nasal passages, he staggered back to the rope ladder illuminated by the light shining through the open trapdoor. His hand tremor having failed to abate, he struggled to grab hold of the twine, but grab it he did, and he quickly started climbing. *Has the spectre departed?*

A set of footsteps clopped across the floor above, and suddenly the American woman stood at the trapdoor and peered down. 'What's with the fancy cooking?'

'It's Doktor Pflug, he's funked the cobbler,' Fingal said.

'Oh?' The American woman folded her arms across her bosom, as if waiting for Fingal to explain the peculiar colloquialism.

He did not explain. He just staggered from the hole with the odour of burning human flesh wafting into the room behind him.

The American woman turned pale and stepped back. 'Pflug took sick, did he?' She yelped, as if she had only just intuited what had happened, then she raced off.

The chocolate Siamese stood on its hind legs, reached out

with its forepaws, and sneezed as cats sometimes do. Then the mercurial creature made a curious angry wail—as if to ask Fingal whether anything in the world could ever serve to restore the semblance of order.

An hour later, a procession of steam-powered motorcars from the constabulary pulled into the castle drive. Most of the officers tended to the heap of ashes that constituted the physician's remains, but back in the stair hall a burly detective lieutenant pulled his dragoon revolver from its leather sheath and tapped the butt against Fingal's shoulder. 'Look here, chap. Whilst you fritter away the time, there's a poor sick lass wandering lost out there in the moorland.'

'Aye.'

'Thanks to you, we'll have to look through every last bloody henroost to check she's not cowering among the boiling fowls. What's more, thanks to your folly, we find ourselves in the grips of a right odious calamity. Far and away the worst ordeal in living memory. Thanks to you, we've got ourselves a vile beast buzzing about, some kind of fiend aiming to compel everybody to off themselves by fire.'

Another detective came along and poked Fingal with a cudgel. 'You got no reason to get yourself hot-tempered, but you've got to leave this keep and henceforth live elsewhere.'

'How do you mean?'

'Pay whatever hearth tax you owe, resign your post, and sell the ruddy castle.'

'Sell?'

'Aye. Whether you got yourself a surveyor's report, you're bound to find some reckless sod willing to pay the buyer's premium. If not, you'll auction the dismal place for whatever hammer price you get. Whereon you'll draw up the papers.'

'You expect me to sell me own birthright? *No.* I can't footer with the family business, eh? No, we saintly Scots honour our traditions. Aye, all me fine forebears, we've managed this gladsome loch-side establishment for three hundred years.'

'That don't make no odds,' the detective told him. 'No, you've to flit. For good and always. Because you'd be the source of all the unbounded devilry around here.'

'*No.* A hotelier, I'd be. And I rather fancy this place, mind you. This here would be me home.' His heart quivering, Fingal wrapped his hand around the newel post. 'I can't just walk off into exile.'

'Why not? Even if there's no law against conjuring the express kind of spirit you've brought forth, you assuredly deserve a taste of retribution.'

For the rest of the day, Fingal took refuge in his bedchamber. Back and forth, he paced the length of the room.

In the evening, when he returned to the hotel desk and sat to attend to some work, a third detective approached. 'Time would be getting on. If you don't want me to lay charges, you'd best pack up your steamer trunk and be off. If not, I swear we'll deliver you to the incident room. Aye, and I'll be sure you get a minimum tariff of seven years.'

Fingal tapped upon the pewter urn awhile. *For Christ sakes.* He stood and turned his back to the detective. *What if I were to contact a solicitor, or what about a family-liaison officer?*

Again the detective tapped Fingal's shoulder. 'Listen to what I say. We got orders from the office of the Sheriff Principal in Peterhead. It's time for you to bugger off.'

With a sigh, Fingal took the pewter urn into one hand and the Instruktor into the other, and exited the castle. At the rowan tree, the chocolate Siamese leered at him from within the now barren, desolate crown.

'What're you doing up there, mouser? Can't you feel the

icy cold of winter coming on strong? Get yourself out of them shrubs and collect Fräulein Wunderwaffe before the poor lass drops dead from exposure, why don't you?'

The chocolate Siamese continued onto the jagged bough dangling just above the place where Fingal stood and glowered at him even more.

'What's this? You think *I'd* be to blame for the poor girl's disappearance? *No*. A right, honourable gentleman, I'd be. And I wisnae wrong to do what I done because I done it in good faith. Aye, and that's why me rival, the malevolent wretch, he should've …'

A sharp, frigid, wintry wind assailed the tree, and the mysterious cat coiled its long tail around the bough.

A moment later, the burning man rematerialised at Fingal's back. 'Do forgive the trespass. I only wish to ask one thing of you. Let me go *free*.'

Fingal dropped the pewter urn at his feet and tapped the tip of the Instruktor against his chin. *Patience*. He stared into the cat's eyes, which grew wide as the wary animal studied the apparition.

The evening mist rolled westward without a sound and grew darker, the silvery colour something like that of a perforated, celluloid, black-and-white filmstrip stuck in a projector and gradually melting.

The burning man whistled awhile and then stopped. 'I think maybe you always knew how dodgy I'd be. How could I function any other way? I'd be something godly, far more intricate than a person's elemental nature, his deepest impulses, his instincts primeval.'

In that moment, Fingal should have turned around very slowly. Then he might have raised the Instruktor.

The burning man whistled anew and then ceased with

the music. 'I know what you've always longed to learn from me. Unconsciously, you've always wanted me to help you resolve the riddle of the universe.' Once more, the burning man whistled a tune.

Fingal shook his head. *There's that melody again.* The Instruktor fell from his hand, and he did nothing to collect it. A powerful wintry breeze rattled the boughs of the rowan tree. He looked deeper into the cat's eyes. *Might* you *know the name of that tune? Perhaps you store the name in the depths of your soul.*

The chocolate Siamese averted its gaze, and given the way the cat studied the barren crown, the creature suddenly seemed all so wise—as if the animal's innermost psyche housed a boundless, primal, even *godly* body of esoteric wisdom. More than enough to resolve the riddle of the universe.

At Fingal's back, the flames grew brighter.

The burning man sighed. 'You mustn't send me back inside you. If you let me go free, perhaps I'd be willing to share with you the answers to those crucial three questions philosophic, all them grand mysteries metaphysical what've always intrigued any and all visionaries. Aye, I'll help you to envisage the origins of the cosmos. All what preexisted this universe. And I'll let you know the meaning of life. And I'll let you determine some grand way to explain Man's attested purpose as well.'

Fingal knelt to the earth, but he did not reach for the Instruktor. Instead, he contented himself to touch the urn. By now, the pewter felt like hard-rime ice.

The chocolate Siamese glared at him—the same expression with which others had always employed when looking askance at all his temerity.

He pointed at the cat and shook his finger. 'I can't just

forgo the chance to learn the riddle of the universe, eh? *No*. There's been a change of plan, mouser. I can't just dominate me foe and send him back inside me.' Now he studied the rowan tree. *No, I've got to collect me foe and then bide me time. I can't send the burning man back just now. No, not until I've made him share out every last bit of his wisdom.* Slowly, Fingal turned around.

Yet again, the burning man whistled—and now Fingal recognised the tune. *Yes, I know that piece.* He activated the Instruktor and put the entity back inside the jar. At which point he himself whistled a measure. *Aye, there's nothing like a fine, Scottish song of farewell.*

II

Chapter Eight

For nineteen years Fingal wandered the land. Time and again, he sought to teach the burning man how to call upon willpower so as to develop and to maintain a kindly disposition—but the burning man refused.

In the winter of 1927, a hopeless exile yet, Fingal settled in the town of Newbattle. Despite how tolerant the majority of the people in that part of Scotland, he rarely spoke to anyone—not even his neighbours. To engage the locals would have been undignified, for everyone had heard the rumours regarding the whole sordid affair back at Bonnie Castle. Even worse, the authorities had never puzzled out just what had become of the little girl. As such, all the townspeople would be sure to assail him with the most heartrending questions—ones for which he had no answers.

To be sure, the enduring mystery regarding Fräulein Wunderwaffe's vanishing had never ceased to torment Fingal. As a direct consequence, he had already decided against marriage and had already ruled out the idea of fathering his own children. What else could constitute a better penance?

On the seventh of January, the captive finally broke free from the pewter urn and materialised in the sitting room. And the weary spectre did not sound healthful, its laboured breathing a kind of thrumming.

'You there. How'd you manage to escape?'

'Just why should I tell you that? Let me go free for good, why don't you?' Slowly, the fugitive wrapped his hand around Fingal's throat. "Do you know what I'd be doing just now? I'd be afflicting your mind with despair. Aye, a kind of despair strong enough to endure as long as you stay here in Scotland. I've estranged you from your homeland, I have. Sentenced you to confusion, I have. Aye, endless wanderings. Undying melancholy. What fate could be worse, eh?" With that, the fugitive dropped his hand to Fingal's wrist and drew him outside.

The fiery being let go then, and for a moment contented itself to study the modest structure where the Scotsman now lived—a lopsided Queen-Anne-revival built upon a tree-lined street named Parthenon Avenue. Then the apparition touched Fingal's hand, and while Fingal marvelled at the sensation—the burning man's fingers felt like fine silk dampened by a humid rain—the entity darted off down the walkway.

Fingal raced after him and traipsed through town for more than an hour before finding the entity. Then it took another fifteen minutes to subdue his miscreation, for over the years, the spectre had developed a measure of resistance to the Instruktor's beguiling effects.

Though he did recapture it, over time the spectre continued to break free. Every now and then, it would even manage to elude capture for several hours.

Late one day, after a long expanse of time in which the malevolent being had gone off, a procession consisting of three

Rolls-Royce Silver Ghosts appeared at the end of the street.

Fingal inferred that his projection must have been goading the motorists, in the same way that it had delighted in taunting the tenants back at the castle. More than that, the entity had chosen *three* potential fatalities so as to enhance its power to impact the whole of British civilisation. Once the populace witnessed as many as three immolations, who could say just how many cases of emotional contagion might follow from the triumvirate?

Though cold winter rain fell, Fingal walked out onto Parthenon Avenue and approached one of the vehicles. 'You'd be in grave peril,' he told the driver. 'Me insidious projection preys upon impressionable souls just like you. So, if and when he comes around, you mustn't look upon him nor listen to onythin' he says. No, he only aims to *prime* you. Then, when he senses you're ready, so he'll cajole you into destroying yourself, and in the worst fashion as well. *Flee*, mate. Get yourself to someplace where he'll find neither hide nor hair of you.'

From back inside the house, the rasp of the burning man's breath awoke—and for a time, the soft grating almost sounded like winter flowers, camellias, swaying in the wind.

The motorist whistled the tune to 'Auld Lang Syne'. Then, once the gentleman had completed the song, he sped off.

The illusory stench of burning human flesh oozed and dripped and bled into being at the back of Fingal's nose, and then enveloped the whole of his person. *Bloody hell.* Fingal returned inside, activated the Instruktor, and commanded the entity to go down into the cellar.

The entity did as it was told, but still, the illusory stench, each one of its invisible, airborne particles, breathed and trickled and percolated all throughout the house.

Meanwhile, three loud, distinctive-sounding vehicles

drew up alongside the kerb.

The Silver Ghosts. Fingal walked into the foyer and opened the window. 'Don't let's get ourselves in a dither,' he shouted.

A sound as of a leaky tap commenced and kept time with the rumble of the motorcars' engines. The source of the botherment proved to be an icicle dangling from the cornice. A beam from one of the Rolls-Royce's headlamps was melting the delicate formation. The ongoing beat of the melting ice made Fingal wince. He stomped upon the floor grate. *How do I save them poor bastards out there?*

From the direction of the sitting room, the illusory odour of burning human flesh poured forth until the strip of tissue at the back of his nose bubbled like a cloud of steam. The stench grew moist, as if some unseen being had dipped each invisible particle into poppy-seed oil.

Fingal choked and coughed and wheezed. Like a drowning man, he raised his arms and flailed them all about. When his condition only grew worse, he opened one of the windows. But fresh air failed to help, so he collected his tortoiseshell cat, and they took refuge outside on the front doorstep.

One after the next, the three Silver Ghosts slipped into gear and sped off. No sooner had they done so than a battered Ford Model T turned the corner some five blocks north and then proceeded forward. With a clamour as of a film-projector bulb explosion, the motorcar stopped at the curbstone before Fingal. The driver-side door opened and a middle-aged woman wearing an oatmeal-coloured ulsterette climbed out from behind the wheel.

That'd be the American cow. What was her name? Jean . . . Selwyn.

Though many years had gone by, the overbearing woman had not changed much. Aside from having arranged her thinning, brittle, greying hair in a most unbecoming Eton crop, her left eyebrow still arched as it had before—as if for no other reason than to emphasise her stubborn, mischievous nature.

He longed to say something sardonic, to insult her. *Why not call her a munter?*

Only when the woman stopped near the mull post and offered him the kind of smile that a lovesick schoolgirl might give some indifferent, older youth did he relent.

'Your kilt looks a bit wrinkled,' she told him. 'No, you don't look well.'

'*No.* In low spirits, I am. I'm fifty-odd years now as well. Getting old, I am.' He ushered her through the door, took her ulsterette and draped it over a box of machine parts, then gestured to the kitchen. 'How about a cup of tea?'

What a mess, the kitchen: yesterday's crock of oxtail soup sat in the sink, and a puddle of goose fat had left a yellowy discoloration amid the otherwise white, stone-tile floor.

Jean collected a piece of salted fish from off the cooker. 'You ought to get yourself help, just like we got down home in Kentucky.'

'This ain't Dixie, and I can't afford to hire no servants.' He turned to the pantry and grabbed a tin of lotus-blossom tea along with a box of Japanese allspice.

'I don't want nothing. Hell, you ought to save your best tea for some fine lady friend one night when you and her get to sugar talking to one another and all that.' The American woman continued to speak, but the rumble of motorcars drowned out her voice. The three Silver Ghosts had returned onto Parthenon Avenue, and now idled alongside the house.

It's terrorism, I say. Fingal put the tea and the allspice back into the pantry and showed Jean to the rear of the house. 'Let's go on out to the back green, eh?'

As they stepped outside, Jean placed her hand over her left breast, the woman plainly overwhelmed.

The property consisted of a vast, Japanese-style garden, complete with lily pond, gazebo, and a thicket of white-birch trees.

'What a splendid sanctuary, eh? Three winters ago, the previous tenant took a brief respite from his sundry labours and went and designed this here. Got his inspiration from a book down there at Newbattle Library, a study of them regal estates the City of Yokohama knocked together along the edge of Tokyo Bay. Aye, the house agent told me the whole story. The last tenant designed this here to look like a right, precise replica of some Filipino aristocrat's herb garden, the whole expanse looking out over Mitsubishi Shipyard, I think it was.'

Jean Selwyn shook her head. 'This place must've cost a pretty penny.' The winter breeze played softly through her blouse and long yellow skirt. She walked off along the garden path and pointed to an empty bottle of rice wine lying in a patch of ryegrass. 'That there's the brew you've been drinking of late?'

'Aye, these days, I'd be swilling saké like a cultured, urbane shogun.'

'But it don't seem right you drinking a pinch of this kind of thing out here in an Oriental garden like this. Maybe I'm looking at it all wrong, but this ain't like you at all.'

He removed a cat hair from his coat's lapel. 'I've lost me castle. And with it me identity, me name, me fine Scots traditions.'

'So I suppose all them years of exile must've got to you.'

'Me present footing would be much worse than all that. No, I'm not just struggling to preserve me identity. I got vital business to tend to. Moving toward the essence, I am.' Fingal's nose dripped.

And at the very same time, the outside cellar door blew open, and the fiery apparition climbed up the wooden stair and continued out into the garden.

Bugger all. Fingal grabbed hold of Jean's elbow and pulled the American woman behind the gazebo.

She drew a deep breath and then peeked back in the direction of the house. 'So your old friend's fixing to do you wrong?'

'*No*,' Fingal answered untruthfully. 'The bloody bastard there, he's got no telling powers anyway.' With the sleeve of his fisherman's jumper, Fingal swabbed a cold rivulet of sweat from his brow. Then he removed the Instruktor from his kilt purse and lined up his shot. *There we are*. He depressed the control button.

Thankfully, the relic proved to be more or less effective; for a time, the burning man raced about like a cat chasing its own tail.

Jean studied Fingal's face. Then she rounded her shoulders some and twirled a strand of her hair. 'You sure have changed. All them wrinkles make you look like you was some crazy *Shinto* monk perfectly content to live out here in this fine garden bower and never want for nothing.'

'Aye, that's the real me, for I've been working with diverse prototypes of the analogue computer, and in recent days they've brought me true identity to the fore. I know it.' at last, he turned back to the burning man. *How good it would be to send the goddamn projection back inside myself. But I can't. No, not just yet.*

The burning man grew still, then chanted a series of Welsh-language prayers before lying upon the earth.

Fingal turned back to Jean. 'Listen, when I talk about

them computers, you must believe me. Why would I fib? All of them mock-ups and technologies futuristic have helped me to know me one true identity. A natural-born visionary, I'd be. Aye, I'm the kind of chap who *must* learn the meaning of things . . . No matter what price I've to pay me accursed foe.'

'Horse feathers. What you're saying makes about as much sense as—'

'No, them analogue computers have brought it out. They've taught me the lucid way I've always yearned to process knowledge. For I was born something like a Japanese philosopher king, a ruler blessed with an artistic soul, aye, a soul clever enough to appreciate the binding worth of . . . *symbols*.'

'*Symbols*?'

'Aye, analogue technology has made me grasp the import of *analogy*, myth and metaphor, archetype.'

The burning man returned to its feet, its movements slow and precise, and continued inside. A dull, yellow light reeking of burning human flesh suddenly flashed.

Goddamn. A series of jerking spasms raced up and down Fingal's arms, but even so, he managed to return through the back door. 'Where did you go?' He continued into the sitting room. 'Would you be in here? Get back to the cellar, why don't you? Get yourself back inside your hollow.'

Jean stopped in the sitting-room doorway. 'What's happened?'

Without responding, Fingal raced off to check the rest of the house. When he could not locate his nemesis anywhere, he paused not far from the foyer.

Jean approached him and tapped his shoulder. 'Why you looking so forlorn?'

Fingal looked to his feet. 'Why'd you visit today? Could

it be you stopped by to gloat some? I'm sure you read all the papers, all the editorials them blighters write about me. Every month or so, someone holds me up to public scorn. A remembrance of Herr Wunderwaffe one day, an homage to Doktor Pflug some other day, and then . . . yet another report all about some fine chap claiming he's beheld the leopardess.'

Jean breathed rapidly and placed her hand over her left breast. 'I didn't come by to get on your one last nerve.' She squeezed her breast. 'I think you ought to send your foe back inside you. Hell, yeah. Them philosophical dreams of yours, they'll never help no one.'

Fingal walked over to the staircase, sat upon the bottommost step, and scrunched up his nose. 'You've changed plenty, haven't you? Back on the loch, you never did me no favours. Yet now you wish to help me with me burdens?'

Jean sat beside him. 'Yeah, comes a time when a lady ought to lay it down. So I did just that. These days I got me a forgiving heart.'

From the direction of Fingal's study, the tortoiseshell cat cried out, and at once Fingal returned to his feet. He found the creature cowering behind the tea trolley. 'What's gone wrong?' he asked, stroking the animal's brindled coat. 'You got yourself a nervous complaint, have you?'

The ghostlike projection, engulfed in metallic-blue flames, materialised beside the wine table, whistling a traditional tune.

Fingal grabbed the Instruktor from his desk, rested his thumb tip on the control button, and pointed the weapon at the burning man's heart. 'Don't make me suppress you with me armaments, eh? Get yourself down to the cellar.'

'How much more of this seclusion do you think I'll stand for?' it retorted. 'It can't be right the way you incarcerate me inside a stagnant, forbidding urn. I don't suppose you realise the interminable tedium. What punishment the all-encompassing solitude. Let me go *free.*'

'You'll not make me pity you none,' Fingal whispered, pointing the Instruktor at his foe's chest.

Out in the street, the three motorists revved their engines. The spectre held its chin up and walked over to the window.

Fingal depressed the Instruktor's control button, but no starfish-orange light flitted about like an animal reeling around within a zoetrope. Neither did the burning man dissolve into a puff of smouldering carbon.

The uncanny being's weight-bearing joints did seem to flash the white colour of a cinema-house screen. And then the entity fell to its knees and crawled off to the cellar door.

Jean walked into the room. 'You shouldn't keep your old friend laid up the way you do. Send him back inside you and forget all that jazz about learning yourself all them big secrets philosophical.'

Fingal's muscles tightened. 'I can't betray me charge.' He narrowed his eyes and studied his hands and fingers for a moment, then turned away and leafed through some of his books, until he chanced upon a tattered autochrome depicting Bonnie Castle.

The image should have pleased him. At the very least, it should have served to remind him of all that the castle had once meant to him. As far back as he could remember, it had been a refuge from the cruelty of the schoolyard. No longer did the structure feel like home, though. As a consequence, he could not muster so much as a hint of melancholy. His thoughts turned to the leopardess. *Where are you? Please answer. Fräulein Wunderwaffe, do you read me thoughts?*

If indeed the little girl lived as a telepathic leopardess, just what message might she have transmitted at that moment?

Perhaps the little girl would not know what to say. Would she even remember him? Even if she did, maybe she would question his strange obsessions.

Outside in the street, a winged creature—it looked like nothing more than a nightjar—soared past the three motorcars. And the portent must have affrighted the drivers, for one after the next, each one of the Welshmen slipped into gear and drove off.

He dropped the autochrome to the floor. *Fräulein Wunderwaffe, where are you? Please answer.*

Down in the cellar, the burning man wailed—and for a moment, the spectre sounded like a little girl in peril of death.

Fingal's arms and legs trembled so. *Fräulein Wunderwaffe, please tell me that you read me thoughts. Where are you? Please answer.*

Chapter Nine

On the penultimate day of January, Fingal awoke to what he believed to be an aural hallucination—a distant roar as of a fierce leopardess calling for her cubs. A dozen times over, he attempted to clear his throat, but his mouth had grown dry. He walked into the washroom and downed two whole cups of water.

Downstairs in the foyer, he stopped before the front-door letterbox and collected the morning paper. The headline read:

HOLYROOD BANS FINGAL T. SMYTH'S
EVIL-TWIN MACHINE!

Fingal's hands trembled as he read every word of the detailed *exposé*. The Scottish Parliament had unanimously decided to ban the venturesome type of experiment by which he had brought forth the burning man.

In addition, Scots law would demand that Fingal himself answer to the charges if and when his creation came to wield any kind of harmful influence on any innocent party.

The newspaper fell from his hands, and he slumped to the floor. *What if those bloody fools in the Silver Ghosts immolate themselves? If something like that were to happen, then the authorities would surely send me off to the worst penal colony in the empire. And for the rest of me miserable life I'll have to content myself with a daily crock of pheasant broth and a stale crust of rye. Meanwhile, the burning man would be free to wander wherever.*

As Fingal rocked back and forth, the aural hallucinations returned. And what a piercing, accusatory tone. The leopardess grunted as if she had only just discovered the lifeless bodies of her cubs, and then she hissed as if she believed Fingal to be the depraved poacher who had committed the atrocity.

For most of the day, Fingal sat in his bedchamber. *Fräulein Wunderwaffe, do you read me transmission? Wherever you might be, please forgive all me folly. Ever since I was a wee thing your age, I've deserved good favour. Please forgive me trespasses, hen.* He cleared his throat and awaited a response that never came.

At two o'clock the glow of the sunbeams falling through the windows assumed a series of theatrical colours such as a Shakespearean lighting designer might conjure by arranging candles within varicolored glass vessels. Even more disturbing, a faint pattern seemed to materialise *within* the light—a series of bestial, black rosettes as of a leopard print.

At four o'clock, when the postman dumped the mail into the front-door letterbox, Fingal leapt to his feet and raced back down to the foyer. *The leopardess, she's probably changed back into Fräulein Wunderwaffe. Aye, and she's sent me a telegram.* But he found nothing but the electric bill. He shook his head, then slipped his fisherman's jumper over his polo shirt and raced outside to accost the postie. 'Please, sir. Check your mailbag a second time, won't you?'

'No, there's no more for you.'

'That's Irish bull. Look through your satchel. Something's bound to be there. What about a German-language message from a little girl?'

'Listen mate, when the dispatch arrives, someone or other should bring it around. Now then, good day.'

Fingal clenched his teeth and balled his fists, then turned in the direction of the train station. He walked through a dozen old, discoloured Christmas decorations that blew about in the breeze and then paced along the walkway for twenty minutes or more.

When he finally returned inside, the light had grown darker—or had the illusory rosettes grown in size?

He mixed a half-empty bottle of rice wine with a half-empty bottle of sherry and downed the whole concoction, despite the fact that it tasted something like the warm, diseased blood of some freshly slain beast.

At six o'clock he crept into the sitting room, crumpled up some of the layouts and scale drawings he had brought from the pewter works, and cast the papers at the tortoiseshell cat. 'Everything's wanting.'

The poor creature darted off through the spare parts scattered about the sitting-room floor and then ducked behind the davenport.

One by one, Fingal collected the tea sandwiches from the workbench and hurled them at the animal. Then he shook his fist. 'All them years ago, I builded me what I'd require to speed me adversary from me psyche, and all for naught. He won't teach me onythin.'

He hurled the warming pan at the poor cat, and when the creature raced across the room and took refuge beneath the writing table, Finegal grabbed a brass blowlamp. 'Have you any appreciation of what it feels like to long to make some kind of contribution to Scottish engineering? It's a right bloody toilsome life, you ought to know. Precision tools strewn about all over the auction. Aye, and so many goddamn components mislaid here and there and always some bloody subcomponent to mend. You got no bloody idea how disconcerting me lifelong labours would be.' He hurled the blowlamp at the cat, which yelped and then darted off into the shadows.

A bead of sweat rolled across Fingal's temple. He removed his jumper and paused to study a few of the cables surrounding the garment's frayed rib neck. *I'm right beclouded, I am.* He dropped the garment to the side and studied the patterns in his kilt, the intricate lines of gold and blue crossing one another over a series of little, black squares printed against a field of lush evergreen. *I'm lost, I am.*

An odour as of various noble gases seeped through the house. Fingal's tongue registered an earthy, almost-sickening taste—something like chrysanthemum tea.

Little by little, he thought of a leopardess, how strong and pungent each one of its exhalations might be. *So might that be you? Have you come back, little girl?*

For ten minutes he checked the house, as if the leopardess ought to be curled up somewhere in the shadows here or there. *What if she'd be lying wounded on the lawn?* No sooner had he reached the front door than a loud purring like that of a powerful jungle cat suddenly resounded from somewhere outside.

He looked out the foyer window only to find no sign of any leopardess. Rather, a motorcar with a loud, powerful engine had pulled up. *Aye, one of them Silver Ghosts.* Fingal cleared his throat a few times and then marched outside to the curbstone. 'I'll not permit you nor anyone else to trifle with that blasted fiery spectre no more,' he shouted. 'So you might as well get your buggy in gear and bugger off. I'll not let no one immolate himself. No, sir. Do you think I wish to rot away in the nick? Piss off then, eh?'

The Welshman rolled down the driver-side window and whistled the tune to the parlour song 'Till We Meet Again'. When he'd concluded the tune, he rolled the window up and sped away—at which point Jean's familiar-looking Model T pulled up to the house.

Alas, when Fingal invited her inside, his double materialised down the hall, near the back door. Aflame as usual, the spectre called out to the woman and bowed—something like a tamed jungle cat that recognised her as a huntress capable of operating with great stealth.

'You got nothing to say to this bird here,' Fingal told his twin. 'Get yourself back in the goddamn cellar.'

'You think I'd try something untoward?' the entity asked him, then he turned away and passed through the wall.

Fingal raced down the corridor, removed the Instruktor from his kilt purse, and opened the window looking out over the Japanese garden. 'Don't you putter off too far, or it's back into the urn with you.' A winter breeze drifted into the house, and Fingal brushed away some of the dust overlaying the windowsill. 'Why'd you call today?' he asked, turning back.

'I've been thinking on what you said the last time I came around, all that high-minded business about analogue computers and myth and metaphor.'

He turned back to the window and gazed outside at the Japanese garden. A thin sheet of freshly-fallen snow coated the wooden bridge spanning the lily pond, and a pair of Mikado-yellow ribbons danced about in the current. Only when the two ribbons sailed off westward did he turn back. At that point, he fiddled with his cuffs and then forced a smile.

Jean tapped her tongue against the roof of her mouth, and then she fussed with a pleat in her skirt. 'In my younger days, I only ever thought about the shape of things to come. But over the years and all, I've grown weary of all that because even if somebody invented some fantasy world where the moneyed could live like characters in a picture show, I'm not sure I'd want to buy in.'

'Me neither. The wondrous life there would have no *meaning*. The kind of world you envision would be a most inclement dystopia, for a person requires *purpose*.'

'Yeah, and that's why I envy you so. No matter your hardships, you got *purpose*. Yeah, you got yourself the hunger to put your opposite number back inside you. And what's more, you got the hunger to think about the mythic and all. You know all about how the unconscious mind makes a person think in metaphor and then act up in a roundabout way.'

Fingal turned back to the window. His nemesis was gone. The Instruktor in hand, Fingal walked outside and checked the gazebo. Aside from the remnant fumes of some or other sweet spice—it happened to be a fragrance vaguely reminiscent of coconut oil—he detected nothing unusual nor mysterious in the air.

Jean slipped back into her ulsterette jacket and followed him. 'What's wrong? Has the burning man broke loose?'

With the tip of his index finger, Fingal traced the contours of the traditional Japanese incense burner standing atop the tea table. 'There's nothing wrong at all.'

'You know what I'd like to do?' Jean asked. 'I think I'd like to apply a few of your ideas about myth and metaphor to *cinema*.'

He did not respond. No matter the soft, winter rain that

had only just commenced, he departed the gazebo and sought out the fugitive among the white birches.

Quickly, Jean followed. 'Here's how I'll do it,' she told him. 'First, I'll watch the movie and all. Be that as it may, later on, I'll ask myself just what myths and symbols my *un*conscious spirit might be thinking on. Because what a person's mere waking mind espies in a movie show ain't ever the same as them myths and symbols what the *un*conscious mind smokes out. Don't that sound about right?'

'Yes and no. You must remember that only a person with a *healthful* unconscious looks for the mythic in art. I'd wager a sick fool's unconscious mind detects only the struggle with the *self*. He sets up a baby projector down in the cellar, watches a war picture, and then gets up off the sofa and murders everyone in the house. Like a German soldier storming a Belgian castle.'

For a moment or two, yet another round of aural hallucinations blared—the cries of a wounded leopardess calling for her cubs.

Fingal continued through the thicket, until he discerned someone's gaze upon him. And then he reeled around. From one of the master bedchamber's awning windows, the tortoiseshell cat looked into his eyes—as if the creature held the power to discern that sibylline aspect of his psyche, perhaps even his very soul.

He cleared his throat, turned slowly to Jean, and grimaced. 'Got me a stark, heartfelt confession, I do. You wouldn't believe how goddamn malicious I've been to me mouser of late, always dumping on the poor little bastard whenever things go wrong.'

'So what? A cat don't care about nothing. I'm sure a critter like him tends to be indifferent to things. Just like the brute what sprung from your unconscious mind.'

Fingal drew closer to the American woman. 'Tell me, when you're back home, does the fiery spectre ever call upon you?'

'Good heavenly days, no.'

'What about when you're giving some film theory address at this or that university?'

'Can't you help me none? You've grown so good and wise, working like you have with them revolutionary analogue computers. So teach me about symbols. If you'd tell me just a pinch of what you know, I'd be mighty obliged. If you'd help me, maybe someday I could write the kind of film theory everyone's dying to read.'

The light around them grew bright and flickered a few times, as if the moon had only just broken through the clouds.

Fingal turned from Jean. 'Can't talk now, eh? I got to keep me twin from running off, and at the moment, I can't even find him. What if he's already ten miles away? Maybe he'd be having himself a dish of creamy rice pudding in some tearoom in Motherwell. For all I know, he's convinced half the patrons there to make a bonfire of themselves.'

The rumble of a motorcar's engine resounded from the direction of the apple orchard running alongside the back of the garden.

Fingal's breathing grew heavy. *Has a Silver Ghost happened along the pathway out there? What if the goddamn, bloody motorist aims to rendezvous with me contemptible projection?* Fingal sprinted forward through the white-birch trees.

Sure enough, the same auto from earlier in the day idled near the dry-stone wall marking the property line, and his fiery double stood at the driver-side window.

Fingal hopped over the wall and trained the Instruktor on the being. 'What're you bloody well doing here? You think I'd let you ride off with some innocent soul? What, you think I'd let you get someone to reduce himself to ashes? No, no. Go on back to the cellar, deuce and all. If you don't, I'll give you such a bollocking you'll wish you was dead.'

The flames engulfing the projection's body assumed a shade of beet red. 'Why must you persecute me like this? Tend to your ladylove and teach the woman the substance and merit of symbols, why don't you? Yes, but let *me* go *free.*'

Fingal depressed the control button, at which point the spectre thrust out his tongue and then fell back against the Rolls.

The driver climbed out of the vehicle and shouted a litany of Welsh-language profanities, then he reached into his houndstooth overcoat and removed a plain pocket envelope containing what appeared to be a Bakelite dessert spoon. 'I beg you. Permit me to bring the glorious burning man home with me to Wales. *Please*. If you would be so good, let him go.'

Fingal held the Instruktor high. 'I don't mean to make you do your dinger, but I must insist you shut your goddamn gob.'

Slowly, the Welshman shifted his thumb from the neck of the spoon to the bowl, as if the harmless implement might truly be some kind of formidable weapon.

'You shan't fool me with that twopenny heirloom,' Fingal told him. 'No, no. I say you're blustering.'

'I shouldn't think so,' the Welshman whispered.

'*Please*, I don't mean to kick off no row. No, I only wish to help you so that you might live a good life.'

'Go to Putney on a pig, I say.' With that, the driver rushed forward like a cricket bowler, raised his non-balling arm, and hurled the spoon at Fingal's left breast.

Barley. Fingal's heart quivered, and his knees buckled, and as he fell to the earth, he grunted like a jungle cat.

A shadowy figure marched forward out of the thicket with

a loping stride: the fellow proved to be a second Welshman. 'Why must you persecute our acclaimer?'

Fingal collected the dessert spoon, leapt to his feet, and hurled the harmless instrument at the second Welshman's feet. 'Me goddamn double, he's got you good and minced. Keep your head, mate.'

The second Welshmen turned to look upon Fingal's double for a moment or two and then turned back. '*Behold*. Our enlightener; he's an angel of fire. Yes, I'm quite sure he must be one of them uplifting seraphims. And he means to prepare us for immolation only because nothing else could ever save our heathen souls.' Just like that, the misguided fool proceeded to recite what sounded like a Welsh-language prayer.

The projection levitated as much as two feet, then the fiery spectre sailed forward and pushed Fingal into the dry-stone wall. The force of his skull impacting against the masonry had him writhing about, lost in a state of delirium. He imagined himself floundering before Parliament. The illusory voices of at least two-hundred irate lawmakers cursed him in the most jarring terms, as if his creation had already destroyed the better part of the Scottish populace. At the same time, the voices of two hundred or more jungle cats roared as if defending their territory.

Jean slapped his face. 'Come to!'

When he finally awoke, Fingal found himself alone with the American woman. 'Where's everybody gone? Have the Welshmen driven off with me double?'

'*Nope*.' Jean handed him the Instruktor and then pointed at it. 'I went and fiddled with that thing there till I made the holy terror get on back into the cellar.'

Fingal slipped the device into his kilt purse, and Jean had helped him to his feet. He held fast to the dry-stone wall. 'I fear it shan't be long before the blackguard goes free for good.'

'Nah, you won't let it happen.'

'But he's damn ruthless, that one.'

'*So*? You're one tough customer too.'

'No, no. For years, I've mulled over them analogue computers, aye, till they redesigned the very way me psyche functions such that now I comprehend the wisdom of myth and symbols but can't do onythin' else. And I do mean damn all.' Fingal climbed over the wall and staggered back through the white birches. When he noticed an empty bottle of *saké* lying over to the side, he fell to his knees and took hold of the rice wine. *Drink up.* Alas, the inside of the bottle reeked of spoiled cabbage—and it made him shake violently.

Jean stormed off in disgust, and ten minutes passed by before he mustered enough strength to return to his feet and continue inside. He stopped in the foyer as a pair of footsteps approached the front door. Suddenly, a graceful, pallid hand dropped the early-evening edition of the *Financial Times* into the letterbox. And there it was: an old photograph of Fräulein Wunderwaffe graced the front page.

Fräulein Wunderwaffe. Fingal sank to his hands and knees as he read the article, grunting like a weary leopard.

Chapter Ten

One winter day Fingal brought the pewter urn up from the cellar and into the conservatory, where he had recently rebuilt his invention, power source and all. He placed the pewter urn on the floor within a beam of light that poured down through the glass roofing. *Why not message the leopardess? So then, do you read me thoughts? What should I do, hen?*

He received no answer, but a solitary wreath of smoke reeking of phosphorus arose from a vent in the power source.

Don't turn that side to London, eh? He pinched his nose shut, until a strong gust rattled the conservatory's glass walls and rooftop. Then, as the lingering phosphorus odour diffused, he placed his hand upon his temple. *Maybe I should send me foe back inside me right here, right now. Would that be good? I could go back to the life I once knew, eh?*

Again, no answer came. Still, at his feet, the pewter urn rattled some—as if the captive yearned to escape.

Fingal pressed his fingers harder against his temple. *Soon enough, me foe must go free for good. And who knows what should follow? Mass hysteria. Pandemonium. Aye, the kind what grows, until it dominates cities and nations far and wide. Like a pandemic. Imagine me creation cajoling countless peoples to immolate themselves, as if that should be the only answer to their tribulation and heartache. Oh God. That's what's bound to happen.*

A shrill, brassy pop, as of an explosion, rang out. The captive blew through the pewter jar's lid and darted off into the sitting room.

Fingal followed, and the burning man turned to face him. 'Don't come any closer. I'll never let you put me back inside that goddamn vessel. No, I'm going free.'

Fingal blinked several times. 'I can't let you go nowhere.' He removed the Instruktor from his kilt purse, but his head throbbed, so he grabbed a bottle of rice wine and downed a pint. For the rest of the day, the standoff continued, with the spectre refusing to return to the urn.

Jean, dressed in her oatmeal-coloured ulsterette, stopped by the house early that evening and invited herself inside. But before she had the chance to speak, her eyes dilated.

Fingal studied her face. 'Me foe, he's mesmerised you. No, there's no doubt about it. Aye, he's gotten deep down into your soul.'

The burning man took the American woman's hand and walked her back to the front door without a word.

Fingal pointed the Instruktor at the burning man's back and activated the device—but the undependable weapon again had no effect. The burning man guided Jean off along Parthenon Avenue and into the heart of town.

The locals panicked when they espied the diabolical figure, the majority shrieking and racing off. A fellow operating a Bentley Down along Commercial Street nearly crashed into the maisonette, the building where Newbattle's Village Green

Preservation Society maintained its offices.

Fingal took hold of Jean's arm. 'Please, hen. Don't let some torchbearer beguile you. Don't trifle with a creature all so hollow-hearted.'

'Hush,' Jean insisted. 'He's just acting neighbourly.'

'*No*, he only means to put me back on me heels.'

'No, he's promised to take me to an Ealing Studios thriller. And he says he'll help me interpret some of the myths and archetypes buried inside them flickering, celluloid images and symbols. He didn't use them words, but that's what he meant.'

'*No*, don't let me wicked miscreation take you to some fleapit.'

'Go home,' the spectre shouted without so much as a backward glance, and he escorted the American woman one block to the east.

Once more, Fingal grabbed Jean's arm. 'The chancer, he don't wish to help you with no film theory. He only means to prime you. Then he'll bring you to ruin. Aye, one of these days, he'll get you to immolate yourself. Like your ritual burning should serve as some kind of sick prelude to them three Welsh chaps.'

'Quit your bellyaching,' Jean cried out. 'Me and this gallant here have decided to be friendly, and there ain't nothing unseemly about it.'

When the party reached the crowded picture palace, almost everyone fled. Still, as the apparition escorted Jean into the empty stalls, the uncanny being commanded the old lady sitting at the pipe organ to remain.

As the elderly lady commenced the overture to the score, Fingal sat down behind Jean and tapped her shoulder. 'Let's go on back to me flat,' he whispered into the American woman's ear. 'We'll have ourselves a lovely tea ceremony out there in the gazebo, and we'll even flavour the brew with Japanese rose.'

The cinematograph suddenly rattled in a lilting, cadenced, rhythmic way over the music—the clamour as hypnotic as the rumble of a locomotive.

The movie began with a shot of a pensioner in a covert coat walking into a train station's booking office, and the first intertitle appeared upon the silver screen:

Our hero shall not take the local line,
for he's purchased a ticket on the Nighttime Express.
Castle Fields, here he comes!
Tomorrow morning, he'll have himself a jovial homecoming!

The story continued with a soft-focus shot of the elderly gentleman walking past the train station's refuge track, where the body of a lifeless animal lay sprawled across the sleepers. The carcass resembled that of a Persian leopard, and because of that, Fingal could not help but think of Fräulein Wunderwaffe. He wept.

On the screen, meanwhile, the elderly gentleman climbed aboard the train and wandered into the crowded dining car.

Jean nudged the burning man's shoulder. 'Ain't the direction of photography all good and fetching? Don't you think them shades of grey recall the black-and-white hues of a genuine dreamscape? To heck with the Kinemacolor process.'

Fingal's nemesis did not say anything, but the diabolical creature's scalp shone so bright that it illuminated the theatre for a moment.

As the picture show continued, a figure appeared at the end of the dining car—a portly gentleman wearing a bowler not unlike the one that Fräulein Wunderwaffe once wore.

Another intertitle appeared:

Behold the dodgy Yorkshireman!
Could he be some agent provocateur?
Has he come to perform an act of terrorism? Oh, what to do?

Fingal recoiled, for he had not anticipated that the story might prove to be the kind of tale in which someone struggles with the presence of death. Sweating profusely, he removed his coat and fisherman's jumper.

The cinematograph let out a pulsating, high-pitched, animalistic drone.

Fingal winced. 'Oil the damn feed sprocket!' he cried out, turning to the projection box, only to be blinded by the harsh glare.

When he turned back, the film cut to a shot of various frantic passengers assailing one of the railway porters. Then the film turned to a shot of a gentleman pulling the communication cord, albeit to no avail.

A third intertitle appeared:

There's no hope!

Soon enough, an exterior shot made it plain that the train had put on speed: a crank pin detached from one of the power car's driving wheels.

Yet another title card appeared:

It's a runaway! What if it derails? Oh!
What if the track should buckle?

Fingal loosened his necktie and leaned forward. 'I'm by

the wind, I am,' he whispered into Jean's ear. 'This picture makes me hackles rise.'

'Oh, my Lord.' With that, the American woman turned back. 'Ain't you a sight? And all on account of you don't approve of the feature.'

As she turned away, a close-up shot revealed a wreath of blinding-white smoke swirling through the cracks in the engine's footplate. On the screen then, the elderly brakeman quickly succumbed to smoke inhalation—and how realistic the character's dying.

Fingal's throat tightened. 'Let's go watch something else,' he whispered, leaning forward to whisper into Jean's ear. 'What about a right, proper, old-fashioned drawing-room comedy? How about Sybil Thorndike's new picture?'

'*No*,' Jean told him, over her shoulder. 'This here story suits my fancy, and I ain't going nowhere.'

No sooner had she spoken than another exterior shot showed the runaway train speeding past the signal box at what looked to be Newcastle.

Fingal leapt to his feet and cursed his foe. Then he slumped back into his place, dropped his hands into his lap, and wept anew.

At the same time, a point-of-view shot revealed the central character hobbling into the cluttered caboose.

A fifth intertitle appeared:

Release the buffers and chain!
Hurry! Hurry! Hurry! Before it's too late!

The harrowing caboose scene continued, but the hero's efforts to uncouple the car from the rest of the train proved futile. And now the insistent pipe-organ music ceased, leaving no sound but the rumble of the cinematograph. On the screen, the hero placed his trembling hand over his ticket pocket and mouthed a prayer.

Fingal closed his eyes. *How do I thwart me foe's scheme to dispatch the American woman, and how to save the three Welshmen for that matter?*

From the direction of the projection box, just for a moment, some of the moving parts within the cinematograph let out a shrill, cacophonous, metallic clamour that sounded something like the din of swordplay.

Fingal opened his eyes and tapped his rival's frigid, fiery shoulder. 'Hey there, let's bugger off to someplace secluded and initiate ourselves a barnie. Wouldn't you be keen to cross swords? Come along, mate. Aye, we'll find ourselves some rapiers and have a go at one another, just like we was fencing in some right fine sporting arena.' Fingal grabbed his coat and jumper, slowly exited the stalls, and continued through the lobby doors.

Three blocks north, he stopped beside a gutter filled with empty Pepsi-Cola bottles, gritted his teeth, and awaited the burning man.

In time, the entity drew near. 'What do you care about your frail, womanly acquaintance sitting back there in the cinema?' the creature asked. 'She's nothing but a haybag. Why do you give a toss?'

Fingal peered into the gutter. 'Look at the refuse here. To most peoples, it'd be nothing but rubbish. On the other hand, as far as the stream of unconscious knows, a right gracefully-shaped old Pepsi-Cola bottle could very well be some kind of ancient idol. Which means the goddamn thing must be *sacred*.' Fingal turned his gaze to the spectre.

The entity clenched its fists, its eyes as luminous as neon

lamps. 'You think you'll impress me with your newfound insight into myth and metaphor?'

'Imaginably.' Fingal did his best not to blink, but he failed.

'You'll never enthuse no one. You might be a pioneering inventor and all, but you're not clever enough for my likes. Lately, you've grown as daft as a brush.' The apparition collected one of the bottles, the flames glowing much brighter up and down its arm.

Fingal removed the Instruktor from his kilt purse. 'Go home. Get on back into the pewter jar, I say.'

'The device in your hand there can't do nothing to me no more.'

'Think I'm bluffing, do you? Get on back to the goddamn house.'

'Give your baleful banter a rest.' The malevolent being stepped back and then cast the bottle at Fingal's feet. The glass exploded against the pavement.

In vain Fingal endeavoured to work the Instruktor. *Goddamn.*

The spectre grinned. 'Let's have ourselves a merry chase, eh? If you catch me, maybe then I'll tell you whatever you wish to know.'

'What's all this?'

'You heard me clear enough. Catch me and maybe, just maybe, I'll answer all your questions philosophical.'

'You mean it?'

'*Yes*. Catch me and maybe I'll fill you with the wisdom of a prophet, one what's attained a truly-evolved conscious. Yes, and more than that, I might even teach you the power to translate all that pinnacle of intellectualism into that one empyreal metaphor. Aye, a metaphor to serve as that one glorious myth by which to explain the origins of the cosmos together with the meaning of life together with the purpose of civilisation.'

A Silver Ghost stopped alongside the gutter, and the driver flashed his headlamps. The entity climbed inside, and the vehicle sped off.

God, no. Fingal walked the rest of the way home, continued through the front door, and collapsed at the foot of the stair. 'What do I do?' he asked the tortoiseshell cat, the moment the creature stopped at the top newel post. 'How do I control the fugitive?' The cat walked off.

Fingal climbed the staircase and entered the room where he had collected several analogue-computer prototypes. His heart beating faster, he grabbed one of the contrivances and cast it against the wall. It splintered into pieces.

The tortoiseshell cat appeared in the doorway, licked the tip of its tail, and then pawed at some of the debris strewn about the floorboards.

'You there, mouser. Do you suppose I ought to forgo me quest for wisdom? Aye, maybe you think I ought to make some minor adjustments to me invention and then send the rakefire back inside me.' Fingal toppled another prototype. Tears came, and he knocked over a third computer.

The cat retreated into the hallway, and Fingal huddled against the wall and surveyed the wreckage. 'Even if I learned me the riddle of the universe, and even if I was to envision some ideal myth so as to explain the whole creation, why should anyone listen to all me wisdom and knowledge? Aye, I'd be guilty of having caused so much *death*. It's a bloody miracle I haven't received a summons as of yet.' He returned to his feet, continued into the master bedchamber, and opened one of the sash windows looking out over the garden.

A majestic winter night should have stretched forth. As it so happened, though, a bone-white mist enshrouded the earth and sky. Try as he might, Fingal could not even discern either the apple orchard or the dry-stone wall standing along the property line. The night grew dark and cold and as malodorous as oil sand, so he climbed into bed and became lost in a dream where he found himself standing on a freshly-paved asphalt street in Paris, not far from an empty stone planting box.

A leopardess cries out, the beast's voice reverberating all throughout the French classical architecture that comprises the skyline—the towering cathedral spires, the spiked gables, the parapets.

The leopardess grows quiet, as if it has transformed itself into a Frenchwoman.

From the direction of le rond-point des Champs-Elysées, Madame de Pompadour approaches. How mesmerising the large Marquise diamond around her neck—the gemstone resembling almost perfectly the shape of her lips.

'Have you come to save our souls?' she asks.

'I doubt I could. Me projection, he's already destroyed the British Isles, and there wisnae onythin I could do to stop the calamity. Everyone would be dead by immolation.'

'What a pity. You liberated a terrible spirit from your deepest unconscious but then chose to play the part of a person who should never determine the way to send the execrable thing back inside.'

'No, that's me true *identity. A visionary, I'd be.'*

'I fear as much. So now the spectre must destroy everyone in la Bibliothèque nationale, most of the people sitting in le Théâtre du Palais-Royal, and whosoever might be strolling along l'Avenue de l'Opéra. Soon, every last, blameless Parisian should be immolated. And afterward, le fantôme should board the train to Marseille. Then he'll sail away because he shall not content himself to destroy only the French Republic. On the contrary, he must continue to

travel to one nation after the next, until every last polity would be a wasteland.'

I fall to my knees. 'Me creation, he's bound to destroy countless lives. Pardonne mes péchés.'

The diamond around the Frenchwoman's neck gleams as radiantly as the moon.

I return to my feet. Then, as the courtesan begins to hum the tune to 'la Symphonie fantastique', I plant a fatherly kiss upon the gemstone and then . . .

He awoke from the dream and made his way downstairs to the conservatory where he fussed with the undependable Instruktor. *How to make it work?*

The tortoiseshell cat emerged slowly from behind the power source and turned to some of the refuse scattered about the floor—a tattered direct-mail ad from a gas fitter.

After a while the cat hopped onto the windowsill. Then, as if longing to go free, the creature let out a grinding, deafening, monotonous yowl.

Fingal held the Instruktor close, and placed the palm of his free hand flush against the cold of the glass wall. *Fräulein Wunderwaffe, do you read me thoughts? Where would you be on a night like this? Tell me what to do, leopardess.*

The draughty room grew colder, and the glass walls rattled. Soon enough, the winter wind assumed the odour of bitumen and woodsmoke, something sour too.

Fräulein Wunderwaffe, do you even remember me? Please send me a message, me little hen.

No response followed other than a gust that rattled the glass rooftop, and the cold, winter current babbled like air through old, diseased, compromised water lines.

Fingal looked up, just in time to witness the moon vanishing behind three little blue clouds. *Fräulein Wunderwaffe, please say something. Don't leave me here all alone and sombre. If you'd just send me your thoughts, aye, it'd bring me such elation.*

Again no response followed other than a distant train whistle, the percussive sound rumbling like the wail of a dying jaguar.

Chapter Eleven

Late one winter afternoon, the aural hallucinations returned: from all throughout the sky, a leopardess cried out for her cubs. And then, a yelp as of elation, as if the leopardess had only just discovered her young ones safe and secure.

Rejoice. Fingal walked into the foyer and knelt before the front-door letterbox. *I know what you mean to tell me. Aye, you wish for me to know that it's well-nigh time for me to make a wee bit of progress in all me endeavours to capture the burning man. Perhaps you want me to find someone to help me and fill me with sound counsel. Would that be right, hen?*

The next day, he rang Midlothian University to make enquiries regarding celebrated electrometallurgist Professor Milo Ignatius Squyres.

A few nights later, on the evening of the Lord Rector's gala reception for the Midlothian faculty, Fingal ironed his kilt and donned his best Oxford-cloth shirt. Then he invited himself to the banquet in the hope that Professor Squyres might attend.

The Lord Rector's manor house proved to be as luxuriant as Fingal had expected: plush carpets and a grand piano, a pair of wrought-iron gates leading into the dining room, and a long, flat-grain wood dining table that must have seated forty or more.

In the hope that it might make him look discreet, Fingal accepted an appetiser. Then, with the dish of firm, crumbly Cheshire cheese in hand, he meandered through the crowded halls and chambers until he located Squyres.

Initially, the scholar failed to impress. For one thing, the fine gentleman had an overly-waxed moustache; second, the vain fellow wore a most inappropriate, cloud-white ensemble and tail coat.

The various quirks notwithstanding, Fingal related his story. Afterward, he rubbed his palms together. 'Do you know of anyone who could help me? *Anyone.*'

'Well, I just published a monograph that quoted a German chap. He's a Berliner. A fine engineer. Herr Spieler. Yes, that's his name.'

'And you think the Berliner would be willing to help me? Remember, countless lives would be at stake. It's imperative that I capture the burning man. As quickly as possible.'

The eccentric professor grew quiet, then he guided Fingal over to a wireless receiving set neatly arranged atop a pier table with canted corners. 'By any chance, do you ever listen to Radio Luxembourg?'

'Can't say that I do.'

'Well, each night I listen to that very service. Ofttimes till dawn. It's the only way to know what's what out there on the Continent. And though I cannot remember the precise date of transmission, I do recall one evening when a rather glib presenter orchestrated a most exhaustive interview with Herr Spieler himself.'

'Yeah? And what did he talk about? Did he know how

to release a projection of inborn knowledge? If so, did the Berliner know how dominate the damn thing? Aye, and did he know how to make the damn thing talk and share out all its primal wisdom?'

Squyres shrugged, as if he did not quite understand the question. 'Well . . . Herr Spieler came off as not a little bit *coy*. And let's not forget, he's very young. As I recall, he's only been dabbling in your line of work for the last two years or so.'

Over in the corner, the Lord Rector's Georgian grandfather clock stirred to life and played a simple tune. And as the chimes proceeded to count the evening hour, Fingal asked Squyres a dozen more questions and belaboured the fine points of each answer.

Eventually Squyres grew quiet, and from somewhere outside the hum of a motorcar's engine awoke.

Could it be one of the Silver Ghosts? The dish of Cheshire cheese fell from Fingal's hand, and he held onto the edge of the pier table.

When he finally forced himself to walk over to the dining room's large bay window, he scanned the length of the thoroughfare: there was no motorcar, only a solitary, black, cast-iron lamppost, its beacon of light glowing a faint, dreamlike Victoria blue. *Maybe I only imagined the disturbance.* He walked over to the cloakroom and slipped back into his royal-navy duffle coat. *Go on.*

Outside, the air felt dry and lifeless. Above, a cloud shaped like an Arab frame-drum lingered over the campus.

He cocked his ear and listened for another aural hallucination—the call of the leopardess. Then he kicked at a few sequins strewn about the walkway and continued east. Six blocks on, he stopped before the machine works. Alas, he noticed nothing unusual. An array of rusted engine manifolds lay strewn about to the right, and to the left, the ruins of what looked to be a 1914 Britannia cyclecar lay between a sheet of brushed nickel chrome and a large heap of merchant pig iron. *So where's the Silver Ghost then?*

From what sounded like two blocks away, the unmistakable rumble of a motorcar's engine resounded. And soon enough, the Rolls-Royce rolled up to his side.

Twice, he knocked upon the opaque driver-side window. 'Hello?'

The window rolled down—no more than two inches, though. 'Let your prisoner come live with me for good,' the motorist announced in a thick Welsh accent, his breath reeking of ginger brandy. 'Please. Leave him be.'

'Don't be deceived. Me heartless double, he only hopes to cajole ye into immolating yourselves.'

'You think I'm fritter-minded, do you? Like I haven't got a grain of sense? No, no. I've invested quite well, haven't I? Never once did I overbid my hand. And now I've got me great riches. As a matter of fact, I own me half the town of Queensferry.'

'Please, sir. Find your two mates and tell them that I'm working steadfast to work through whatever stumbling blocks remain before me. In the meantime, you and them two others, ye must resist me double's vile influence.'

'You're no one to talk about my associates. The one fellow owns himself a profitable slate-mining operation in Welshpool, and the other chap owns half of Rhymney. That's right, we got more money than *you'll* ever make your whole life long.'

'Aye, the lot of you would be right successful. I never said you wasn't. However, you've still got *insecurities*.'

'That's character assassination,' the motorist almost shouted.

'Don't be incensed,' Fingal pleaded. 'It's just that me diabolical twin, he aims to manipulate ye. Don't let him do it though. No, no.'

'You engage in the injury of my reputation, as if you must be something better. Yet I'm sure you've got your own share of sorrows, eh?' The motorist recited a bit of James Joyce's prose:

> *Secrets, silent, stony sit in the dark palaces of both our hearts: secrets weary of their tyranny: tyrants willing to be dethroned.*

Fingal nodded. 'Yes, of course. Everyone's got foibles. And that'd be just what me double aims to exploit. I'm quite certain he's chosen you and the other two fine, high-principled businessmen to immolate yourselves, so that the whole bloody affair should inspire a multiplicity of people to do the very same.'

The Welshman shook his head. '*Rubbish.*'

Fingal held up his hand. 'Listen, gudgeon, and listen good. I only wish to save your bloody life.'

Without warning, the Welshman let out a piercing, primal shriek, a cacophony as great as any aural, leopardess-call hallucination from before.

The beastly cry made Fingal's eardrums burn, but he stood his ground and tapped the driver-side window. 'Don't be spiteful, mate. Aye, and don't lose faith. As tense as you'd be feeling, you mustn't falter.'

The motorist quickly rolled up the window, slipped the Silver Ghost into reverse, and sped backward some twenty feet. The headlamps flashed, as if the driver hoped to blind him, and then the maniac gunned the engine, as if to terrorise him into submission.

Fingal did not so much as fidget. 'Go on home. And come the noon light, if the ghoul comes calling, don't engage him.

In them moments of excitement, tell him to shut his puss.'

With a wild, high-pitched screech, the Rolls-Royce burst forward. And as the tires squealed, Fingal held up his hands and averted his gaze.

A slowly-unfolding vision followed, showing the motorcar obliterating him and instantaneously melting the whole of his person into a ball of languid fire.

Do I live? Like a character in a Greek tragedy, he fell onto his knees and held his palms up. 'Might this be a fainting spell?' he asked himself, in a whisper.

By the time he came to his senses, the speeding vehicle had already continued around the corner.

The bloody bastard must've missed me by no more than two *inches.* Fingal returned to his feet. *So where do I go?*

Guided by some unconscious, esoteric impulse, he returned to Midlothian University and stopped before the gates. *The dreaming spires of academe.* He clenched his fists and, for a moment or two, recalled his childhood habit of sitting all alone in the schoolyard and laughing out loud at this or that subversive thought, until some hooligan might stop by.

Always the little philistine would roll his eyes and belch. 'Are you daft?' he would ask.

Fingal belched now. Then he lifted his kilt and emptied his bladder onto the wrought-iron gate's bottom rail.

From two blocks south, meanwhile, the rumble of a motorcar's engine resounded, and a second Silver Ghost drew perilously close, the headlamps bathing him in a prismatic glare. The second driver let out his own primal shriek, and Fingal let go of his kilt and raced off through the gates.

When Fingal reached Centennial Hall, the grandiose beaux-arts structure standing in the heart of the campus, he paused to read the words emblazoned across the building's epistyle:

M. Laszlo

EX SAPIENTIA MODUS

A hymn, William Blake's 'Jerusalem', commenced from somewhere inside.

Might them voices belong to the Midlothian Orpheus Choir? All the time scratching at his scalp, Fingal walked over toward the building's Venetian-style doors and advanced into the anteroom. From there, he continued along the corridor to a chamber with eggshell-white walls and a marble floor. *Splendid.* He greeted the caretaker, who sat atop a heap of sheet music.

Over to the right, meanwhile, the director conducted the rehearsal—the old man sweating profusely, as if no other task could ever be as crucial.

And now the choral society belted out the last quatrain:

I will not cease from Mental Fight,
Nor shall my sword sleep in my hand:
Till we have built Jerusalem,
In England's green & pleasant Land.

When the glorious hymn concluded, Fingal rubbed his ears, then returned outside, all the time hugging the corridor wall.

The air remained as dry as before, and not even the softest winter breeze played among the ivy growing wild up and down the walls of the various buildings. All throughout the campus, a low, throbbing, set of pulsations thrummed—either the steady rattle and hum of a proper cold-blast furnace or the experimental echoes of a newfangled electric-arc furnace.

Fingal wandered into a courtyard comprised of cracked terracotta tiles. For a moment or two, he listened for the Rolls.

Should I risk walking home? If I do, the Silver Ghost must surely run me down.

A chap looking to be the nightwatchman passed by, paused to check his timepiece, and then strolled along.

From the direction of the electric curling rink that stood over on the west side of the campus, a din awoke—most likely a friendly bonspiel.

Fingal shivered some, for no matter how warm his duffle coat, he had not thought to wear his fisherman's jumper that night.

A copy of the *Daily Mail* tumbled by in the breeze. He grabbed it, wrapped himself in the papers, then lay down in the warm, inviting shadow of an electrical generator. He almost fell asleep, but the college chapel's bells rang out and jerked him into wakefulness.

Two seconds later, from a glinting, deep-purple glow in the surrounding darkness, a nimble creature of indeterminant size walked forward. Step by step, the animal drew closer.

At a distance of some eight feet away, it became clear that the creature must be a Scottish wildcat—a diseased one, too, with balding patches in its coat.

Fingal patted his kilt purse, where he kept the Instruktor. 'I know what you've come to tell me. Maybe you've come to say I ought to ask the chap down there in Berlin to help me mend the device inside me bag here. Wouldn't that be so?'

The wildcat looked at him with opalescent eyes, its expression an emotion somewhere between self-satisfaction and simple disdain, then it turned away and licked a thinning part of its coat.

'Come the morning light, I'll post me request for an audience with the Berliner. And he'll help me. That's right. The bloke there, he'll help me find some way to make the requisite modifications to me Instruktor. And I'll go forward with them wee changes, and I'll execute every adjustment proper and piecemeal and in the most exacting detail, and at long last me double should act good and genial.'

The Scottish wildcat lay down upon its back, as if for no other reason than to display a dozen or so lumps protruding from beneath its skin.

Fingal settled back into his newspapers and felt at his throat—the place where the spectre had held him so as to poison him with despair. To be sure, his nemesis had succeeded. *I'm nothing, I am. I don't even deserve to sleep in me own bed. No.*He fell asleep and dreamt of the Welshmen standing atop the bonnets of their respective motorcars and setting themselves aflame, the insidious spectacle inspiring a pandemic of like abominations all throughout the land.

At the break of dawn, he awoke to find a pair of driving gloves lying a few inches from his nose. *Hello*. At some point in the night, the gentleman in the second Rolls-Royce had been there. Fingal cast the old newspapers to the side and leapt to his feet. 'Come back, you guileful bastard,' he called out, reeling around.

If the Welshman were hiding somewhere, he did not show himself. Still, a pair of aged, bespectacled celestial-chemistry professors happened by.

The diminutive one pulled at his long, unkempt beard. 'Did you ever find a way to improve the resolution of those solar daguerreotypes?' he asked his colleague.

'Negative,' the second professor answered. 'Whatever I do, the blasted flares never fail to ruin the image. Had the same troubles back at the University of Leeds, I did.' He suddenly noticed the driving gloves. 'What fun.' The seemingly-oblivious old man tucked the driving gloves down into his tweed coat's breast pocket, and then he strolled off into the dining hall.

Once the elderly scholars had ambled off, Fingal sought out the maniacal driver. 'Where'd you go? You skulking in the shadows somewhere? Come face me, why don't you? Let me help you triumph over any and all presentiment. You ought to know there's no reason to despair. Day by day, I'm making progress.'

His belly rumbling, Fingal debated whether he ought to follow the scholars. *Why not pilfer a wee bit of breakfast?* The hunger spread throughout the lining of his stomach, so he continued inside.

Over at the sideboard, the celestial-chemistry professor helped himself to rumbled eggs and a slice of cinnamon toast, so Fingal did the same. He blushed, though. And with his free hand, he could not help but poke at his neck. *I'm an intruder, I am.*

Over by the speckled brass coffee urn, the elderly scholar finally paused to study Fingal's face. 'Don't I recognise you from the papers?'

'No, no. I shouldn't think so. No, not at all.'

'*Yes.* Feargal Smitty, wouldn't that be the name?'

'Aye, so it would,' Fingal confessed, with a smirk.

'Yes, you're the mad scientist who released the projection of his deepest self, all the innate knowledge.'

'Aye, that I did. Frightfully sorry. Still, I must take exception to your remarks.' Fingal struggled to think up a rejoinder to the 'mad scientist' remark. Nothing came to him, however.

The scholar pointed at him. 'Why'd you do it, Highlander? For what reason did you do something so dodgy? *Why*?'

'Why *not*? A learned chap ought to be curious about baubles and such, no?'

'On the whole, but there's no future in your brand of Hermeticism. I'd say you're on a hiding to nothing. Remember, if you're too heavenly-minded, you'll never do anyone any earthly good.' With that remark, the professor frowned and walked off.

Fingal helped himself to a cup of burnt, bitter coffee and then made his way over to a table beside a window. *After breakfast, I'll send a telegram to Berlin. Aye, that's what I'll do.*

As he picked at his rumbled eggs, a pair of cocksure-looking students all decked out in fashionable raccoon-fur coats from America sat down beside him.

What a couple of toff-nosed knobs. He braced himself. How long before they engaged in the most vulgar exchange, the kind of talk that he did not wish to hear? He looked out the window and studied the winter sky, soon fixing his gaze upon a cloud shaped like the Arabic letter *rā*.

One of the students finally tapped his shoulder and grinned. 'Fingal T. Smyth, the one and only. Yes, indeed, I'd recognise your face anywhere. What a great honour that you should come have a spot of breakfast among us.'

'A great honour? How so?'

'How so? You're only the most forward-thinking researcher of our time.'

'No, I'm not. No, I've gone and conjured a deadly, grandiose delusion.'

'No, for years and years, I've read all about you in the trade papers. As a matter of fact, back when I was in grammar school, I longed to write you. Couldn't quite muster the courage, though.'

'So what's new with your evil twin?' the second student asked, picking at his black pudding.

'For aught I care,' Fingal answered. 'Me and me old friend

continue to spar like a pair of barn cats.'

'Oh?' the second student asked. 'At daggers drawn, are ye? Still, there's no reason to be sullen.'

'How do you mean?' Fingal asked. 'I got no reason to feel nothing but unrelenting despond.'

'No, you'll achieve your ends someday,' the first student told him. 'Yes, I'm quite sure you'll resolve your troubles and get through each and every obstacle. I know it.'

'That's right,' the second student agreed, tapping Fingal's arm a few times over. 'Unlike all the complacent old bastards at the Scottish Royal Academy of Sciences and the like, you wish to add something genuinely *new*. That's why you test the frontiers of science. You pursue great discovery, and that's why you'll carry the day. By hook or by crook.'

Fingal thanked the two gownsmen for their good cheer. Aside from the odd muttered word, though, neither he nor the two youths spoke any further—even as the sun shone brighter and brighter, a beacon of hope.

Chapter Twelve

When Herr Spieler's invitation arrived, Fingal held it against his left breast. *Hallelujah.* With that, he continued into the conservatory and looked to the glass rooftop. *Time to pack me fort-nighter. I'm going on the journey, I am. The chap down there in Berlin, he's just written to give me his pledge to get me Instruktor working proper. And then I'll get the better of the goddamn fiend and send him straight back inside me. Maybe it's all for the best, eh?*

From that moment on, things should have gone smoothly, but no. Feverish chills racked his body. Then when he visited the passport desk, he could not recall his name. And when the clerk asked after his destination, he had no answer. The stupor intensified, and he stepped outside. Standing beneath a lamppost, he held his timepiece tightly in his hand. *I got to collect me thoughts. Could it be that unconsciously, aye deep down, I don't even want to travel onto the Continent?* He closed his eyes and sought to crush the timepiece. *What should I do, fräulein?*

At one o'clock, when he returned home, he descended

into the cellar and stopped before the empty wine rack—the very place where he had once stored the pewter urn.

The spectre should have been inside, and its fiery, malodorous aura should have glowed from within the jar. 'You don't know what to do,' a ghostly voice should have whispered. 'Shall you forgo your big ambitions and content yourself to send me back? *Maybe*. Truth be told, you haven't any idea. Aye, and it's got you flailing all about.' At that point, the ghostly voice would have laughed and laughed and laughed.

'You got no reason to gloat,' Fingal would have said in that moment. 'I'll not let you harm no one. Not the mad bastards in the Silver Ghosts, and not no one else neither.'

Three days later, once Fingal had secured his travel papers, he collected the undependable Instruktor and caught the evening train. When he reached the Port of Dumfries, he booked passage aboard a tramp steamer bound for Hamburg. The succeeding voyage did not take too long. And when he reached the train station in the heart of the teeming German port city, he purchased a ticket on the Berlin Express.

Not an hour later, as the train rolled along, a cool, fiery presence sparked to life not far from his right ear. 'No one has the knowledge to help you any,' a ghostly voice told him. 'Deep down you realise all your efforts must be futile. Even now you must admit you've gone further in your kind of investigation than anyone else ever managed. And you know well enough that when you meet the young German, the pointless consultation should only serve to *emphasise* your isolation.'

Fingal sobbed. 'What I'd be up against, it wouldn't be a square go.'

The cool, fiery presence flickered some and then seemed to dissolve into his ear drum.

Three nights later, on the evening of the appointment, Fingal gave himself a close shave and then walked from his hotel to *Tie Traummädchen*—the alehouse where Herr Spieler had agreed to meet him.

Herr Spieler proved to be even younger than expected, a fact greatly enhanced by the German youth's thin arms, slumped posture, and pronounced overbite. While he sipped his *Berliner Weiße* and explained his theories, Fingal scraped the base of the Instruktor against the edge of the table. Despite Herr Spieler's obvious eagerness to please, how could he be of any use? Fingal found it impossible to conceal his discontent; he sat back and shuddered.

'What's wrong?' Herr Spieler asked him.

'If you don't mind me pumping you with a rather unmannerly question, just how old would you be? In my opinion, you don't look a day over fifteen.'

'I'm *seventeen*.' The engineer wrapped his hands around his earthenware beer mug and averted his gaze. 'So you feel I've brought you here under false pretences?'

'No, but I've got busy work to do.' For a moment, Fingal studied the painting on the wall, a watercolour depicting the Battle of Vienna. 'I ought to go now. Back home, maybe someone from the University of Dundee would be willing to help me some.'

'*No*. Stay and help *me*, won't you? Only *you* should be clever enough to help me settle my petty affairs.'

Fingal sat forward. 'How do you mean, laddie?'

With a sigh, Herr Spieler gestured toward the window. Outside on the walkway, nine tall, perfectly-poised women dressed in chiffon gowns, cocoon hats, and foxgloves stood beside the window. Moreover, each fine lady's eyes glowed like yellow-green topazolite.

'Upon me word,' Fingal whispered, the feverish chills from before having returned all over his body. 'Who'd that lot be?'

'*Guess*,' Herr Spieler replied, the young man's voice all so raspy—as if the muscles that controlled his voice box must be tightening.

Fingal glanced back at the women. 'To all appearances, them handsome birds out there ought to be working for the Deutsches Theatre.'

Each one of the nine women kicked off her court shoes, and they walked barefoot off down the street in a stately procession.

Herr Spieler arose from the table, slipped into his topcoat, and exited the alehouse.

Fingal followed along. 'So just who the devil would them nine ladies be? Won't you tell me what's astir?'

'You wouldn't betray a confidence, would you?'

'Not a word to the vicar. Not one blessed word.'

'*Mitkommen*'—come along—Herr Spieler whispered, and he followed the same route that the band of shapely women had taken.

Against his better judgement, the pangs of Fingal's conscience convinced him to follow the troubled fellow through the crowded streets.

Three blocks on, Herr Spieler stopped before *Das Kabaret Lebensmüde*. 'Do you know the legend that says no German composer may compose more than nine symphonies? According to tradition, a German composer receives inspiration for nine and no more than that. And if ever he attempts to write another—'

'He'd be a deader?'

'*Korrekt*. As a matter of fact, the curse did not even spare Ludwig van Beethoven.'

'Aye, but how would any of this pertain to them nine

ladies we'd be chasing through the city this fine winter night?'

Herr Spieler looked to the sky, open-mouthed. Then when the troubled young man sought to speak, it seemed that his voice had grown too hoarse for him to manage.

Up ahead, the nine women stopped in the heart of a quiet, austere intersection. One of them waved to Fingal. 'Draw nigh,' she called out in a theatrical tone, her accent vaguely Greek as much as anything.

At first, he hesitated. And when he failed to advance, she looked to the sky. '*Wenn du zu himmlisch . . .*' If you're too heavenly . . .

Fingal marched forward, through an oily puddle shaped like a bassoon, and did his best to bow like a gentleman. 'Avow your identity, won't ye?'

Before any of the women could speak, a copper bell high atop a nearby Lutheran cathedral pealed discordantly. The procession continued down the cross street. Herr Spieler waved to Fingal, and then all eleven continued along to a darkened flat with scrolled gables.

The darkness, the mist, and the shadows all around shone like the art of low-key lighting—the optical engineering of silent film, its dark tones, its blend of natural and artificial illumination.

Fingal nudged Herr Spieler and motioned toward the transom window. 'Who the hell lives here, then?'

'My older brother lately dwells at this address,' Herr Spieler answered, his voice even raspier than before. He pointed at the name engraved in the door panel:

HIMMELREICH

'Don't be fooled by the grandiose *nom de plume*,' Herr

Spieler continued. 'My brother, he's a symphonist. Hence the absurd pseudonym.' Herr Spieler tapped out a jazz-waltz drumbeat against the water-metre box. Then the peculiar youth stopped. 'So *now* do you know who the women must be?'

Fingal fidgeted some and then pulled his arms and legs toward his centre. 'I can't make sense of onythin. Explain all this intrigue.'

Up above, a light suddenly shone from a window with an ornate hoodmold, and the glow resembled the otherworldly flash associated with shadow photography. Then from within that very same flat, a polytonal melody commenced to play on a poorly-tuned pianoforte.

Herr Spieler winced, as if he had just chipped a tooth. Then the young gentleman collapsed to the pavement. In obvious hysterics, he rolled about amid a jumble of broken glass.

At the same time, one of the ethereal women approached Fingal and poked his breast with the tip of her gloved finger. 'Do you know the impious fool who lives here?' she asked, the scent of olive oil lingering on her breath. 'Do you think *you* might save his life?'

Fingal shivered. 'Just who the hell would you be, eh?'

The woman reached into her left foxglove and removed a postcard-sized print of a watercolour depicting a lofty summit. 'This comes from le Musée des Beaux-Arts, the famed gallery in Dunkirk. Look closely. This splendid peak would be Mount Helicon.'

'Aye, home of the Nine . . . *Muses*.' Feverish chills made him shiver again, but the sickly sensation concluded. 'Herr Spieler, he must've dreamt about ye. Would that be so? Aye, he done something like what I done. Aye, he fashioned a machine to draw ye forth from his unconscious mind and bring ye to life.'

The woman dropped the print to the earth. 'Imagine how wicked Herr Spieler must've been to envision us slaying his own flesh and blood, and for no other reason than to preclude the innocent soul from bringing to fruition his tenth symphony.'

Herr Spieler gestured toward Fingal and panted. 'Each day, my brother grows that much closer to rounding off his tenth. Which means he doesn't have long to live. And no matter how often I admonish the fool, nevertheless, he won't relent. Because he seeks to punish me for my fleeting treachery.'

Fingal stepped back. 'Why should I concern myself with your woes? What about me captive back home? Me nemesis imperils peoples everywhere. As such, I haven't got time to address no goddamn tenth symphony.'

Herr Spieler crawled over to Fingal's feet. 'Help me. No one else should ever be accomplished enough to send the Nine Muses back into my dreams.'

Fingal felt at his ribs. 'I can't help you. In point of fact, I can't do nothing right. Back home, I'd be gainsaid at every turn. Hell, I'd count myself lucky just to find someone willing to help me mend me Instruktor.' He looked to the nighttime sky—just in time to consider the black, tonal values of a cloud presently drifting westward.

Herr Spieler grabbed hold of Fingal's ankles. 'Maybe you won't help me only because you despise us Germans. You're still bitter about the war, yes? Maybe you've visited the Tomb of the Unknown Warrior. Still, I do very much deserve your sympathy. Can't you imagine the anguish I've felt, as my ruthless, fanatical brother continues to compose his ingenious, fertile symphonies, measure by measure by measure, always bringing the total number ever closer and closer and closer to nine? And now he's gone *beyond* his limit.'

One of the Muses kicked Herr Spieler's hip. 'If you truly

loved your brother, then you would've determined some way to temper your jealousy. For that matter, you never would've fashioned projections of us.'

As the pianoforte music continued from up above, Himmelreich quoted a passage from what Fingal believed to be a setting of Shelley's 'Music, When Soft Voices Die'.

Again, the Muse kicked Herr Spieler. 'Soon, our foolish melodist should be ready to orchestrate his score. Any day now he must perish from this world.'

'No, let him *live*,' Herr Spieler pleaded, his voice increasingly hoarse and unsteady.

'You should be thankful that we permitted him to live as long as we did,' the woman continued. 'Usually, a wicked composer forces our hand the instant he chooses the keynote for his tenth.'

The pianoforte music ceased, and a faint, wavering voice from inside the flat uttered a solitary word: 'Verboten.'

Fingal crossed his arms. *Why must we do what's forbidden?* He dropped one hand to his side and covered his mouth with his other.

For thirty minutes or so, the nine women debated whether or not they ought to slay their quarry that very night. When the women finally decided against acting just yet, Herr Spieler scrambled to his feet and followed the procession down through the alleyway—at which point Himmelreich commenced another night-piece.

Fingal continued inside, where he paused to let his eyes adjust to the darkness of the antechamber. *What am I doing? I ought to turn back.*

The weathered balustrade proved to be warm to the touch, so he climbed the spiral staircase. Oddly, Himmelreich had left his door open. The flat smelled of black lager, smoked sausages, and pipe tobacco.

I got so much to do. Turn back. Fingal nodded to himself but then continued through the door.

Before the upright piano, the composer sat upon what looked to be a Danish-style dining chair rather than a proper piano bench. On the floor, to the side of the chair, stood a dusty Vienna horn. To the side of the horn stood a tufted-leather ottoman.

After a while, Himmelreich discontinued the tune and looked up. 'You must be my brother's contact, the Scotsman.'

'Aye, that'd be so.'

'It's true what he says about you? All the time, he claims you've done much more than give life to nightmares. He says you've somehow created a representation of humankind's inborn knowledge.'

'Aye, so I did.'

'And where do you keep the likeness?'

'Don't be alarmed, but these days he'd be mucking about all over. That's why I haven't got much time before he makes someone go off like a rocket.'

'Oh? So you cannot consign him to his rightful place?'

'No. Always aback, I am.' Fingal drew a deep breath. 'I got me a question. Why don't you *forgo* the tenth symphony? Aye, forelay the Muses' scheme.'

'No,' Himmelreich answered. 'Someday *die Musen* must dispatch me. There's nothing to do, no way to change anything.' The composer stood up and polished the dusty Vienna horn with his sleeve. Then the young man removed the gold studs from his shirt and placed them inside a cufflink box sitting upon the windowsill. 'Das ist das Ende.'

The whole of Fingal's body stiffened. 'Why do you act so calm? Wouldn't you be longing to *live*?'

A winter breeze reeking of coal dust drifted through the window, the current stirring the pages of a paperback novel lying in the corner.

'You shouldn't concern yourself with my impending death,' the composer continued, his tone slow, out of pitch, perhaps even a touch too low. 'Soon I'll be gone.'

'Aye, but what if the Nine Muses resolve to harm someone else?'

'They'll not do that.' His head held high, the doomed composer walked over to a receiving set and horn speaker assembled atop a table on the far side of the room.

'Do you listen to Radio Luxembourg?' the composer asked, after a long pause.

'No.'

'What a pity. I say so only because they mention you. *Frequently*. If you weren't so intimidating, I should think they'd ask if you'd be willing to grant them a proper interview.'

'I'd say no. I don't never gad about me bloody failures. Who cries stinking fish?'

'Very well, but last week, I heard a most enthralling dialogue with a Frenchman who might be of service to you. Have you ever heard of Monsieur Félix Barthélémy Zéphir? To the best of my knowledge, he lives in Paris. Whatever the precise arrondissement might be, you'll not have any trouble finding him. So visit him. Perhaps he could help you.'

'No, after a night like this, why commit to another bootless errand?' His head hanging low, Fingal returned downstairs and continued into the street.

Himmelreich appeared at the window and snapped his fingers. 'Do go to Paris,' the composer implored him. 'Make no provision. You can't afford to laze about like my vindictive brother. That's because *der unmensch*, the brute you have unleashed, he must be ninefold stronger than even you imagine.'

'Yes, I know,' Fingal shouted over his shoulder. He paused to make believe that he held the pewter urn in his hands. If so, he would open the vessel and peek inside. What a paradoxical sight the miraculous, ever-burning creature would be in that moment; neither would it look merely natural, nor mindlessly *super*natural.

'Tell me the riddle of the universe,' Fingal would whisper.

'Maybe you should've asked the Nine Muses that question,' the entity might have answered. 'Don't the Muses bring about all great discoveries?'

'I disbelieve all that. A child of modern times, I'd be.'

'Yes, you believe that the unconscious mind houses all wisdom and directs a person's thoughts and decisions. Oh, yes. The unconscious mind directs all. *That's* what you believe.'

The untuned pianoforte recommenced with yet another displeasingly modernistic, polytonal melody.

Fingal looked to the night sky. *Shall I move on to Paris?* He shivered and shrugged and frowned. *Fräulein Wunderwaffe, what do you suppose I ought to do? Please send me your thoughts, leopardess. I'd appreciate your counsel. So talk to me some.*

At his back the melody splintered apart into what sounded like fifteen wholly dissimilar minor keys. Had the composer got lost in confusion? Whatever had happened, suddenly each tone hung in the air, until the music reached its logical conclusion.

Chapter Thirteen

At the stroke of midnight, with the late-February breeze blowing in his face, Fingal boarded a passenger train bound for Paris.

Over and over, he tapped upon his knee, until he fell asleep. At dawn, he awoke and looked out the window. *Might this be Leipzig?*

At half past two o'clock, the train pulled into Luxembourg, at which point some kind of signals-and-points failure caused a big delay. Not until midafternoon did the journey resume, and not until six o'clock that evening did the train roll into the French capital.

For a little while, he passed the time in a quiet brasserie and polished off two bottles of crème de violette. The establishment did not remain quiet for long. Soon enough, a series of loud aural hallucinations bounced off the walls: the cries of a leopardess, the creature urging him to hurry onward. *Aye, I'm going.*

At half past eight o'clock, he checked into a modest hotel just off la Rue de la Créature de R*êve*. When he reached his room, he ignored the lump in his throat and rang Monsieur Zéphir—the youthful engineer to whom the doomed composer, Himmelreich, had alluded back in Berlin.

No sooner had Fingal asked Zéphir to examine the flawed Instruktor than the Frenchman groaned. 'Why didn't you *write*?'

'Because I'm desperate, don't you know? Afflicted by dark, sombre dreams and ghastly visions, I am. Like me sins should bring about the end of the world. So help me. *Please*.'

'If I could, of course, I would. But this would be a most unfavourable *période difficile* in my life. Only this morning, not two hours ago, I heard the most terrible news.'

'If you don't mind my asking, what happened?'

'It was a report out of Berlin,' Zéphir answered very softly. The line went quiet, as if the young engineer must be feeling profound distress. 'In the darkness just before dawn, someone murdered my favourite composer.'

'Your favourite composer?'

'Yes, Himmelreich. The symphonist.'

'The German bloke struggling to complete his tenth?'

'*Yes*. Someone came into his flat and put him in a stranglehold. Radio Luxembourg even quoted a few of the officers in charge of the coroner's court.'

Fingal dropped the receiver from his hand, looked to the far wall of his hotel room, and studied the watercolour there—a canvas depicting a dishevelled old man and his three-legged dog stumbling along what appeared to be le Boulevard du Montparnasse. To the left of the watercolour sat a wall clock which suddenly stopped, and the most displeasing, lifeless quietude filled the room.

Fingal took the receiver back into his palm and feigned a croup cough—as if the semblance of frailty might somehow excuse the incivility of his ringing the young Parisian at this inopportune time.

'Are you well?' Zéphir asked him.

'No, but don't pother. I'll go on back home to Scotland.'

'*No*. Since you travelled so far, I shall help you. Why don't you come to my house tomorrow morning?'

'With pleasure, monsieur, and thank you a thousand times over.' Fingal placed the receiver on the switch hook.

Later, when he climbed into bed, he could not fall asleep. The mere thought of what the spectre might be doing back home had him thrashing about. Twice, he fell to the floor. And when he did it the second time, he even managed to bruise his jaw.

At almost the midnight hour, a caterwauling commenced, and the clamour seemed to come from just beneath his hotel-room window. *How about that for une très belle chanson?* When the cacophony would not relent, he rang the night clerk, but no one answered. *Has the staff already departed?*

The caterwauling continued at tedious length, and when Fingal could not take it any longer, he hurled the brass warming pan at the window.

Ten minutes later, he walked outside and discovered the culprit, an almost-hairless, half-starved cat with but two whiskers. 'Why you singing the black psalm?'

The pitiable thing grew quiet. Did it think that he might help it find its way home? If so, where did the wayward creature live? Like other feral Parisian cats, perhaps it sheltered in one of the historic cemeteries—either Montmartre or Père-Lachaise.

The cat wandered off, and Fingal, curiosity picqued, followed it two blocks east to a nickelodeon theatre called le Studio des Ursulines. The animal stopped and looked up, as if to read the words arranged upon the marquee:

À l'affiche dans ce cinema, Iphigénie en Tauride!
On display in this cinema, Iphigénie en Tauride.

The thought of viewing a Greek tragedy did not seem to excite the creature. It looked down, gave Fingal a sidelong glance and hissed. Then the cat licked its right front limb, groaned, and collapsed.

Fingal intuited the animal's wishes. The poor thing happened to be dying, and it longed for company lest it succumb in solitude. Fingal realised that he could not simply return inside the hotel. *If I did, the guilt should only add to the torment I'm already feeling.*

Fingal stroked the animal's chin. 'Aye, I'll stay. Who better to do it? I know all about dying. I'd be the one who brought the angel of death into the world.'

A plain, unassuming woman dressed in a tea gown and holding a feathered purse in her hand emerged from an alleyway opposite the deserted boulangerie. As soon as the woman noticed Fingal's duffle coat and kilt, she cracked a wide grin. 'Happy days, I've found me a countryman.'

He resisted the urge to greet her with a bow. *She's on the game, this one.* A soft current blew through his thinning, grey hair.

The woman removed a cutty pipe from her purse and pointed the lip at him. 'Could you help me find my way? I'm looking for the Catulle Mendès Society.'

'Never heard of it.'

'You don't know about Catulle Mendès, the tragic poet? Almost eighteen years ago to the day, he booked passage on the night train to le Quartier Saint-Germain-des-Prés. I think he aimed to return home to his wife and children, but the damn fool went strolling along through the corridor just as the train pulled into a tunnel so dark that he never even quite realised when he'd reached the caboose, '*le wagon de queue*', as the French say. Anyway, I think the poet must've presumed it another passenger car, so when he stepped out the door, naturally, the chap figured the landing to some other carriage ought to receive his foot. Alas, the wistful poet stepped into nightmarish nothingness and fell to his death, he did.'

From what sounded like a few blocks north, the rumble of the Métro resounded, and then the whole walkway rattled.

A moment or two later, as the city returned to quietude, a thin maiden dressed in the uniform worn by pupils at l'École Pratique des Hautes Etudes—The Practical School of Advanced Studies—passed by. When she paused to check the copper-stained address plaque, 10 Rue des Ursulines, it became clear that the girl had either steam burns or quite possibly a grave case of fever blisters running through her face and neck.

Fingal blanched, but what to do? At that hour, any number of strange, tormented souls would be wandering the city.

Like a weary, woefully-driven slave, the sickly maid staggered across the street and into the park. Evidently, a magician calling himself Monsieur Letrompeur had come to demonstrate the miracle of teleportation. On a makeshift stage, he had arranged a wooden armoire painted deep purple with myriad gold stars.

'What's sauce for the goose,' the Scottish woman muttered. Then she crossed the street and joined the girl.

Fingal attempted to do the same, but the miserable cat howled, as if someone had kicked it in the ribs. He flashed a smile. 'Hush. Let me look at the exhibition. I'll be back in no time, won't I?' The cat continued to gripe, but Fingal walked into the park and jostled for a place at the front, not far from the Scottish woman.

Monsieur Letrompeur produced a basket filled with cotton candy, and he placed it atop a footrest standing inside a large wardrobe. Then he closed the door and pulled from his cummerbund a contrivance that looked almost identical to the Instruktor.

The Scottish woman elbowed Fingal's arm. 'I don't care a pall mall how much you might pay me to do it, I'd never step into a machine like that one there. Who knows where the hell you'd get to? Wouldn't it be like Catulle Mendès falling off the brake van?'

The illusionist depressed a button on the droll device in his hand, waited a spell, and then opened the door. Of course, the cotton candy had vanished.

As if the maiden from l'École Pratique des Hautes Etudes disbelieved all, she feigned a round of laughter. 'Mon barbe à papa!' she cried out in a coquettish tone. 'Mon Dieu!'

A dozen other spectators booed and jeered and heckled the magician, but Fingal returned to the street just in time to catch sight of the forlorn cat dragging itself off behind a slow-moving pair of blind grenadiers. *How to forsake the poor mouser?* At once, he followed along.

Some two blocks north, the ailing veterans held hands and continued into the metro station. As if loath to step into the concourse, the dying cat turned back, then glowered at Fingal before collapsing on the pavement.

At that point, the Scottish woman came along and pulled on Fingal's sleeve. 'Do help me locate the Catulle Mendès affair, won't you? Afterward, maybe we'll get ourselves a good, strong cuppa.'

Like a person in prayer, Fingal knelt. 'No, I can't do that. I got to stay here with me confidante, don't I?'

Almost laughing, the woman wrapped her hand around her cutty pipe's tulip bowl and pointed the lip at the dying animal. '*He'd* be the reason you won't help me?'

'*Aye*. Wouldn't be right for me to simply forsake the poor wretch.'

'But it's a damn mouser. The wee rascal don't deserve no one's pity.'

'Who's to say? What could be more innocent than a loving, purring cat?'

'Don't you know onythin'? Catulle Mendès helped Claude Debussy found l'Ordre Kabbalistique de la Rose-Croix, because them fine artists knew that Christ alone ought to command our undivided sympathies. Erik Satie had it right as well when he founded l'Ordre du la Rose-Croix Catholique.'

Fingal stroked the dying animal's ribs. 'I've got to stay here and bear witness. Think of a composer denied his tenth symphony by the Nine Muses. In much the same way, tonight, I shall observe the terminus to this mouser's nine *lives*.'

The woman cast the cutty pipe at the cat's nose. 'What kind of Scotsman lets a half-dead pest draw his sympathy?' The irate woman collected the pipe, marched off around the corner, and did not return.

The rumble of the arriving train resounded from the platform above, and the squeal of its brakc rang out like the song of a sleepless, unmated mockingbird.

Plainly entranced by the commotion, the feral cat continued into the dimly lit station and climbed the cinder-block stair. Fingal followed, but the heel of his left shoe detached from the rest of the sole. 'C'est la guerre.' He placed the chunk of wood into his flask pocket and plodded along.

A moment or two later, when he reached the platform, he joined the cat not far from the tracks. Over and over, he wiggled his toes. *How long till this goddamn languid night finally ends?*

The sickly cat turned to the two blind grenadiers, who had climbed into the observation car and huddled together on the filthy floor.

Fingal caressed the cat's ear. 'You going somewhere?'

The dying stray sneezed twice in rapid succession.

Gently, he wiped the animal's nose, after which it wheezed and climbed aboard the train.

'I know. You mean to travel off to Saint-Germain. Aye, you hope to end your life just like the poet, Catulle Mendès, went and done.' After some hesitation, Fingal followed along and gathered the animal into his arms. The doors closed. *Bugger.*

The locomotive hissed and jerked back and forth and then pulled out. One of the two grenadiers passed wind, filling the air with a medicinal odour. At the same time, the locomotive hissed and wheezed and descended into a tunnel.

Goddamn. He held the cat close and studied the impenetrable blackness. *I'm as blind as them old soldiers.*

The cat pawed at his neck, so he blew into the animal's ear. 'Should me hard luck never cease?' he asked in a whisper. 'It's the dead of winter, and you got me riding off to nowhere.'

Outside, the rail squeal grew deafening—the call of the sleepless, unmated mockingbird having turned to absolute desperation.

As he staggered about this way and that, Fingal thought of the Great War. *Aye, them awful trenches.* He had not served, and until this moment, his sense of guilt had always precluded him from fantasising about combat. Now he could not help but ask himself just what it would have felt like to reach for his shrapnel-scarred Tommy helmet and to climb from the wet, mouldy duckboard and onto the fire step. *And then . . .*

over the top.

Unlike the doddering poet, Catulle Mendès, the grenadier must have registered awesome dread. His terror could not have lasted *too* long, though. From out of the fog enshrouding the torn fields—the clouds of hot, thick chlorine gas obscuring all the German pillboxes—the enemy would take aim and fire off his periscope rifle, and then the French soldier would fall into a length of concertina wire. *And that'd be that.* Fingal saluted and whispered a few of the hallowed words etched into that monument at Westminster Abbey:

'For the unknown war dead, wherever they fell.'

At Fingal's feet, one of the ailing soldiers kicked and cried out in a combination of Swiss French, Belgian French, and a little bit of Flemish.

Does the poor soul even know where he'd be just now? Fingal hung his head. He half-yearned to leap through the door at the very end of the train. *Why not?*

The observation car emerged from the tunnel with a neon-blue flash of light. And before long, the train pulled into the station at 8 Rue de l'Ancienne-Comédie.

Fingal disembarked with the cat bundled up in his arms. Once he had limped out onto the street he placed the creature beside a public street urinal.

As if for no other reason than to add to the overpowering stench of stale discharge lingering in the air, a 1916 Radieuse spewing a torrent of honey-coloured exhaust passed by. Not ten seconds later, a noisome 1918 Zèbre came along and traces of a rust-like odour suddenly streaked the air.

The cat made a long, drawn-out yowl and then looked all about, as if hoping to find someplace to hide. Then the cat collapsed onto its side.

Fingal gathered together a few crumpled broadsheet newspapers and made a modest bedroll for the dying creature. For a moment or two he even caressed its warm belly.

The cat's hip joint bobbed, and the miserable creature's tiny, delicate, glistening-pink member slowly arose from a patch of pewter-grey hair.

Fingal winced. 'Why must you put me to shame? Why must you expose your majesty like that? Would this be a sign you're fixing to expire here and now? Aye, your body's growing frail. You got no choice but to surrender your modesty and show me your wee boabie.' His belly churning, he debated whether he ought to take the cat back to the hotel. What would be the point, though? He felt at the soft flesh of the cat's toes, and then he sighed. 'If I could save you, well of course, I'd do so. Sure, I'd take you home and introduce you to me tortoiseshell, and then I'd get on with the business of nabbing me double, and I'd save them goddamn dullards always driving about in them Silver Ghosts and . . . '

Empty-handed, Fingal returned into the train station, and as he did the dying cat let out one last agonised wail. He should have stayed and kept vigil. *But I'm weary, I am. I got to sleep.*

In the morning, when he arrived at *le manoir privé* where the youthful Frenchman lived with his parents, the aural hallucinations returned: a young leopardess calling out as if its vocal cords had stiffened. Fingal knelt before the front-door letterbox and covered his ears.

When he finally knocked, the French youth answered before long. Like a starstruck child, the callow Frenchman bowed. 'Thank you for visiting. I have read so much about you in l'Encyclopædia Universalis. Yes, and I'll have you know that every time someone from le Congrès International de Philosophie Scientifique delivers a paper on you and your work, always I attend.'

Fingal smirked. 'Good on you, then.' For a moment or two, he studied his youthful host's slender frame. *Bloody hell, he's but a manchild.*

Zéphir blushed, as if he could read Fingal's thoughts. Nevertheless, Zéphir ushered him inside, and Fingal followed the youth upstairs to his room.

What a mess the young man's bedchamber: a muddy Peugeot bicycle lay beside the door, and to the left lay a cracked hourglass.

Fingal turned to the east corner, where the young Frenchman had mounted a watercolour depicting the University of Liverpool. *Lovely.* In the opposite corner, a warped Himmelreich recording lay beside the gramophone.

Zéphir shuffled his feet, then donned a homburg some two sizes too big for him. Fingal removed the Instruktor from his kilt purse. Zéphir muttered something about 'le spectre chromatique', and then brought the device over to his wobbly bureau.

In that moment, Fingal should have demonstrated his impatience. If nothing else, he might have alluded to all the troubles back home, but a slouching, little poodle wandered into the room and opened its mouth to reveal a bit of thrush upon its tongue—a dozen or more little, white lesions.

Fingal thought of the feral cat. *How could I leave that poor mouser to die all alone?* Though his eyes produced no tears, he wept—for he suddenly realised that he had left a lonely friend to die. *Aye, and in utmost isolation.*

Chapter Fourteen

Once the young Frenchman had completed his modifications to the Instruktor, Fingal travelled from Paris to Cherbourg and booked passage home. Determined to recapture his nemesis, he held the device in his hand all throughout the voyage home. Several times over, he paced the entire length of the ship's deck.

Not three hours after reaching the Port of Dumfries, he travelled by train to Wales. As soon as he reached coal country, he consulted a solicitor in Cardiff and explained the whole dilemma regarding the three Welshmen.

The solicitor smirked, as though he knew just what to do. Then he sat back some and rubbed his hands together. 'Let's put the frighteners on,' he told Fingal.

Together they sent a series of alarming, unsigned, unsourced letters to the shareholders who had invested the most capital in those various mining operations owned by the three disturbed coal barons. In no uncertain terms, the correspondence explained how demented the trio had become, and the letters implored everyone to band together and to abduct the three fools.

'Then what?' Fingal asked.

'Don't worry,' the solicitor answered. 'I got me a cracking good answer. In the end, we'll commit all three to a nursing home.'

As soon as Fingal arrived back in Newbattle, he rang Jean. 'Got me a right perfect stratagem, I do,' he told her. 'Once the shareholders abduct the three Welshmen, me foe should be so incensed, he'll just have to come around. Aye, and when the burning man reappears before me and curses all me artifice, that's when I'll strike.'

Alas, nothing happened—at least not at first. On the evening of Empire Day, though, Fingal spotted a familiar-looking Rolls idling across the street from Village Hall. When it drove slowly away, Fingal followed the vehicle to the picture palace, but the Rolls-Royce didn't stop; it just sped off down an alleyway. Fingal looked at the establishment before him. *It's the one what showed the tale of the runaway train.* He approached a delicately-built usher who had only just stepped outside to smoke a cigarette. 'You still showing the same feature?' Fingal asked him.

'No, governor. Not since Wednesday last.' The youth took a long drag.

'How did the story end? Did the hero leap from the caboose and plunge into some wee tepid lake, or did he perish when the engine impacted at the end of the track? I'd think the train would've crashed at speed, eh? At least tell me the archetype within the story. Could it be that the picture means to teach us some long-forgotten allegory? How about a myth regarding the perils of unbridled technology?'

'I can't tell you nothing, governor.'

'But if you don't, I'll go bloody mad.'

'What a brilliant pity.' The usher discarded the cigarette without even putting it out, and then he sauntered back into the lobby.

Fingal stepped on the burning cigarette butt and ground it into the pavement. Then he walked back to Parthenon Avenue, where one of his neighbours, Mr Sorley, happened to be standing beside the engine compartment of his Crossley Motors HP Phaeton.

As Fingal passed by, Mr Sorley spat upon the curbstone. 'Why don't you collect your blasted machinery and bugger off already? No one wants your kind living here. You imperil everyone.'

'But I don't mean to put no one in harm's way. Honestly.'

'Go on and leave us. For too many anxious years, you've lived here with that infernal genie or whatever the hell it'd be.'

'Yes, but I got me Instruktor working good now.'

'Your creation, he's comprised of inborn knowledge? So why does the burning man take the form of a fiery demon? And why's he always buzzing about from pillar to post?'

'It's a mystery. I haven't got the answers. Nevertheless, as soon as I trap him, he'll have himself the deuce to pay for all his mischief.'

'Yeah? What about them bloody Rolls-Royce Silver Ghosts your wicked creation has running up and down our fair street? The accursed thing aims to get the drivers to brass off someplace and immolate themselves, don't he?'

'Maybe so. Nevertheless, I've already hatched me a guileful scheme to resolve the whole sordid affair.' Fingal turned away, at which point a set of headlamps suddenly shone from the end of Parthenon Avenue. *Could it be a Silver Ghost?*

The motorcar proved to be Jean's Model T, and as soon as it pulled up to Fingal's house, the American woman cut the engine and climbed out from behind the wheel.

Fingal hurried over to greet her. Then he ushered the American woman inside and took her ulsterette.

'Shall I fire the gas jets and make you a pot of carrot soup?' Jean asked him.

'I don't want nix.' Fiingal removed his own coat and staggered off. When he reached the foot of the stair, he turned back and raised his hands. 'You stay down here and have a care for the spectre, eh?' Fingal retired to his room, his hands balled into fists.

After a while, he nodded off. And at some point in the night, yet another vivid dream took hold of his psyche, and he found himself in Marseille outside the impregnable gates of le Palais Longchamp.

Madame de Pompadour exits the museum, and the socialite makes her way forward, the woman's hands restless and her breath the scent of melted parsley butter.

How bright pink the big Marquise diamond around her neck, too, the flawless gemstone resembling almost perfectly the shape of her lips.

'So do you expect me to unlock the gate and let you *inside?' she asks me through the rails. 'Why did you even come here anyway? No, don't answer. I know why. You came to boast about your scheme to trap the projection.'*

'Indeed. I mean to save the world, I do.'

'Well, let's hope so.' The Frenchwoman steps back some. Then she looks to the hoary, overcast sky, and as she does, a blue phoenix descends from the clouds. Madame de Pompadour, her diamond blazing like a sodium fire, gathers together some passion flowers from the museum garden and helps the mythical bird to build its funeral pyre.

At that point, the salty, ashy odour, no matter how

illusory, proved to be just strong enough to stir Fingal from his slumber. *What was that? It must've been a vision of triumph.*

In time, he arose from bed and went downstairs, where he found Jean sitting in the conservatory.

Slowly, she stood. 'You'll never guess what happened while you was asleep. A solicitor rang you.'

'What did he say?'

'The fine gentleman told me to tell you that it won't be long till the shareholders come around.'

'So they've brought together a band of swains to come to Newbattle and collect them three mad fools?'

'Sure did sound that way.' Jean walked over to the window that commanded the best view of the garden, and she lifted the sash.

A predawn breeze swirled about the conservatory and stirred some of the mechanical sketches strewn about the floor.

Fingal breathed in the earthy aroma of late-winter rebirth. How soothing the current felt, not so cold at all. He stepped outside and walked to the heart of the wooden bridge spanning the lily pond. *Where could the spectre be?* He took hold of the weathered railings, and he shook them so hard that the bridge jolted and jounced. 'Come join me here,' he pleaded, hoping that his miscreation might hear him. 'Let's have ourselves an early morning tea party, why don't we? Do you want breakfast? I'll get you a sherry trifle.'

No response came. But over to the side, a big green frog climbed onto a rock and looked out over the pond. Several times over, the frog grunted.

Fingal smirked at the creature. 'Why don't you dive to the bottom of the stew, where it's good and warm? Aye, you'll sleep the winter away.'

Three days later, the solicitor rang to say that the

conspirators had already subdued one of the coal barons. Then the cabal secured another. The next day, the schemers abducted the third.

Fingal did not rejoice, for he knew his nemesis would be in a fit of temper. At nightfall, he sat in the foyer and awaited the entity's homecoming. For a time, he lay beside the narrow space between the bottom rail and the sill sweep. *Come on through there. Aye, like a wee puff of smoke, you'll materialise the way you do.* He removed the Instruktor from his kilt purse and examined the improved activation switch.

When dawn arrived, he marched over to the wine table, tore apart the autochrome depicting the castle and the rowan tree, and cast the pieces of the photograph at the cat. Several fragments caught in its tortoiseshell coat. At three o'clock, the much-maligned animal departed, as quietly as a ghost. Would the innocent creature ever return?

That evening, Jean stopped by the house again. And no sooner had she invited herself inside than a metallic groan resounded from the direction of the conservatory. Her eyes as wide as could be, she followed Fingal into the room.

His ill-fated invention, the one that had enabled him to bring forth the burning man, expelled a gas of some kind. Then the purge bulb shone the brightest blue, at which point the spring stirred to life. Three compression waves glided through the wire that connected the power source to the arched gateway. Then the purge bulb blinked five times and went dead. Would the ageing machine ever function again?

Jean looked to the glass rooftop. 'I got me a bad feeling.'

The next day, Fingal returned to the foyer and awaited his prey. Along the baseboard, near where the paint had peeled some, he located a solitary, brindled hair. *Me wayward cat.* Before long, he walked into the kitchen and filled the ceramic cat bowl with a tin of Indian-Ocean oil sardines. *Please come home.* Before long he melted into tears.

On the last day of winter, he walked out into the garden. 'Are you out here, me wee mouser?' He gazed out across the apple orchard to the ruins of the cider mill. *What if me cat's taken refuge there?* He crossed the property line, trudged up the winding pathway and stopped. Not far from the cider mill, a billowy plume of raspberry-red smoke with orange stripes swirled about in a gentle eddy. *Me projection.* Fingal reached into his kilt purse and produced the Instruktor.

A cool, rejuvenating gust tore through the apple orchard, but the plume grew perfectly still.

What's all this? Fingal stared at the mysterious, unmoving wisp—until it diffused into the air.

Moments later, not three feet to the left, the spectre materialised. Wholly engulfed in blue flames, the entity flared its nostrils. 'What's become of my three friends? Did you consume my prey?'

'Forget them, eh?' With the tip of his thumb, Fingal caressed the Instruktor.

'*Blimey.* I came so close. Another week or so, and each one of those fine Welshmen would've delivered himself.' With a loud sigh, the burning man passed through the dry-stone wall and continued into the garden.

Fingal followed him onto the wooden bridge spanning the lily pond. 'Don't try me patience. Get on back into the cellar.'

'This here's the kind of garden where a haiku poet should be thankful to live,' the fiery apparition announced. 'A haiku poet, he'd seek to achieve absolute concord with nature, for he'd feel at one with the sun and the moon and the sky. And what of your lovely pond? In the eyes of a haiku poet, the pond might serve to stand in for the Sea of Japan. And that'd be crucial, for the first verse of a haiku must house a graceful image of the *eternal*.'

'You fancy yourself some kind of poetry professor? Aye, maybe someday you'll get yourself a post at Tokyo Imperial University.'

'In a garden like this, the mirthful poet might feel at one with any living thing. And even if he never befriended either a flowering plum tree, or a little Japanese snow crab, or some wind-ravaged scarecrow, still the poet would witness many instances of transitory life. And all that would be so very crucial as well, for the second verse of any properly structured haiku must house the *ephemeral*.'

'No more dawdling,' Fingal shouted. 'Get on back into the cellar.' With his free hand, he pointed at the house.

'*You* could never write a heartfelt haiku. Even if you could put something eternal into the first verse and something ephemeral into the second, it takes a visionary to enkindle the third and final line. To write the first two would be as easy as shelling peas, but the third line demonstrates just how the ephemeral *relates* to the everlasting. Yes, the wondrous, almost unimaginable bond between them.'

'How do you mean?'

'Don't you follow? One moment, the poet feels such earnest adoration for nature. And then his unconscious mind sows the seed, and the seed grows, until he comprehends the way he and any other living presence truly relate to the undying world. And now, because he fathoms as much, so he comes to hold the power to compose the last verse. So he completes a sound work, and when he does, he feels *free*. As if his soul has escaped his body and has already returned to the gods of Mount Fuji.'

Fingal depressed the control button, and if the modifications to the Instruktor had proven to be effective his nemesis should have drifted back inside the house, but nothing happened, at least not at first. Then the burning man contorted and shrunk until the projection had twisted itself into the shape and glow of a faint, miniscule cinema-projector bulb.

The aureate, phosphorescent spark of light drew very close and then oozed and bled and trickled through the skin at the heel of Fingal's thumb. The entity had invaded Fingal's person.

At first, he merely tilted his head. *It's only illusion, like trick photography.* Then an ache awoke in the pit of his stomach—a feeling as of a big mushroom-shaped polyp having suddenly sprung into existence, a tumour comprised of fire and flesh and closely-woven linen.

Below the wooden bridge, the frog from before returned to the rock looking out over the pond.

Fingal fixed his gaze upon the animal—the little spot upon its brow. 'What's happened to me? Abounding in repugnant fumes, am I? Why you looking at me funny? Perplexed, are you?'

The frog turned away and grew very still, as if it registered the whole of the natural world as a fleeting dream sequence. And then the frog leapt into the waters with an alluring splash.

Early that evening, with a soft spring rain falling onto the glass rooftop, Fingal entered the conservatory, arranged his precision tools on the floor, and then attempted to mend the electrical-ballast mechanism—perhaps the most crucial component, the one that had done the most to help him conjure the burning man.

Eventually he realised that the machine no longer functioned at all. With no better option, he walked off into the cookery nook and read through some of his papers. *What'd be the answer?* For fifteen minutes or more, he chewed upon the end of his wooden-barrel pencil.

When he finally returned into the conservatory, he kicked the machine's base—the very place where several pieces dovetailed in the most fragile way. 'What a plonker,' he whispered.

The troublesome machine's exhaust passage seeped through the air duct, and the conservatory filled with an odour as of purified hydrogen sulfide. Not long afterward, the power source's evaporator coil failed—first it produced a grating whistle, and then the whole component trembled as if too old and too infirmed to go on.

From the direction of the cellar, a series of crackles resounded—a dedicated circuit perhaps responding to some electric signal. Then the whole system overloaded, and the mishap plunged the house into darkness.

From somewhere inside his body, the spectre called out: 'Your work's all over grumble, or so it seems.'

And deep inside his belly now, the mushroom-shaped polyp seemed to grow in size—by as many as three whole inches.

Fingal flinched, as if some vile entity had touched his hand. He clenched his jaw and tried to look through the glass rooftop, but instead he fell to the floor, his eyes shut as tightly as he could.

From deep inside Fingal's body, the entity called out again: 'You've got no idea how nettled you got me feeling at present. Much to my chagrin, you've saved them Welshmen. All three. And now I've got to avenge that trespass, haven't I?'

Several drops of cold rain leaked through the glass rooftop, and soon a relentless shower dripped onto Fingal's brow.

The mushroom-shaped polyp inside his belly seemed to grow even more, so much so that the anguish proscribed any attempt to move out of the rainfall's way.

At last, Fingal thought of the leopardess. *Fräulein Wunderwaffe, do you read me thoughts just now? Listen, hen. For donkey's years, I've laboured goddamn hard. With every measure of me strength, I've struggled so. But where did it get me, eh? Me toils, they've brought me to this place. A place of defeat, eh?*

The storm grew stronger, and the raindrops increased in number, many of them hitting him right between the eyes.

Listen, leopardess. From this occasion forward, I'll not be calling on you. Got to burn down me bridges, I do. No, there's no turning back. I've got to commit and do what's necessary to dominate me miscreation and make him teach me the riddle of the universe. Aye, and that's a dodgy proposition because me invention don't even work right no more. And if the burning man goes free from me body, just what should me goddamn undependable Instruktor do? It's bound to send him back into me belly, like he'll be the death of me.

Harder and faster, the cold rain poured and pelted him, until Fingal placed his hands over his face. *Someday I'll be triumphal. Even if it takes decades, I'll find the proper way to modify me machine and gateway. And I'll make the spectre help me puzzle out the riddle of the universe, aye, and in the selfsame moment that I'm sending the spectre back inside me, where he can't do no more harm. Aye, and it's got to be me because the sore villainous malefactor went and issued from me own fleshy noodle, didn't he? If anyone should be on the cuff to redress what's happened, it'd be me.*

At last, Fingal managed to push himself away from the rainfall. *Aye, someday I'll be free. That's right, somehow, some way, I'll puzzle out the whole riddle of the universe. And then everybody should go free, for I'll share the revelation with one and all.* With that, he opened his eyes.

By then a fragment of the electric power had returned; a

solitary table lamp bathed the conservatory in an uneven glow not unlike that of an improperly-lit film.

Deep inside his belly, the ache intensified—as if the mushroom-shaped polyp had suddenly grown into something indomitable, a cast-iron anchor hook.Fingal wrapped his hand around his throat and thought back to the time the burning man had grabbed him there. *I know I'll get better one of these days.* He rubbed his belly and thought of the leopardess. *Goodbye.*

III

Chapter Fifteen

JEAN. Evangeline, Connecticut. Spring, 1947.

Jean departed the campus at five o'clock, walked seven blocks back to her Dutch colonial on Wren Haven Drive, and stopped to check the mailbox. Among all the marketing circulars and utility bills, she discovered a thick letter from a British probate-court magistrate; evidently, the lay judge had learned her name from his liaison at the Bank of Scotland and had written to tell her that the courts had reason to believe that Fingal T. Smyth must be *deceased.*

A current blew through the hemlock tree over to the right, and the leaf of paper fell from her hand and settled atop a patch of melting snow, then it reeled around the mailbox and drifted off down the street.

She gasped for breath and placed a finger against the faint, almost-invisible cleft in her chin. *Fingal's dead?* Until that moment, she had not regretted having returned to America. Already, she had lived here in Evangeline for nineteen productive years. *In so doing, though, I've lost all contact with the only man I ever loved.*

She walked over to the doorstep, where the courier service had arranged a large number of paperboard boxes. *What's all this here?* She immediately intuited the answer; under the mistaken impression that she must be Fingal's common-law wife, the justice had resolved to ship *her* all that remained of *his* possessions. The whole idea left her tittering. She looked to the place in the sky where she had espied Coma Berenices three nights before. *Fingal.*

That evening, she hired an odd-job man from Horse Creek to put the paperboard boxes into the corn-crib barn standing back from the driveway. Once he had done so, she concealed the lot beneath a duck-canvas drop cloth and then locked the barn's alley doors.

Early the next morning, she awoke to a persistent, hypnotic clamour. The commotion sounded like the humming of a motor circuit—a device similar to the ones that often emanated from the physics laboratory back at Evangeline Women's College. She climbed out of bed and bound her long, charcoal-grey hair into a dowdy, old-fashioned chignon. Then she continued downstairs. *Where's the noise coming from?*

The disturbance would not relent, and came to sound like the hum of a propeller-driven airliner.

She sat at the kitchen table and closed her eyes, and pictured herself travelling upon an airplane, seated in the exit row. *That noise, though.* She opened her eyes, stood, and walked outside onto the Connecticut-stone pathway and over to the snake-rail fence, where she scanned the pear orchard bordering her property.

A cool breeze blew through the yard, awakening the scallop-shell wind chimes dangling from the butternut tree. The mysterious din from before underwent a series of shrill spurts, violent fits, and quiet intervals. And then the clamour ceased altogether.

That's better. She studied her desolate garden. Now that winter had passed, she had plenty of chores to do: plant the ice flowers, fill the wheelbarrow with garden hash, and then tidy the sundial. *How will I ever find the time?* She returned to the women's college, for she had so much work to do. Some nine years earlier, she had founded the school's film theory department, and in addition to today's various symposia she had scheduled a meeting with her speech pathologist. And Jean could not afford to miss the appointment, for lately she endeavoured to alter her entire way of talking, lest her Kentucky catchphrases and colloquialisms continue to tarnish her otherwise scholarly reputation. *I got to recondition myself.*

At one o'clock, Jean's speech pathologist sent her off to the other side of the campus to meet with Professor Gertie T. Fenham.

Only a week before, a department search committee had hired Gertie T. Fenham to conduct the school's investigations into hypnotherapy. She employed a most ingenious method, too. She recorded a series of messages that only the patient's *unconscious* mind could hear; consequently, when the patient listened to the recording, all the silent affirmations would be sure to communicate directly with the unconscious mind itself—which would serve to reprogram whatever quirks the subject in question might have acquired in life.

When she arrived at Gertie T. Fenham's office, Jean shuddered. The hypnotherapist owned no light other than a funeral parlour lamp, which illumined the tables and chairs with a dull, seaweed-green glow.

The hypnotherapist studied Jean's eyes for a long time, as if the scholar detected great anguish there, a series of lamentations moving through her soul. 'You don't look well.'

'Please don't be alarmed or nothing. I just received some hard news about an old friend from years before, when I lived in Scotland. That's all it was. So what's on offer?'

From behind her desk, Gertie T. Fenham grabbed a record player and set it down in the glow of the funeral-parlour lamp. 'Look here.'

Jean leaned forward and studied the record player very closely: it happened to be a state-of-the-art Carryola Porto-Pick-Up, and it boasted a speed-change lever that glowed a distinctive shamrock green.

The hypnotherapist handed her three vinyl discs. 'I've implanted a series of subliminal messages into these wax recordings.'

'What kind of messages?'

'These attestations all but guarantee you'll achieve intellectual growth. They'll inspirit you with the hunger to *improve* yourself.'

Before Jean could say anything, the electricity went out, and the funeral parlour lamp ceased to glow. *Oh God, what's happened?* For a moment, the whole campus grew quiet, except for a strange thrumming, some kind of experimental apparatus.

After a while, in a sudden moment of realisation, she very nearly dropped the vinyl discs from her hand. The clamour she presently heard happened to be the very same din that she had heard earlier that morning.

When she returned home that evening, she walked into the study and listened to one of the recordings. Then she sat at her antique writing table and continued work on a paper she had been writing for the past week or so—a piece all about a film's ability to change a cinephile's temperament by exposing the person to primal archetypes reminiscent of those woven into age-old morality plays and time-honoured cautionary tales.

In time, she looked to the ceiling. *Why should the* Saturday Evening Post *even be willing to print such an exotic essay?*

Over on the table where she had arranged the record player, the stylus reached the end of the recording, but the quietude lasted only for a moment. Then the uncanny disturbance from before, that mysterious din, recommenced.

At first she endeavoured to ignore the cacophony. Given the clamour's indescribable power, though, all her efforts proved futile. The din made her think of Fingal. Subsequently, the hair all about her scalp bristled, until an overbearing compulsion drove her to do something that she had never even attempted before. *I'll compose something creative.*

With the odour of peacock-blue ink dripping from her stylograph, she proceeded to write the script for a surreal photoplay.

The story begins at Evangeline Women's College. Naked, I stand in my favourite lecture hall. And when a white pine's bough scrapes against the stained-glass window, I step outside and consider the crescent moon.

What a commotion. The whole campus resounds with a menagerie calling out to one another: a school of aoudads quarrelling with a pandemonium of koodoos, a big party of muskrats protesting against a coalition of wombats, several peccaries squabbling amongst themselves.

From behind the sugar maple tree standing on the island in the heart of the pond, Fingal reveals his presence.

'Fingal T. Smyth, as I live and breathe.'

'How you lasting?' he asks me.

'Just managing. And you?'

'Not bad, considering I can't find me invention. Neither the

power source nor any other component. Where could it be? Would you know? Help me find it, won't you?'

For a time, I admire his fine, silvery hair—the way it tumbles all the way down to his shoulders. And then I collect myself. Humbly, I bow. 'You'll find your invention someday.'

The scent of tree sap drifted in through the window, and she dropped the fountain pen from her hand. *He seemed so alive. Fingal.*

In the morning not long after she awoke, the hypnotic clamour recommenced. Determined to resolve the mystery once and for all, she walked downstairs and continued outside. There, she glanced this way and that. *Where's it coming from?*

When she continued down the length of the driveway, she espied nothing peculiar—only the tuxedo cat from the mock-Tudor across the street.

At first the cat just sniffed at the dead wisteria entangling the gatepost. Then the creature looked all about, as if it, too, heard the uncanny humming. And then the animal moved its whiskers forward into attack position and advanced toward the barn.

Jean followed the animal to the barn's alley doors and held her palms perfectly flush against one of them. The plank pulsated gently, as if the sound waves from within were strong enough to penetrate the grainy wood.

She stood tall. *Of course.* She turned to the cat. 'Do you realise what that damn fool magistrate shipped me? Each and every part to Fingal's invention, that's what. I'm sure of it. We must be hearing some highly-energised motor.'

She returned into the house, and for an hour or more the sound waves commingled with the hypnotherapy recordings.

The next day, she travelled the hourlong journey into New York City. Still mulling over what to do, she made her way to the Postal Authority on the Avenue of the Americas. *Why not send everything back to Scotland?* She stopped before the doors and placed her hand over her left breast. *What? Return all the boxes? That'd feel like an act of betrayal.*

In the end, she resolved to take in a picture show. Hopefully, a diversion like that would help her to feel at ease. *What about Humphrey Bogart in* Dead Reckoning*?* To the very best of her knowledge, the crime drama would be playing at a theatre just three blocks down from the old Harlem jailhouse.

Fifteen minutes later, she stopped beside a lamppost that stood not far from the cinema and looked about. A burning sensation in her gut told her that someone had fixed his maniacal gaze upon her.

And there he was: a gaunt old man wearing harlequin eyeglasses stood peering at her from a splintered window on the top floor of a nearby brownstone.

It's Fingal. She raced into the building and climbed the stair to what she believed to be the flat in question. Several times over she knocked. 'Fingal! My Fingal!'

After a slight delay, an unseen tenant opened the door as far as the taut, brass chain would permit. 'Scram, lady.'

'Open the door.' She looked up through her eyelashes at the brass chain. 'We've got so much to talk about. Do you realise I'm changing the way I talk these days? Yes, I'm committed to attaining *wisdom*.'

'Don't that beat all? You must be working some kind of racket. Ah, go on before I call the coppers.'

'Listen, please. You've got to open the door. Show me you're alive. You've no idea how affrighted I've been ever since that letter arrived.'

'Ain't that the limit? You're a pistol, you know that?' With no further ado, the tenant slammed the door.

For a time she paced up and down the length of the corridor. *My God, that wasn't Fingal at all.* When she returned outside, she paused beside a pipe leaking a stream of wastewater into the walkway. *I'm bad lost.*

Several days later, back home in Connecticut, the clamorous drone recommenced—loudly enough that her writing table rattled.

She walked into the laundry room, changed into a linen blouse and a plain-woven, pleated skirt, and stepped outside into the cool spring air.

Like a night exterior in some gangster film, a sharp, high-contrast light bathed the backyard in impenetrable, overlapping shadows and bright, almost blinding highlights.

The whole effect made the muscles between her legs tighten. At the same time, a scent as of jasmine or some kind of natural aphrodisiac glided through the air, and she tasted something like vanilla on the tip of her tongue. Her nipples growing firm, she walked over to the barn's alley doors.

The tuxedo cat already stood there, so she looked into its hazel eyes. 'Do you want me to go in there? Oh, but there's no reason to rush. Let the moment breathe.'

The cat lay down on its back, revealing its swollen belly and graphite-grey nipples—the animal had a litter growing inside it.

The revelation made her question her solitude. *Why did I never marry? Why* not *bring life into this world?*

Within the barn, the humming grew increasingly fitful—punctuated, uneven, and hard to follow.

Unsure of her next steps, she walked out across the bluestone patio and stopped before her oval-shaped in-ground swimming pool. She slipped out of her shoes and stockings, sat at the end of the diving board, and let her toes trail through the dark waters.

The tuxedo cat drew near, pressed the bridge of its nose against the small of her back, and nudged her.

'What should I do?' she asked the cat. 'Have you an opinion? Do you think I ought to open those boxes back inside the barn?'

From the opposite side of the swimming pool, a little pink camellia petal floated toward her. For a time she endeavoured to catch it upon the bridge of her foot, and when the delicate fragment sank, she glanced back at the cat. 'Wouldn't it be good to put Fingal's handicraft back together again? If nothing else, it'd demonstrate my enduring devotion.'

The tuxedo cat made a series of birdlike squawks, then stood on its hind legs and scratched her shoulder.

She studied the barn. *Has the drone diminished some?* Once more, she looked to the waters; miraculously, the camellia petal from before resurfaced. She returned to her feet, let her toes extend over the end of the diving board, and considered her faint, almost-imperceptible reflection. 'Do you know why I have no choice but to put Fingal's invention back together again? Maybe it's because, deep down inside, I *disbelieve* the notion that he's dead. Yes, that's why I've got to help him. Because someday he'll come looking for that ole apparatus, and he'll be hoping to put the projection back in its place.'

A cool spring breeze blew through the distant orchard, the current stirring the crowns of a dead pear tree. Slowly the air filled with the dizzying aromas of wild strawberries and fresh figs.

Her heart rate quickened. *What will Fingal look like on the day he arrives? Perhaps the old fellow would appear as serene as a wise, aged, Tibetan monk.*

On the other hand, what if Fingal's eyes were darting? If so, she would sit him beside the pool here. 'You've nothing to fear,' she would tell him. 'No, there's no reason to be frantic with worry. As a matter of fact, I've already completed your work. That's right, I've gone and rebuilt everything, power source and all.'

The quiet drone ceased altogether now, and she pushed with her heels to make the diving board bounce some.

A moment later, once she had collected her shoes and stockings, she walked back to the barn and wrapped her hand around the downspout. *Unlock the alley doors.* She did so and continued inside.

The sound waves had blown the drop cloth to the side and left the duck canvas lying in a heap.

Let's do this. She searched for a good utility knife but could not locate one. With her bare hands she tore into the first box and reached into the packing straw.

As she did so, a grey house wren fluttered past her shoulder. Had the songbird been trapped in here the whole time? Before long it fluttered off and went free.

The breeze kicked up, and the barn filled with the scent of raw oysters. She opened another paperboard box and so on, until machine parts and packing straw alike lay strewn all about. *Where to begin?* She shook her head and cursed her ignorance. *What do I know about engineering, the design of automated systems, and so on? I'm all thumbs. If only Fingal were here*. She envisioned him standing at her back.

'What're you doing, hen?' he would ask her.

'What's it look like?' she would ask in turn.

'Listen, hen. The last time I looked at this machine, none of the modifications worked in the least. *No*. Whatever you might think to do, it won't make one blind bit of difference. It's not cricket neither. I builded the entrails of this here mad contrivance with oil-rubbed bronze, I did, aye, and I greased the moving parts with the finest palm oil. Precious black butter as well. The bloody lot ought to function as right as rain.'

She rubbed her eyes, and with her sleeve dabbed at some of the sweat dampening her brow. 'I want you to know something,' she said, as if Fingal really were standing at her back in that moment. 'I'm committed to helping you. So get your Instruktor working. Please find the burning man. Yes, and then you'll come here. And I'll have this whole apparatus working right enough that you'll be able to send the projection back inside you.' For a time, she studied the machine parts scattered about before her—the spring, several transformers, five little cylinders. *Good God, I'll have to hire a whole band of draftsmen to help me do this.*

After a while, the very idea made her muscles ache. *I've got to do this by myself. The reconstruction of Fingal's invention must be a labour of love. Yes, because I know my nature well now. And I know that I love him . . . for his intellect.*

At her back, a flurry of activity transpired—what sounded like an act of violence followed by a yelp of anguish.

She turned to look. The house wren had narrowly escaped the tuxedo cat. She turned back to the matter at hand. *How do I do this?* She thought of the one thing that she knew: the structure of a film. *Might that help?* She scratched her nose. *Think. Assemble the pieces. Work.*

Chapter Sixteen

By the first few days of April, Jean had rearranged the various components across the barn floor, and every other day, if she had the time, she slipped into the same plaid, drawstring-waist shirtdress and returned to her toils. *I've got to press on.*

One afternoon, she stared at the dissimilar shapes for two hours. *I've achieved the isolation of variables, but how do I put the pieces together?*

A few days later, she brought her Carryola Porto-Pick-Up out into the barn, and from that point on, she listened to a pair of arithmetically precise baroque suites as she pondered the task at hand. Hopefully, the music would inspirit that part of her mind that processes the most intricate engineering quandaries. *And then, like wildfire, I'll develop the prowess necessary to reassemble all.*

Regarding her work back at Evangeline Women's College, she cancelled even her most popular seminars. When some of the regents protested, she ignored them. Despite any underlying impulse to take control of her life and reconnect with her colleagues, she could not overcome her newfound obsession. Moreover, she refused to accept the notion that Fingal might possibly be deceased. *He lives.* And without question, he would come around someday. *And when he does, everything must be ready for him.*

One afternoon, as the cool April rains awoke the earthy scent of spring all throughout her property, she lifted the phonograph's stylus from the recording and contented herself to listen to the downpour drumming against the barn's rooftop.

When the hard rain ceased, she put a Monteverdi piece on the turntable. *Think. Put the pieces back together. Go on.*

At four o'clock, when she returned to the house, a spot of flickering, iridescent light such as an aura appeared in her field of vision. *Am I having a migraine?*

Little by little, the anguish spread through half her head, until she sought to look *through* the spot of flickering light.

A pair of sunbeams shone through two of the study's windows, making the knotty-pine floor resemble an ancient Greek theatre's wooden, sunlit stage—the floorboards cut from some rarefied ebony tree.

From the depths of her being, a prickle compelled her to drop to her hands and knees and contemplate the various patterns in the study's knotty-pine floor. She placed the tip of her nose against one of the wooden planks running parallel to her writing desk. *How to transform myself into a scientist?*

The prickle turned to a tingling sensation, and then the tingle turned to formication. *Yes, I've got two thousand or more pharaoh ants crawling all over me.*

She crawled over to one of the windows and endeavoured to wait out the tribulations. Soon enough, though, a dozen or so lumps throbbed and pulsated and twisted and burned beneath the skin to the left of her spine. *No, no. It's just my imagination.*

At dusk, as the light of the setting sun suffused her property in shades of bright tea-rose pink, she mustered her strength and returned to her feet. Then, the spot of flickering light obscuring her field of vision yet, she staggered outside. *Someone's here.*

The tuxedo cat from across the street sauntered up the driveway, the animal's nipples dripping a steady stream of milk.

The flickering light waned just enough that she could reach for the cat's tail and follow it into the barn.

The cat stood still, its swollen teats leaking a few more droplets, and studied the bits and pieces of Fingal's invention.

She drew near. 'For all my enthusiasm, I've yet to rebuild anything. And do you know what'll probably happen when I do? Maybe I'll damage the damn thing irreparably. And then where should Fingal be?'

Jean knelt beside one of the creamy little puddles the animal had dripped onto the barn floor. With her index finger, she placed some of the warm, nourishing fluid on the tip of her tongue. *What a bitter taste.*

Late that night, just as the lingering spot of flickering light in her field of vision assumed a shade of purple, she sat at her writing table and composed a second photoplay.

At the lecture hall back on campus, I disrobe and step outside, and as I walk along, a majestic building springs up some forty feet to my left.

The structure happens to be a duplicate of the London School of Tropical Medicine, and none other than Fingal himself stands naked upon the doorstep. The sun has badly scorched his long, thin nose. Still, with his silvery-white hair tumbling to his shoulders, the Scotsman has never appeared so beautiful.

'How are you these days?'

'Oh, I've never felt better,' he answers. 'May the same befall

you.' Out of the blue, he kisses me. Then he looks up to watch a dozen or so little crested guinea fowl soaring through the sky.

'Why'd you leave your island?' I ask, pointing to the pond. 'Have you come to help me put your invention together? I hope so, for I'll never be resourceful enough to do it alone.'

'No, no. I'll be off now. On the journey, I am.'

'Oh?' With that, I place my brow against his left breast and listen to the beat of his heart. And then I whisper a line of verse penned by Walt Whitman:

'Now voyager sail thou forth to seek and find.'

He returns into the London School of Tropical Medicine, and the building dissolves and leaves behind in its place a tiny African-bone bead exuding the scent of an almond.

The stylograph fell from her hand, and she found herself overcome with a violent coughing fit.

The next day, she sat on the kitchen floor and listened to the white noise emanating from beneath her electric Frigidaire icebox. *Think.* She revisited the key elements in structuring a fine film: the heroine who longs for something, the details that reflect that desire, the things that she does to attain that desire, the race against time as she strives to resolve her woes. The thought experiment did nothing to improve things. *No, I'm as befuddled as ever.*

At midday, she took the train into the city and wandered a flower market for twenty minutes. She could not resist the compulsion to study the buds and note the way each piece fitted together—the filament, the style, the ovule, and stem. Until the bells from the Ukrainian Catholic Church tolled, she could not break free. *Go home. Get back to work.*

She wandered towards the station, but when traversing a

deserted alley, the burning man appeared before her. Rather, the spot of flickering light in her field of vision assumed the shape of the burning man. At which point the fiery spectre smiled. *Come with me. Do not resist. Let's take the Uptown.*

Her hands and feet tingled and burned. *Just like the side effects of sedation.* Despite all, curious to its intent, she permitted the light to guide her, and she took a train all the way to Times Square.

When she arrived at the loud, bustling intersection, the spot of flickering light brought her over toward the Warner Brothers Hollywood Theatre.

At last, she stopped.

A peroxide blonde dressed in a raincoat with snap-button cuffs emerged from an office building up ahead and climbed into a waiting Studebaker Starlight. As the young lady drove off, Jean approached the office building and read the words painted in seaweed green over the door:

DUNLEAVY CONFIDENTIAL

Oh, a detective agency. Jean paused for a moment or two. A big part of her longed to hire a sleuth to travel off in search of Fingal. How good it would be if the operative were to send her a telex revealing the Scotsman's whereabouts. She laughed, for she knew she would just have to be patient. *Someday, Fingal's bound to come find* me.

The spot of flickering light shone a little bit brighter in her field of vision. *Do you wish to know whether Fingal lives yet?* it asked in her mind.

Oh, I'm quite sure that he's alive.

Yes, yes he is.

Oh, that's good to know. So where would he be at this moment?

Please, please. You must tell me where he's living.

I haven't much time; I'm beginning to lose power. Still, I'll tell you where he's living … but only if you *promise to forgo all your endeavours to rebuild his confounded machine.*

From the alleyway to the left, the spring breeze awoke, and in an instant, the spot of flickering light assumed the shape of a splashed-white racehorse with a sleek barrel.

Jean closed her eyes and rubbed both of her eyelids. Then, when she opened her eyes, the miniscule racehorse assumed even more detail; most astounding of all, the beast possessed a braided mane. Jean laughed like a little girl on her birthday, and she studied the animal's crest. More than anything, she longed to kiss the patch of white on the horse's nose.

The dreamy apparition served to remind her of a noble charger that she had encountered many years earlier. She recalled her childhood in Kentucky and revisited the warm, spring day when a silver-buckskin filly had appeared out along the road running past the family farmstead.

Once the stable hand had let her have his fly whisk, she had swatted at some of the gnats darting about the animal's hip. 'Please come live with us here,' she had whispered into the creature's ear. 'If you wish to pasture breed, I should think you'll be the most splendid broodmare on our team and—'

A dozen times over, the little racehorse reeled around, then the apparition grew still. *Do you love Fingal? If so, you ought to know that he'll never love you back. Even if it takes him an entire lifetime of toil to return me into his unconscious mind, I know that he'll not shirk his charge for anything. Not even love.*

A bearded old man dressed in tailored coat and linen trousers emerged from the same alleyway from which the breeze had erupted a moment before. He paused to observe her very closely, as if he regarded her as mad. 'Do you know where you are?' the old man asked her. 'This here's Manhattan Island.'

She turned her back to the old man. A few town cars passed by, but despite the exhaust, the spring breeze seemed to fill up with the scent of feed—a bale of hay spiced with mountain laurel. *By golly, just the kind they always sold down home.*

A second time, the racehorse in her eye reeled around. And a second time, the apparition grew still. *No, no. Fingal should never love you. He's wholly committed to learning and does not care for anything else. Day by day, he expects me to tell him the source for the process of biotic evolution.*

At her back, the old man tapped Jean's shoulder. 'What's wrong, ma'am? Have you lost your way? Are you looking for Carnegie Hall? I'll take you there, if you wish.'

'Please go away,' she told the kind stranger. 'Honestly, I'm not suffering any kind of strain at all. My vision's just grown a little bit blurry, nothing more.'

From around the corner of a grey credit-union building, a Dodge Deluxe emerged and then sped by. The clamour of the motorcar's engine resounded so loudly that she very nearly lost her balance and fell onto the subway grating.

No, no. Fingal should never *love you. Do you know what he prizes? He longs to learn the laws of nature, all them principles and statutes what govern the movements and machinations of time itself. He yearns to know from whence everything emanates. And he expects me to teach him, just like that. Ah, but the conscious mind learns from the unconscious mind by degrees.*

Once again the old man tapped Jean's shoulder. 'Do you know where you are? Look at the statue of that army chaplain across the way. Do you recognise this place?'

She glanced at the statue. 'Yes, this here's Times Square. I'm not ill. I just thought that maybe I'd stand here a spell and rest awhile. Please leave me be.'

A lady in a flounced skirt and felt hat happened by, and she looked just like a friend from Jean's past, from her very first pony club. When the lady crossed the street, Jean followed her into Times Square, where the lady vanished into a large crowd. *Come back.* As she looked this way and that, Jean almost collided with a Chinatown-style pushcart filled with bean cakes; she turned to the diminutive bean-cake peddler and apologised.

The bean-cake peddler merely shrugged, and then looked down to brush a bit of debris from his Mandarin-style coat.

Jean sat beside the pushcart and sought to focus upon the racehorse apparition hovering in her eye. *What happened to Fingal?*

A cabal made him go into exile. Various members of the Scottish Parliament along with a few ladies from the Order of Scottish Clans, they had a meeting one night. Aye, they all came together in the ruins of Holyrood Abbey.

So where did they send poor Fingal?

They sent him far away, and in so doing, they sent me *far away. Oh, but soon I'll have the strength to escape him. For good and all. And then I'll be* free.

Jean studied the pavement; in the afternoon light, the asphalt assumed the colour and texture of Tennessee marble. She thought back to the racehorse from her childhood. *Back then, life was always so simple. And now this.*

The apparition in her eye flashed the colour of Chinese dragon fruit, and then the little racehorse shape shook the tip of its tail's skirt. *You have no idea how much I suffer. Fingal expects me to tell him things that no one should know,and then he aims to put me back inside his noodle. Forevermore, forevermore.*

Tell me where the cabal exiled him. If so, I could write him. Yes, I'll write him love letters.

No, no. Permit me to speak. I ain't no one's goods and chattels. I'm telling you that I've had me a bellyful. So forgo the work you've commenced. Forget all about helping Fingal send me back inside him. By your leave, let me go free. Free. With that, the racehorse reverted back to its original shape—a spot of flickering light. And then the light was gone.

Jean returned to her feet. *Come back.* When the flickering light failed to return, she stumbled forward, into the pushcart.

The bean-cake peddler cursed her beneath his breath, but she ignored him and hailed a taxicab to return her to the train station. *Go home.* She did just that, and for the next six days she did not leave the house.

When she finally visited the barn, she stood for a moment and surveyed the machine parts scattered across the barn floor. *What about a baroque Italian flute concerto?*

The tuxedo cat came along and lay down at her side, as if for no other reason than to reveal how bloated its belly had become.

She ignored the animal and fitted the first two thrust bearings together, laughing like a little girl. *Empiricism, the powers of observation, that's how I'll put the pieces together.* She rocked back and forth. *Yes, just like a clever diarist who devotes herself to the description of the present, I'll find some way to analyse the matter at hand.*

The cold, unforgiving late-April breeze sailed into the barn, whistling like a cheap, plastic flute, and the air filled with the earthy scent of spring, a thousand wildflowers.

Go on. Synthesise thesis and antithesis. By nightfall, she had rebuilt the power source and arched gateway. *I'm almost ready to rig the electric spring and connect the one component to the other.*

As if greatly impressed with her work, the tuxedo cat

stood and purred. And as the creature's affectionate vibrations reached a crescendo, Jean lost herself in reverie, imagining Fingal standing at her back.

'So you've just about done it,' he would say. 'How did you puzzle it out?'

'Wasn't anything unorthodox,' she would answer. 'I simply rededicated all my faculties and let my instincts guide me.'

'But you've still got to send a signal through the wire, and then you've got to make every wee part work just right.'

'Yes, but I will.'

'I hope so anyway.'

'You doubt that I should ever make the machine capable of sending the projection back inside your unconscious mind?' she would ask then.

'Not even a wee bit,' Fingal would tell her. 'Answer the call of destiny. Aye, complete the endeavours what fate has called upon you to face. Embrace your toils, hen.'

Almost convinced that Fingal did indeed stand at her back, she reeled around to look. Not six feet away, a porcupine peeked at her from a pothole in the driveway and shook its coat of long, sharp quills.

The ingenious quills made her recall the myth of Prometheus—the secret of fire, the one technology that might offer Man the power to dominate the animal kingdom.

The porcupine grunted like a hungry, pot-bellied pig, and then the curious creature ambled off.

She turned back to the power source and knelt before the oblong contrivance—just like a bondservant kneeling before her master. *How do I make this confounding thing function as it should?*

The answer eluded her, so she closed her eyes. *Burning man, come back. Let's enter into a friendly colloquy. Tell me what to do. You've no reason to fear me, and you've no reason to wish to go free. Let me put you back where you belong.*

From somewhere deep inside the power source, a few of the moving parts sputtered to life and chortled like two little kangaroos.

Then the barn grew quiet, the only sound either a wireless or a record player next door playing a bit of country music.

Burning man, please come back. She closed her eyes tighter. *You've just got to help me. Do you know why? When Fingal learns that I've gone and mended his invention and all, he'll fall in love with me. Yes, he'll love me for my intellect.*

When she finally opened her eyes and permitted herself to stand, she could not bring herself to turn her back to the power source. Instead, she bowed and stepped back, not unlike a beaten slave girl—an odalisque unworthy to consider herself human.

Chapter Seventeen

Just after breakfast, Jean stepped outside to stretch her arms and legs and to consider the morning light.

How delicate the shadows; all throughout the sky, the glow shone as if diffused. As if some film producer had willed the whole effect by hiring someone expert in the use of bounce light. She shook her head and struggled not to hyperventilate. *Shall I test my workmanship today?*

Like a wondrous portent of all things good, a white-breasted nuthatch fluttered down from the Dutch colonial's flared eaves and circled about.

Yes, go. She continued into the barn and activated the power source, which stirred to life slowly, the drone thrumming something like the rumble of a crematory. Again, she struggled not to breathe too heavily. *Here goes.* With tears in her eyes, she engaged the lever that transmitted the electric signal through the wire and over to the gateway.

A spark shone all along the length of the spring. Though nothing else happened, she lifted her arms triumphantly and hummed the tune to a sacred, baroque hymn, feeling quite certain that she had in fact rebuilt the contrivance properly. *Now what?*

The spark glimmered and flared and then changed colour and diminished, until the flash of light palled entirely. From somewhere inside the apparatus, a trilling commenced—what sounded like the voice of a child, a maniacal little boy afflicted with echolalia.

Something's gone terribly wrong. She placed her hands against the section housing the valve chest. *All that racket, could it be coming from the resistance box?*

For the better part of the long, quiet day, she tested the suspect component but made scant progress.

In the evening, the compulsion to write another photoplay came upon her. *So why not indulge myself?* She sat at her writing table, took the stylograph into her hand, and went to work.

> *Well after one o'clock in the morning, I race over to Evangeline Women's College and stop in the harsh glare hovering like a fogbank at the edge of the campus.*
>
> *From out of the shadow-filled backlighting, a naked Fingal appears.*
>
> *Quickly, I draw close. Then I remove the lady's riding habit that I'm wearing. 'So here we are,' I whisper. 'Both of us in the altogether.'*
>
> *'You wish to ask me something, do you?'*
>
> *'How do I mend the resistance box?'*
>
> *'Let me think.' He runs his hand through his long, wild hair. Then he motions toward the distant New York City skyline. 'Look at them towers rising into the sky.' As he speaks, he sprouts wings and begins reciting a line of*

verse from Walt Whitman:

'Now voyager sail thou forth to . . . '

A moment later, he wraps his hand around my wrist and takes me flying into the surreal cityscape—the uneven glow of low-key lighting reaching through the swirling smoke.

We alight in the heart of Herald Square—the intersection impossibly quiet, not even one motorcar idling in the street.

'The people should be out and about on a pleasant spring night like this,' I say. 'So where could everyone be?'

Fingal guides me over to Gimbel Brothers Department Store and points to an RCA television receiver in the window. 'Me nemesis, he's bluffed the rats. Aye, he's infected the city with incurable hysteria. Before long, all those who viewed his presentation should surely immolate themselves. Martyrs, they'd be. Innocents lost forever.'

The fountain pen fell from her hand, and she pushed her chair back. Her nose flaring, she returned outside and drew several deep breaths. *Should I return onto campus?* If she did, perhaps she could visit the school planetarium and take inspiration from the show. She looked to the sky, focused on the faint gleam of Hesperus, and thought of Henrietta Swan Leavitt—the woman who had counted every last star in the Clouds of Magellan. *Was it 71, 717?* Whatever the figure might have been, the lady astronomer had accomplished a monumental feat—and she had done so despite all the sexism and misogyny that characterises the scientific world.

From out of the shadows of night, the pregnant tuxedo cat's eyes suddenly shone, and the animal drew near.

'Look at you, content to bear kittens. Meanwhile, all throughout this nation, so many devoted lady scientists persevere. And no matter all the sexual intimidation and sexual extortion in the workplace, those women contribute something all so crucial. These days, we've got lady stargazers at Mount Holyoke, and Wheaton College, and even the College of the Holy Cross.'

The pregnant cat panted and drooled and then ambled off, back through the darkness and the contrasting patches of harsh light.

The next day, Jean travelled into the city and continued to Herald Square. For an hour, she wandered about Gimbels, a floorwalker following her the whole time. When she stopped beside a display of heart-shaped, chinaware candy dishes, her heart thumped. *How do I make that damn machine work?* Her left arm smarting, she staggered across the sales floor and then ducked into the fitting room. Her nipples ached—as if her own loneliness had released a torrent of pheromones from the deepest recesses of her mind.

At last, she looked to the ceiling. *Fingal, come to me. Please. Love me.* When she returned outside, she hailed a taxicab and asked the driver to take her to a cinema house some five blocks away. *Maybe if I lose myself in a picture show, the answer to all my troubles should come to me of its own accord. As if from the depths of my unconscious mind.*

When the taxicab pulled up to the curbstone, she detected a foul stench, an odour as that of contaminated mollusc meat, and her groin broke out in a sweat. 'Take me away from this place,' she pleaded.

'Yeah? So where to then?'

'I don't rightly know.' Her left arm tingled, and she rubbed her elbow. Once more, she breathed in the stench. 'Take me to Oyster Bay.'

'On the level? Belle Harbor, Queens would be better. If you want to chase the blues away, nothing beats the Rockaways except for maybe a little place off Bagatelle Road. I know a place that always does my heart good.'

'So,take me to Belle Harbor.'

'No problem, lady.' As if proud that he had talked his mark into a costly fare, the cabbie smacked his lips. Afterward, he drove slowly and stopped for each yellow light.

When they finally arrived at the boardwalk, she paid the fare and then walked over to the railing.

A tugboat passed by, her engine churning with a monotonous commotion that made Jean think of the bewildering contrivance back home. *How do I mend the damn thing?* Someday, she would have to ring a machinist. *No, don't do it.* She just knew that once he had helped her with the resistance box, she would only have more trouble with it the very next day—and then she would have no recourse but to ring him yet again. And then, by the time the machinist finally returned, of course, the electric circuit would function properly. *And I'd still have to pay.* Then, just before leaving, the machinist would endeavour to manipulate her into signing some dubious insurance contract.

At some point the scoundrel would look her in the eye and smile. 'Wise up,' he would say. 'A dame like you could use some genuine indemnity. If I'm lyin', I'm dyin'.'

And what if she did indeed purchase the protection? A week or so later, if and when she resolved to ring him and to make a claim, the lout would exhale loudly and then make a tutting sound. 'I'm not your goddamn *tutor*,' the swindler would tell her.

'Bewail my ignorance if you must, but I paid for the safeguard,' she would protest.

'Yeah, but I didn't know you was serious about the crazy contraption you're working on back there in your cowshed,' he would counter. 'That ain't no everyday johnny pump. If you ask me for my professional opinion, lady, you're just throwing good money after bad. But don't take it personal or nothing. You know what I'm saying? I mean don't take it to heart and whatnot.'

At that point, she would drop the telephone from her hand. Speechless, she would slump to the floor and brood for thirty minutes or more.

A winged creature's shadow streaked across the harbour; the visitor proved to be an everyday herring gull.

She watched it for a while, until she heard footsteps and turned to look. An elderly gentleman hobbled over to the railing, a bunch of windflowers in his hand and a lady's patent-leather shoe tucked up beneath his arm. *Could he be a widower having come to mourn his lost love?*

Gradually, her scalp broke out in a cool sweat. From the back, the elderly gentleman looked just like Fingal. *Yes, it's him.*

Without looking back the old man placed the lone shoe at his feet and then cast some of the spring blossoms onto the waters below.

Jean felt as if her womb filled with a breath of dryness, as if the whole of her insides must be shrivelling. She looked at her lap. *Fingal, Fingal, Fingal.*

An odour as of raw sewage crept into the air, and now the old man lost his grip on the bouquet. Had he detected the scent of her loneliness, the release of some erotic signal?

She glanced at the small of his back. 'Fingal? Stop pretending to be somebody else. Take me over to the luncheonette. Let's drink a strawberry phosphate. Then maybe we'll sort out what to do about the resistance box.' She looked to her lap again. 'Just what should I call you? Have you got some kind of alias?'

He turned toward her very slowly. 'I'm Artemis Puzzlewood.'

Overcome with chills, Jean wheezed and then cupped her hands, at which point the old man dropped an arrowhead into her left palm. His actions did not seem strange to her at all since he had to dissemble lest the burning man locate him. She squeezed the wedge-shaped stone with all her might and whispered her Connecticut address.

Whoever he was, he wrote the address down and then placed the slip of paper into his coat pocket. 'My late wife, she came from Englishtown, New Jersey. But we lived all over, me and her. For seven whole years, we lived up there in Cheshire County, New Hampshire. And in the days of 1933, we lived in Barnstable, Massachusetts, and bred racehorses. Yes, and we bred them in Woodstock, Vermont, too. My late wife, she'd often act as prim as a maiden aunt. But don't let that fool you. No, she studied the Tango. All day long, every day, she'd think about the beauty of it all. I guess she found the movement of them lithe Argentine dancers' bodies all so mesmerising.'

For a moment Jean sought to look up. How good it would be to study Fingal's face. Try as she might, though, the chills would not permit her to do so. She fixed her gaze upon a run in her stocking.

At last, the old man hobbled off, and when he was gone, she dropped the arrowhead to the side and returned home.

Early that evening, she sat at the kitchen table and made a crude sketch of the resistance box. *When Fingal arrives, we'll get to work on this.*

The hours passed by, and Fingal never showed. Late that

night, she admitted defeat and walked upstairs. Overcome with night sweats, she paced about her room. Five times over, she folded and unfolded her bedquilt. Afterward, she slipped into her chenille 'intimate-hours' housecoat and returned downstairs.

In her study, she opened a letter that had arrived one week earlier—a request from one of the professors at Evangeline Women's College. The scholar had written to ask her to conduct a symposium on some or other Adolph-Zukor production.

Now she flinched. If she failed to comply with the request, the regents would probably sack her. *Oh God.* Outside the groves of academe, she had no social life—no connection to anyone.

From the direction of the barn, a steady cacophony commenced, the sound waves so formidable that the window's dew-streaked upper sash clattered.

She walked outside, returned into the barn, and considered the contours of the power source. Soon enough, she set the tip of her thumb against the pressure gauge. As if soothed by her touch, the noise experienced syncopation and then gradually waned and fell quiet.

Jean removed the resistance box and placed it upon the floor. On her hands and knees, she proceeded to dismantle the troublesome component, then paused suddenly to imagine Fingal standing at her back. *What do I tell him if he does come to me tonight?* Slowly, she took apart the resistance box. 'As much as it kills me to admit, I haven't found the way to make your invention work,' she would tell him. 'Still, I'd give my eyetooth to help you.'

'But if me machine doesn't work, what am I doing here?' he might ask.

'We could live the Middlesex life, just like proper New

Englanders,' she would tell him then. 'In the evening I'll prepare a supper of pickled oysters and pea beans. Yes, and each and every Sunday, I'll serve you daisy ham with Boston bread.'

'You never once ceded hope that I'd be alive, and for that I'd be thankful. Nevertheless, you haven't done onythin' to help me send me foe back inside me mind.'

A set of steady, unmistakable, all-too-real footsteps approached. With a gasp, she stood up and turned to the driveway.

An old man stood there, a bumbershoot in his hand. He dropped the umbrella, pulled at his necktie, and stroked the knot. 'I came to beg your pardon. I didn't mean to give you the air. Far from it. I thought I'd buy you a candy apple, but when I got back, you were already gone.'

'Who are you?'

'You know something? My late wife had a lovely, little cleft in her chin . . . just like yours. Golly.'

'I think we're talking at cross purposes.'

'Tell me something. What did you do with my Pequot-Indian arrowhead? Could I have it back? It was a gift from my late wife.'

By now Jean realised what had happened. 'Artemis Puzzlewood. Would that be your name?'

The doubtful guest dithered awhile, and then he drew close. 'You know what? I can tell by the way you talk, you got a faint accent. Like you come from bluegrass country. Only you've learned how to hide it. Still, I just know you come from Dixie. Possum Trot or someplace not far from there. Maybe even Christian County, Kentucky.' Without another word, the lonely old man walked over to the edge of the swimming pool and plunged into the deep end.

Jeab held her hands tight against her chest, then leapt in

to save the poor fool, almost forgetting her desperate purpose. The waters felt so soothing that she came to believe that she must be floating amid the membranes of her mother's womb. By the time she managed to refocus, she could not locate him. And before long she had to break the surface, struggling to catch her breath for a time.

A halting cry rang out in the night. Could it be the tuxedo cat from across the street? Had the creature just gone into labour?

The wailing grew louder, and Jean went under again, but when she located the hapless fellow, he would not budge: Mr Puzzlewood had entangled his hand in the drain. *He drowned himself.* Again, she broke the surface. Then she waded over to the in-pool ladder, but it almost gave way—for a screw had come loose.

In tears, she made her way over into the shallow waters—and as the tuxedo cat wailed one last time, she crawled out of the pool by way of the Roman-access stairway, waters dripping from her body. *What do I do now?* She had to alert someone, either the county sheriff or the local desk sergeant. *Or what about the Connecticut State Police?* She attempted to stand, but her knees buckled. Then she rolled onto her back and studied the sky.

If only a shooting star would streak by—a sign that her visitor's death must have been foreordained. After a while, a strong breeze awoke. Then a lacerated bluebonnet petal came gliding through the air—no meteor, though.

Jean felt her left breast and recalled her erstwhile attempts at transforming her speech patterns. *What good did any of those absurd hypnotherapy recordings do?* She thought of the cinephiles who delighted in screening their favourite sequences while listening to alternate music scores or incongruous pieces of music. *I'm just as vain.*

Finally, she staggered back to the barn and knelt before the various bits and pieces that once comprised the resistance box. And now she let out a shriek, as if the jumble must be the outward reflection of something inside her—the fragments of her broken heart. Then, like so many times before, she imagined Fingal standing at her back.

'I think I know your trouble,' he would say. 'All your fears and loneliness, that's what's got you muddled.'

She thought back to her life in Scotland—Fingal's displeasure with her selfishness. And now she closed her eyes. 'Maybe I should ask the hypnotherapist to prepare a disc to help me to undergo complete *moral* transformation. Until I become as selfless as a nurse. Yes, I'll ask my good friend, Professor Gertie T. Fenham, to make a new hypnotherapy recording, a test pressing at the very least. Wouldn't that be good?' Jean turned around to look, but she noticed no trace of Fingal.

Instead, a dog stood there—the beagle that lived some three houses over to the east. The animal drew close, sniffed her feet, and wagged its tail. Had the animal detected the presence of some thrilling scent streaming throughout her body?

From far away a little girl called out to the beagle by name, and the dog darted off into the vaguely blue shadows of night.

She turned back to the disassembled resistance box and rearranged some of the pieces. 'Please tell me what to do,' she thought out loud. 'Please, Fingal, at least tell me where you are on a night like this. Where are you? Where are you? Where are you?'

Chapter Eighteen

FINGAL. The Island of Saint Helena. Spring, 1947.

Late one morning, Fingal awoke and realised that his double had gone free from inside him; deep in the pit of his stomach, the familiar ache was gone.

For a moment or two he raced about the ruins of the Georgian manor house—the residence to which the Scottish officials had confined him almost two decades before. Over and over, in every last darkened chamber, he called out—but his twin did not return. *Aye, me double, he's gone for good.* Fingal paced up and down the corridor. *Has me twin gone into Jamestown?*

After a while he walked into the piano room and studied the faded canvas depicting Napoléon I and la Grande Armée firing off their light-siege howitzers at the Battle of Austerlitz. *Where's me twin gone?*

Ten minutes later, Fingal grabbed the dusty, timeworn Instruktor and exited the manor house. 'Come back,' he cried out. 'I'm a frail old man of seventy, I am. You can't honestly expect me to chase you all about.'

The burning man did not answer, the only sound a pair of crested guinea fowl calling to one another.

Fingal walked a half mile west to a shallow crater lake filled with glistening-black volcanic debris, and then stopped beside a wild orchid. And there it was: the fiery projection hurried past the adjacent observation well, continued east along a winding footpath, and then ducked into a thicket of sneezewood trees.

For more than two hours, Fingal searched the woodland, the sunlit rocks and boulders shining like white marble.

At two o'clock, he lay beside the lakeshore and rubbed his belly. A new kind of ache had awoken inside him—a sensation that made him feel as if he had swallowed a farrier's hoof knife. *It's the anguish of guilt. I've got to admonish the populace.*

When he returned to his feet, he marched off along the roadway leading past a few of the coffee plantations and back into Jamestown.

As soon as he reached the market square, a steady ring resounded from a bright-red phone box, so he stepped inside and placed the receiver against his ear.

'Don't tell anyone that I've gone free,' his twin whispered over the line. 'If you say anything, I'll kick off a pandemic potent enough to destroy every last islander. No one should escape my wrath, and that's a promise.'

'Where did you go? Have you decided to have yourself a day at the races? Come back, won't you?'

'No, let me run wild.'

'Never, do you hear? *Never.*'

'But *why*? You'll stay here and live the philosopher's life. Wouldn't that be just what you always wanted to do?'

'Aye, but I can't let you harm no one on top of what you've

already done. No, no. I got me a conscience, haven't I?'

The line went dead. Then, as Fingal exited the phone box, an ocean breeze blew across the square and tore through a grove of baby lime trees, until the gust knocked over a few of the more fragile ones.

How long before me creation destroys another innocent? How long? He crouched amid the dead trees, until the wild wind diminished in strength.

At last Fingal stood and then turned to consider the natural-history museum. *Has me foe concealed himself there?* Fingal continued through the doors. 'Would you b-b-be in here?' he asked in a faltering whisper. When no one answered, he proceeded through the austere hall to the most celebrated exhibit in the collection—the skeletal remains of a long-toothed whale seemingly hovering ten feet off the floor, the massive bones intricately mounted upon an almost-imperceptible, metallic frame.

The late-afternoon breeze sailed through the window, and the whale bones rattled like a cup filled with coffee seeds. An ancient, tragic light poured through the windows, until the whole exhibition, each and every bone, shone like the white marble that had always provided each theatre in Athens the finest skene.

The glow nearly made Fingal fall to his knees. He looked to his feet. *Jean, do you read me thoughts? Help me, hen. You've no idea the trouble what vexes me. Here I'd be, an exile in Saint Helena. And Saint Helena finds me lost. Not only has me double gone free, he'd be good and rested. Runs as fast as a racehorse, he does. God only knows how many multitudes me double should destroy now.*

An acquaintance, a retired distiller from the Isle of Skye, waved and approached. 'What's an old rounder like you doing here?'

'Looking for someone, I am.'

'Oh? So who'd be the focus of the enquiry?'

'You wouldn't know him. No, he's a friend from the old days.'

'But I'd be on speaking terms with every Christian soul here.'

'Please don't let's take offence but piss off, why don't you?'

'No, let's you and me visit Crown Colony Tavern. We'll share a bottle of Graham's vintage port, and we'll have ourselves a game of draughts.'

'No, no. Pushed for time, I am.' With no further explanation, Fingal exited the museum and returned to the manor house.

At twilight he washed his face in the hand basin and then walked out onto the cantilevered balcony. *Jean, do you read me thoughts? You can't believe the stakes I'm living with these days.*

The island breeze whistled through the pieces of his broken time-and-tide clock and stirred a few of the letters and unaddressed envelopes lying at his feet—some twenty years' worth of messages that he had prepared for Jean but had never sent.

He took one of the faded picture postcards into his hand and, despite the dim light, sought to read the verso. The elements, both the sun and the rain, had rendered the words illegible, so he dropped the postcard to the side and slouched beside the balcony post.

Late that night, the whistling of the winds grew into wailing, and amid the cries and lamentations the crackle of fire resounded.

He ducked back inside and grabbed the Instruktor. Then he tiptoed downstairs, and though dressed in nothing more than his frayed nightshirt, he continued outside, stopped beside one of the grand columns, and studied the premises.

When the sound of faint, inappropriately-giddy laughter awoke, he marched forward. The disturbing presence guided him a half mile northbound along a pebbled lane to a derelict internment camp, where the English Occupation Force had housed dozens of its highest-ranking prisoners back in the days of the Boer Wars. 'Where'd you be hiding?' he asked as he turned this way and that and looked all about.

How to locate the burning man, or anything else for that matter? In recent years, the establishment had become a wrecking yard filled with colossal heaps of scrap metal.

Slowly, he proceeded past the battered wreckage of an 1898 Bushberry Electric and then stopped beside a jumble resembling a rusted-out Alldays & Onions chassis. From the corner of his eye, he noticed a sea-foam green spark. *Could that be me accursed double?*

A fierce gust of wind commenced, and alongside the crumbling, westernmost stockade wall, a spark shone as dazzling as the Mediterranean noon—the burning man.

A shivering spell came over Fingal, but even so, he managed to depress the Instruktor's activation switch. When he did, the ageing component cracked apart and fell to the earth. *What the hell?* He breathed in and almost gagged, for the fallen pieces reeked of moulding powder—the rarefied, experimental kind once popular in French engineering.

His double drew closer. 'Having trouble with that half-arsed device there?' the spectre asked. With that, the creature snickered and hurried off.

For the next few days, Fingal searched the island. Alas, the entity was gone. Had it departed for parts unknown?

One afternoon, Fingal visited a desolate stretch of ocean

shoreline where a Royal Navy cruiser had run aground two nights before and the current now whipped through the vessel's damaged bulkhead. Fingal looked out across the churning waters. *Where'd you go?*

A pair of elderly islanders, Marmaduke de Villiers and Gyles Smuts, happened along and stopped beside the shipwreck. 'You're looking inconsolable,' Mr de Villiers told Fingal. 'What's gone wrong, old chap?'

'Let me guess,' Mr Smuts spoke up. 'Could it be a touch of wanderlust?'

'Can't be,' Mr de Villiers said. 'Why would anyone think to leave our tranquil foreland?' For no especial reason, Mr de Villiers removed a bugle from his peeling, discoloured, mouldy Gladstone bag and sounded 'Reveille'. What a fine tonal colour it was—the timbre every bit as triumphal as that of an elephant.

Fingal thought back two years to someone from *Le Figaro*—a lady reporter who had travelled to Saint Helena to prepare a story on the East India Company's involvement in the tusk trade. When she had stopped by the manor house to photograph the grand piano's ivory keys, she had mentioned an earlier assignment in South Africa, where she had conducted a probe into the curious case of two young Afrikaans sisters, Jacoba and Godelieve Prätorius, who had gone lost in the days of the Transvaal gold rush.

'What enchanting girls,' the lady reporter had told him. 'According to legend, they wandered out into the wild one evening and metamorphosed into elephants.'

Evidently, a tribesman walking along the road to Johannesburg had espied Jacoba's face looking out from an elephant calf's eye.

Twelve days later, out along a meandering, half-flooded

road to Ladysmith, Swaziland, a young bushman had noticed Godelieve's visage slowly revolving within some other elephant calf's eye.

Fingal had never believed the disturbing tale. Still, the story had awoken in him a certain fascination with that majestic world so tantalizingly close to the island. *Aye, the Dark Continent.*

Mr de Villiers concluded 'Reveille'. Then he polished the bugle's tuning slide with his sleeve before returning the musical instrument into his Gladstone bag.

At that point, the sun grew brighter and brighter such that a whole expanse of the shoreline shone as milky as white marble.

A moment or two later, a flock of wirebirds streaked across the sky, the winged creatures followed by a flock of what looked to be zebra doves.

Fingal approached the surf and looked northeast. Had the fugitive wandered off into the heart of Africa? For a time he sought to discern the coastline rising out on the horizon. *If I find that world so intriguing, then perhaps me twin feels the same.*

Mr Smuts collected an empty bottle of Portuguese brandy from the sands and cast the liquor bottle at the spot to Fingal's right. 'You there. Why you gazing out to sea? You look restless. Like a death-or-glory boy getting ready to conquer some beachhead.'

'That's right,' Mr de Villiers agreed. 'I'd say Fingal has puffed himself up with pride to the point where he's ready to take up arms.'

A sleek, fast reefer ship flying the flag of the Orange Free State sailed past the jetty, and as soon as she was gone, Fingal checked his bony, wrinkled hands. *Would a gentleman of some seventy years even be strong enough to venture off into Tropical*

Africa? Probably not.

Mr de Villiers drew a little bit closer to Fingal. 'I think I know what you'd be feeling, old soldier. The tedium of island life, it's no good for me neither. No, at times, I wish I'd never mustered out. I'll tell you what our kind was always meant to be: *Gentlemen-rankers out on the spree; Damned from here to Eternity.'*

In truth Fingal had always preferred the monotony of island life. For the past twenty years, the repose had helped him to daydream and to wonder what might constitute the best myth by which to explain the origins of the cosmos. As of yet, though, he had still not stumbled upon the metaphor.

The ocean breeze whistled through a length of driftwood, and from down the coast, a pair of cuckoos called out.

Mr de Villiers placed his hand on Fingal's shoulder. 'I wish I'd never made colonel nor second lieutenant for that matter. If only I'd fallen in battle. Why did I even deserve to survive at all? When I think of it, far too many soldiers fell in the Second Boer War. Far too many.'

All the talk of the dead made Fingal cover his eyes, at which point his thoughts turned back to his double. *Maybe if I invoke me powers of intuition, I could locate the fugitive.* Before long Fingal dropped his hands to his sides. *Jean, what should I do?*

A few tropical birds flew by, and as they did, Mr de Villiers removed what looked to be a proper Dutch-issue brass shell case from his hip pocket. 'It's right dishonourable, living on the dole.' His bottom lip quivering, he cast the odd memento into the ocean. '*Die Atlantiese*,' he whispered.

Fingal walked out into the surf and let the froth wash over his feet. Then he marched ever further out into the waters, until they reached his waist and a large fragment of seaweed from some underwater kelp forest entangled itself in his kilt pin. *Where has me twin gone?* He looked northeast again; his intuition told him that the entity would have most yearned to visit the Congolese coast, perhaps some harbour town or port city. *Aye.*

That afternoon, he booked passage on the next ship bound for Pointe-Noire, and then he visited the telegraph office to reserve lodgings.

At midnight he returned to the ruins of the manor house. *What might the Scottish authorities do once they learn I've departed the island?* For twenty minutes or more, he walked up and down the dark corridors. *What should the authorities think?* Perhaps they would presume that he had booked passage aboard some vessel bound for the Celtic Sea, or maybe they would think that he had stowed himself away on a passenger ship bound for the coast of Portugal, some idyllic fishing village. *Aye, let them think I've fallen between the cracks.*

Out on the balcony, he called out to his double. When no response came, he knelt beside his broken time-and-tide clock. 'Come here, ghostly being. Blithely explain to me the origins of the cosmos, eh? Tell me the purpose of civilisation too. Or do you even know? Aye, back within the recesses of a person's unconscious mind, that storehouse where a person packs away all them primitive, animal impulses what remain through millions of years of hominid evolution, maybe we haven't even got the answer.' Fingal smashed the time-and-tide clock to pieces with all his might.

In the morning at half-past eight, he travelled back into Jamestown and wired his lifesavings into the Bank of the Belgian Congo.

A few days later, he packed his satchel and made his way to the waterfront, but down by the ship's gangway the same two elderly islanders from before stopped him.

Twice, Mr de Villiers poked him with the bugle. 'Whither you bound, then? You intend to sail to Africa? At *your* advanced age? Are you serious?'

'Quite so. I'll call upon me six senses, and I'll survive.'

'You're barking mad,' Mr Smuts said.

'Maybe so. Still, I'm off to the jungle to brave me a life of high adventure.'

'But can't you imagine the many perils awaiting you out there as you footslog about the wilderness?' Mr de Villiers asked. 'What if you fall into a pool of quicksand?'

'I'll take the rub.'

'Oh. You've done this kind of thing before, have you?'

'What about Guinea worms?' Mr Smuts asked then. 'I shudder to think of them burrowing beneath your skin.'

'Yes,' Mr de Villiers agreed. 'Listen to Gyles, here. He knows whereof he speaks.'

'By all means,' Mr Smuts said. 'What a wild place, Africa. Just where do you aim to get buns for tea? Not six days hence, you'll be living on beetroot and bunny grub.'

'Yes, that's the life in the hinterland,' Mr de Villiers added. 'And what happens when you grow weary of the bachelor's fare? You'll not find no black treacle anywhere about.'

Fingal looked out to the surf, where a tattered anti-torpedo net along with a dozen or so booms bounced in the surf. 'How much worse could Africa be than our grim, violent world?'

Mr de Villiers grabbed hold of Fingal's arm. 'In two weeks, you'll be crying blue murder. But who should be there to secure your mortuary passport?'

Fingal pulled away and struggled to go free. 'Unhand me.'

When Mr de Villiers finally did, the old man stomped his foot upon the pier. 'I hope a camelopard sodomises you.'

'If and when it happens, I'll just close me eyes and think of Scotland.' With that, Fingal climbed the gangway, and once aboard the vessel, he turned toward the pilot house and saluted the ship's captain.

No sooner had the ship's captain saluted Fingal than Fingal turned away and shook his head from side to side. *What am I doing? I'm travelling into a world ravaged by colonialism, racism, wickedness. And in tracking down the entity and preventing it from bringing harm to others, I'll be playing the part of some patronising saviour figure, aye, the very last thing that the people of Africa require.* Almost laughing, Fingal gripped the ship's railing. *I'm damned if I do, damned if I don't.*

A flock of large white seabirds glided by, followed by yet another flock. Then, just off the starboard bow, a trumpeting commenced. The commotion proved to be the call of an elephant seal peeking from the gulley of a wave.

Greetings, bold spirit. For a moment or two, Fingal waved and sought to catch the animal's attention, but to no avail.

At last, he turned away, and then he fixed his gaze upon the soft horizon's blinding scintillation. *Hear me then, burning man. I'm coming for you. No quarter.*

Chapter Nineteen

When his ship made landfall at Pointe-Noire, Fingal visited a moneychanger's shop. Then he walked into the marketplace and purchased an ankle-length kaftan of ivory white. Lastly, he bought a handwoven shoulder basket in which to keep the Instruktor.

For the first week, he accomplished very little. Time and again, he studied the people; their eyes shone with the memories of colonial crimes impossible to forget.

When he finally managed to move beyond the crowded port city, he let his intuition guide him. One hunch after the next failed him, however. Despite all, he persevered.

One warm, rainy Tuesday morning, he searched for the fiery spectre in a forest of tamarind trees standing some three miles north of Elisabethville. The next day, he explored a vast field of feather grass on the outskirts of Astrida. A week later, when he reached Léopoldville, he paused to mull over his dilemma. *What if me accursed foe never even came to these shores?*

A gust of wind, the current fragrant with the hot, spicy scents of the jungle, blew through the narrow streets and nearly toppled Fingal. When he regained his footing, he let the balmy gale pour over his person for a while. *Of course, the burning man must be nearby. How could me foe deny tropical Africa's allure?* Fingal stood up straight and tall, turned northwest, and studied the distant wilderness. *I can't even breathe from the beauty.*

At three o'clock he made his way down to the riverfront, where he encountered a game young Belgian woman by the name of Mèlusine Saintenoy.

'I'm commanding an expedition to the Mountains of the Moon,' she told him. 'Yes, indeed, that's always been my dream.'

Fingal studied the young lady. *Could it be she feels guilty regarding all them unspeakable crimes what took place in Congo Free State?*

The idea did seem plausible. Despite her bold posture, Mèlusine did have rather a dull complexion. Moreover, her narrow face and elongated neck made her seem much too fragile for the Congo. The young lady also had bags underneath her eyes.

Finally he stepped back some and bowed politely. 'Listen, hen. Anyone who aims to scale them heights and find the source of the Nile and all that would have to be very *strong*.'

The young lady shook her head. 'No, as soon as we get close enough, I intend to *fly* to the summit. In a hot air balloon.'

'Sounds fraught with danger.'

'Not at all. Back home in Châtelet, I took the time to study the map, and I'm sure I'll find the bluff in question. And after I land there, I'll climb the grand staircase to the legendary moon temple.'

'Moon temple?'

'*Yes*. Just imagine it. A sanctuary with domed turrets, each one carved from tiger-eye quartz. Or maybe topaz or cinnabar.'

'You mustn't believe such fanciful things. There's no magical temple up there in the mountains.'

'*No*,' Mèlusine told him. 'When I studied at Ghent University, I learned all the great legends pertaining to the Congo. And I shall find the temple, and I shall excavate the garden and unearth the sacred tombs.'

Though he disbelieved her talk of ancient shrines and equated the ignorant woman's romanticism with a kind of soft, idiotic bigotry, Fingal longed to join the preposterous expedition. He knew that the dreamlike mountain range would surely appeal to his creation. *Aye, me quarry, he's bound to be there.*

On the night before Mèlusine sailed off, Fingal returned to the pier. 'If you let me join your party, I'm sure you'll find me a steadfast squire. I may look bloody old and frail, but I'd be good and strong.' Quietly, he sought to demonstrate his fitness. Three local porters lugged the balloon bag aboard the riverboat, and he helped another to bring the wicker basket up the gangway.

With a wall-eyed expression, Mèlusine laughed—and in a snide tone too. Still, she permitted him to join in the quest.

The next day, as they sailed off, Fingal stood at the bow and rejoiced. *Soon, I'll blast the burning man and send the devil back inside me.* Instinctively, Fingal wrapped his hand around his throat. *No, the burning man can't escape. I'm stronger now, strong enough for anything.*

The voyage continued, and how gracious the Congo River. At nine o'clock one of the local crewmen dragged a handmade net and enmeshed several big tiger fish. And when the riverboat crossed the equator a soft, sultry rain commenced.

Mèlusine, dressed in a gown of ribbed *sicilienne* silk with a scoop neckline, danced about the deck for fifteen minutes or so. Then she joined Fingal alongside the mainmast and drew forth from her slide-slip pocket a brass pendant shaped like a mermaid. 'Have you ever paused to imagine how it'd feel to go through life with your legs fused into a fishtail?'

Before he could manage a response to the peculiar question, the riverboat berthed at an ornate wharf built by the now-defunct African Violet Society.

What a dark place. The impenetrable fog looked as thick as treacle mustard. More than anything, the dark mist did not look true to life. If anything, the whole wilderness appeared as a film-studio soundstage—one in which the director had conjured the rolling fog with myriad blocks of dry ice.

Fingal disembarked and studied a shaft of light falling through the mist, the faint sparks bouncing off various atmospheric particles in the air. He turned to Mèlusine and helped her collect her things, and then she ushered the party into the derelict plantation house that the horticulturalists had left behind.

What disturbing décor: in the dining room, the ladies from the African Violet Society had mounted a sweeping view of Bloemfontein Concentration Camp—an oil on canvas depicting a band of badly-starved Boer women languishing in the shadow of a guard tower.

On the other side of the manor house, various artefacts looking to be the stuff of colonial plunder lay strewn about the floor: a Senegalese shield, a Watusi spear, and a potjie filled with ostrich eggshells and medicinal sneezewort.

The evil of it all. Fingal's weight shifted from the balls of his feet to his heels, and as he teetered, he placed his hands over his face.

When he finally confronted the Belgian woman and

alluded to her own people's crimes against Africa, she stuck her nose up in the air. 'What about all the terrible things the Germans did to your country? What about all those formations of Nazi Junkers and Messerschmitts flying over the Strait of Dover and onward across North Downs Way or Land's End or whatever your people call it.' She lay upon the floor and struck a classic death pose. 'This here's how the Russians found Eva Braun's body, *die Frau* lying perfectly lifeless in a beautiful black silk gown embroidered with pink roses. Yes, the Russians found her in that bunker on the edge of Spandau District. Where the roadway leads into the Austrian autobahn.'

Fingal blushed and bowed, and then he excused himself. At dusk, he grabbed one of the expedition's bolt-action Mausers and shot a plump Congo peafowl—and what a savoury supper it made. Afterward, Mèlusine brewed a kettle of chocolate-mint tea.

That night he could not sleep due to the humidity. Despite the ongoing rain, he walked outside and made his way into the heathland. For a time he sought to peer through the silvery mist. How good it would be to lay eyes on the fabled mountains.

Mèlusine came along dressed in a pair of drainpipe trousers and a blouse with a rumpled collar. She collected a goliath beetle from a bed of Egyptian starcluster, and, holding the insect in her palm, turned to Fingal. 'What a magical place, the Congo.'

He kicked at the brush. 'It's childish to romanticise West Africa.'

Up in the mahogany tree, a marsh owl called out—as if to jeer him. Then the marsh owl dove from the mahogany tree and snagged the goliath beetle. Swiftly, the winged creature fluttered off into the vines.

Mèlusine held up her hands, the humid breeze playing through her blouse. Then she spread her fingers apart and examined her nails, then held her forearm to her nose and sniffed at her wrist the way a woman tests a new perfume. 'Why did you wish to join in my quest?'

He looked into the crown of a nearby heather tree and debated whether he ought to commiserate with the adventuress. *Aye, why not confide in her?* Alas, by the time he felt ready to say something, she had already returned inside.

The solitude did not last long. An elderly, fair-skinned woman dressed in moleskin trousers and a blouse with a fox-fur collar emerged from out of the dark, swirling mist. Whoever she was, she did not belong to Mèlusine's expedition. She placed her tattered cowhide bag atop a rock and drew close.

'Who might *you* be?' Fingal asked.

'I'm Tolhurst,' she answered in a sharp Brooklyn accent.

'Should I know you?'

'Not if you're one of them British naturalists. But if you are, I wonder why you ain't got no specimen bag. Did the viceroy refuse to grant you a licence? Yeah, and now you're worried if anyone catches you picking the strangler ferns, you'll get deported.'

'*Please*, what're you doing out here in the jungle? By any chance, have you noticed a burning man, a spirit, a fiery apparition?'

'I don't know what you're talking about.' The woman walked back to the rock and removed an African thumb piano from her satchel. After stretching her fingers, she performed the tune to 'Sophisticated Lady'. What a pleasing sound—the fanciful instrument's tonal colour resembled that of an authentic Caribbean steelpan. When the woman concluded her song, she slipped the thumb piano back into her satchel.

'Hey pops, have you ever visited the land o' darkness?'

'*Where?*'

'*Harlem*. The borough. The one with the cotton clubs.'

'No, I've never travelled to the New World. I got a friend there, however.'

'Back there in Harlem, I'd always stop by the Congo Room. At first, I was happy just to dance to the killer diller music. But one night the joint's jumping, and I'm listening to a fellow in a zoot suit, and he's all jazzed up and playing good country blues on his trombone, and the whole epiphany comes on like gangbusters, and I realise that when we listen to swing, the unconscious mind must hear the percussive rhythms of Africa and think of itself as being *here* in a jungle like this, Guinguinèo or wherever we are. Anyway, that's when I knew I had to explore the rain forest someday. So now I'm here, just like some big visionary bucking to resolve some mind-blowing riddle.'

Fingal scratched at his scalp. '*Listen*. Throughout your wanderings here, you must've noticed a burning man. A fiery ghost. Something like that.'

The woman checked her *art-deco* timepiece, belched, and then scowled. 'What's the date, pops?'

'Whitsunday, I believe. That'd be what you Americans call Pentecost.'

'Yeah, well I got to go.' Tolhurst quickly gathered all her things together and hurried off through a patch of honey mushrooms and back into the mist.

Fingal chased after her awhile. 'Beware the burning man. Don't let him befriend you nor beguile you any. He'll use you to help him destroy multitudes, all over this continent.'

Did the American woman even hear a word? In truth, Tolhurst was already gone.

The next morning, the fog looked as bleak as the plague of darkness such as it appeared in Cecil B. DeMille's silent biblical epic, *The Ten Commandments*.

Mèlusine's three best porters prepared the hot air balloon, and when the Belgian woman came along, she activated the burner and filled the envelope. Then she climbed into the wicker basket and checked both the skirt and the parachute-valve cord. At that point, she dismissed the porters. Then she turned to Fingal. 'Allons-y.'

He hesitated. Never before had he entrusted his life to such an aircraft. For a moment, he averted his gaze. When he turned back, he fussed with his kaftan's collar and sleeves.

Like a lonely mermaid, Mèlusine smiled. 'You look tense,' she told him, running her hand down her hipline. 'What's wrong? Do you fear the current should blow us off course, and we'll crash into Timbuktu? Can't happen. I've got a dependable Magnetkompass.'

The burner roared louder, and he felt the growing heat of the flame against the tip of his nose. *I've got to go. Find the burning man!*

Finally, he grabbed his shoulder bag and climbed into the gondola. The aircraft swayed and rattled and ascended into the gloom. Powerless to move, he felt the same kind of wonder that a caged animal might register in that moment it goes free from the laboratory and looks upon creation for the very first time. Soon, he shot a glance below and gasped. The tops of the trees looked like fox-fur pompoms—either that or a thousand or more colossal balls of eiderdown.

A pygmy falcon fluttered past and then continued onward through a rolling cloud of fog that shone the color of greenish-black onyx marble. Then an African cuckoo-hawk called out from a patch of velvety, pale-cream mist, as if begging the explorers to reconsider. After a while, the soft rain turned to snow, and as the snowflakes swirled about, the hot air balloon drifted past the silhouette of a glacier shaped like a colossal impala horn.

Exposed to the elements as she was, Mèlusine slipped into a heavy, Belgian Army greatcoat, and Fingal bundled up in a mud-cloth fleece blanket.

The wicker basket climbed ever higher, until an immense shape came into view—that mountaintop which the Italian colonists once called Margherita Peak.

Five minutes later, Mèlusine landed the basket upon an icy precipice. Once she had tethered the gondola to a boulder, she reached for Fingal. 'From here the pathway gets very treacherous, but I know every foothold, every toehold. So follow me.' With that, Mèlusine illumined her princess-feather oil lamp and guided him out onto the windswept plateau.

No sooner had they arrived at the summit than the clouds broke apart, and in the most sublime way, the light of the sun suddenly shone all across the ridgeline. What a glorious vista! Far below, on the other side of the mountain, the headwaters of the Nile spread out through the African grasslands. Had anyone ever witnessed such an exalted spectacle? Had anyone ever revelled in such godlike beauty?

Fingal stood tall and relaxed his shoulders. *Does this interlude not mirror the workings of the psyche?* He trembled all over. *Aye, in the very same way that a dream must be a glimpse of the unconscious mind, a window into that alien sector of the psyche, so this fleeting panorama affords me a view of East Africa . . . as if it, too, must be but a vision.*

Mèlusine only pursed her lips and scrambled about, as if looking for the moon temple. Before long, though, the young lady must have realised that no such place of worship existed.

Eventually, her knees buckled—at which point the clouds shifted, and a boundless pall re-enveloped the heights.

The cold, dissonant winds played through Fingal's kaftan, and his feet grew numb. *How long until the effects of mountain sickness have me in a stupor?* He cringed. *Perhaps it won't be long before I hallucinate the goddamn moon temple.*

As his feet grew increasingly numb, a primal force of some kind, a hot, palpable presence, swirled about at his back.

Gads, it's me vile miscreation. Fingal debated for a moment whether he ought to remove the Instruktor. *Why not bluff like I've got it working right?* He hunched his shoulders and turned around. 'I've b-b-been looking high and low for you.'

'What're you doing here?' the burning man asked, his brow taut.

'Does my presence surprise you? Yes, you thought I'd never locate you. No, you thought I'd live my life all despondent. Always wandering around in circles, chasing you here and there and wherever. But you got it all wrong. My study of metaphor has made me *wise*. And my years of exile have made me *strong*.'

The burning man pointed at Fingal. 'Do you aim to send me back inside you? *Yes*. So go on then. Catch me if you can.' Without another word, the fiery figure dwindled into the unseeable.

Fingal found himself alone. Had the diabolical creature already descended into the grasslands?

Mèlusine walked over from the other side of the plateau. 'Where's my precious moon temple with its lovely altar room?'

'Forget the joss house. Get me eastbound.'

'*East?* Into the Uganda Protectorate? *Why?*'

'Because I'd be tracking a right terrible beast.'

'No, you just wish to leave me. For shame.'

'No, hen.' Without any further ado, he grabbed the young lady's arm and sought to pull her back to the hot air balloon.

She dropped her oil lamp, and it shattered against the rocks. 'If I'd found the precious moon temple, do you know what I would've done? I would've collected enough treasures to pay off my student loans, and then I would've used the rest to pay Africa's dues and obligations. And because of that, the people of Africa wouldn't require debt relief, and the people of Africa would never suffer the ignoble reputation that comes with debt relief.'

Fingal shook his head in disbelief. 'Where do you get these ideas? Your daft brand of saviourism shall never do no one any good. Let the people of Africa live their own lives.'

For thirty minutes or more, they quarrelled, but when they finally climbed back into the basket, Mèlusine delivered Fingal down to the river basin.

The lakeshore did not appear as dark on the east side of the mountain range, so there was no reason to dawdle. He thanked the Belgian woman and then marched off along a pathway winding past a derelict emerald mine.

A Bantu girl hurried past him. Had she noticed the hot air balloon? Did she even know what it was?

He glanced over his shoulder. The Bantu girl knelt before the aircraft. He shook his head. The misguided Belgian woman had chanced upon an innocent, sorely-oppressed, and technology-deprived African sister.

The tragicomic confluence of events made Fingal pause, and he could not decide whether to laugh or cry. *What does any of it matter?* He had to locate his own reflection.

He turned away and continued on, past the wreckage of a wooden oil derrick. He paused anew. His belly suddenly ached, as if he had swallowed fifteen or more mouthfuls of medicinal mushrooms and orange-peel fungus, white-coral fungus too. *Aye, that'll be the way it feels when I put the burning man back inside me.* Despite all, he could not permit himself to rest just now. *Onward.* He made his way into the wild.

Chapter Twenty

Over the course of the warm, rainy African spring, Fingal pursued his twin through the lakeside villages of the Great Rift Valley. Day by day and week by week, the anguish in the pit of his stomach grew, until he felt as if he had swallowed an African ceremonial knife that had metamorphosed into a deadly African hunting knife that had, in turn, metamorphosed into something like a traditional African *sickle-shaped* throwing knife.

Despite all his discomfiture, he marched forward, and by mid-April he had tracked the entity to a game preserve in Kenya.

He found the ghostlike presence in the heart of the park, sitting inside the hollowed-out trunk of a colossal baobab tree, the spectre enshrouded in powerful blue flames.

'What're you doing in there?' Fingal asked. 'Has the timeless beauty of Africa overwhelmed your senses? Aye, the sensual mystery of it all, it's got you feeling undone.'

The burning man pointed past Fingal's shoulder. 'Look at the sunlight. Consider the way it glows such that the stones of Africa shine like white marble. Not unlike the Athenian stage, the building where the players change their masks and costumes. And that's what I'd be doing, my friend. Now I *revitalise*. Now I breathe new life into my being.'

In no way did Fingal doubt his double. As soon as the entity grew strong again, it would surely recommence with its primal, predatory impulse to bring those around it to ruin. And then countless immolations would be sure to follow. *And all that on top of the myriad crimes that colonialism has already visited upon this land.*

Fingal collapsed before the baobab tree and curled up into a ball. And he did not move a muscle, until a pair of spotted Madagascar cuckoos came along to poke at him.

For the next few days, he prepared for the worst. One afternoon in Nairobi, he purchased a collection of mechanical odds and ends with which to repair the Instruktor. *Aye, soon I'll have the burning man back inside me belly.* When he returned to the baobab tree, Fingal held his head high. 'I've already got the means to reduce you to a feeble flame. With nowhere to take refuge. You might as well comply with me commands.'

The burning man should have gasped—as if a feeling of presentiment had come over it. Instead, the entity exited the shelter of the tree trunk and climbed to the topmost bough.

Not twenty minutes later, an African crowned eagle streaked through the sky, and the burning man gave chase and quickly vanished.

Where's the bloody bastard gone? Southbound? Fingal sought to deny his feelings of dread. Surely, his wayward creation would return.

The afternoon passed by, and nothing happened. At nightfall, Fingal backed away from the baobab tree. Quickly he made his way over to the Safari Club, where he collapsed in the doorway. 'Get me alee.'

The tall, thickset game warden, Mr Foulkes, arose from the sofa and, illumining the establishment with a solitary hand-painted candle, walked over to the double-action piccolo upright and picked out the tune to a traditional Swahili dirge.

'Take me to the Serengeti,' Fingal implored him.

'Can't do it, old boy. Not unless you got the lolly.'

'I'll pay you later. First, we've got to go south. The fate of Africa, maybe even the whole world, depends on it.'

'Have you taken leave of your senses? Why don't you rest awhile? Sleep here tonight, and in the morning, I'll make you a breakfast of Scotch eggs. And if you behave, I might even treat you to a spoonful of treacle.'

For lack of any better way to respond, Fingal crawled forward and shook the game warden's pith helmet from the hat-rack.

A few days later, as Fingal languished beside the baobab tree, Mr Ffoulkes stopped by in a jeep all fitted out for a proper expedition.

'So you'll take me southbound?' Fingal asked him.

'By all means. I got me a charter just in from German East Africa.' With that, the game warden turned and pointed toward a jeep idling alongside the Oloololo Gate. 'That's the chap there. Herr Zugvögel.'

'Herr *Zugvögel*?'

'Yes, he's some kind of philosopher fellow. Anyway, he's brought along his young daughter, Leopolda. Unfortunately, she's none too healthful. I thought maybe you'd be willing to mind her. So what do you think?'

Fingal observed her closely; the little girl had dressed herself in a beaded mud-cloth hat and king's *dashiki*.

What mystery her big blue eyes; they betrayed a thought

process rooted in the most sentimental kind of melodrama, yet simultaneously rooted in the most insolent kind of irony.

'Just out of curiosity, what'd be wrong with the lass?'

'Who knows? Herr Zugvögel says she's afflicted with *autismus*.'

'*Autismus*? I'd say she's got herself a brain tumour.' No matter his misgivings, Fingal packed his things. *What other option have I got?*

At midday the two jeeps pulled out into the grass plains and continued through a field of weeping love grass. At two o'clock, miles from nowhere, the expedition stopped to refuel. Then, once Fingal had stowed the half-empty jerrycan, all four gathered beneath a cabbage tree.

'Tell us something about your writings,' Fingal said, turning to Herr Zugvögel.

'*No*, you English speakers could never make sense of my work,' the German philosopher answered. 'Let's talk about the war. Do you know something? It never would've happened if the reparations committees had not destroyed the Weimar Republic's economy.'

'Oh, enough of that,' Foulkes told him. 'Go on, old boy. *Translate* some of your big ideas for us. Give it a go. Enlighten us.'

'No, I can't translate it,' Herr Zugvögel insisted. '*Nein*.'

'You could tell us *something*,' Fingal said. 'Tell us the origins of the universe, why don't you? Tell us the meaning of life, or how about the purpose of civilisation?'

'No,' Herr Zugvögel said. 'The reason would be simple. The German tongue permits a devoted *philosoph* like me to contrive my own words. Which grants me the power to fashion epic compound words to denote or connote intricate concepts that commonplace words never could. As such, the

German tongue permits me to construct compound words that signify the properties comprising the Socratic truths. Put another way, *hurra*, the exalted German tongue grants me the power to show all the ways the eternal truths tend to overlap and blend together to form the *illusion* of new ideas.'

Fingal turned to Leopolda; the little girl had wrapped her left foot in a frayed, blue bath towel embroidered with the words *Hotel de l'Aeroport Algiers*, and she had bound her right in cloth resembling cotton brocade. *Could it be she suffers from some kind of birth defect?*

Whatever had happened, the little girl looked to the sky and pointed at a cloud shaped like a vast diamond solitaire. 'Let me share a secret,' she said, her voice hoarse and breathy. 'The mother tongue has no word quite so grand as *diamantenpracht*, the German word for diamondshine.'

'Diamondshine?' Fingal asked. 'What's that?'

'The *gleam*,' she answered. 'Don't you get it? We Germans grasp the fact that no one ever truly beholds a diamond. Actually, we may only ever witness the shine or *pracht* that the jewel emits, and that's why our language *must* have a designation like *diamantenpracht*, yes, indeed, for the gemstone's *gleam*, it's all so *real*. As real as Ilsestein granite.'

When the little girl grew quiet, an awkward silence persisted—the only sounds the whisper of the African breeze, along with the protestations of an irate speckled hen walking through the brush.

Foulkes climbed back into his jeep. 'Let's soldier on, shall we?' When no one responded, the game warden took a sip from his hip flask and then sounded the horn a few times over.

With the approach of dusk, the party stopped in a field of African moon daisies looking out across the Serengeti. Once everyone had pitched their tents, the game warden kindled a campfire and prepared a supper of hyacinth beans and pigeon peas.

Later, when Herr Zugvögel retired for the night, he talked in his sleep. As if indignant regarding the war, he rambled on and on about Rommel's Afrika-Korps—the field marshal's glorious Panzer divisions—and the fine engineering that went into *der Kübelwagen.*

Foulkes polished his Webley Bull-Dog pocket revolver, then withdrew into his own tent.

Fingal studied the German girl. *As soon as the lass adjourns for the night, I'll walk off and find me accursed twin.*

After a while Leopolda squatted beside Fingal and removed her hat. The little girl was bald. Despite all, she grinned, as if she did not feel even the least bit self-conscious. Then she recited what sounded like an ancient incantation.

Fingal stoked the fire. 'Aren't you knackered? Why don't you climb into your bedroll and get some sleep?'

A westerly breeze sailed through the encampment, and a billowy storm of feathers sailed out from the little girl's tent. One appeared to be a Persian robin's semiplume, and another looked to be a thumb feather that had once belonged to a black-footed albatross. The little girl retrieved all the wayward treasures and placed them inside her ostrich-skin satchel.

Afterward, Fingal picked up a piece of warthog ivory and pointed the end at her carefully-swathed feet. 'What ails you?'

As if greatly embarrassed, Leopolda turned away. '*Ich bin ein gesundes . . .* '

He again gestured toward her feet. 'Might you be afflicted by ram's-horn toenails?'

She circled the fire. And despite the materials wrapped around her feet, she walked with animalistic grace, the way a flamingo might strut along the shore of some placid, pristine lagoon.

'You're as funny as a piece of string, lass. Why do you walk the way you do? Do you study ballet? That'd explain the perfection of your leg muscles, eh? Like enough, you aspire to make *première danseuse* someday.'

The nighttime current kicked up, and the air filled with the odours of toxins, potent chemicals such as those that a Zulu warrior might extract from the poisonwood tree.

Leopolda licked her lips like a sailor savouring the taste of spiced rum. Over and over, she inhaled.

He studied her in profile. Did her nose not tilt up like an Egyptian vulture's beak? He sat back. 'Did you ask your father to take you on safari? Why so? What beasties do you hope to observe? How about a black-billed flamingo? Aye, there's nothing so bewitching. If you catch one, maybe you'll cut out its long, salty tongue and cook it for supper, eh? Would that be so, lass? Have you got a craving for poor man's goose?'

Without a word, Leopolda reached into her pocket and handed him a newspaper clipping of a story pertaining to the conquest of Abyssinia and a legend regarding an Italian girl who had got lost in Babille, where she had, by all accounts, transformed into a flamingo.

Fingal shuddered and, with his fingertips smudged with ink, returned the newspaper clipping. 'Don't even think of such things, hen.'

'Tell me about the animal *you* seek,' she whispered.

'What makes you think that I'd be seeking some creature?'

'You must prize your quarry so. I know because in my travels I've never encountered anyone so sad as you, so *hopeless*.' She walked away then, vanishing into a bamboo grove.

Go on, find the spectre then. He hiked off in the opposite direction, toward a thicket of mustard trees. Soon, though, he tripped over a tamarind root and twisted his ankle. In tears, he crawled back to his tent. *Sleep*.

At the break of dawn, he awoke. And when he crawled outside, he realised that a fierce animal of some kind had torn apart all the safari chairs.

What could've wrought such damage? He studied the wilderness. *Maybe a spotted hyena and its cubs came through here, or what about a drove of elephant shrews?*

A pink bristle feather drifted languidly past the tip of Fingal's nose. While the plume sailed about in the cold breeze, he knelt to the earth and examined some of the debris lying about the ruined encampment.

To the left, the contents of the game warden's billfold lay strewn about: a photograph of the Niger River, a faded *De Beers Consolidated Mines* business card, some tattered papers from a local retail bank, and a postcard boasting a view of Mount Kenya.

Not two minutes later, Foulkes emerged from his tent. He surveyed the disarray, threw up his hands, and then collected his things.

'What could've done this?' Fingal asked him. 'How about a flamingo?'

'Only a flamingo possessed by the devil could've caused this much destruction.' The game warden drew his revolver and placed his thumb against the hammer spur. 'For what it's worth, if the beastie comes back, I'll blast the gizzards out of him.' With a hiccup, Foulkes returned the weapon to his holster.

Herr Zugvögel emerged from his tent and frowned. Then he removed a brick of surgical cotton from his breast pocket, whispered his daughter's name, and marched off into the papyrus swamp.

A pink flight feather drifted past and settled at Fingal's feet. He studied the plume—its perfect vane, the wispy, immaculate afterfeather. *Could it be that the burning man has taught Leopolda how to metamorphose into a flamingo?*

He limped over to the game warden's jeep, removed a pair of field glasses from the glove box and scanned the virgin wilderness. He espied nothing unusual—a corps of giraffes to the north and an oryx to the east. As the sun grew stronger, he hobbled off through the endless moon daisies, until he stumbled upon a shallow bog, where a large skein of flamingos bathed. Thankfully, most of the wading birds ignored his trespass—no nasal honking, no grunting.

He studied the crater highlands and sought to gauge the distance, then focused his gaze upon the snowcapped peaks of Kilimanjaro. *Has she wandered off that way? Perhaps she's always longed to summit that mountain there.*

A hot wind blew across the plains. The current shrieked like a thousand birds of prey, and the field glasses fell from his hands. He stumbled backward a few steps.

Over to the right, a little gazelle fawn suddenly appeared. What a magnificent, godlike creature; a series of perfectly-symmetrical rings adorned its horns. The animal looked about as if it had heard something terribly sinister, a distant bushfire. Without any warning, the fawn raced off.

Leopolda emerged from behind a weeping-fig tree and studied Fingal. Pouting, she said, 'Your eyes look red. Are you ill with yellow fever?'

'No, lass.'

'Maybe it's a bad case of dysentery. Let's find an African herb to remedy your condition.'

He grabbed her arm. 'Why'd you wander off? I got no time for larking about. Bloody hell, I got grave business in these parts.'

Leopolda broke free and walked over into the shadow of a thorn cactus. 'Tell me what beast you seek. Does it come from the Horn of Africa? Did the animal migrate from Xoogad? If so, the poor thing must be footsore by now. How much trouble could it be for you to trap it?'

He shook his finger at her. 'You've got to stop acting all mysterious. If you don't, people will despise you. And ever since the war ended, loads of people already despise you and only because you'd be a *German*. That's right. On reflection, your kind would be just like the people of Africa. Do you follow? People demonise them too. Anyway, you mustn't give anyone any reason to abhor you. No, you've got to mend Germany's reputation.'

A siege of purple herons flew southbound, and he turned to look. His double, the spectre, stood on the dusty pathway, the creature wholly engulfed in glinting, pearly-purple flames. Fingal groaned. How to ensnare his target without venturing into the Serengeti, the most demanding wilderness in the world?

Leopolda pointed at the burning man. 'Who might that be?' she asked. 'Do you think it might be a Hottentot witch doctor?' Leopolda waved at the burning man.

The burning man heckled Fingal with a litany of insults and epithets, until a series of harsh convulsions racked Fingal's body.

'Enjoy your lolling about whilst you may,' he cried out once the uncanny seizure had ceased. 'Before I breathe me last, I'll nab you and stuff you back inside me.' No sooner had he quieted down than he doubted himself, for who could say whether the faulty Instruktor would ever work properly? For all he knew, he had a better chance of trapping his projection with a burnt-wood spear.

Out in the distance, the purple blaze intensified. 'Catch me if you can and put me back inside you, and then I'll tell you the answers to all your questions,' the entity shouted, its voice resounding like a distorted, tinny voice on a telephone line. 'Ah but if you'll not rein me in, *remember*, I'll destroy the whole continent.'

Fingal turned back and knelt beside a tropical orchid. His belly churned and rumbled as if he had swallowed something unripe, something deadly.

He closed his eyes and prayed that soon the burning man's blinding glare must diminish, until the light came to shine as prosaically as a heap of fake diamonds.

When he finally opened his eyes and turned to look, the burning man shone as blinding bright as a bottle of pear brandy standing in the heart of an ancient Greek stage. *Aye, what a goddamn tragedy.*

Chapter Twenty-One

JEAN. Evangeline, Connecticut. Spring, 1947.

One evening, Jean walked out into her garden and paused to picture Fingal materialising in the shadows. 'Are you feeling ill?' she would ask him if he stood there.

'That's a funny question,' he would answer. 'Have I got puffy eyes?'

'Yes. In fact, you look you've just come back from the dead. Like you've only just regained your pulse. And now you wish to go back to being dead.'

'Aye. It's true. I haven't any hope. Standing down, I am.'

'No, that can't be.' She turned from the garden and studied the barn.

'You hope to divine some way to make me old invention function. Wouldn't that be right, hen? What's the point, though?'

She walked into the barn, activated the Carryola Porto-Pick-Up, and listened to the waterfall at Puerto Iguazú, one of her hypnotherapy recordings. The roar of the mighty cataracts diffused with subliminal messages exhorted her unconscious mind to once and for all push a winning stratagem up into her level of awareness. She paced awhile until the stylus bumped against the label, then she played the flip side.

At one o'clock in the morning, the Carryola Porto-Pick-Up finally seemed to die out on her. Outside, meanwhile, the moonlight assumed a seemingly artificial hue, as if some film company had lit the world with a beam projector.

Why not look upon the stars? She walked over to the swimming pool and climbed into her foamed-plastic lounger. As the soothing current carried her off into the deep end, she studied the cloudless June sky. 'Don't let Fingal die. Hear my prayer. Do you know what I heard? Just last week, I heard that a band of scholars at New York University have founded something quite revolutionary. They're calling it the Department of Occult Sciences. Oh God, do you think they could help me?'

Throughout the sky the beam-light grew increasingly faint, as if the imaginary film company's lamp was faltering.

If I were to audit the lectures, perhaps I'd learn how to make Fingal's invention work properly. Her heart pounding that much harder, she nearly fell into the waters. *Why not enrol in the unconventional course of study?*

Over in the barn, the seemingly-broken record player stirred back to life and the stylus returned to the first groove in the vinyl. A moment later, as the roar of the mighty waterfall washed over her person, the subliminal messages burrowed ever deeper into her unconscious mind. *I'm getting better, stronger, wiser.* She shook her head. *No, I'm not.* She closed her eyes awhile and then opened them very slowly.

The night sky shone as a night sky might appear in a picture show—one in which the film director had placed a blue filter over the camera so as to make sure to give his illusory night sky the quality of absolute cold solemnity.

She looked about, as if the burning man must be nearby—as if *he* must be the film director. *Yes, and he's decided to reduce all contrast and to fill the night with the kind of calm that follows from the absence of warm light. No, there's no balance to the colour tones.* Once more she studied the nighttime sky. The whole expanse seemed all so unreal, as if the whole world were nothing more than a scene from a moving picture, an ambitious film director's wide shot. The very thought made her shake all over.

In the morning she rang the university and requested an interview with the occult sciences department chair, an obscure clinician by the name of J.G. Źymbalist. Once she had made the appointment, she giggled like a little girl. Then she brought the Carryola into the study and played another hypnotherapy recording—this one the surf along the Sea of Cortez, the crash of the waters diffused with various, heartfelt, moralist affirmations. When she returned to her writing table, she wrote her final photoplay.

Again, I stand naked in the lecture hall back at Evangeline Women's College. And when a little Ghana-glass bead appears at my feet, I take it into my hand, and the jewel teleports me out into the plains of Africa, where a winged Fingal soon appears.

'What're you *doing* here?' *the angelic old man asks me.*

'Don't be cross. I've only come to bring you good news.'

'You shouldn't be here. We got freakish man-eaters prowling about these parts, and them beasties would be most ill-tempered. That's because they got no manes, and that's why the pride has banished them, for how to tolerate such anomalies?'

'Never mind all that. Listen. I've rededicated myself to occult science. In time, I'll know how to make your brainchild

work right.'

Fingal looks at me and shrugs his shoulders. 'Even if you did all that, who's to say I'm not already dead? And if I live, who's to say I'll ever find the burning man?' With that, Fingal crouches to the earth and studies a set of lion tracks in the tawny, sunbaked soil. Then he darts off into the brush.

At which point a docile lioness walks me home, where . . .

She dropped the stylograph and looked about. A soft, warm light fell through the room, as if she had lit a solitary candle. *The kind I'd light to pay tribute to the dead.* She returned to her feet and backed away from her writing table. *Shall I light a blessed candle?* For fifteen minutes or more she wandered the empty house. *Shall I perform an act of remembrance?*

At last, she lit a thin, white candle and placed it in one of the windows to the side of the front door—a sign to show Fingal's ghost that she missed him so. *But would his ghost even know how to find this place?*

Later, as she walked off to collect the evening paper, she discovered the carcass of the tuxedo cat lying in a storm-drainage ditch. *An automobile must've struck the poor thing.* When she collected the cat's body, it felt unreal—like a moist, rigid doll. With slumped shoulders, she walked over to the mock-Tudor across the street and knocked three times. No one answered, so she placed the lifeless body before the storm door. Then she retraced her steps and collected her paper.

On the day of the appointment with the occult sciences department chair, she slipped into a floral-pattern gown and shoes with tapered heels. The scholar had agreed to meet her beneath the Washington Square Arch at three o'clock. As fate would have it, though, she reached the city much too early. With nothing better to do, she resolved to stroll about awhile.

In time, she bumped into an elderly gentleman dressed in

a threadbare, oilskin watch coat and a tattered kilt not unlike the one that Fingal had always worn.

Might this coincidence constitute some kind of omen? She placed her hand over her mouth and pressed her thumb against her cheek. *Might this random New Yorker be the one to help me make real progress?* She dropped her hand. *Yes, this must be some kind of* meaningful *coincidence.* She bowed some. 'Hello.'

The elderly gentleman fussed with one of the buttonholes in his coat, and then the inner portions of his eyebrows lifted. Most peculiar of all, he suddenly adopted a blank stare.

The light shone colder again, as if the burning man himself had created the sky in some film studio and employed a blue filter by which to bathe the world in a glow calm enough to put every living thing to sleep.

The elderly gentleman tapped his chin. 'Are you lonely? Do you grieve? Maybe you ought to follow me. Come, please.'

She followed him to a cinema house at Waverly Place in Greenwich Village. Alas, as she proceeded through the mostly-empty stalls, she realised that she had lost track of him. *Did he go back to the lobby to beg a smoke from the cigarette girl?* Before long, she glanced at her winding watch. *It's almost three o'clock already.* She gritted her teeth, for she realised that she ought to be at Washington Square. *How could I have permitted this to happen?*

The theatre lights dimmed, and the picture show commenced: *Forever and a Day* starring Ida Lupino.

From out of nowhere, the gentleman reappeared at Jean's side. 'Why you chasing me about?' he asked in a Cockney accent. 'Was you the one what pinched the Enigma machine from my flat back there in Cripplegate?'

'I'm sure I don't know what you're talking about.'

'Why'd you do it? Do you mean to fence the goods or

encipher the code? Working for them bastards in the deadly Wehrmacht, are you?'

She realised that the fool must be demented. For all she knew, he merely feigned his inflection. As for the kilt, perhaps he had purchased it from some local clothier.

He took hold of her wrist. 'You'd be a duplicitous one, and I'd know because I got me the power to sniff out a saboteuress. That's why the English Army made me to serve as the air-raid warden back home.'

'You must be afflicted by a grievous chemical imbalance. I think maybe you'd be susceptible to *delusions.* Could it be you hear voices? Even if that were the case, you must stay calm and speak to me. That's because our whole encounter, it's what Jung would call a case of synchronicity. So speak to me. And then maybe I'll learn what's become of Fingal.'

'*Fingal?* Whoever he'd be, he can't fool me none. I've beheld nightmarish devilry your likes can't imagine. I'm the *witness.* I'd be the one to attest to the crimes them German bombers committed. Do you remember the one what nosedived into Whitehall or the bastards what went and strafed London Bridge the very next day? Listen up. I beheld every doodlebug what rained onto Thames Street and the one what fell on St John's Wood as well. And when the light of day came around, I myself helped the MI5 to measure the blast radius.'

Once more, she checked her winding watch. *I'm a damn fool.* For a moment, she pictured the occult sciences department chair back at Washington Square. *He'll be feeling cross with me just about now. Go*. Outside, she sought to hail a taxicab, but one after the other passed her by. *Take the subway!* She descended to the platform below but boarded the wrong train and ended up in Chelsea. *Oh God.*

As she rode back toward Washington Square, she sought

to convince herself that the gracious scholar would be waiting for her. If so, she could tell him that she had experienced a long delay at one of the railway depots. *Or maybe I'll contrive a big sob story all about some gruesome train collision out in East Manchester.*

By the time she reached Washington Square, she found no sign of J.G. Źymbalist. She sat beneath the Hangman's Elm—the oldest tree in the city—for an hour. *Have I any hope? Maybe there's no hope at all.*

When she finally returned home, she walked out into the barn and her thoughts turned back to Fingal. *What if he were standing here?*

First, he would laugh. 'So did you blow your chance to meet with that scholarly chap from the university?' he would ask.

'Yes, but you've no cause to fret,' she would answer. 'Tomorrow morning, I'll ring the school and apologise.'

'You'll have to do *more*. If you hope to convince J.G. Źymbalist to reschedule, you'll have to give him a jolly good story. No, you'll have to tell him the truth.'

'Yes, that's right. So I'll explain my habit of helping the demented. And I'll mention how good it would be to pioneer a drug to remedy a nervous constitution.'

'That's all well and good, but I doubt your moralism ought to impress him.'

'How do *you* know?' she would ask. 'Maybe he's got a relation who suffers from dementia. Or a friend who's grown into a worrywart to the point of willing his body to reduplicate the symptoms of some awful malady.'

Deep inside the power source, the combustion chamber stirred to life and pulsated, producing a sound something like that of a waterfall.

She looked to her feet and rubbed her temples awhile. Then she exited the barn, only to witness an occultation, a bright, shimmery star vanishing behind the moon.

An animal brushed past her ankle. By the look of its coat, there could be no doubt that the creature must be one of the dead tuxedo cat's motherless kittens—the runt, no less.

Yes, of course. She knelt to the earth. 'You've no reason to despair. I'll mend the machine. And Fingal, he'll capture the burning man. Yes, we'll rise to the occasion.'

The kitten turned away. Without a doubt, her tone of voice had only served to confound the animal. The kitten turned back, and Jean gathered the outcast into her arms. *There, there.* She stood and swayed and hummed a loving lullaby.

IV

Chapter Twenty-Two

Jean graduated from New York University after studying every last aspect of the occult sciences as they pertained to Fingal's invention. Not three weeks after commencement exercises, she pegged her mechanical-arts degree to her writing-room wall.

The next day, she made one last modification. Then, her head held high, she backed out of the barn. *Everything ought to work properly.* For the rest of the morning, she took refuge inside the house. *I just know Fingal must come soon.*

At one o'clock she sat at the kitchen table and clasped her hands together. *What if he shows up and nothing works right?*

At dusk she returned outside and considered the sky. How soothing, how hazy, how exquisitely diffused each ray of light. The whole world appeared to her as a motion-picture background filmed through ground glass. She should have registered a sensation as of deepest bliss. Instead, she slumped to the earth and buried her face in her hands.

When she finally looked up, night had fallen—but not one star cluster shone.

On the eve of her eighty-first birthday on the 9th June, 1967, a frail, withered figure arrived at her door. By the look of his fleshy, drooping eyelids and the many liver spots on the backs of his hands, the wrinkled, decrepit caller might have been a hundred and one years old.

'Fingal?'

'None other,' he answered. 'Do forgive all me unsightly blemishes. The years haven't been kind. But you've grown into an elderly jam as well, eh?'

She fussed with her wig's velvet ear tabs. 'Yes, I'm old. And ever since my hair fell out, I've had to hide my barren scalp.' She pulled here and there, endeavouring to adjust the foundation net. 'This here's the top rug on the market, the best by a country mile. The wigmaker told me that he fashioned this piece from the coat of a Himalayan yak.'

'Aye, you were never lovelier. And how do *I* look?' Fingal performed a slow twirl as if to show off his threadbare coat and old, familiar kilt.

When he turned back, she studied the colourful, handwoven basket in his hands. 'You've got the burning man inside there? Where did you find him?'

'Out and about,' Fingal answered, hobbling into the house.

'I'll get some tea on call,' she told him as she closed the door. With that, she guided him into the kitchen, debating whether she ought to ask just how he had located her. She paused beside the kitchen table. 'I always knew you'd come find me, but what took you so long?'

'Had to track me foe, didn't I? And then I had to subdue the bastard besides. And I'd be blessed if the goddamn Instruktor didn't have it in for me the whole time. But I've got him. Aye, so I do.' Fingal placed the basket on the kitchen floor and nudged the lid with the side of his foot.

An awkward silence followed, for she could not stop biting her nails. Nor could she take her eyes off the basket.

Fingal ambled over to her pantry and grabbed a Twinings of London variety pack, then he continued over to the kettle. 'I'll brew the tea, eh? Then we'll chew the rag. Aye, it's always good to catch up with an old friend.'

'Are you hungry?' she asked him. 'You look positively famished. As empty as an old drum. What about some sour milk cheese? Or would you prefer a dish of butter pecan ice cream, or how about a piece of divinity fudge? Or we could go to Woolworths and sit at the lunch counter.'

The hazy light of the summer sun poured through the window, and as the kitchen grew brighter, she placed her hands upon the tabletop. 'I hope you know I've been working hard all these years. I guess I felt some kind of duty to mend your old machine. Anyway, I think your whimsy ought to perform as it should.'

He switched off the stove. 'Show me what you've done, hen. *Please*.'

A shudder moved through her body. She walked over to the kitchen counter and wrapped her hand around her chrome, beehive-shaped blender. When she turned back, she breathed in. Fingal smelled sweet and musty, and his distinctive odour made her mouth fill with the taste of something like chloroform gas.

At last she fixed her gaze upon the handwoven basket. 'Suddenly, I realise that I've got everything to lose. It's the moment of truth.' With that, she guided Fingal out to the barn and held her breath.

His hands shook as he looked upon the power source. '*Behold*. You've done it, haven't you? Yes, indeed.'

She exhaled. 'Yes, I've done it. Or at least I hope so.' She averted her gaze and studied the light falling through the barn. *Oh my.* The glow that reached through the space appeared to her not unlike the glare of some film company's spun-glass fill lights—as if the vindictive film director aimed to expose every imperfection that might have otherwise concealed itself in the shadows of the key light.

Fingal looked to the hem of his tattered kilt. 'Howbeit, I seem to possess that very contrivance by which to send the projection back inside me mind.'

'I wish that I could promise you certain success, but I can't do that.' Slowly, she backed away. *Why not leave him alone?* She crossed her arms and returned inside. When she reached her writing table, she fixed her gaze upon the mechanical-arts degree and let her body sway some. At the same time, her arms and legs trembled. *What if I've failed in all my efforts?*

A light as of a beam shining through ground glass crept into the room—as if for no other reason than to expose every detail of her life, every pencil strewn about the writing table.

After a while, she walked upstairs to her bedroom and slipped into a poplin blouse and a long, grey skirt. When she returned downstairs to the kitchen, she stared at an icing spatula for five whole minutes. Then she walked out the front door. Without even saying goodbye, she took the train into the city.

She wandered Washington Square for an hour. Eventually, her feet aching, she ducked into Pravda Café. As she sipped her spiced espresso, she admired some of the photo prints adorning the wall—shots of Moscow State University, the Volgograd skyline, Pushkin Square, the Kremlin Library.

When she finished her coffee, she approached a display of cookie gift baskets. She ran the tip of her tongue over her remaining teeth: they had grown so brittle. *If I were to bite into one of the treats, all the enamel would be sure to crumble apart.* She turned to study a fine watercolour hanging on the wall—a cool-toned scene of Leningrad Train Station complete with an elderly woman struggling to climb into a passenger car. How anguished the expression etched into her muted, wrinkled face—as if the old lady had only just learned that her whole life had been a lie, a lost cause, a failure.

Jean tapped the watercolour's frame. 'What's got you feeling all so conscience-stricken?' she asked very softly, as if the elderly Russian woman might answer.

Over in the corner, a beatnik removed an ornate balalaika from its case, and the waifish young man strummed the melody to a Russian folk song. As he did so a strong fill light poured through the coffee house.

Jean turned to study one of the agitprop prints and then a solemn, nighttime cityscape that included a view of Saint Isaac's Cathedral.

A college girl walked up alongside her and pointed at the golden cross mounted atop the spire. 'Die Religion ist das Opium des Volkes,' the young lady whispered, with a giggle. Religion is the opium of the people.

Jean wrapped her hands around the young lady's wrists. 'What if I've failed? What if nothing works right? Then what?'

Late in the evening, when Jean returned home to Connecticut, she found Fingal sitting at the kitchen table.

'Went the day well?'

'No, can't say that it did.' She sat at the table, fussed with one of the lace doilies, and then placed her hands upon the tabletop. 'Tell me that the machine works right.'

'You're looking a wee bit glum, hen. Do you fear that maybe we'll fail?'

'Yes, that's right.' She removed her hands from the tabletop and felt at the crow's feet around her eyes. Then she looked to her feet. 'I'm very sorry that I walked out on you earlier today. How could I think to leave you at a moment like this? I ought to be looking after you as you fight the good fight to put the burning man back inside you.'

'*No*. I'll not have you dancing attendance on me. Even if I look to be some old codger, there's a fresh hand at the bellows.'

One of the yak hairs in Jean's wig came loose and sailed off upon the current presently drifting in through the window. 'Do you approve of my toils?' she asked, as the solitary strand alighted along the very edge of the sink. 'Does everything more or less meet with your satisfaction?'

'Haven't decided yet, but what's it matter?'

'Do you know why I fret so? It's because I love you. Yes, I love your *intellect*. So tell me that everything's working right. Don't make me fear that I've gone and failed the love of my life. Tell me that I've done what's needful to . . . further your agenda.'

In response Fingal merely ambled outside and stopped beside the brightly lit swimming pool such that the whole of his being suddenly shone the colour of a Russian blue cat, the gleam of its coat.

For the next week, he continued to check over her work, and never once did he offer any solace. Did he even believe that she loved him? Even if he did, what did any of that matter? As the days passed by, he ignored her.

For her part Jean travelled into the city and frittered away the hours at some of the revival houses. Three times she watched *Mourning Becomes Electra*. The acclaimed picture failed to inspire, as did several screenings of *Penny Serenade* and *Mine Own Executioner*.

One night she returned home and locked herself in the

study. For a time, she listened to the radio—highlights from the Monterey Pop Festival, some aged master of the Indian sitar. She danced and swayed to the hypnotic music, and as she did, it seemed as if every bone in her body rattled softly. *California, California, California.*

In the morning she adorned the house with pink honeysuckle, then stopped by the guest room and knocked upon the pocket door. 'Are you feeling stronger today? What do you think? Are you ready to pass on through the gateway?'

'Maybe tomorrow. What about you? Maybe you ought to find some way to ease your mind. Why don't you get a book to read?'

At nine o'clock she drove her 1957 Chevrolet Bel Air to a bookshop near the town square. On a whim she purchased *An Archaeological Investigation into the Popular Arts*, an acclaimed overview of the various expeditions lately excavating some of the silent-era film sets stretching out across Los Angeles County.

Later, she stopped along the banks of the Connecticut River and sat beneath a plum tree. A cool, summer breeze blew across the waters. She read the biographical sketch of the authoress, Ms Poppy Ostrum from Albertus Magnus College. Then Jean read the detailed proem written by Pavel Hexenturm, a somewhat obscure film-theory-and-media-arts professor who presently taught at Gustavus Adolphus College. *Hexenturm, that name does sound rather familiar.* Before long she closed the book and returned to her feet. Then she let herself dance and sway. *Yes, like a little girl.*

A flowery storm drifted by, several dandelion seeds entangling themselves in her wig. She plucked one of the wild summer plums, but when she found it tasted much too sour, she dropped the fruit into a patch of hogweed. *Hexenturm.*

Early that evening, as she drove home, she very nearly had

a fatal collision with a taxicab. When she reached the house, she staggered into the kitchen.

And there was Fingal. He had dressed himself in her duster robe, and he lay across the floor—as if it pleased him to rest his weary back against the cool tiles.

'*Hello*. How long till you pass through the gateway and all?'

'Not till I'm sure that everything would be up to scratch.'

'The furnishings work fine. I know it. Every steely nut and bolt. Yes, indeed, everything's fit for purpose. It's just got to be.'

'So you think you're the biz, do you?'

'Just tell me that I haven't failed you.'

'*Aye*. The lot's perfect. To a cow's thumb.'

'I know. Let's ring someone from International Business Machines and have *him* check my work.'

'Go on now. It's time for you to revisit your own passions. Aye, go free. Find something to fulfil your urges, your *weaknesses*.'

She made her way into the laundry room, slipped out of her summer gown, and wrapped herself in a robe of Calais lace, then she walked outside and gazed upon the night sky. *It's a picture show.* Once more, she danced and swayed. *Oh yes, what a spectacle. Neither the moon nor the summer stars ever shone so bright, so buoyant, so blissful.* She inched over toward the neighbours' house, the Stroud family's brick colonial, and for the very first time she realised that someone had fashioned a wooden fortress in the crown of a chestnut tree looking out over her backyard. Had the Stroud family's little boy built the crude structure?

She approached the chestnut tree, mustered her strength, and climbed the ship's ladder dangling from the largest bough. Inside the refuge Micah Stroud had left a host of treasures: a deck of Old-Maid cards, a book about the Bermuda Triangle, a first-edition of *A Canticle for Leibowitz*, a book on ufology, and, over to the side, a tinfoil hat.

From the direction of the swimming pool, Fingal called out her name and clapped his hands. 'Where'd you go?'

She peeked through the window and studied him; once more, the whole of Fingal's person shone as beautifully as a Russian blue cat's lustrous coat. She snapped her fingers and waved. 'I'm up here,' she called out. 'In the tree.'

When Fingal espied her face in the window, he scowled. 'Crivens. You look piss funny up there.' He made his way across the Stroud family's property and then stopped and looked up. 'What's wrong, hen?'

'The fear of failure, I think it's got me falling apart, reverting to my childhood, acting like a little girl.' She turned from the window and espied a crayola-crayon sketch that Micah had thumbtacked to the opposite wall.

The image depicted an old man, and beneath it, a crayola-crayon caption read:

Tom Fury of the Lightning Rods

For a moment, she thought of Volta—how he had struggled to disprove the notion that lightning held within it the power to enkindle life.

Moments later, as a west wind sailed through the tree house, she studied some of the peculiar images thumbtacked to the walls: a view of Yucca Mountain, a map of Area 51, and a sketch depicting the astrobiology laboratory in Boulder City, Nevada. The wind kicked up, and a spider's silken strand blew into her face.

Fifteen minutes later, she returned to her study and

leafed through the book that she had purchased earlier that day. The breeze stirred the curtain as she read the proem by Pavel Hexenturm again. *Where have I heard that name?* She reached for the telephone, and despite the late hour, rang an acquaintance from Evangeline Women's College—an accomplished film critic and art historian by the name of Emmanuelle Schwab.

The telephone call must have awoken Emmanuelle from a deep slumber, for it took some time before she had collected herself. 'What do you want?' Emmanuelle asked, yawning noisily.

'Who might Pavel Hexenturm be? Does the name sound familiar to you?'

'Yes, he wrote a memoir about the lost scene from RKO's *King Kong*, the part where all the crewmen fall to the bottom of a chasm, and a cluster of giant spiders come along and devour everyone. *Yeah*. I guess the sequence must've come off so grisly and grotesque that one of the suits, possibly David O. Selznick himself, cut the scene.'

Jean gripped the handset so tightly that her fingers smarted. Long before, she had read about Hexenturm's quest to find the lost sequence. He had travelled to Hollywood, hoping that one last dupe negative might be extant. Subsequently, he had rifled through every last one of the various studio archives. *But he never discovered anything.* She dropped the handset to the floor and then hung up the phone.

The ongoing breeze grew strong, meanwhile, and some of her papers took flight; for fifteen minutes or more, her unpublished essays drifted all about the study. Then a powerful, invigorating scent as that of wild Russian sage sailed through the window, and she collected her papers and weighed them down with a Scotch-bonnet seashell that she had brought home from the beach years before.

A little bit later, when she retired to her bedroom, she lay in bed and thought of the lost scene—the giant spiders devouring the crewmen. Her eyes adjusted to the darkness, and she looked around and effortlessly espied every contour of every object in the room. She pictured Fingal's mysterious, handwoven basket standing just there on her bedroom floor.

At any moment a clutter of spiders would push back the lid and crawl out. And they would appear all so clear to her—every strand of hair, every detail, as if she found herself in the midst of a picture show directed by the burning man himself, a show for which he had carefully flashed and fogged and pre-exposed the film so that every last spider might glow all so brightly, despite the darkness.

All atremble, she tossed and turned. *The spiders, the spiders, the spiders.* She kicked her feet uncontrollably. *I can't sleep.*

When she returned downstairs, she found Fingal sitting at the kitchen table. 'Have you any idea what kind of dread I'm feeling? It's something like the fear of spiders. If my work were to fail you, then I'd be failing the only person I ever *loved.*'

Fingal flashed a vacant smile, as if he had not even been listening and had not even heard a word.

Chapter Twenty-Three

Sometime after Independence Day, perhaps the sixth of July, Jean walked into the guest room and tapped Fingal's foot. 'Put the burning man back inside you. Activate the power source and pass through the gateway.'

'No, I'll not do aught till you get yourself to California. Stop holding me up to shame, hen. Go already. No more dawdling. Go on and get back to your true passions, film theory and such. Unearth that lost scene from the bloody RKO picture.'

She sat upon the edge of the bed. 'Tell me something. How should I ever be content to dedicate my life to something so *trivial*? Try to sympathise. I'm so confused. In a way, it'd be good to do as you say, but even so, what would any of it matter what with you on the cusp of accomplishing something monumental?' She returned to her feet and walked outside.

With heavy steps, she paced alongside the swimming pool. *So do I travel out to California?* She stopped, crossed her arms, and looked out across the lawn, where a very soft light poured from the sky, in the same way that a glow as spare as candlelight illumines the stage manager in that moment the aged actor appears before the audience and introduces *Our Town*. For the second time, she thought of leaving for California. *Maybe it's all for the best.*

A cry rang out from the crown of the dying butternut tree; it sounded like that of a willow thrush.

Jean scanned the boughs, but she could not detect any songbird. For a moment or two, she picked some of the dried, brittle bark from the trunk, but her thoughts soon turned to Fingal's obsessions. She stood still. *If all my efforts were to fail, then civilisation should never learn the riddle of the universe.* Twice, her bosom heaved.

At midday she drove to New Haven Airport. No matter the infernal heat, she sat behind the wheel and watched a few of the departing flights reach altitude. *Burning man, can you read my thoughts? If everything fails, what do you mean to do to this world? You'll inspire countless numbers of people to destroy themselves, won't you?*

No one responded, so she turned the radio on and fiddled with the dial. A correspondent out of Saigon issued a report regarding a Buddhist monk who had immolated himself the day before, in protest of the war.

She interlaced her fingers, and each one stiffened. Her skin growing hot and dry, she peered into the rear-view mirror and imagined a large, purple tarantula crouching in the bench seat. Only when a high-wing cargo aircraft roared by overhead did she awaken from her reverie.

A few days later, back at the house, she read a most intriguing notice in the papers:

Flatbush Revival House showing RKO's
King Kong at eight o'clock!

She decided to ignore the advertisement. There would be no point in watching the movie, knowing full well that it lacked the most extraordinary sequence—the one in which the crewmen fall into the chasm, only to be devoured by giant spiders.

In the late afternoon, she sat on her front doorstep, and while holding an empty milk bottle against her left breast she revisited the notion that somewhere in Hollywood there might exist a dupe negative by which to view the lost scene. A rush of adrenaline made her heart beat faster and faster. The more she thought of the gruesome lost scene, the more she cringed. A second time, her fingers stiffened. She returned the milk bottle to her side.

At that point, the call of a cock robin resounded up and down Wren Haven Drive, the clamour followed by the din of lawn tractors. Then a gaunt, jumpy fox squirrel stopped to look at her. When it stole away, her own loneliness compelled her to follow the creature—and she pursued the animal as far as the Llewellyn family's storybook house, then the pest darted off into the mushroom garden. She walked two blocks west, past the Whitaker family's Victorian cottage and Mr Hemphill's quaint Craftsman.

Little by little, she broke into a terrific sweat. Beneath the wig, her scalp itched and burned badly. As if all that were not enough, the scent of Ms McAdam's spice bread drifted through the humid air. *Oh God, that aroma sure does make me thirsty.*

At last Jean stopped beside a web-enshrouded evergreen shrub, and a black widow's silken strand sailed down her blouse. Slowly, the sticky thread descended along her spine.

The whole of the neighbourhood grew quiet, meanwhile, until no noise reverberated other than the drone of a distant steamroller. Then the drone of the steamroller fell silent, and no sound remained save the hiss of rain guns. *Or could it be the soft jeers of spiderlings huddled in some egg sac lost in the brush?* She looked to her feet. *What do* you *think, burning man?*

At six o'clock she walked home and took the keys to the Chevrolet Bel Air from the kitchen table. Then she drove back to the bookshop at Evangeline Town Square.

What a stroke of luck; the bookseller had a copy of the Hexenturm memoir, the hapless film critic's account of his quest to locate the lost scene from *King Kong*.

Back at the house, she read the entire book in less than six hours. Then, as the night grew hotter and increasingly humid, she slipped out of the warm housecoat she had ordered from the May Company catalogue. Dressed in nothing more than her foundation garments, she approached the hallway window overlooking the backyard.

Below, Fingal stood alongside the brightly lit swimming pool. As usual, the whole of his person shone the shade of a Russian blue cat—the gleam of its coat.

She turned from the window and walked downstairs. Fingal ignored her, so she looked this way and that. There could be no denying the sensation of someone or some*thing* gazing upon her. *Could it be a venomous orb-weaver crawling through the shadows?*

At her feet an everyday house spider cast out a strand of silk. Then, as the thread captured the faint summer breeze, the creature sailed off into the night.

She turned to study the colossal web presently enshrouding the better part of Micah's tree fort. She walked over. *Shall I go up again?* After a long delay, she finally climbed the ship's ladder that dangled from the largest bough.

Micah had filled the space with new reading materials:

a volume by H.P. Lovecraft, a frayed copy of 'The Day the Icicle Works Closed', and two reviews of a local summer-stock production, *The Effect of Gamma Rays on Man-in-the-Moon Marigolds.* He had removed the Tom-Fury-of-the-Lightning-Rods sketch from the wall. In its place, the little boy had thumbtacked a view of Star City, including a half dozen cosmonauts standing before a space capsule boasting micrometeorite shields.

Where do I turn? Where do I go? She climbed down and walked over to the driveway, where Fingal stood urinating into a pothole.

When he finished, he looked at her. 'What's wrong? You look like someone did the dirty on you. Like someone bulled your tea, aye, and now you got the piss shivers.'

The arched gateway rattled inside the barn and shone with a white glow brimming with shimmery sparks.

Fingal walked over to the power source and fiddled with the lampboard until he had suppressed the flares.

When he returned to her side, she gestured toward the gateway. 'If I go, do you promise to pass through?'

'Aye, that I do.'

'And you'll remember that I won't be gone for too long?'

'Aye,' Fingal told her. With that, he walked over to the swimming pool, took hold of the long plastic leaf-skimmer, and sought to collect a dead shrew mole floating upon the waters.

She looked to the night sky. No matter how selfish the sensation, she could swear that almost every point of light shone for her alone—Alpha Centauri, all the dazzling asteroids, Isis and Calliope and a hundred or more nameless ones as well. And what if the astronomical bodies were to call out?

'Go west!' the chorus of voices would tell her, if they

could. 'Out there, you'll find your destiny!'

At last Fingal nudged the dead shrew mole into the net. Then he drew the body forth from the waters and dumped the detestable carcass to the side.

Jean walked over, tugged on his sleeve, and briefly rested her brow against his shoulder. Afterward, she returned into her study and listened to the wireless—a broadcast from the Club Atlantis, a jaunty *danzón* band from Miami performing, while a poetess with a French accent recited selections from Jack Kerouac's *Mexico City Blues*.

The radio signal went dead. Twice, then, the oval-base table lamp flickered—the way theatre lights sometimes do.

She reached for the dish of Russian black bread sitting on her writing table, but the treat tasted all wrong in the sweltering night, each mouthful mouldy and tinged with silky, little pieces of cobwebs. *It's time to go.* She walked upstairs and packed her bags.

A few minutes later, once she had changed into a linen skirt and a simple-enough blouse, she climbed into the Chevrolet Bel Air and drove off. Only as she passed by the drive-in did she slow down to look.

A long line of autos inched their way toward the ticket window, and, lit by the marquee's chasing lights, a series of large, crimson letters announced the feature:

TONIGHT ONLY! HOW TO STUFF A WILD BIKINI

A pair of headlamps suddenly illumined the road, and a motor truck filled with tangerine-yellow summer flowers emerged from her blind spot. As a dreamlike blossom drifted through the vehicle's bed rails and landed beside a dent in the Bel Air's hood, she turned onto the westbound highway.

When she reached New Haven Airport, she cut the engine and gripped the wheel for a moment or two. *Burning man, do you read my thoughts? I'm off to Hollywood just now, and do you wish to know why? I'm going there because no medium has greater influence and power than picture shows. So I'll go there and talk to the young people who choose to live there. And maybe I'll promise them that someday very soon, Fingal should be triumphal. Yes, I'll share the happy news with everyone. I'll tell the young people that soon Fingal and I should be preaching the greatest revelation of all.*

Ten minutes later, once she had purchased her ticket to LAX, she followed the signs to the domestic departure hall.

Not far from the flight-operations room, she sat and listened to the sounds of computers and other futuristic devices emanating from behind the door. *I'm flying off to Hollywood, and there's no way you'll stop me. Do you hear, burning man? Soon, I'll be tending to the loneliest people in the world. Those most susceptible to your influence.*

A diminutive blonde dressed in a fashionable moon-lace partygoer walked from the end of the concourse and sat beside her. 'Hey there, ma'am. By any chance, are you on your way to San Francisco?'

'I'm going to Los Angeles. Are you going out to San Francisco? Do you wish to take part in all that summer-of-love business?'

'No, I'm flying out to Visitación Valley. Flight 714. I got to find my kid sister. Man, she's got a real bad case of manic depression. And I'm pretty sure she's joined a cult. Can you believe that?'

When the young lady walked off to the snack bar, Jean thought back to a radio show that she had heard some two weeks before—a riveting, detailed interview with a pair of high-ranking medical staff from Gracie Square Hospital. For twenty minutes the chief nurse had spoken about the runaways who join cults and follow charismatics. At one point the director of operations had claimed that no reputable institution would even treat such runaways as outpatients for fear that the confounded youths would revert and then flee back to whatever commune or mock-religious order had come to wield such sway over them.

A bottle of Schweppes Bitter Lemon in her hand, the diminutive blonde returned from the snack bar. 'You shouldn't go out to LA. I'll bet the pilot won't even be able to see the approach lights what with all the smog.' The young lady crossed her legs and held the bottle up against her brow. 'I'll bet you're planning to take some grand tour of the movie stars' mansions, huh?'

Jean considered telling the young lady the truth. She would explain that she longed to gauge how lost society had become, and she would explain her obsession with learning whether the resolution to the riddle of the universe might be of any use to anyone. *But a girl like this one here, she'll never understand. Maybe she'll think that* I'm *caught up in some kind of cult.*

At last, Jean sat back some. *Why not tell the young lady a fib?* Jean kicked her feet, like a little girl might do. 'I'm going out to Hollywood because I'm looking for something. I seek one of the great treasures. A lost dupe negative from *King Kong*, a perfect copy, one without any infidelities, one that shows the lost scene.'

'The lost scene? What lost scene?'

'The one that RKO cut from the picture.'

'RKO cut a scene from *King Kong*? Why? Did it include a lens flare? I hear that's what happened to a lot of those old-time movies.'

'No, it's nothing like that. RKO cut it because it was too macabre. It's the segment in which the crewmen plummet into a chasm, and a bunch of giant spiders come along and gobble them up.'

'You'll never find it. Back in the olden days, the studio executives discarded anything unseemly because they didn't want to offend the authorities.'

'No, I'm sure I'll find what I seek. First, I'll check the Technicolor Company's corporate archive on Doheny Drive. Or I'll visit Phonofilm on Venice Boulevard. Or maybe the film critic down at the *Los Angeles Times.*'

The blonde swallowed some of the Schweppes Bitter Lemon, and then she belched so quietly that she did not even trouble to excuse herself.

Directly above, amid the perforated ceiling panels, one of the public-address system's speakers crackled to life. 'American Airlines Flight 714 to Toronto with continuing, non-stop service to San Francisco now boarding,' a stolid, androgynous voice announced.

A gentleman dressed in a textured pinstripe suit emerged from the door to the business lounge and continued off toward the gate.

Jean watched him pass into the skybridge and then turned to the blonde. 'It's time for you to board your flight.'

The blonde placed the bottle of Schweppes Bitter Lemon on the floor. 'You know something? The more I think about the spiders devouring the crewmen in that lost film clip, the more it reminds me of something really profound. Man's deepest fear. The notion that he might die in a state of *shame*. Like during his greatest crisis, he'll feel so panicked that he won't even be cool-headed enough to muster the nerve to *resist*.'

The public-address system's speakers crackled to life a second time, and the monotone, androgynous voice announced the final boarding call.

Slowly, the blonde removed a Polaroid from her pocketbook and studied the image. 'You want to know how totally ditzy my crazy kid sister has become? Just last year, she auditioned for a blue movie. *Mondo Topless*. Not the kind of smut that shows penetration, but still. Yeah, and two weeks ago, the crazy kid had herself a spontaneous abortion.'

Jean shifted her hips. 'So go rescue your sibling . . . yes, before the cult makes her do something awful.'

'Yeah, if she does do something awful, she'll never beat the rap. No, she'll wind up in a jailhouse full of butch-broads. And then it'll be one weirdo orgy after the next.' With that, the blonde raced off, and she passed through the gate and into the skybridge.

Jean placed her flight bag upon her lap. *I know what you think, burning man. Yes, you think I'd be going to Hollywood only because I'd be confounded, erratic. Well, if that's what you think, you've got it all wrong. I'm making a leap of faith, that's all. A leap of faith.*

From within the souvenir shop, a radio crackled to life with a piece by Fauré—an especially mournful movement from his *Requiem in D Minor*.

Jean closed her eyes and thought of all the penniless, demented runaways wandering about out west. *How confounded the multitudes must be these days, so many people looking for the answers.* She wondered if the trouble might follow from their family history—the scourge of alcoholism. For that matter, perhaps some of the runaways would be fleeing mothers addicted to some kind of daytime sedative. And now she thought about the many pharmaceutical companies and their habit of suppressing just how addictive their products could be. *Yes, the business of healthcare has grown so depraved.*

Over in the souvenir shop, the music turned to static. She opened her eyes and thought of Fingal. *Someday soon, if I've done good, he'll be sending the remains of the entity back inside himself. So how long before he grasps the revelation he seeks?*

The airport grew quiet. Then a flurry of sound rang out: the departures-and-arrivals board, its newfangled, split-flap display.

Jean rocked back and forth awhile. When she stopped, she fidgeted. *I can't fail Fingal, no. If I've failed Fingal, then we fail society.*

Little by little, her thoughts turned to RKO's director of photography. *Doesn't he live in a bungalow off Blue Jay Way?* If he permitted her to rummage through his attic, perhaps she would find the lost scene from *King Kong* lying behind a dusty, obsolete Moviola. Or maybe she would find a release negative lying atop the prototype to Max Fleischer's rotoscope. *Yes, the lost scene from* King Kong. *If only that really were all that I desired.*

Two hours passed by before the Pan Am airliner bound for Los Angeles taxied past the vast window. What a terrific clamour, too, the combined roar of the engines; they bellowed like colossal spiders, monsters hungry enough to consume all of humankind.

Chapter Twenty-Four

No sooner had Jean reached her room at the Beverly Wilshire Hotel than she realised that she must have grabbed the wrong flight bag when disembarking the airliner. She sat down on the edge of her bed, opened the zippered pocket and discovered an esoteric diagram pertaining to an IBM data-conversion system linked to some covert government laboratory in Los Alamos. *Oh no.* She raced downstairs and hailed a cab.

Back at LAX, the gentleman working the lost-and-found desk politely accepted the item but could not help her to locate her own property.

Empty-handed, she returned to the hotel and made her way through a maze of potted lady palms in the lobby. *Think positive. Any day now, maybe Fingal should meet the moment and triumph and learn all. I've got to tell someone the good news.*

She paused beside the front desk and looked about—the light shone all wrong, as if she presently found herself in a night-for-day interior, a movie scene shot at night but lit so as to conjure the illusion of daytime. *Have I got lost in a dream?* For three hours straight, she sat in the lobby and contemplated the incomprehensible sensation.

At dusk an elderly nun approached. 'You look nonplussed, if you don't mind my saying so. Just like the dowagers that haunt Mystic Seaport back home.' Before Jean could respond, the nun tapped Jean's elbow. 'What a pity all those widows. They're so lonely and sullen. But even in their dotage, they could be performing good deeds. Why not care for *others*? At the very least, a widow could be feeding the hungry cats chasing about the shipyard.'

Jean pictured a Russian blue cat wandering the pier—a bloodied, badly-mangled Connecticut warbler in the creature's jaws.

The nun guided her outside onto the walkway. 'I'm off to Redondo Beach to watch the moonset. Did you ever watch the moon sink below the horizon?' Before Jean had even had a chance to answer, the nun climbed into a taxicab and was gone.

A green smog invaded the dusky sky, and as the evening breeze grew forceful, a draft card drifted past Jean's shoulder and continued off along Wilshire Boulevard. *I'll make believe it's a sign, a portent.* She followed the debris three blocks east to a length of oily, grooved pavement stretching out before a taverna reeking of Dungeness crab. From all directions more odours awoke: hydrogen sulfide, chemicals, warehouse fires. *Oh, that's just the way the world should smell if and when the burning man goes free.*

A taxicab pulled up. 'Hey, big spender, you from out of town?' the driver asked. 'Hop in and I'll show you the City of Angels. Just twenty-five clams. Yeah, we'll do Tarzana Boulevard, or, if you want to treat yourself, we'll take Ventura

Freeway North. Or how's about maybe you and me cruise the Miracle Mile? Or, if you're in the mood for something really wild, we could size up all the heads roaming Sunset Boulevard. We'll have lots of laughs.'

'Could you maybe help me find someone desperate for good counsel?'

'Down on the Sunset Strip, they're desperate for anything and everything.'

'So take me to the Sunset Strip.' She climbed into the back and did her best to ignore the refuse strewn about the floor—an old taco shell, a pair of 3D glasses, and a tattered, yellowed page from *The Doors of Perception* by Aldous Huxley.

The cabbie smirked, added her to his log of fares, and then he pulled out into the street.

She gazed out the window and noted the random things passing by—a set of neon lights that spelt out the words *Draft Beer*, a deserted impound lot, a Mobil sign too.

The cabbie fussed with the radio dial, and a jumble of sounds and voices arose from the one working speaker: a verse from Guy Lombardo's 'Begging for Love,' followed by a comic named Soupy Sales, and then a broadcaster announcing his station's call numbers to the strains of bumper music.

When the taxicab reached the Sunset Strip, the driver proceeded along slowly. What a multitude; among the teeming crowd, countless boys and girls with bloodshot eyes wandered about. Many of them wore badly-worn Duluth packs or else pushed rickety shopping trolleys filled with personal effects.

'Where do they come from?'

'Squaresville, USA,' the cabbie answered. 'Yeah, I think most come to make the dope scene. Whatever the story, a lot of the girls end up hooking. They got to make bread somehow, you dig? *Tricks*. This town's crawling with them.'

'But don't the girls know to honour their fathers?'

'*No*. The girls around here, they just want to get baked. Whether she cleans her own weed and she's got her seeds rolling off her favourite album cover, or whether she aims to score a cheap contact high, either way, the chicks get their kicks. Good times with bad company. Blaze a bowl. Smoke bud. Pull it down into your lungs and hold it. That's all these freaks want.'

'No, I don't think so. They want much more. I'd say the runaways, the flower children, the drifters, they're *lost*, so they come here hoping to find something to *believe* in.'

The traffic halted, and the cabbie turned the radio dial to an evocative piece that might have come from the score to that arthouse picture, *Juliet of the Spirits*.

The music made Jean think. *Young people want to know the meaning of life, but society offers no answer. Only lame advice.* Slowly, she turned to her right.

In front of a club called the London Fog sat a girl in a filthy skirt and peasant blouse. She could not have been a day over fifteen, but even so, she looked childlike due to the fact that she wore her ginger hair in a pageboy bob. Even more poignant, she caressed her left funny bone, as if she suffered from nursemaid's elbow.

Immediately, Jean's own elbow smarted—as sharply as it had during the flight, when the cabin crew had come along and she had rammed her arm against the drink-service cart.

She imagined Fingal sitting beside her. Would he not detect something profound in the concurrence of circumstances? If so, he would poke her in the ribs. 'Pay the bloody fare and get out of this rust bucket,' he would tell her. 'Go on.'

For a moment, she closed her eyes. *What if my modifications make it much too trying for him to pass through the gateway? What if my work drives Fingal to madness?* She opened her eyes and handed the driver thirty dollars. Then she climbed out of the cab and approached the pitiable girl. 'How do you do?'

As the taxi drove off and sped through a boulevard stop-sign, the girl hummed along with the mellotron music resounding from inside the club. Then she grew quiet, and with her weary eyes, looked Jean over. 'Ain't you too old to be hustling?'

'*Hustling*? I haven't come to cause you any trouble.'

'Did Minnie Kilbride send you? Listen here. You tell Minnie that's it. I won't make another run. From now on, I answer only to the gods of rock. Find somebody else to unload the smoke. I ain't carrying bricks no more. Spread the word, old lady. No, I don't want that kind of action. Like, I can't afford to get busted for possession again. No more, man. Like, no way. Like, not even if you was to plunk down five bills. Not even for fifteen large. Not even if you was to throw in a 1965 Pontiac Bonneville, pink slips and all.'

With a sigh, Jean pointed at the crook of the girl's elbow. 'Let me help you. Maybe we could find a free clinic willing to treat you.'

'What's this all about, grandma? Like, if there's something you want or whatever, you ought to consult the wizard. Mr Glasscock.'

'Can't say I've ever heard the name.'

'Well, let me clue you in. He's got a cure for everything. Like, some bughouse. Yeah, but it'd be real righteous of you not to tell anyone. Because lately he deals in black tar heroin. Here's the deal, though. If you get hooked on the junk, and the wizard thinks like maybe you're bound to overdose like

Brian Jones or whatever, so the wizard helps you come down. Yeah man, and like you won't even feel no hairy withdrawal symptoms or nothing because—'

'Uh, I think I might be a touch too *mature* for your friend's services.'

'No way. He treats oldsters all the time. It's just that you got to pay the price on the street. Play it as it lays. That goes for everybody. Pill poppers, shopping mall zombies, unmarried librarians, long haul truckers, a cafeteria Catholic here, a mattress actress there. Like, everybody, man. So you want to go? Dance it over in your mind.'

Jean fussed with her wig as the booming traffic continued to pass by. *Why not speak to this Glasscock fellow?* First, she would chide him for all his unsound methods. Then she would lecture him on the perils of drug diversion. *And I'll remind him that mere opiates should never help anyone triumph in the struggle with the self.*

As gracefully as a rhythmic gymnast's twirling ribbon, a fragment of yellow caution tape blew past Jean's shoulder. *How beautiful.* She attempted to say something but suddenly realised that she spoke with a lisp. *Oh God, I'm reverting back to my childhood.*

She turned back to the girl. 'Please excuse me. It's just that I'm feeling so much dread these days. Suddenly . . . I've got everything to lose.'

The girl felt at her elbow. 'Yeah, you don't look well.' The girl raised her hand to her face and picked at some of her acne scars. 'So should we check out the wizard?'

'Yes, take me to the wizard,' Jean answered, struggling to make the lisp go away.

'No sweat. What's your name by the way, or like do you go by an alias?'

'Call me Jean Selwyn. And what about you? Have *you* a summer name?'

'Uh, you could call me . . . how's about . . . uh . . . Heather Paisley-Jones.'

'Very well. Good to make your acquaintance, Miss Heather Paisley-Jones.'

'Yeah, likewise.' Heather guided Jean across Sunset Boulevard and into an all-night launderette reeking of chlorine bleach. 'Like, where's Glasscock at?' she asked a dishwater blonde dressed in a tie-dyed tee and yoke skirt.

'The dealer? Like, he blew town.'

'Yeah? So . . . like, where did he go?'

'Hell, if I know. Maybe he went to Santa Cruz to get new threads. I'm pretty sure one of his disciples works as a stock clerk at the Fashion Bug there.' Without another word, the blonde walked over to the wall, tore apart a movie poster for *Striporama*, and replaced it with a movie poster for *The Left Hand of God.* Afterward, she passed through the soft, pleasing clatter of a beaded curtain that served as the doorway into the launderette's back room.

When the dishwater blonde failed to return, Heather guided Jean outside and introduced her to a buxom redhead named Mercy Ann Gillies. After a round of small talk, Heather took the redhead's hand. 'We're looking for a pill kick. Like where's Mr Glasscock? Like he's in town, yeah?'

'No, didn't he split? Yeah man, like he's living in some freak farm commune out along the road to Idyllwild. Or else he's hiding from the fuzz back at Black Sands Beach.'

At that point, Heather took Jean down to a broken-down bus and waved to the Korean girl sitting in the door well. 'Hey sister, like I'm trying to get a line on the wizard.'

'That dude? Like, I heard he cut the scene and thumbed

a ride to San Francisco. Don't ask me why. Like, hey man, for all we know, he went to reset the emergency third-rail power trip. Or maybe he's dealing. Or maybe he's got an old lady up north. What about that chick who bobs her freaking hair in a French twist? She lives near Russian Hill or Fisherman's Wharf or someplace like that. Shit, I don't know.'

'Yeah right. Whatever. Keep the faith, sister.' With that, Heather guided Jean three blocks further along and then stopped a brunette dressed in a pleated archeress gown. 'Like, hey man, do you know where the wizard might be? And don't do me like he ain't around.'

'Try the Alta Cienega Motel,' the brunette said, scratching at some of her glittery-blue eye shadow. 'Me and him shacked up there a week ago, and, like, what a shindig.'

'Hey man, like who cares about last week? Like, where's the wizard at right now?'

'Right now?' For a moment, the brunette scanned the sky. 'He's probably off riding his atomic-fuelled surfboard. Yeah, man, like maybe he's gone to have himself a cosmic rap session with Galactus.' All the time laughing, the brunette walked off.

Heather turned to Jean. 'Don't lose your cool. We'll find the wizard. If you want, we could check Ventura Boulevard. Like sometimes he hangs out down by the burn barrels.'

A vice girl dressed in a jungle-green gown and white vinyl go-go boots emerged from a nearby café. She tossed a slice of banana bread into the rubbish bin, and then she vanished down the alley.

Heather walked over to the rubbish bin and dug through the refuse. When she located the discarded treat, she popped it into her mouth, chewed some and swallowed.

For shame. Jean looked to the polluted sky and sought to discern the stars.

Heather belched. 'You know what I could go for right now? Scottish beef stew. Yeah, and for dessert, a dish of Dalmatian pudding.'

Jean sat on the curbstone, not three feet from a rat's rotting carcass. She looked westward, hoping to catch a glimpse of some glorious, astronomical body having only just arisen over the ocean. *How about Alpha Centauri or Isis or Calliope?*

As fate would have it, a decaying comet flashing like tally lights fell through the smog.

Heather sat beside her. 'Hey, old lady. By any chance, are you a nun? Are you looking to enlighten me and all that?'

'No, I'm no bride of Christ.'

'That's a relief because like even though I was born on a cusp, everything's cool.'

'No, you lack *direction*. I'd say you haven't anything to believe in because no one's ever taught you the answers to life's big philosophical questions.'

'Hey, man, like I got the wizard to help me come to terms.'

'But what does *he* know about anything? He's not much better than a pusher, no? A scoundrel like that, he traffics in barbiturates and such.'

'Listen, if you think I'm one of those nobody runaways, I'm not.' Heather caressed her swollen elbow. 'Sure, the guards down at the studio shine me on. But someday, I know I'll make it. One time I almost got an audition for Diamond Joe Esposito, and that's no jive. And I happen to know the street where Paula Prentiss lives, and, like, I got a friend who knows a cat who lives next door to Dorothea Duckworth's press agent.'

Jean remained silent and fussed with her wig, until she inadvertently managed to pull loose several unruly yak hairs.

Heather wrapped her hand tight around her elbow. 'Yeah,

and I know where the English actress, Vivien Pickles, buys her shoes. It's only a matter of time before I get my big break. And before you can say knife, I'll be working on some groovy soundstage, and I'll be totally balling, and, like, I'll have my own crash pad on Hollywood Boulevard, and it'll be way better than those cold-water dumps the realtors advertise in the *Evening Outlook*. Believe it.' With that, Heather stood and marched over to a coin-operated newspaper rack and jiggled the door handle. Her efforts to pilfer a copy having proven futile, Heather continued along the street.

Jean followed her into a vast, empty parking lot that must have served as a farmer's market by day. Here and there, an array of placards advertised various types of produce:

Gala apples all the way from New Zealand!
Sweet lady apples from Malibu Canyon!
Juicy purple heirloom tomatoes, only a dollar a pound!

Heather, her left arm shaking uncontrollably, looked down and studied one of the cigarette butts lying at her feet. 'Man, if I had any bread, like I'd invest in big tobacco.'

Jean struggled to speak but could not do so. Until Fingal had realised his revelation and had shared his avowal, she had nothing to offer—no association of ideas by which she might commence a meaningful exchange with someone.

As if from out of nowhere, a night-mist-blue G.T. 500 Mustang with an opaque windscreen pulled up and stopped to idle.

'Well, what do you know?' Heather walked forward, inadvertently bumping Jean's bruised elbow. 'Hey man, like I got to split because this here's my big daddy, and like he's probably hopped up on a bad bag or something.'

For the first time, Jean noticed several needle-puncture wounds in the girl's arm, and the revelation made Jean tremble all over. 'Just remember to make the best of things.'

'Yeah, go easy yourself, and don't take a ride from strangers.' At that point, the young lady climbed into the vehicle's passenger side and closed the door.

As the pony car backed away, Jean sat upon an empty crate and imagined herself sitting at the kitchen table back home, Fingal in the opposite chair. 'Have you any idea how spiritually deprived this nation has become?' she would ask him. 'We've got to help people triumph over the fog of *addiction*.'

Most likely, he would shrug. 'Have you found the lost scene from *King Kong*?'

She closed her eyes and envisioned the border—the Mexican drug cartels smuggling contraband into California. *Who do they work for? Russia? China?* Before long, her thoughts turned back to the here and now—the vagabonds and runaways. *How splendid it would be to build a state-aid community, where they could live and work. And in the name of public morals and civic-mindedness, the state legislature could require that all college students must complete a semester-long practicum in which said students teach the homeless people fanciful things such as arts and crafts. And Sacramento could establish little villages for the demented, too, and if they took their anti-psychotic medications, the state could reward them with field trips. Yes, indeed, how good that would be.*

In the shadows just to her left, an object suddenly came into view—a worn, imitation-leather overnighter covered in record-album hype stickers. Had the burning man left the bag there?

Jean reached inside it and drew forth its only contents—a bloodied halter top. At once, she dropped the garment.

From several blocks away, the deafening cacophony of squad-car sirens awoke, and traces of riot gas wafted through the air. Jean returned to her feet and continued back out onto Sunset Boulevard. *Ah, yes, the boulevard of broken dreams.*

Chapter Twenty-Five

FINGAL. Evangeline, Connecticut. Summer, 1967.

Late one night, every impulse told Fingal to attempt to make a successful passage through the gateway. *Aye, the time has come.* He climbed out of bed, reached beneath the box springs, and grabbed the soapstone krater in which he had confined the entity. *I'm poised for victory, I am.*

Beaten and battered from his erstwhile obsession with testing every last detail of Jean's work, he paused in the downstairs hallway and drew a deep breath. *Have I even got the strength to continue?* In the den, he watched the last scene of the late show—*Forbidden Planet,* a science-fiction fantasy all about a Prospero figure who releases a monstrous reflection of his most primal urges.

As the ending credits rolled, a voice arose from the krater: 'How long till you return me back inside yourself?'

'In a trice, burning man. Tonight, I shoe the goose.' He checked himself over. As it so happened, he had dressed himself in the things that Jean had recently purchased on his behalf—a silk-polyester robe and a pair of fuzzy pink faux-fur slippers. *I look like a bloody fool.* Despite all, he continued outside.

The summer night thrummed with the stridulation of two thousand or more crickets, and straight ahead, the swimming pool's bright lights shone upward through the waters. Over to the left, a steady breeze stirred a few of the lilac trees.

With a system of pulleys, he removed his invention from the barn and placed both the power source and the arched gateway in the backyard.

From within the cabana, a childlike voice called out his name. He turned toward the hut to investigate and then passed through the sheer curtains dangling from the cabana's rooftop.

The voice belonged to the little boy from next door, Micah Stroud. He sat at the taffeta-glass table dressed in a pair of plaid pyjamas.

'You there, laddie, why you dossing about in the middle of the night?'

'I came over to ask if you caught *Forbidden Planet* on the late show.'

'What do you care about the late show?'

'You missed the greatest picture ever made.' Micah stood and reeled around a few times, as if looking for something. 'Have you noticed my invisible cat anywhere about?'

'Listen here. You remind me of a prodigy from long ago. A whiz kid, you'd be. But that's just the trouble. Forget all about me. Go home, laddie. Go to bed. Maybe in your dreams you'll find your mouser.'

'Yeah, she's probably just about the best cat in the world. Yeah, she's got a knack for telekinesis. And she's really huge. Probably as big as a brontosaurus. Do you know how I made her? *Simple*. I did it the same way they did it in the late show. She's a product of all my thoughts and stuff. And I built her brain out of millions and billions of integrated circuits, so she'd be part-robot, yeah, with the ability to speed-read and remember all kinds of things. And since her brain happens to be a sophisticated computation device and all that, she's got herself the power to hail on all frequencies and broadcast her innermost thoughts into someone else's mind. Just like the power of telepathy. She's got posi-traction, too.'

'*Enough*. I got no time to play silly buggers.'

'Hey, do you think maybe you could raise my invisible cat on that crazy radio gadget thing you got there?' Micah pointed at the Instruktor where it protruded from the front pocket in Fingal's robe.

'This here's no radio, laddie. No, no. What I got here would be nothing less than the weapon what'd save the world.' His hand trembling some, Fingal reached into his pocket and produced the apparatus—what a fine example of make-do engineering. Years before, in the heart of the Serengeti, he had mended the instrument with pieces of Tanzanian soda ash and Kenyan titanium ore.

Fingal slipped the Instruktor back into his pocket, and Micah walked off through the cabana's translucent curtains. The little boy stopped at the edge of the pool, crouched beside the brass skimmer lid, and removed the basket, then brought it over to the table.

Fingal scowled. 'Put the damn thing back.'

Undeterred, Micah reached into the basket and pulled out a hairball glowing a metallic, prism-white silver. 'I think maybe my invisible cat must've coughed this up into the water.'

Over to the left, the power source suddenly creaked with a shrill clamour resembling the high-pitched drone of an atomic clock, and the arched gateway filled with a royal-yellow radiance.

Micah picked his nose. 'What do you know? I think my invisible cat must've triggered the trembler switch on your time machine or whatever the hell that thing would be. Remember me to tell my cat to walk on her tippy toes from now on, okay?'

The soapstone krater in his hand, Fingal walked over to the gateway. *Why the devil did me invention power on?* Whatever had happened, he placed the soapstone krater upon the earth and removed the lid—and just like that, a fragile wisp of orange smoke curled into the air. *There you be.* With the help of the Instruktor, he compelled the gassy fumes to wrap themselves around his person.

'Hey, what's that stuff floating about your waist?' Micah asked.

'I made me a good conjure, I did.' Fingal dropped the Instruktor in a bed of dead elderflowers. Then with the sounds of stridulation growing louder—or so it seemed—he drew a second deep breath. Without a backward glance, he stepped forward then, into the gateway's ethereal incandescence. *Way out and up we go.*

He felt as if he must be falling. Given the whole effect, he should have registered absolute horror. Regardless, as he imagined himself nosediving through the wondrous glare, he experienced no disquiet. Instead, he laughed the way he would do if someone were tickling his ribs. And for what felt like an eternity, he plummeted through the gleam. *How long before me body gathers enough velocity to curve the space-time continuum?*

At the tip of his nose, a torrid, smouldering current collided with an eddy of cool, fresh air, and the impact served to gently bend a dozen rays of light.

Brills. He closed his eyes and imagined himself an explorer having mastered the art of trans-dimensional travel.

And now I traverse the corridors of time, each one of them big celestial hallways what connect the universe. Aye, I'm travelling from the present and onward back to the mysterious atom what preceded this world. He raised his arms. *So . . . how much time has transpired between the formation of the cosmos and that preexisting realm? Whatever the answer happens to be, soon, I'll arrive at that primal, foregoing domain. And in so doing, I'll come face to face with the Godhead.*

All around, the air grew cold—so cold that he wondered if he felt hot. *Could it be the magic of time dilation I'd be feeling?*

The rate of the illusory free fall increased, and he opened his eyes. *I must be moving at the speed of light.*

All around, the effulgence shone brighter, which made his muscles tighten. *How long till I dissolve into cosmic antimatter?*

Little by little, his arms and legs seemed to grow, until it appeared as if they stretched out for miles. *Aye, dead brilliant.*

Slowly, the fumes unwrapped themselves from his body. Then they rose a foot or so above his brow, only to assume the shape of a tiara that gradually served to enhalo him.

Twice, he shook his fist at the smoke. 'Go on back inside me then. Get on back where you belong, you bloody git.'

Some of the fumes obeyed, at which point he tasted something like burnt, bitter ash upon his tongue—a salty sensation something like French onion soup. Then, as the exhaust dissolved into his scalp, the rate of the seeming free fall grew unbearable, until he stumbled forward through the gateway and fell into a patch of butterfly weed.

At his back, the royal-yellow glare expired. And now the backyard grew dark again, as if the whole expanse were an outdoor theatre, but the electricity had just gone out, leaving all the players to talk to one another in the dark, everyone invisible to the audience.

A palpable odour lingered about him—a potent, dizzying blend of ash-baked vegetables.

Deep inside his person, a sound as of a clockwork pump thumped a few times, and then the peculiar, muffled clamour fell silent. Had an aspect of the projection only just dissolved into the deepest recesses of his psyche? Despite the dim light, he examined the smoky cloud of gas particles presently coiling about his shoulder. *Has the swirling haze diminished?* He shook his head. *Of course, the fumes have diminished.* He pulled at the stubble on his chin, and then his arm fell to his side. *A fine boffin, I'd be.*

The night grew darker—as if someone had replaced the moon with some obsolete technology, a moderator lamp.

He lay as still as could be. For a moment or two, he felt as if he had been buried alive, and he could feel the weight of the earth bearing down upon him. *Are me lungs collapsing?*

After a while, he wondered if the sensation felt more like drowning—as if having placed weights upon his ankles so as to hasten his descent, he dove to the bottom of the ocean. *And I can't hold me breath no longer.* With that, he grabbed the Instruktor and compelled the remaining wisps of orange smoke to flit back into the krater. Then he replaced the lid, rolled onto his back, and sought to make sense of the sky—the countless stars. *What a graceful glow.*

All around, meanwhile, the crickets' ongoing stridulation grew louder and increasingly felicitous, something like the sound of sleigh bells.

He hummed a few measures from Telemann's *Weihnachtskantate*, but he could not manage more and gasped for breath.

Micah walked over. 'What happened?' The little boy's cheeks flushed. 'Did you maybe travel into the past? Did you go so far back you arrived at the future?'

'You think I'd be a chrononaut, do you? No, no. I had me a diversion, that's all.'

'Somehow you don't look the same. Could it be you're suffering the side effects of time travel?' Micah walked off for a moment or two, but when he returned, his eyes flashed. 'I just had me a big talk with my invisible cat, and she says the energy field you went through probably transformed you into a robot like the one in the late show, *Forbidden Planet*. Either that or you went and maybe mutated into some lifelike doll, the kind Peter Pan Playthings Ltd puts out, the one where they rig up a mechanical pump so that it looks like the crazy thing has an honest-to-goodness heartbeat.'

'Why don't you go on home? Aye, go on. Get back into bed, lad. Dream of time travellers, spellfarers.'

'Yeah, and my invisible cat says one of your eyeballs has probably turned into something a little bit like the lens from one of them box cameras. And now that very eyeball clocks stuff perfectly. Even from about fourteen million miles away.'

Fingal shook his finger at the little boy. 'Why must you engage in all kinds of confabulation? Don't chant the poker, laddie. No, no.'

'You know what else? My invisible cat says half your bean must've remade itself into some kind of computation device, like the ones they make down there at Texas Instruments.'

'I'll tell you what's happened. I've grown more whole than I were before. There's much less to burden me, and so I rejoice. That'd be what you espy, laddie. Aye, you notice the thrill of redemption streaming through me bones.' Fingal turned onto his side. 'Now go on home and get to bed, laddie. *Forthwith*. Let me rest and permit all me thoughts to go free, aye, so that the long-awaited revelation should announce itself.' Fingal returned onto his back and looked to the stars. 'I must let me unconscious mind permit the whole epiphany to surface. Even now, I must resolve the riddle of the universe. And I must seek to fathom the one true metaphor by which to explain the origins of all the cosmos.'

Micah walked off, and as the crickets' ongoing drone grew deafening loud, Fingal curled into a ball. *I'll let me thoughts wander.* He shifted to his left. *Mustn't make no haste.* He kicked off his slippers. *Aye, the perfect myth shall come to me in the fullness of time.* He shifted to his right, until the earth felt soft against his weary back. *Aye, what bliss.*

In time, a sound somewhere between a tooth whistle and a pucker whistle arose from the depths of his being.

Fingal tapped his temples. *Would that be you then? So what're you doing down there in your council flat? Do you recall the deal we had? If so, go on and tell me the origins of the cosmos. Aye, let the answer issue forth.*

Patience. *Soon, you shall envision the force that preexisted the world. And what a sullen, fiery presence.*

Sure enough, Fingal envisioned that preexisting force; the godly creature resembled the fiery projection itself. Still, the whole idea did make perfect sense. If the recesses of a person's unconscious mind did in fact house the secret to unravelling the riddle of the universe, then it stood to reason that there must be a telling parallel between the prime mover and the fiery, diabolical projection, the burning man.

The stridulation grew quieter and quieter, until the crickets sounded like a pair of amateur violinists suffering from stage fright.

At the same time, from the depths of Fingal's being, the sensual music returned—the sound of someone whistling.

A second time, Fingal tapped at his temples. *Why'd you*

always seek to cajole everyone into setting themselves aflame? Did it have something to do with the Godhead? Could it be that some like pathology always afflicted Him? Did He ever set Himself ablaze?

And what if He did? What if the godlike force that preceded the cosmos had always yearned to resolve the riddle as to whether something eternal might be omnipotent enough to destroy itself? To learn the answer and to resolve the paradox, that woefully unstable force that preceded creation would have had no choice but to explode in the selfsame light that served to create the cosmos.

So the Big Bang itself . . . the whole thing was a kind of immolation rite?

Yes, *but in the end, the godlike force neither succeeded in destroying itself nor failed to do so. Instead, the fiery attempt at non-existence merely* transformed *the preexisting world. And in phase, that erstwhile pinprick of primal, ineffable energy came to assume the guise of this . . . unpalatable universe.*

Fingal stared at the soapstone krater. *Listen, burning man. Now I understand you. Way down there in the grey matter of me psyche, you've never forgotten the cataclysmic explosion what served as the commencement of things. Aye, you grasp the sorry fact that the creation of the world and the immolation of the gods was always one and the same. No, the creator never intended to create the world. He only ever hoped to top himself . . . by* fire.

So you've learned something. What does it matter, though? Don't you feel greatly fatigued? Overwhelmed? I doubt you'll ever manage to learn all.

With whatever strength that he could muster, Fingal took the krater into his right hand and then grabbed the Instruktor with the left. Slowly, he returned into the house.

Back in the den, the doleful sound of dead air roared from the television's speakers, so he switched off the Magnavox and sat upon the sofa. Before long, he pictured Jean sitting at his side. 'With dogged determination, I got some of the infernal apparition back into me being,' he would tell her. 'Aye, a part of the burning man, he's doing porridge now.'

Over in the corner, the floor lamp's lightbulb dimmed. Suddenly, the glow that once illumined the room shone as weakly as an archaic, clockwork-driven light source—the kind that a playhouse might employ to light the audience members' way during intermission.

The sound of music echoed throughout his body—electric chimes playing in time with a set of lightning bells. What an impossibly intricate beat—the timing associated with modern jazz, or perhaps even Old-African polyrhythms.

He dragged himself off the sofa and crawled past the end table. When he reached the door, he paused and pictured Jean standing at his side. 'What about you there, hen? Have you located the lost scene from *King Kong*?' The more he thought it over, the more he doubted that she would even trouble herself to answer. Instead, she would turn away and flip through a dog-eared street atlas of Los Angeles.

After a long delay, he made his way back into the guest room. His breath coming in gasps and grunts and rasps and retractions, he placed both the Instruktor and the soapstone krater beside the wickerwork hamper.

A moment or two later, as he lay in bed, a noise as of an eruption rang out from someplace outside. *Has one of me neighbours switched on her Electrolux carpet-sweeper, or could it be some badly-overheated star has gone nova?* He chose to believe the latter, for the idea seemed fitting. He closed his eyes and endeavoured to hum along with the cacophony.

Chapter Twenty-Six

Early one evening, Fingal returned through the arched gateway. When he exited the other side, he imagined himself a film actor suddenly exiting the frame, and then he fell to the earth and lay there. For the duration of that time, he sought to speak but could not do so. No matter how forcibly he endeavoured to move his lips and tongue, his mind commanded no power over the rest of his body. *It's Jean, she'd be to blame. I know it. She must've done something wrong.*

After a while, he sought to turn his head enough to look at the power source. When he realised that he had grown too fatigued to manage, he contented himself to draw in a series of deep breaths. *No, it's me own damn fault.*

He fell asleep. In his dreams, he imagined himself a player in RKO's *King Kong*, the giant spiders devouring him.

At nine o'clock he awoke, staggered back into the house, and put the krater on the knickknack shelf in the den. *Rest awhile.* No sooner had he slumped into the club chair than he hallucinated the presence of a movie camera in the room. *It's the burning man, he's making movies.* The preposterous notion did seem possible; perhaps the diabolical burning man intended for his film to be nothing more than a slow-motion zoom-in shot, a study of Fingal's face. 'Don't over-light me, eh? If you've got too much glare, no one should have a good look at all me bonny lines and contours.'

For several hours he contented himself to watch the light falling through the dimly lit room, until a fragment of the orange pall arose into the air, as if through some minute crack in the soapstone vessel. 'Don't do nothing to test me resolve. I might be feeling a bit knackered, but even so, I'll not let you go free.'

The vapour swirled about the room, so much so that the current toppled the plastic tray-table strewn with the remains of yesterday's brunch—three charcoal-roasted beets that had come to smell like stoneware clay.

He rested his heels on the footstool. Then he switched on the Magnavox, just in time to catch the closing credits to the late show—*Now, Voyager*.

When the exit music ceased, 'The Star-Spangled Banner' commenced. At the same time, the picture turned to a heroic shot of Old Glory. When the hymn concluded, a blizzard of noise suddenly dominated the screen.

Despite the roar, he crawled forward and rested his brow against the television set's tuning controls.

Still very much free, the puff of smoke drifted close to his shoulder, and a disembodied voice spoke up: 'You'll never complete your labours. Summoning me was nothing next to making me dissolve back into your mind. I've grown *strong*.'

The cacophony of the electromagnetic snow seemed to grow louder, so Fingal attempted to turn the volume down. He could not even raise his hand, though, and he fell back onto the floor.

'Could it be you find me a wee bit irksome?' the voice asked in a whisper.

'Silence, I say.'

'Yes, I've got you look gravely ill. I do believe you're fordone.'

'Naff off.' Fingal slipped out of his robe. Naked but for his fuzzy pink faux-fur slippers, he crawled back outside. When he reached the power source, he lay in the grass and studied the plugboard. *What if I make some adjustments so that the next time I pass through the gate, the experience shan't leave me feeling all so bloodless?*

After a long delay, he reached for the bottle of Japan wax with which he had often greased the various moving parts. Then he applied a liberal portion of the compound to the device that managed the radiosensitive radiation. His muscles stretching as if soon they must surely tear apart, he held his breath and dumped the rest of the gummy tallow into the copper-alloy tube that measured the mechanism's electrostatic levels. *There we are.*

Dressed in a gown with a Peter Pan collar, Mrs. Stroud emerged from her house. She walked over to one of the chestnut trees, passed by the hammock chair dangling from one of the boughs, and checked the weatherglass that she had nailed to the trunk.

Fingal fell to his hands and knees. *What's she doing? Might this be some kind of data-science project? Maybe she's working for IBM Corporation.*

With folded hands, Mrs. Stroud looked to the sky. 'Help my summer flowers grow,' she implored the stars. 'I beg you, from the bottom of my heart.'

Fingal wrinkled his nose. *She's moon-gardening.* And now he heard footsteps. Micah emerged from behind Jean's barn, the mischievous little boy dressed in Madras-plaid pyjamas and wearing a Roy Rogers gun belt wrapped around his waist. When he espied Fingal lying there, Micah scrunched up his forehead and waved.

Fingal crawled over to the arched gateway and gathered together some tree litter and butterfly weed so as to conceal his nakedness.

The insufferable little boy stopped not three feet away, pulled a toy laser from one of the gun belt's holsters, and pointed the weapon at Fingal's gut. 'Don't move a muscle or I'll open fire.'

'Why you always knocking around like a Greenwich goose? Go home and get back in bed.'

'That's enough out of you. *Beware*. What I got in my hot little hand here just happens to be the Wolverine Toy Company's latest space-pilot plasma death ray. Friction-powered, for when the going gets rough. So don't make me zap you.'

'*Please*. I'm too old for all your foolery.'

'Hey, what's happened to your eyes?'

'My eyes? How do you mean, laddie?'

'Well, they're all flashing and stuff. Yeah, they're blinking like you've become part-robot. Like you have yourself a powder-coat finish, and we'll have to find a place to mend your broken parts. Like a big metal-fabricating company. But don't worry. My dad owns a bunch of shares in some real neat ironworks in King of Prussia, Pennsylvania. My dad says it's good stock too. "A sure thing", he says.'

Fingal pointed at the little boy. 'Why you chaffing? Listen, laddie. As soon as you get the chance, you ought to go home and get back into your bed.'

Before Fingal could say anything more, the wisp of smoke from before sailed out the mudroom window, and the sinister presence swirled about his ankle.

Several times over, he jerked his foot. 'No more of your goddamn guff,' he told the remains of the entity. 'Get back inside the house.'

Micah planted his feet in an open, wide stance, trained the toy gun at the fumes, and then squeezed the plastic pistol's trigger.

Fingal turned away to scan Mrs. Stroud's flower garden. The woman had plainly returned inside, so he turned back to Micah. 'Here's your one chance to get back into your diggings, laddie, and if you do so all good and gingerly, your maw shan't notice onythin'.'

Micah slipped the toy gun back into its holster and removed from the other a contrivance resembling a children's walkie-talkie. 'Look at this thing here. You might think it's just another wireless, Flashmatic television-remote, maybe the kind you find in your mom's junk drawer, but no. Yesterday, I modified this here gizmo so I could use it to talk to my invisible cat.'

'There's a good fellow. Aye, you'd be a quick study. That said, won't you bugger off and go home?'

Micah lay on his back, held the remote to his ear, and acted as if he had detected the imaginary cat's voice. And then he placed his hands on his belly. 'You should hear the crazy stuff my invisible cat says. She probably knows more than you and me put together. Who knows how the hell she does it? Unless maybe she's some kind of idiot savant. Yeah, maybe someday she'll found the greatest toy company ever. And she'll make robots that look real sharp.'

The vapour uncoiled itself from Fingal's ankle, drifted over to Mrs. Stroud's birdbath, and reeled around the pedestal.

'Where do you think you're going?' Fingal followed, only

to espy something balanced upon the very edge of the basin. The poised, carefully positioned yet slightly teetering object proved to be a book called *The Motions Of The Moon And The True Aspects Of The Planets.*

The title alone made him think, and he paused to imagine the silence and solemnity of other worlds—all the planets and their sprightly moons. *Aye, Europa and Titan and Miranda and Saturn's Phoebe too. So many others.* He looked to the night sky. *The chemicals what fell from all the constellations, just why did them life-granting substances settle here?* His fingers dancing, he reached for the book.

From all directions, meanwhile, the cacophony of stridulation commenced—what sounded like myriad crickets, enough to overwhelm the entire world.

He clenched his jaw. *No everyday ephemeris could ever resolve the mystery as to why life initiated here.* He thought of the creation. *If the Big Bang had in fact been the immolation of some godly force, could it be that some imperishable aspect of that noble, eternal substance had willed the bountiful compounds to descend through the Milky Way's galactic halo and to continue down into Earth's gravity field?* He dropped his hand.

From all directions, the crickets' stridulation grew louder—as if they longed to tell him something, to reinvigorate him perhaps, or to admonish him regarding some unseen peril.

He made a fist. *A quantum of energy resembling a deity's stream of unconscious must have willed all life to commence here on this planet. But why? For what purpose? Why?*

A beam of lunar light fell through the boughs of a pignut-hickory tree standing off to the side. How mesmerising the beauty of it all—especially the way the gentle, creamy radiance shone through the crown.

Again, he turned to the night sky. *How now*? Like anyone

else who had ever gazed heavenward, he asked himself what might explain the grand scheme of things—the intricate process of biotic evolution, the precise patterns of nature, the hominid creatures' languid, prosaic transformation into humankind. The crickets' drone growing louder, he reeled about and then fell to the earth. Before long, he saluted one of the celestial bodies directly above. 'What means this business of sentience? *Why* does any living thing exist?'

Micah drew near and nudged Fingal's thigh. 'Hey, what gives? Are you dying?'

Fingal gathered some of the spiderwort together to better conceal his nakedness. 'Get yourself inside your house. Go to sleep.'

The little boy fussed with his Roy Rogers gun belt. 'What're you doing over here in my mom's garden?'

'I'm watching the way luminosity falls from the firmament. Think of how the sun's blinding rays fall onto our world. That's how life must've commenced. The immolated God's unconscious mind must've commingled with the stardust. And then the unconsciousness fell from the sky and dropped off into the Sea of Hebrides. And way down there in the abyss, the energy, the chemicals, the light must've inspirited this otherwise *in*organic world with the vital spark.'

The breeze whistled and wailed and stirred the spiderwort, and Micah once more held the remote to his ear. A moment later, he slipped the device back into its proper holster. 'My invisible cat says the big, huge secret of life would be shamanism. 'Each and every living thing has its very own soul,' she tells me.'

'No, that kind of superstition don't meet with the realm of possibility. I'd be talking about the immolated God and the smouldering remains of his psyche, and how it happened to settle here and take the various avatars of all what *lives*, all them spores primordial floating about, all them flavoursome herbs some peasant lass might plant by seed.'

The back door opened, and Mrs. Stroud returned outside. 'Micah Buckley Stroud, what're you doing out here past your bedtime? I'll give you one minute to get back into your room.'

The little boy breathed heavily. 'But what about Fingal? He gets to stay up till dawn, and like all the best timefarers and chrononauts, Fingal gets to wander off into the future whenever he pleases, and he travels backward in time, and he gets to pervert the course of history, and he gets to erase people from existence, just like they vanished into a parallel universe made up of antiparticles and stuff.'

Gasping for breath, Mrs. Stroud leered at Fingal. 'Just what've you been teaching my child? And put some clothes on. Have some respect for yourself.' With that, the irate woman grabbed Micah's arm and dragged him inside.

A little while later, once the pall had wrapped itself around Fingal's neck, he crawled back onto Jean's property and returned into the house.

In time, the fumes uncoiled from his person and proceeded to swirl about the volume lying upon the kitchen table—a copy of *Betty Crocker's Cook Book* open to the page containing the recipe for Cornish game hen.

His belly growling, Fingal crawled over to the pantry and downed a box of Kellogg's apple-currant 'delicious anytime' pop-tarts.

'Let me go free,' a disembodied voice pleaded all the while.

'No, I shan't ever free you. For I've devoted myself to wisdom, the virtue of which ought to preserve me from all your deceit. And despite whatever you may think, all me faculties would be in square nick. And even if I'd be well-nigh past a hundred years old, nevertheless, the whole of me psyche works as right as a quartz movement now that I'd be diverting *you* back inside me noodle, and when the last remnant settles into place, I know I'll be feeling as pristine as a knee-sock what's just come back from the launderette. And I'll be feeling fresh as an eel, all of me blood a-leaping.'

Slowly, the wisp of smoke drifted about the pantry. First, the fumes circled a box of custard powder. Then the diabolical presence swirled about a jar of pickled onions before exiting the pantry altogether and sailing over toward the electric toaster oven. Not three seconds later, the fine wisp of smoke assumed various shades of purple before guiding Fingal out into the hallway.

When they reached the den, Fingal slipped back into his silk robe. Then he walked over to the knickknack shelf and tapped the soapstone krater. 'Get back inside here, you.' But the emanation merely darted about faster. Fingal shook his head. 'Get on back into the damn jug, I say. Let me work. Let me give a keen thought to all me obsessions philisophical.'

The wisp of smoke drifted over toward the krater and then darted off into the opposite direction.

'May the goddamn Curse of Scotland put you in your place.' Fingal made his way over to the television set and looked into the tumultuous, electromagnetic snow. In that moment the ardent cloud of pixels should have appeared as nothing more than a shapeless maelstrom, but no; the dead air resembled a living entity, a ghostly alien organism.

The longer that Fingal studied the dizzying display, the more he longed to believe it a benevolent being, a creature sophisticated enough to perform ambitious calculations. He placed his palm flush against the screen. 'If I should learn the great maxim that I seek, what do I do with said knowledge?'

The wondrous commotion provided no response, so he slammed his fist against the side antenna input and then switched the set off.

The sudden quietude must have intimidated the remains of the spectre, for the fumes darted off into the furthest corner of the room.

Fingal grabbed the Instruktor and depressed the activation switch, at which point the wayward pall finally returned into the soapstone krater. Quickly, Fingal closed the lid as tightly as he could. *Why not sleep?* He crawled off to the guest room but decided that he felt much too tense to retire for the night. Perhaps if he checked the ultra-high-frequency channels, he could find something amusing to watch. *What about a horror show hosted by Vampira?*

When he returned into the den, he knelt before the Magnavox. *Aye, let's have ourselves a right fine picture show.*

The unit popped and sputtered, as if some of the inner filaments and phosphors must be contracting. When the power returned, Fingal searched all the channels. At that late hour, though, no one broadcast anything other than test patterns. *What about* Space Ghost *or* Petticoat Junction*?* He would have settled for *The Patty Duke Show* or *I Dream of Jeannie*. As much as anything, he hoped to find a channel broadcasting either *Jonny Quest* or *The Flintstones*. When all hope was lost, he switched the volume off and contented himself to observe the silent interference. Gradually, the static came to resemble something like a multitude of larvae feeding on some carcass.

He adjusted the contrast dial. 'Why the process of biotic evolution? Given the fact that the primal light of creation and the immolation of the gods must be one and the same, then why didn't the deity's remains simply *decompose*?' The silent interference proffered no response, so he rested his brow against the television.

'Already, I fathom the origins of the universe,' he continued after a long delay. 'And maybe I've always grasped the attested meaning of life. The whole damn thing, it wasn't never onythin' more nor less than the nexus between the origins of the universe and the very purpose of civilisation. Aye, that interzone between the two. But what'd be the purpose of civilisation? Tell me *why* life had to commence, won't you? *Why* civilisation?'

Fifteen minutes later, he made his way back outside, where the ongoing stridulation thrummed as loudly as ever.

He imagined the ringing of the crickets to be the echoes of the Big Bang, and he sought to conceptualise the cosmos—the fibres holding the stars in place, the dark matter and dark photons and omnipresent energy that govern all the ineffable patterns by which natural phenomena recur, everything coming and going, as if by design. Every last bit of existence would be but an aspect of the same age-old, exacting process—the process by which the doomed God's afterglow, the primal radiation, seeks to do something *other* than to simply evanesce.

After a while, Fingal lay upon the earth and looked upon the starry sky. *Why life*? *Why civilisation*? *Why*?

Chapter Twenty-Seven

To the best of his knowledge, Fingal had just succeeded in sending the last remnant of the entity back into his unconscious mind. So he lay upon the earth. *Feeling right infirm, I am.* Like some intrepid explorer having only just arrived from some faraway planet, the crushing, all-oppressive weight of Earth's gravitational pull pinned him down. *I know what's happened. The burning man has beheaded me.* For a moment or two, Fingal considered the notion that a person might register consciousness after death. *Could something like that be possible?* Like a maudlin schoolboy, he thought of the French Revolution—the guillotine. *What if poor Marie Antoinette experienced a moment of awareness as the executioner lifted her severed head to show it to the unforgiving crowd?*

In time Fingal resolved to check whether his head did in fact remain attached to his body. *If so, I'll scratch at me stubble.* Alas, he could not even manage to lift his hand.

Little by little, as the late-morning hours passed by, he detected the scent of wine in the air, and then he tasted something like pomegranate juice at the back of his mouth.

Aye, I'm half-dead. Just like poor Persephone.

At midday the sun shone upon the lawn with a blinding light that made the whole expanse gleam like an ancient Athenian stage. All through the long, hot afternoon, he sought to stand. Time after time, he succeeded only in falling back.

At eight o'clock a dozen clouds came along, and he wondered if the sudden darkness resembled the kind of volcanic ash that had often polluted the Greek skies, leaving both the ancient panicked actors and the ancient panicked audience running for shelter.

Late that night, he managed to crawl all the way to the back door. *Finally. I'm going from strength to strength, I am.* He made his back inside and breathed in; the house smelled like ash-roasted beetroots.

The clock in the buffet cabinet struck the midnight hour, and with whatever strength he could muster, he crawled onward into the den. In front of the Magnavox, he lay upon his side and grinned. 'You'd be the best idiot box ever there was, with 'magna-colour and astro-sonic sound', so go on and show me something, eh?'

In time he settled upon the late show—*Gunga Din*. Alas, the old movie's abhorrent use of blackface sickened him, and he writhed about the floor. Just as the film reached its finale, the sequence in which the servile soldier sounds his bugle high atop the Hindu temple, Micah knocked on the windowpane.

Fingal buttoned his nightshirt, slipped his feet back into his fuzzy pink slippers, and then crawled back outside.

'Hey, are you feeling well?'

'Why do you ask, laddie?'

'Because you look terrible. Like you're sick. It's your eyes.'

'What's wrong with them, eh? Do they appear a wee bit dry?'

'They're *dull*, like iron ore. I'd say your eyes look like the stuff the Martians make their flying saucers out of, and I ain't cracking wise.'

'Aye, right. I should be chuffed, like I've left me troubles high and dry. Instead, I'd be feeling plenty doleful. As a matter of fact, I feel like six kinds of shite.' Fingal lay against the earth and pointed at Micah's house. 'Go on home. Get some sleep. Dream of time travellers, momentfarers.'

A cold, brisk breeze stirred the wire cable extending to the arched gateway, and a deafening thunderclap rent the night. A multitude of storm clouds blew in from the east, and soon the nighttime sky assumed the colour of peanut-butter fudge.

A hard summer rain commenced, and a bolt of lightning revealed a badly-corroded, penny-farthing bicycle lying off to the right.

'Bloody hell, where'd the two-wheeler come from?'

'I found it out past Olde Town Colony,' the little boy said. 'Somebody left the crazy thing down at the scrapyard over there. The freaky bike was lying inside a hollow, right there in a patch of barnyard grass. Yeah, right next to an iron lung, the kind you sleep in if you get the poliovirus and no one knows what else to do.'

'So you thought you'd bagsy some old racer?'

'Yeah, I thought you and me could fix it up it and ride it around. And I thought we'd attach a sissy bar to the fender struts, like a big, huge Electra-Glide. Yeah, and maybe we'll get a sidecar for you.'

Another peal of thunder resounded, and as the rain fell harder, Fingal crawled over to the bicycle and wrapped a hand around one of its decayed handlebars.

Micah pulled his jumper over his head and followed along. 'Hey, what's happened to you anyway? Are you transforming into an automaton?'

'*Please*. This wouldn't be no trifling matter. I daresay I've fallen into deep, debilitating sorrow. Me latest passage through the gateway took the very piss out of me.'

Micah kicked the bicycle's frame a few times over. 'I don't know what you're talking about. You're talking crazy and looking glum. That's all I know. You remind me of the kid in that crazy commercial the Playskool Toy Company always runs in-between Saturday-morning cartoons.'

Fingal lay low and studied the antique. 'I think I know why this fanciful speedster fascinates you so. Everyone prizes a momentum engine because we all presume that we could better ourselves if only we trek somewhere far away. But no, you can't change your nature by going places. As soon as you arrive at your destination, you'll find your very essence would be just the same as it ever were. No, no. Your disposition can't ever change, no matter how many galaxies you might visit.'

The summer storm grew louder and louder, and out past the swimming pool, the high winds made the arched gateway wobble back and forth. Eventually, the arched gateway collapsed with a thud that rattled Fingal's bones.

He pulled up a handful of weeds, then lay still. His thoughts wandered, and he became lost in fantasy—a simple game of make-believe. He imagined that he had come from the star Aldebaran and had travelled to Planet Earth on the magical penny-farthing bicycle itself. *As such, I'll have to find a suitable place in which to take shelter. A warm, dry grotto, where I might laze about. And come the morning, I'll have to look for sustenance.*

A harsh gust of wind blew through his hair. Then yet another powerful thunderclap rent the night, and a bolt of lightning illumined the expanse of Jean's property in a blinding, fleeting manner, something like the technology of strobe lighting.

He barely noticed and returned to his game of make-believe. *I got to learn the local tongue. Once I do, I'll have to determine me proper place relative to the various classes of this world. Furthermore, I'll have to note the dissimilarities in learned behaviour between those with riches, those with some means, and those with none. Moreover, I'll have to determine the variances in learned behaviour between those dwelling in the cities and everyone living in the countryside. Aye, and I've got to learn the orthodoxy here in glorious suburbia.*

Little by little, the torrents and torrents of rain turned to a mere downfall, and eventually, the storm abated.

Finally, once I've properly assimilated to the local customs, I'll have to ascertain me purpose. Shall I work as a salesman? Aye, I'll sell electric tickers. These days, who wouldn't spoil for an electric Timex?

Little by little, quietude dominated the night, but the quietude sounded not unlike some tense interlude that precedes the arrival of some horrible beast and its mate.

All the time panting, Fingal took hold of the bicycle's cracked stem. *At any moment, I'll hear them two beasts. Yes, I'll hear their footfall. Each footstep complementing the other, just like the thumping of traditional African cross rhythms.*

Fingal let go of the handlebar and turned to Micah. 'By any chance, do you hear fine music, lad? That's not the miracle of jazz and ragtime. We'll not be attending a twopenny hop, lad. No, no. A great beast approaches. A lion and its mate.'

Nothing happened. For ten minutes, no disturbance resounded other than the rain dripping from the gutters. Then the wail of sirens rang out. In short order, a rescue ambulance raced through the neighbourhood, and then the sirens' drone grew faint, as if the vehicle had continued into the development to the south.

Fingal trailed his hand over the bicycle's rusted chain stay. 'That blood wagon should've stopped to collect me ratty remains. The burning man has gotten the better of me. Aye, there's no doubt about it. I'm ready for the butcher's cart, I am.'

Micah removed his rain-soaked jumper. 'That's crazy talk. Let's go inside and make some crab soup. That's the kind of chow my mom makes for me whenever I come home in the rain and whatnot.'

Fingal sought to stand, but he fell onto the penny-farthing bicycle such that the jagged, frayed chainring dug into his gut.

'Why you acting so sleepy?' the little boy asked him. 'What's the big idea?'

'I'm buggered, I am. Through and through, I say. Given the collective effect of me three passages through the gateway, I've fallen into an accursed state of entropy. Like a drunkard lying about the streets of Thamesmead. I've come all unglued, haven't I?'

For a moment or two, Micah sought to drag him across the rain-slicked grass—and as he did, Fingal bawled and groaned.

When the little boy finally let go, Fingal howled and wheezed. And then he quoted a line of poetry from Siegfried Sassoon, 'Bring me the darkness and the nightingale.'

Micah scrunched up his nose and shook his head. Then he removed what looked to be a wireless remote from the back pocket in his blue, needlecord trousers. 'Look at this crazy thing here.'

'No, no. Leave me to die here, lad. Go on.'

'I made me a new, walkie-talkie gizmo out of some crazy Zenith-Radio-Corporation device. I found the crazy thing over in the landfill, so I modified the contraption with some real good Martian-style fittings and stuff. Anyway, I think I'll call my invisible cat and ask her what she thinks we ought to do.' With his hips and shoulders perfectly aligned, the little boy turned away and held the remote to his ear. When he turned back, he knelt to the earth. 'There was a whole lot of interference and crazy commercial radio traffic, and I think my bandwidth might've reached transmission capacity too, but even so, I'm pretty sure I heard my invisible cat promise me that you'll be feeling better in about ten minutes.'

Fingal took the remote into his hand, but he found the weight of the chrome-steel frame much too heavy. With the ball of his thumb, he sought to depress a few of the buttons but could not manage. 'Take it back to the rubbish tip.'

Micah steepled his hands, as if imitating a grownup. Then he took the remote back into his hand and held the device to his ear a second time. 'Do you want to know what else my invisible cat says?'

'Not particularly. Don't take offence though. I can't talk just now, for I fear that I'd be dying.'

'Not a chance. If you were ailing, my invisible cat would've told us.'

'Damnation, take it. You haven't got no imaginary mouser friend. For that matter—'

'You know what my invisible cat says? She says you're some kind of artist. Like the hotshot who invented holograms. The kind you get at the curiosity shop. Yeah, you'd be one of them artsy-fartsy type of mischief-makers.'

Fingal crawled about awhile and then rolled onto his back. 'I think the burning man has called upon a pair of beasts to come consume me. Aye, two giant, hungry animals. King Kong together with your goddamn invisible dinosaur cat. Do you hear?'

Micah lay down beside him and pouted. 'I always thought you had the power to subvert the laws of nature. Yeah, I always thought you must be some kind of crackerjack time traveller, but my invisible cat says you ain't nothing like that.'

In a gentle, grandfatherly way, Fingal grinned. 'I'll tell you what I'd be. A theorist, that's what. And I've got to learn the one proper way to explain the origins of the cosmos, aye, and the meaning of life, and the rightful purpose of civilisation. Then I'll compose the perfect myth, the one true metaphor grand enough to explain all.'

A creature of some kind stirred among the boughs of the tall Columbian pine growing near the barn. Fingal studied the wavering grey shadows. *Could it be the angel of death?*

Micah tapped Fingal's shoulder. 'Did you hear something? If so, it was probably just my invisible cat creeping about. I think she pinched my Rock 'Em Sock 'Em Robots playset, and now she's looking to sell the damn thing on the bootleg market.' His head held high, Micah marched over to the evergreen and climbed some forty feet. 'Nope, there's nothing here,' he called out. 'Not even a tiger owl hiding in the shadows.'

Fingal looked to the pine's crown. 'God bless your wee cotton socks. Now get yourself down from there before you fall to your death like bloody Icarus.'

As if out of spite, Micah continued out upon one of the longer, more perilous boughs and then paused to peer into Fingal's eyes. 'Let me tell you a story. About a week ago, I had a really wild nightmare. Me and my invisible cat got into her time machine and travelled about six years into the future, yeah, and we visited that private country day school over on the north side of town, where my dad says I'll be studying as soon as I'm old enough.'

'If you don't get yourself earthward, I swear I'll gouge me eyes out.'

'Do you know what happened? Me and my invisible cat witnessed a future soccer match between our side and the public school. And as my team walks out onto the field, all the public school boys ride their Motobecane scooters onto campus, everyone all proud in their bright blue jerseys and their little white short-shorts. Anyway, my invisible cat was the first one to notice my future self. There I was, kicking around some crazy, futuristic soccer ball. 'Synthetic leather,' my invisible cat told me. Yeah, and then a nasty, short, squat kid I know from kindergarten, a lout by the name of Quentin Guildersleeve, he gets off his itty-bitty little scooter, and he looks over and realises it's me there, so he laughs and laughs. And he laughs so hard, he squeals like a hungry little pig. Yeah, and he roars so hard he can't even breathe.'

Fingal nodded very slowly and sought to mirror Micah's body language. 'I do hope poor, insecure Quentin Guildersleeve didn't wet his nappies.'

'If I'd played, I think he would've. Thankfully, though, my future coach had me sit down along the touchline. Yeah, like the coach felt way too embarrassed to let a total nothing like me into the game.' Micah studied the fallen gateway. 'That thing you built, could you rig it to take us up into outer space?'

'*No.*'

'Are you sure?'

'As sure as eggs.'

'Too bad.' Micah turned back, climbed down from the pine tree, and returned to Fingal's side. 'Why do we dig for oil and tame horses and build windmills? Yeah, and why the age of steam? And what about all those mining towns out there in all those faraway places like Alaska? Why does anybody do anything? I've asked my cat a million times, and she doesn't know.'

With a heavy sigh, Fingal rested his brow against the earth. 'I'm sure life has brought about civilisation for a reason, but I've yet to grasp just what it might be.'

Micah walked over to the penny-farthing bicycle. 'Hey, I think I'll keep this crazy thing here at your place. Yeah, why not? It'll be my gift to you. Like a farewell gift. Because it'll be autumn real soon, and I'll have to begin the fourth grade, and I'll probably have to crash a lot more by night if I'm going to school by day. That's why we probably won't be able to see as much of each other anymore. Except for weekends, of course.' The little boy returned into his mother's flower garden, and without even looking back he continued into his house.

Fingal scanned the night sky. *In the aftermath of God's immolation, how could it be that the process of biotic evolution had to commence? Why didn't the burnt deity's remains simply pass away? Why did the immolated God's burned-out mind will them stars to spew forth them chemicals what brought about life?*

The skyglow shone brighter and brighter. Could it have been a miracle or merely the side effects of light pollution?

Fingal closed his eyes. *What'd constitute Man's purpose? Remember, you promised to tell me all.*

No response arose from the depths of his psyche. Still, a voice should have addressed him in that moment. If nothing else, the voice should have asked him just what he intended to do if he were to suddenly grasp the purpose of life and civilisation.

He shuddered. Twice. *What should I do?* His whole body trembled. *Once every last mystery would be laid bare, should me personal redemption be the only reward?*

The wind whistled, and it sounded something like an

abused dog whimpering in that moment it tucks in its tail.

Fingal felt an urge to move. Having opened his eyes, he crawled back toward the penny-farthing bicycle and gripped the rusted handlebars, and then he imagined either King Kong or perhaps Micah's invisible cat crouching at his back, the monstrous creature having come to tear him asunder. *If some goddamn beast did pounce upon me, what the hell would I do? Would a rush of adrenaline give me the strength to rise to my feet and flee? Aye, the will to live would give me the strength. The will to live!*

A dozen or more times, the boughs of the lofty Columbian pine rattled wildly in the powerful summer breeze.

Aren't long-lived trees immortal? Yes, I think so. In an epiphany he knew that an impulse within the deepest recesses of the immolated God's unconscious mind must have always *regretted* the decision to enter into the fiery, self-destructive rite. *Aye, the will to* live. *And that impulse must have spawned humanity, beings capable of grasping the concept of* immortality.

The wind should have produced a sound not unlike a sigh of bliss. The air grew still, however. And not even the boughs of the Columbian pine stirred.

Fingal imagined Jean standing at his back. 'Like a bolt out of the blue, I suddenly grasp life's actual purport,' he would have told her. 'Aye, the immolated God's psyche, the will to live there, that impulse, went and shaped all of life so that Man might someday found civilisation and let it evolve into an ideal state, a place where all humanity should live as gods. Aye, a bit like the deity what once was.' He returned to his feet and laughed like a child. *The conquest of heaven,* that's *our purpose.*

Chapter Twenty-Eight

JEAN. Los Angeles, California. Summer, 1967.

By late summer, Jean had grown weary with the futility of befriending the disaffected runaways wandering the city. She had no ennobling faith to share with them. *So why should they feel obliged to teach* me *anything?*

One day she paused before a lonely-hearts club on Hollywood Boulevard and looked to the sky. Almost miraculously she intuited the approach of some glorious presence. Three times over, she inhaled—with all her might, too—and soon she detected a strong, acidic aroma. *Could it be lemon? Or what about vinegar? What does it mean?* She closed her eyes and registered the taste of sour plums.

When she finally opened her eyes, the sky had transformed. Far from looking like just another day in California, the blue of the stratosphere shone darkly—artificially, too. As if a filmmaker had tinted all by way of the day-for-night lighting technique.

When the illusion ceased, and the sky suddenly shone as

it should, she looked down and fixed her gaze upon the door to the lonely-hearts club. *The whole miracle, it must've been a sign. Yes, the burning man has vanished back inside Fingal. He's triumphed at long last.*

Gradually, the taste of sour plums in her mouth turned to the taste of sour clover, and from sour clover to gooseberries, and from gooseberries to tart cherries, and from tart cherries to something impossibly acidic. *Japanese pickled plums. Oh God.* Slowly, she turned her back to the lonely-hearts club. *If Fingal has prevailed, does that mean he's gone ahead and puzzled out his great maxim?* She walked over to a chrome pay phone and tapped the dented coin box. *Has he learned all?*

But rather than calling, she turned from the pay phone and looked to her feet. *If I were to ring the house and ask what happened, that'd be a little bit like cheating.* She looked into the blue of the sky again. *A moment like this requires faith, for the quest has concluded. And Fingal has achieved his destiny. And now I must go home and help him teach the world what's true.*

On the nineth of September, the day before she flew home, she visited a crowded settlement house in Cardiff-by-the-Sea and handed out apple fritters to some of the addicts. An hour later, she stopped off at a hospice three blocks from Venice Beach and donated blood to the American Red Cross. Having done so, she felt as faint as anyone else might. Still, she proceeded into a cocktail bar and downed three glasses of blueberry wine.

Just after dusk she hired a cabbie to bring her into the hills. There, amid the wild needle grass, she would meditate on her troubles and prepare for her homecoming. At seven o'clock, the taxicab left her near a large, weathered *Aeronaves-de-México* billboard. At first, she contented herself to read some of the graffiti scrawled across the back of the advertising structure.

Amusingly, someone had written in lime-green crayon: *Ignore alien orders. Keep chasing that peaceful feeling, man.*

When the sky grew dark, she looked out across the city lights and, with no trouble, located the Hollywood Bowl along with several other landmarks.

A nighthawk sailed past, and as the bird of prey called out, she walked off along a quake-buckled road running through a field of coyote brush. The byway happened to be blind; some three hundred feet to the northeast, the damaged roadway stopped before a thicket of ghost pines.

For a moment the strains of music commenced, the sound of a melodica, after which a simple piano song played.

Could it be coming from a transistor radio? As she listened, Jean's mouth filled with the taste of something acidic. *Lemons.* She raised her hands and danced along with the unadorned melody.

The piano song concluded, and as a disc jockey announced his call letters, the Santa Ana winds swept through Jean's wig and played through her blouse and skirt. Careful to avoid stepping on any of the shattered bottles of thunderbird wine lying about, she marched forward—into the woodland.

When she reached the heart of the forest, a glade littered with the tangled ruins of a deer fence, the wireless transmission grew more distinct, and a spot for Ventura County lemons commenced, a husky woman's voice reading off the sales copy. Jean wondered if she ought to bring some produce back to Connecticut. *If nothing else, I could make Fingal a jar of lemon marmalade.*

The commercial concluded, and as an electric-organ piece commenced, she gazed heavenward and laughed like a little girl; no matter the faint ribbons of yellowy smog drifting about, the stars shone all so triumphally. *What a majestic evening.*

The keyboard music grew more dissonant, and she imagined a cult of demented runaways dancing all around, each one of them filled to excess with amphetamines. *How long before the youthful fanatics fall upon me and stab me to death in an orgy of violence?* She laughed. *I've got no reason to fear the runaways.* She revisited her erstwhile efforts to befriend them. *If only I'd had something of value to offer. In the end, they would have confided in me. And we would've learned from one another. And in so doing, we would've tasted a measure of enlightenment.*

Off to her right, a lively animal of some kind stirred within a patch of spotted bell peppers. *Could it be a Russian blue cat?* She fussed with her wig, grabbed her upper arms, and then rubbed her bruised elbow.

Eventually, a black-tailed jackrabbit leapt from the brush and thumped its feet, as if to protest her trespass. Then, as the creature darted off, the organ music faded out. More voices awoke—a spot for a record trader out of Hermosa Beach. Then someone grabbed the dial and changed the station to a trio of surfers debating 'the nature of a wind swell' and 'the best way to ride the hollow curl of a wave' and what to do about 'all the leopard sharks plying the waters off Rincon and Venice Cove'.

Once more she looked beyond the treetops and considered the stars. She thought of the radio waves themselves drifting upward through the furthest reaches of Earth's magnetic field. *And then*? Each and every signal would continue past Telstar and soar through the ionosphere of Valhalla—that great crater dug deep into Jupiter's largest moon. From there, each signal would waft along past Omega Centauri and maybe Antares too—perhaps even far beyond Omicron Andromedae and onward into austere star systems as yet unknown to the radio spectrum.

Why do I indulge myself in this manner? She did so because ever since she had registered the sensation that Fingal had triumphed, she had felt the crushing burden of *responsibility*—and she well appreciated the fact that if she and Fingal were to fail in sharing the wisdom that he had attained, the failure must echo across time.

From far away, back in the heart of the violent city, a thousand or more squad car sirens wailed. Had a race riot only just commenced?

She continued forward, emerged from the woodland, and found herself standing before the wreckage of an ancient city stretching out some three hundred square yards or more.

In every direction stood rows of black-rock lion sculptures, fallen ziggurats, and walls of mud brick. And fifty yards ahead, a truncated pyramid loomed.

Frozen in place, she whispered a Mother Goose rhyme:

How many miles to Babylon?
Three score miles and ten.
Might I get there by candlelight?
Yes, indeed, and back again.

The breeze stirred a blue oak standing to the side. Had Nebuchadnezzar himself planted the acorn that had grown into that very tree? She pursed her lips and shook her head. *Where* am *I?* For a moment, she splayed her fingers over her eyes.

A bin liner blowing about on the current tumbled past her feet and then glided past a workman's ladder lying in a patch of dead orange lilies. At the same time, several Bazooka bubblegum wrappers floated by, only to settle beside a sifter.

At last, she realised that she had stumbled onto an

archaeological site—the ongoing excavations of a silent-era film set. *Might this be a location from* Intolerance*?* At once, she envisioned Fingal standing in the shadows and shining a torch in her eye. 'Do you think this might be the place where D.W. Griffith filmed the sequence in which the procession brings the sacred ark through the gates?' she would ask him, if Fingal really were here.

'Aye, you've got it right,' he would answer. 'This here's where they shot the scene wherein the rival god's high priest puffs himself up with pride and curses the treasure.'

'Yes, the vile filmmaker intended for the high priest and his fawning disciples to be symbolic of all the critics that protested *The Birth of a Nation*.' Jean's muscles tightened, for the very thought of the bigoted director's self-righteousness incensed her. She even shook her fist several times over.

A moment later, as a frayed coconut-candy wrapper tumbled by, she approached what looked to be the sacred ark—an ornate, cuneiform inscription etched into the lid. *I wonder if the expedition discovered the unusual prop earlier today.* She pushed aside some of the little whisk brooms lying at her feet, and then she knelt before the piece of memorabilia. 'Do you think there might be something remarkable inside?' she would ask Fingal, if he knelt here beside her. 'Let's open the ark. I'm sure we'll find some glorious artefact.'

'There's nothing inside that imitation ark but rubbish,' he would say. 'Aye, you'd be lucky to find a pulped-paper idol of Ishtar. And what might *that* be worth to anyone?'

The transistor radio from before crackled back to life with a news bulletin regarding the discovery of an elderly woman's body floating in the Russian River. Afterward, a felicitous spot advertised the Tropicana Motor Lodge on Route 66. Then three gruff voices debated the best recipe for hashish brownies 'like the kind Alice B. Toklas served Pablo Picasso'.

As quietly as possible, Jean crept forward through the archaeological grid, past a solitary spool of drafting film.

A motorcar came into view, a lotus-white Volkswagen Beetle with a convertible top parked near the southern flank. The transistor radio sat atop the Bug's bonnet.

A lone, shadowy figure, a young longhair, stood to the side of the vehicle. Had the expedition hired him to stand guard over the site? Whoever he was, he lit a cigarette and then looked out across the wreckage, as if he might be debating whether he had heard a thief's stealthy footsteps.

Jean remained still and held her breath, until the watchman turned away and moved the radio dial to a broadcaster out of Bakersfield recalling the night sometime before, when, on this very date, 'Koufax tossed his perfect game.'

'Yeah, and what about the way it ended?' the broadcaster's assistant asked. 'Vin Scully keeps repeating the precise time as it appeared on the scoreboard in that instant the final batter struck out. Just like Sandy Koufax and everybody else in Chavez Ravine that night ought to remember that one goddamn detail. The *time,* the *date*.'

She grinned, for what better way to provide the proper consummation for any kind of achievement? Again, she thought of Fingal. *If he* has *succeeded in all of his endeavours, did he note the hour when everything came to fruition?*

The nightwatchman switched off the transistor radio, then he pressed his thumb and first finger together as if he were holding a rolled cannabis cigarette.

She made her way back into the forest and lay beside a pine tree, beneath a bough bearing a night heron's nest. The dark hours passed by uneventfully enough, and suddenly she awoke to the sound of the radio—some media commentator with a flat yet penetrating voice interviewing the dean of women from the University of Connecticut's School of Engineering, an expert on the various kinds of computers that the Russians employ 'at their finest cosmodrome'.

The woman's thick New Haven accent made Jean smile. *I'm so homesick.* She looked to the treetops, hoping to espy a New England titmouse or a Peabody bird.

Gradually, her mouth filled with the taste of something acidic—lemons, some of them fresh and some of them at least a little bit mouldy.

She pictured what it might be like if she were home now. *I'd sit with Fingal over by the snake-rail fence that borders the pear orchard. Together again, we would share a continental breakfast—either honeysuckle apple crisps or English muffins with pecan streusel.* Her belly rumbling, she pushed herself up onto her feet.

In time she exited the forest and walked back to the archaeological site, where she paused to consider the glare of dawn falling through the smog-laden sky.

A dune buggy sparkling with metallic flakes pulled up to the grid, and the driver—a short, thin, bespectacled fellow—leapt out from behind the wheel and hurried over toward the sacred ark. When he noticed her standing there, he tripped over his camera bag. And in the process, he spilled several flashes and filters. Then he paused to check his big, spiral-bound datebook before turning back in her direction and pointing. 'Like, hey, sister, are you that nun from Oceanside?'

'*No.*'

'You don't work for l'Office Catholique International du Cinéma?'

'No, I'm not a nun, nor do I work for any organised religion. Honest.'

'Well, if you happen to notice some Mother Superior wandering around, don't hesitate to tell me because I'm pretty sure she said she'd be coming around this morning.'

A Yukon-yellow Volkswagen camper slowly drove up to the grid, and three college-age women climbed out of the cab. Once the photographer had snapped several images of the ark, the trio removed the relic and placed it inside the hippie van's cargo area.

Jean wrapped her arms around herself and studied the space where the ark once lay. Then she knelt to the earth and felt at the impression. 'Where do those college girls mean to take the treasure?'

'We got a warehouse off Pacific Coast Highway,' the photographer answered. 'The loot ought to be safe there.'

For a moment she continued to feel at the earth here and there, then she leaned back and looked up.

The photographer snickered. 'You won't find nothing,' he told her. 'Almost no one ever does. Months ago, some collegiate kid dug up Constance Collier's eyebrow pencil. That was real far out. Three weeks later, the *Venice Evening Vanguard* did a cracking story about it. Yeah, but ever since then, we ain't found nada.'

'Didn't the ark look true to life?' Jean asked now. '*My*. Didn't the ark look as if it must surely house an idol of legend, a magic fetish?'

'Yeah, that thing was out of sight. The prop masters did a real groovy job back in them days.'

'Yes, the ark came across as something *precious*. Like it held the answer to some great question.' One last time, she felt at the flattened space.

The photographer helped her to her feet and walked her over to his dune buggy. 'How do you like my wheels? This baby has four-on-the-floor stick shift.'

'Please. I must ask for a favour. Take me into the city.'

'Whereabouts exactly?'

'LAX.'

'Yeah?'

'Oh yes, I'm flying home today.'

'So where's all your luggage?'

'I gave everything to the poor.'

'That figures. You *are* the Reverend Mother. Shit, I knew it all along. You're the one from the ecumenical society, l'Office Catholique—'

Jean raised her hand and shook her head. '*No*.'

Frowning as if in disbelief, the photographer helped her into the dune buggy.

While he arranged his camera bag in the back, she felt the warm, malodorous leatherette, then she noticed on the floor, near the clutch, a faded lobby card—a still from the notorious screen adaptation of *Suddenly, Last Summer*, an image of the harrowing flashback in which the abused, frenzied Greek children chase after Montgomery Clift and then proceed to cannibalise him.

Her skin crawled, and she thought of the lost segment from *King Kong*—the giant spiders swallowing the crewmen. *Would anyone ever discover the elusive clip? There's just got to be a release print somewhere.*

The photographer climbed behind the wheel, and he applied a dab of sun cream to his nose. 'Hey, let me ask you something. If you're not from the Sisterhood, what're you doing up here anyway?'

'Why do you ask?'

'Like, don't flip out, man. It's just that I find it hard to believe that a person of your age would come out into the hills just for laughs.'

'What about the old bird from the religious order or whatever it was? Didn't *she* mean to come out here to meet with you?'

'Like, hold up, man. Are you sure you're not her, and do you really want me to take you out to LAX?'

'Oh yes, I'm going home,' Jean insisted. 'I'll prove it.' With a girlish giggle, she removed her return ticket from the welt pocket in her skirt.

A moment later, as the engine roared to life, she looked over her shoulder. An elderly woman emerged from the ghost pines, and though she wore neither a black habit nor veil, the modest-looking woman just had to be the wise old nun to whom the photographer had referred. Jean waved to her. *Too late, old vestal.* The photographer drove along, and Jean picked at the scab on her elbow, until the little wound bled profusely enough to make the young man scream like a baby.

Afterpiece

Late that summer, Fingal collected his thoughts and carefully reviewed all that he had learned. In due course, he proceeded to author *The Perfect Myth*:

> *Billions of years ago, the Godhead yearned to test the limits of Its omnipotence and learn whether or not It commanded the paradoxical power to destroy Itself. With no better alternative, the Godhead chose to explode. Despite the power and the seeming finality of the discharge, the fiery rite proved to be nothing more than the light of the creation; moreover, a sentient force, the field of energy comprising the remains of Its unconscious mind's will to live, subsequently contrived the phenomenon of biotic evolution—and for no other reason than to beget humankind, a race sophisticated enough to make amends and to do so by seeking to live as immortals.*

No sooner had Fingal authored *The Perfect Myth* than Jean returned home. She intuited the fact that something must have happened, for there could be no mistaking how much he had transformed. 'What's happened to you? My oh my. You look all so enthralled, just like some humble saint.'

'That's because I've brought to light the greatest thing since baked beans. Aye, the revelation emerged from me stream of unconscious, which has now aligned with me waking thoughts such that I'm no longer awash with emotion.'

'No longer awash with emotion? How so?'

'At long last, I fathom all, and what bliss to know that I've finally liberated myself from the bondage of indecision and befuddlement, mistakes and miscalculations, and all the rest of me frustrating dysfunction.'

'So what have you learned? Confide in me every last detail. Give me something to believe in. Enlighten me.'

In measured terms, he proceeded to recite and explicate the scope and content of his work, *The Perfect Myth*.

Afterward, the house grew quiet but for the television set back in the den—playing the opening credits to a psychological thriller, *The One Thousand Eyes of Doktor Mabuse*.

Fingal twirled his hair. 'From this day forth, no medium should wield much influence over me. Not even the idiot box.'

'What about a *cult*?' she asked him.

'No, no. Even if some maniacal bastard was to nab me and pump me full of his barking mad propaganda, nevertheless, I'd disbelieve it. Aye, for I know what's *accurate*.'

'So let's begin a movement,' Jean implored him. 'Not a movement to save anyone with some falsehood. No, let's ennoble and edify others. We'll share your newfound wisdom and let any and all perplexed souls share *their* ideas in return.'

Fingal nodded, for Jean's idea sounded sensible. And that

very day, they consulted the local clerk of courts, who helped them to found an ironic, interactive *non*-religion: the *Non*-veneration of the Immolated Godhead.

Before his death Fingal posted dozens of self-published tractates by which to share the non-faith and to extol its non-virtues. Together, he and Jean addressed copies to art colonies, bankers, businessmen, newspapermen, women's shelters, politicians, and nursing homes too.

In late autumn, somewhere out along the Pennsylvania Turnpike, an ageing astrophysics scholar by the name of Gwyneth T. MacDermott pulled her Ford Galaxie into a filling station.

As one of the attendants operated the pump, a second attendant approached the driver-side window and placed one of Fingal's pamphlets into her hand. 'Take this and keep reading till it sinks in.'

'What's this?'

'The author's name was Fingal T. Smyth, and the one true Immolated God's own voice was he. Hell, yeah.'

Despite the roar of the traffic up and down the motorway, Gwyneth T. MacDermott sat at the wheel and read the entire leaflet.

Twenty minutes later, she pulled over to think. Over and over, she recited the few words that she remembered from Lord Byron's poem about Prometheus:

'What was thy pity's recompense?'

She became lost in daydreams and imagined primordial lightning burning down the forests of long ago. Then she pictured the metallurgist who discovered the way to work flint so as to produce a spark. She trembled. 'Oh, the discovery of fire,' she whispered, without even thinking.

Two hours later, when she stopped off in Bethlehem's Colonial Industrial Quarter, she sat beneath a poverty pine and reexamined the tractate. Constantly crossing and uncrossing her legs, she jotted down a dozen notes here and there in the margins.

When Gwyneth went home, she sat in her turnip garden and debated whether the cosmos could have followed from utter non-existence. *Wouldn't the whole idea be akin to the nescience of spontaneous generation?* She looked to the dusky sky. *Could the rite of immolation reconcile the conundrum?* She studied a few clouds. *Might the concept of godlike self-destruction explain how an eternal energy source could have abided* before *time's commencement but then cease to exist in any calculable form* after *having exploded into the natural world?*

A few days later, at the last moment of dawn twilight, her thoughts turned back to the question of spontaneous creation. *Could it be that something as sensible as the law of gravity had ignited the primal light?* She lay in her turnip garden and endeavoured to concentrate all her faculties on the matter at hand. Then she sat up. *Even if the law of gravity were God, what a dull thing to believe.* The late-autumn breeze moved through the treetops, and a fit of jubilation overcame her—a sensation that she had not felt since she had studied Heisenberg's indeterminacy principle.

At last she resolved to join Fingal's novel non-religion. Lest others look askance at the doctrine or call it insubstantial or ill-founded, she would devote the rest of her life to defending the fledgling non-creed. If and when some smug, snarky, condescending know-it-all came along to jeer at the non-congregation, she would calmly explain the value in addressing the *meaning* of things with friendly freethinkers from differing cultures and backgrounds.

Eight months later, a young runaway from the suburbs of Philadelphia, a diabetic girl by the name of Ariel Ippolito, visited Gwyneth's non-chapel in Zionsville, Pennsylvania.

Ariel had always believed that all things must be aspects of the Godhead and that all things must be aspects of free will, and because she longed to share her ideas with others, she had always dreamt of making a non-pilgrimage. When she reached the non-chapel, she paused at the doorstep and rubbed her hands together.

Inside, someone had commenced a melody on what sounded like a Scottish tin whistle, while the non-parishioners recited the words to a non-chorale.

Ariel walked into the foyer and stopped before a card-table upon which someone had arranged reprints of Fingal's writings alongside a selection of other free-of-charge, saddle-stitched chapbooks written by various non-congregants.

The non-beadle approached Ariel, touched her fingertips, and then placed both of his hands over his heart.

'So this would be the chapel?' she asked.

'No,' he told her. 'Not in the traditional sense. A deconsecration minister has already rendered it unhallowed. Nevertheless, *we* approve. Our kind rather prefers to non-congregate in a non-chapel.' And now the non-beadle guided her inside.

What an austere space—no formal choir apse, no baptismal font, no credence table, no shimmery knell cushion. In lieu of a nave filled with rows and rows of pews, everyone sat in a circle and faced one another as *equals*.

Ariel closed her eyes. For the longest time, she imagined that she stood within a colossal spacecraft—one with a saucer hull two miles wide. Soon, some launch vehicle would lift the ship from the spaceport, and then the ship would travel off to some uninhabited, extrasolar planet, or maybe even an extragalactic planet boasting a parent star just like Earth's own.

The non-hymn concluded, at which point Ariel opened her eyes and sat in one of the empty chairs. As a hazy light shone through the bevelled windows, she nudged the woman sitting to her left. 'Pardon me, but what'd be the subject of today's non-sermon?'

'The same as always. The non-priestess, Gwyneth T. MacDermott, she'll tell us all about the Immolated God and then let us share our own thoughts. And we'll discuss life and death, youthful sorrows, the nature of the conflict between good and evil, the *meaning* of things.'

An old man sitting to Ariel's right waved to her. 'If I get the chance, I wish to speak about the unconscious impulses and all that they would have us do. And my wife, she wishes to expound on all the best ways to manage stress levels. Especially as they relate to memories of past trespasses and frustrations.'

Ariel looked to the distressed floorboards at her feet. 'So in this non-church we help each other to comprehend the ways of the world?'

'Yes, we share with one another all our *untimely* meditations. And when we go home, we befriend other freethinkers and invite them to come join in the dialogue that we might learn from one another and heal one another's *puzzlement*. Remember, even when you go free, you're still a slave to your thought process, your unconscious mind, all your beliefs and practices and desires, all your consciously-made and unconsciously-made decisions too. For that matter, how should anyone hope to avoid those decisions that result in unintended consequences? No, we're only free in transitory glimpses. Like we feel in those moments when we comprehend persons, places, and things as they truly are. Yes, that's when we're free. When we *comprehend*.'

Breathless, Ariel recalled her struggle—the shame that she had always felt whenever someone had questioned her fascination with immanence and the nature of free will. For a second time, she closed her eyes and imagined herself aboard the spacecraft. *Soon, I'll retire into my plastic deep-sleep body cocoon and sleep my long, blissful slumber. Then, just as soon as we've reached our interstellar destination, me and the other passengers should awaken to find ourselves heirs to some tranquil planet—an earthlike world comprised of fertile fields . . . yes, magnificent fields that promise a thousandfold harvest.* A sudden hush fell over the room, and she opened her eyes.

The non-priestess had joined the circle. She clasped her arms behind her back, greeted everyone, then moved toward the one empty chair—and how bold and how steady her movements.

Ariel sat up straight. *Yes, let's begin to learn* . . . together.

A Note From the Author

If you enjoyed this book, I would be very grateful if you could write a review and publish it at your point of purchase. Your review, even a brief one, will help other readers to decide if they'll enjoy my work.

If you want to be notified of new releases from myself and other AIA Publishing authors, please sign up to the AIA Publishing email list. In return you'll get a free ebook of short stories and book excerpts by AIAP authors. You'll find the sign-up button on the right-hand side under the photo at **www.aiapublishing.com**. Of course, your information will never be shared, and the publisher won't inundate you with emails, just let you know of new releases.

The story behind 'On the Threshold'

On the Threshold follows from an idea book written while working on an MFA degree in poetry at Sarah Lawrence College in Bronxville, New York; c. 1990.

At the time, there were two kinds of poetry students at Sarah Lawrence. The first type wrote in an obscurantist, free-association style. The second type preferred confessional poetry. Alas, neither style of writing really applied to my interests. The thing that did it for me was the philosophical poem—the type of poem that the other students tended to regard as 'boring'. No matter what the others thought, though, nothing could shake my faith. What could be more fascinating than a poem that seeks to explain the riddle of the universe?

Looking back on that era, the thought occurs that this was about the time that my preferences changed from poetry to prose. That would explain why it became necessary to translate all those philosophical poems into one long novelistic work that could bring everything together. Oddly, it was not visionary, metaphysical fiction that sold me on prose. At the time, believe it or not, *no* kind of prose writing fascinated me quite as much as film theory—particularly phenomenological film theory.

In the early nineties, my sister attended NYU film school—and she would often tell me about cutting-edge writing that followed from the theories of Walter Benjamin and Carl Jung. Much of these theories show up in *On the Threshold*—especially the notion that when we watch a movie, only the conscious mind follows the plot. The *un*conscious mind reacts to the symbols and archetypes and interprets the movie as a reiteration of some primal association of ideas—as if the unconscious mind really does contain within it inborn knowledge, just as Plato had always believed.

Perhaps it is no mystery why *On the Threshold* had to contain a strong, intellectual woman character—and perhaps it is no surprise why that character would be so helpful in bringing about the resolution. All the source material for the book comes from a time when the author just happened to be studying with loads of women at Sarah Lawrence. Moreover, how to deny my sister's influence? The funny thing, though, is that many a feminist reader might oppose the work on the grounds that the women characters are not independent enough nor do they speak to one another enough with regard to women's history and women's issues. Whatever the case may be, the point of my work is not to offend. The point is to resolve the riddle of the universe, and it is my firm conviction that my characters do just that—and they do it for everyone, irrespective of either race or creed or gender.

Acknowledgements

A heartfelt thank you to Tahlia Newland and everyone at Awesome Independent Authors Publishing (AIA Publishing).

About the Author

M. Laszlo lives in Bath Township, Ohio. He is an aging recluse, rarely seen nor heard. *On the Threshold* is his second release and first with Tahlia Newland's Awesome Independent Authors. Rumour holds that Laszlo is a pseudonym inspired by the character of Victor Laszlo in the classic American film *Casablanca*.

Milton Keynes UK
Ingram Content Group UK Ltd.
UKHW010628051223
433778UK00001B/61